THE LADY IN GLASS

AND OTHER STORIES

BOOKS BY ANNE BISHOP

THE OTHERS SERIES

Written in Red

Murder of Crows

Vision in Silver

Marked in Flesh

Etched in Bone

THE WORLD OF THE OTHERS

Lake Silence

Wild Country

Crowbones

THE BLACK JEWELS SERIES

Daughter of the Blood

Heir to the Shadows

Queen of the Darkness

The Invisible Ring

Dreams Made Flesh

Tangled Webs

The Shadow Queen

Shalador's Lady

Twilight's Dawn

The Queen's Bargain

The Queen's Weapons

The Queen's Price

THE EPHEMERA SERIES

Sebastian

Belladonna

Bridge of Dreams

THE TIR ALAINN TRILOGY

The Pillars of the World

Shadows and Light

The House of Gaian

THE LADY IN GLASS

AND OTHER STORIES

ANNE BISHOP

ACE
New York

ACE

Published by Berkley

An imprint of Penguin Random House LLC

penguinrandomhouse.com

Copyright © 2024 by Anne Bishop

For additional copyright information refer to page 465.

Library of Congress Cataloging-in-Publication Data

Names: Bishop, Anne, author.
Title: The lady in glass and other stories / Anne Bishop.
Description: New York : Ace, 2024.
Identifiers: LCCN 2023028959 (print) | LCCN 2023028960 (ebook) |
ISBN 9780593639054 (hardcover) | ISBN 9780593639061 (ebook)
Subjects: LCGFT: Fantasy fiction. | Short stories.
Classification: LCC PS3552.I7594 L33 2024 (print) | LCC PS3552.I7594
(ebook) | DDC 813/.54--dc23/eng/20230810
LC record available at https://lccn.loc.gov/2023028959
LC ebook record available at https://lccn.loc.gov/2023028960

Printed in the United States of America
1st Printing

Book design by Ashley Tucker

To all the dreamers, readers, storytellers,
and friends who have made this journey with me

TABLE OF CONTENTS

THE
LADY IN
GLASS

AND OTHER STORIES

SCRIBERE*

The fleshy shrouds get peeled away
one . . . by . . . one. A crime of
passion, an intimate murder
performed with tender skill.
The hand that holds the razor
is my own, and loves me,
but cannot spare the bone,
the bittersweet marrow I
surrender to daylight to feed
the hungry, to heal myself.

*Latin, meaning "to write"

THE EARLY STORIES

Sometimes I receive an e-mail from a person who wants to write but feels discouraged after comparing their first stories to my novels. Apples and oranges, my darlings. You shouldn't compare fledgling stories to stories that are the result of years of effort to hone the writing craft, not to mention the thousands of pages of drafts that I've written over the past thirty-some years.

This section shows you some of my fledgling stories—the stories that helped me learn my craft as a writer.

A note about finding inspiration: It can show up anytime, anywhere. For example . . .

I was typing some copy at a day job many years ago and was supposed to type "hooting guffaw." My fingers typed "hotting fuggam." I thought that would be an interesting name for a character, and a story grew out of that.

Note: I pronounce "Fuggam" as FEW-gum.

THE LADY IN GLASS

WHO WAS SHE, THIS ONE WHO SLEEPS IN THE glass coffin? How long has she slept? She is beautiful, so beautiful. Her hair is as black as a raven and looks as soft as the clouds. Her skin is as white as the Elderman's best porcelain and unmarked by time or life; and yet her cheeks have the blush of a perfect apple, and her lips are as red as the most perfect rose. Her eyes, closed in her eternal sleep, are they blue with innocence, gray with wisdom, or dark with the mysteries of the world?

Who was she?

She came to us when the earth shifted one day, an unremarkable occurrence in our times. Some men from our village were out hunting. One moment they were walking through a narrow pass between high grassy hills, and the next they were sprawled on their backs as the earth trembled and one of the hills was sliced apart as cleanly as a sharp knife cuts through cake.

And there she was.

They could not believe what they saw. Cautiously they climbed to where she lay, testing each foothold lest their presence on the loosened earth cause a further slide that would bury them, and her. As if in a dream, they used their guns as shovels and carefully eased her from the hill.

When they returned to our village, they came not with the meat needed to fill hungry bellies but with her. Sweating and struggling, they carried her back, fearing all the time that the smallest pebble, the merest twig, would cause one of them to stumble and overbalance the load, which would surely have ended in her destruction.

The Elderman ordered them to carry her into his house to protect her from the elements, particularly the harsh, hazy sun, and everyone crowded in to look at her. Even those who had never been permitted to cross his threshold before forgot propriety as elbow jostled rib and feet were trod on in the effort to get a better look. It took but a few minutes for a fight to break out, and when the bodies thudded against the long table the Elderman's family dined on—the table on which the coffin lay—the Elderman roared his disapproval and banished all but the council of elders from his house.

Even after the door had been closed and barred and all the windows curtained, still the villagers had stood outside, whispering among themselves and wondering, wondering.

She is not like us, and yet she is. She is what we once were, before that terrible, terrible thing happened that is only called the Great Foolishness—a stupid name for that horror in the past that gnarled and bent us so and yet, miraculously, left so much untouched.

She is what we once were, tall and straight of limb; but we are all that's left of humankind. We are all that's left of Man.

We have a library in our village, a rare thing for so small a place. Books are precious. It is a week's travel to a city where they can be bought, and they are dearly priced. Still, we have a collection, a sign of communal affluence. Thrice each week, the Historian or one of his clerks stands before the assembled village and reads from one of them. It is wonderful. When I was young, I wanted to be a clerk (I never dared aspire to be Historian). I had the intellectual gifts required, but my father, who had grown tired and uncaring, thought the fields sufficient employment for me, and his second lifemate (my mother died early—not an unusual occurrence among our wemen) was more interested in advancing the standing of her own child in our village than in tending to me. But he is already gone and I am here, sitting through the night hours, keeping the lady company.

But I ramble. 'Tis a sign of age.

The Elderman tired of having the village underfoot whenever he tried to leave his house. He tired of faces trying to peer into his windows, so he ordered a viewing hall to be built where all could come and see the lady.

Day after day they came to see her. The men came and stared, hungering for her beauty. The wemen came and stared, pain and hatred in their eyes.

Every man has a duty to take a lifemate. Our survival depends upon procreation, no small thing anymore, for if the Great Foolishness deformed and twisted the men, it was even crueler to those who hold the basket of our survival.

They are so ugly. They are humped and bent, their limbs twisted and misshapen. Only their eyes are beautiful, deep and full of strange longings, half-remembered dreams. Men live with them to have a helpmate, to satisfy their bodies' needs, to hopefully produce a child.

It is a great crime among us to desert a lifemate. It is a social disgrace not to perform the marriage duty often enough for her to conceive. It is, at best, a trial for both parties. When a weman feels the need for a man's body, and usually this is only a handful of days in the course of her blood time, she informs him of his duty. On these days he is excused early from his day's work so that he is fresher, more fit to provide the seed. At least once on each of these days he lays his body down upon hers. Then, if they are lucky, her blood time will come and go, and the life within her will quicken. And if they are very lucky, they will have a child. If not . . . Even the childra, the unchild, is allowed to suck once at its mother's breast—if it has a mouth to suck with—before being given a small vial of breeleth, or dragon's breath, a sweet, deadly poison that works quickly and without pain.

So the men would come to the viewing hall from the fields and stare, drinking her in, memorizing her before hurrying to their huts and their beds to perform their duty in a darkened room.

One day, one of the wemen, having discovered that her lifemate could no longer stand to do his duty for her without gazing first upon the lady, stood in the viewing hall before a large crowd and pondered aloud what the lady's lifemate must have looked like. And they could all see him: taller than she but built just as straight, limbs muscled and whole, darker skinned than she, skin that had been gently kissed by the sun, and raven hair as full and sleek as her own. It cut them to the core, for they were no more like him than the wemen were like her.

The weman, gone mad, picked up the jagged rock she'd been hiding and hurled it at the coffin. Her lifemate, grieving for a man's body that could never be his own, threw himself in the way of the rock, protecting the lady. The rock took out one eye and opened his skull. He died that night. A few months later, the weman produced twin childra and died in the birthing.

After that, a guard was stationed in the viewing room to protect the lady as she slept.

And then, one night, the Historian ran through the streets like a man deranged and stood hopping about on the cold ground in his bare feet as he pounded the Elderman's door with his fist. The Elderman let him in, and a few minutes later, his youngest son was running to the huts of the other elders, and a council was called.

The Historian had been reading a book loaned to him by a brother historian and had come across a story about a lady much like our own, so beloved by those who knew her that when she died, they placed her in a glass coffin so that they could still look upon her beauty. And then a man came by and saw her and fell in love with her. He opened the coffin and bestowed a kiss upon her lips, and the lady woke from her long sleep and went to live with him.

A kiss!

The elders were stunned. A kiss does not bring the living back from the dead. It was nonsense. It was blasphemy. It was . . . possible?

So much of what came down to us from that time long ago came in fragments. The historians did their best to piece the fragments together so that we could learn and understand what had come before, but it was so hard, so very hard. They understood that books had contained knowledge and also that we had once recorded the stories the minstrels sing—glorious tales of never-can-be and never-was-but-might-have-been. And who could say what were stories and what was knowledge? At first, it had seemed an easy task; a storyteller has a certain way of talking about make-believe or long-ago, and storytellers do not change as much as the rest of the world—their voices are echoes that have been heard time out of mind. So separate the stories from the knowledge that talks about things, and we will know what was and what wasn't.

Stories of flying to the moon or men exploring the sea's dark secrets sat side by side with words of knowledge that spoke of the same thing. Words that sounded like the storyteller's voice spoke of dragons—but dragons walk the earth now; perhaps not the same kind, but dragons nonetheless. So what was true?

The council of elders pondered this for many days and in the end decided to open the coffin. If the lady was alive, she would be grateful (so they hoped) to be freed, and if she was grateful, she would understand our need for her strength and beauty and take a lifemate and produce children who were stronger and stood straighter and were more beautiful than we.

Thus arose the next problem. It was reasonable that the lady would be most grateful to whoever bestowed the life-giving kiss and would, therefore, choose him as her lifemate. So who would bestow the kiss?

The Elderman graciously offered his eldest son to perform the duty, but many of the other elders in the council also had sons of marrying age and were unwilling to relinquish the possibility of healthy offspring so easily. They fought among themselves for days. Meanwhile, news of their fights—and the reason for the fights—spread through the village. Men measured themselves against one another: Who was tallest; who stood straightest; whose limbs were least misshapen? Whose voice was pleasant; whose speech was witty; who could entertain the lady?

New ideas. Raging jealousies. Imagine the men standing in

the village square, talking of courtship and entertaining the lady while the wemen ache with the knowledge that those same men, coming to them, would barely speak, would look away from them, would penetrate them quickly in a darkened room before hurriedly pulling up their breeches and curling up on their own cots. Oh, how much anger was stirred up along with the half dreams and longings while the elders fought among themselves.

At first, the elders agreed on one thing: the man had to be of good family, and any man who already had a lifemate was not eligible to be chosen. This conveniently eliminated most of the men except the elders' sons and the Historian's clerks. But this proved to be a problem, too, for the fight dragged on through days, through weeks, through months, and one day the council of elders raised their weary heads and realized none of the wemen were with child because none of the young men were willing to marry and become ineligible when the decision was finally made. So they had to recant and say that taking a lifemate did not make a man ineligible to receive the lady's gratitude.

Through all this, the lady slept undisturbed. It never occurred to anyone in the village, including the guards who watched over her, to break the glass and bestow the kiss. Oh, the men still came and stared at her, they came and silently courted her, but to touch? No.

In the end, it was a clerk who was chosen. He was of good family, and his body was not as bent as the rest. The village carpenter was called in to open the coffin. The village crowded into the viewing hall. The clerk, pale from excitement and from the musky scent of envy that settled around him from the other men, was supported on either side by the Historian and the Elderman.

The carpenter placed his chisel against the glass by the

lady's feet and raised his hammer. The hammer was arcing down when Zerth, another clerk, came running into the hall, screaming for him to stop. The hammer crashed on the table, making everyone jump. The chisel, held so tightly in the carpenter's hand, slid across the glass, making a deep white gouge.

Zerth began to babble, almost sobbing, as he handed the book to the Historian and, with a trembling finger, pointed to a passage.

The Historian's face turned sickly green. The words were garbled, more fragments from the other time, but the message was clear. Some things in the past had been preserved in what was called a vacuum. This vacuum kept them just as they had been on the day they were preserved. If the vacuum was broken and the air touched the preserved object, it would disintegrate to dust; time itself would march in, and the toll of years would do its work.

All it would take was a tiny crack in the glass, and the lady might be lost forever.

The clerk fainted.

The carpenter looked at the white gouge in the glass and stumbled from the hall to be sick outside.

Careful, trembling examination revealed that the glass had not cracked. The lady was untouched.

The village filed out of the viewing hall. The council of elders convened at the Elderman's hut. The Historian was called in. Was this a trick, this passage? Did Zerth produce it out of jealousy? In all the months before today, why was it not found?

The Historian hung his head in shame. He did not know. The book was a recent acquisition, he explained, but old and had not been handled much. Such books were given to a single clerk to read. He would write a report and submit it before the

Historian himself read the book. He suggested that recent events might have dimmed Zerth's perceptions, and only when Zerth had been freed of the possibility that he had returned to his task with the required diligence. But the Historian did not know.

Story or knowledge? Vacuum or kiss?

We had a choice: opening the coffin could give her—and us—unexpected, wonderful life; or it could turn the beauty we all looked upon and took some comfort from to dust. It was a terrible responsibility, one the village was grateful the elders had to take.

And so we waited.

Eventually the small everyday concerns of the village recalled the council of elders to their full duties, and discussion of the lady and the fate of the village was reserved for one evening a week.

And we waited.

Story or knowledge? Vacuum or kiss? To choose a fork in the road, knowing the other will disappear with the first step and whatever was beyond the curve will be lost forever.

My grandfather was a small boy the day they brought the lady to the village. Now my own grandson stumbles on sleepy legs to bring me a late supper of warm ale and bread and cheese. He is as I was once, standing so close his breath fogs the glass, loving her as we all have loved her, and wondering, wondering.

And still she sleeps. And still she sleeps.

BEAR TRAP

A LONG TIME AGO—TOMORROW, I THINK IT was—a skinny young orphan girl was walking along a wilderness trail that took her from the village where nobody wanted her to the town where nobody knew her. After she'd been walking a spell, she started feeling tired and hungry, so she stepped off the trail to pick some berries and—*whump*—stepped right into a bear trap.

Now, that bear trap was big, and it was strong. It chewed up that girl's leg pretty fierce. She struggled and struggled, but she was too young and too small, so she spent the night in the woods like that, with those berries just out of reach.

Come morning, the old trapper went out to see what he'd caught, and when he saw the girl, he said, "I could use me a girl like you to do the cookin' and the washin' up and such." So the old trapper pulled up the big iron stake and the chain that was holding that bear trap to the ground, and he took the girl home with him.

At first, the girl was glad to go with the old trapper because she thought he'd free her from the bear trap once they got to his cabin. But that wasn't the trapper's idea at all. He poured some whiskey on the wound to clean it, and then he fixed a long, thick chain to the bear trap before driving that iron stake right into the cabin's dirt floor.

So the girl cooked for the old trapper and did the washing up and such, dragging that bear trap till she didn't think her heart could take one more beat. Whenever she mentioned the hurting to the old trapper, he'd cuff her and call her names and say, "When I found you, you was grubbin' berries in the woods. Now you got a roof over your head and food in your belly. I even give you a blanket to keep warm at night."

Now, this went on for several years. That skinny orphan girl grew into a handsome young woman, and the old trapper started hinting at some other kinds of chores. Well, one day the girl said to herself, "Dyin's better than this," so she took hold of that bear trap, and she wrestled it and wrestled it till she got the jaws apart far enough to pull out her mangled leg.

It cost her part of a finger and a lot of blood, but she got free.

She wandered down that wilderness trail for several days before she reached the town. They were good, neighborly folk down there, and some of the women patched her up as best they could and helped her get a new start.

After a few years of hard work, that girl had a snug little house with a shady porch and a nice big garden where she grew the best vegetables in town. There were even a couple of fellas who'd come calling every now and again. And if that girl always wore men's trousers and thick shoes and never joined in when there was a dance, well, folks just shrugged it off and said she was a good neighbor and a kindly soul, and her small oddities never hurt anybody.

One evening, a traveling man rode into town and started

asking around for the girl, so a few of the folk brought him on over to the house where the girl was rocking on her porch, enjoying the breeze.

The traveling man said, "I come down by the wilderness trail t'uther day and met up with an old trapper who was livin' by hisself. He told me about a girl he took in and took care of and how she just lit out one day and plumb broke his heart. Would you be that girl?"

"I reckon I am," the girl said, ignoring the way her neighbors nudged one another, looking troubled.

The traveling man scratched his head. "Well, that old trapper's doin' right poorly and is in need of some comfort. He said if I was to meet up with you, to tell you he'd be right grateful if you'd come for a visit."

The neighbors all said how that would be a kindly thing to do, but the girl just shook her head.

"Well," said the traveling man, "if you ain't a stonehearted woman. After all that old trapper done for you, why won't you go up and visit?"

The girl looked at the traveling man. She looked at her neighbors. She pulled up her trousers and let them all get a real good look at that leg.

The girl said, "I got out of the bear trap once. Why would I want to step in it again?"

NOT A PRINCESS

ONCE UPON A TIME, THERE WAS A WITCH named Matilda who was the white sheep of the family. She didn't like cackling over a hot cauldron; she didn't like handling eye of newt and toe of frog; she didn't like living in a damp, drafty castle where things went bump in the night and then started moaning and rattling chains; she didn't like walking down dark corridors and slipping on bat poop; she didn't like always having bad-hair days.

She wanted to wear elegant clothes and have a lady's maid who knew how to style hair. She wanted to live in a clean castle with double-glazed windows, central heating, and indoor plumbing. She wanted to be an Important Person.

The only place that had all the things Matilda wanted was a king's castle, but, having inherited the family looks, she knew her chances of getting through the gate for an interview were zip. So she started taking correspondence courses in business administration and public relations, and she developed the Plan.

The Plan was simple. There were a lot of princes in the Twelve Kingdoms and a noticeable lack of princesses. All she had to do was become the companion of a princess who would marry a prince. Once everyone was settled into happily-ever-after, she would transform herself from a companion into a Power Behind the Throne.

Since princesses didn't grow on trees or under cabbage leaves and couldn't be ordered from a catalog, Matilda decided to make her own. So she packed a couple of jars of hair gel and a couple of bags of gold and set off to find a little girl who was Proper Princess Material.

She found Rachel, a pretty, blue-eyed girl about eight years old whose thick golden hair already hung past her waist. Rachel was one of the middle children of a very poor farmer who had a very large family, and before you could say, "Double, double toil and trouble," the farmer had a bag of gold, and Matilda had little Rachel. Using magic foot powder, she sped through the kingdom and finally arrived at the broken-down castle she'd inherited from her uncle Oscar, the ogre.

While Rachel slept, Matilda whisked her up the secret staircase to the top room in the tower, which was the only structurally sound part of the castle since Uncle Oscar's idea of redecorating was to knock down walls. Unfortunately, the last outer wall he knocked down took offense at this redecorating idea and fell down on top of him, squashing Uncle Oscar and thereby saving the tower.

Once the secret staircase was once more a secret, Matilda woke up Rachel and showed her the large room that would be her home until it was time to put the Plan into action.

"You're going to be a princess," Matilda said gleefully.

"I am?" Rachel said. "What does a princess do?"

"That's the best part! Princesses don't do anything!"

Rachel thought about this for less than thirty seconds, got a mulish look on her face (which her parents would have recognized instantly), and said, "Then I don't wanna be a princess."

Matilda huffed. She puffed. She remembered Uncle Oscar. "Every little girl wants to be a princess."

"Not me," Rachel said. "I'm going to be an acrobat in a traveling show and visit every one of the Twelve Kingdoms."

Matilda shrieked.

Rachel sulked.

The evening went downhill from there.

So did the next few years.

Matilda wanted Rachel to lie on the bed and practice languidness and the graceful waving of a lacy handkerchief.

Rachel used the bed as a trampoline and had almost learned how to do a backflip before the bed broke.

Matilda wanted Rachel to practice walking in that ladylike, short-stepped glide that was proper for a princess.

Rachel ran wind sprints.

Matilda spent one day each week washing, conditioning, combing, drying, and braiding Rachel's long, long, *long* hair.

Rachel used it for a jump rope.

Desperate to find a quiet activity, Matilda taught Rachel how to read and then gave her storybooks about princesses being rescued from dragons and other such nasties by brave, handsome princes.

Rachel thought the girls were silly, pretended the fireplace poker was her trusty sword, and happily skewered the large overstuffed chair-turned-dragon until the day Matilda sat down in it and it spewed its stuffing all over the floor.

And every time Matilda said, "Princesses don't do that," Rachel would reply, "*I* am *not* a princess."

And so it went until Rachel turned eighteen. By then, Matilda was living in a little cottage near the castle in order to escape Rachel's pestering and badgering, and the only acknowledged way into or out of the tower was Rachel's long golden braid.

Finally, it was time to put the Plan into action. News arrived that a prince from a neighboring kingdom was going to visit some noblemen in the area and planned to go hunting in the nearby forest. This was the chance for which Matilda had waited for ten long, long, *long* years.

The first part of the Plan was to turn Rachel into Rapunzel because Matilda felt that "Rapunzel, Rapunzel, let down your hair" sounded much better, PR-wise, than "Hey, Rachel, drop your braid!"

The second part of the Plan was to separate the prince from the rest of the hunting party and misdirect him until he came to the tower.

This was a lot easier than convincing Rachel to answer to Rapunzel because the prince was not only geographically challenged; he was nearsighted to boot and never quite grasped that the sun had changed direction on him and the old women who kept pointing out the way were the same person.

With her shoes filled with magic foot powder, Matilda sped along the forest paths and reached the tower a minute before the prince arrived. In her best theatrical voice, Matilda said, "Rapunzel, Rapunzel, let down your hair."

Rachel tossed the braid out the window. Matilda climbed up and stayed all afternoon, knowing that curiosity whetted by frustration made tastier bait.

Late the next morning, Rachel heard a strange sound outside her window. She ignored it because she was still puzzling over Matilda's smug smile and the cryptic hints she'd tossed out about a stranger being in the area.

The sound came again, and then a voice that wasn't Matilda's said, "Rapunzel, Rapunzel, let down your hair."

Rachel looked out the window and fell in love.

He was tall, with long black hair and warm brown skin and four strong legs that looked like they could travel anywhere.

Rachel waved her arms and yelled, "Fuzzy Four-Foot!"

Her beloved raised his head and whinnied.

"Ahem," said a whiny voice.

Rachel looked at the other person standing next to the tower. He was skinny. He had too much nose, not enough chin, and a prominent Adam's apple. He wore a velvet tunic and baggy tights.

Must be the servant, Rachel decided. It was obvious at a glance that her beloved wouldn't be able to put on that little leather chair or the head straps all by himself.

The servant cleared his throat and said in the same whiny voice, "Rapunzel, Rapunzel, let down your hair."

Rachel tossed her braid out the window and waited.

Time passed.

More time passed.

Finally taking her eyes off her beloved long enough to notice that the servant was stuck halfway up the tower, Rachel hauled up the braid and helped the wheezing man over the windowsill.

Once he got his breath and some of his color back, he introduced himself as Prince Twiggly and proudly told her how he'd potted two rabbits in yesterday's hunt. He then proceeded to tell her about other successful hunts. Rachel, however, wasn't listening.

She'd seen rabbits at dawn and dusk nibbling at the forest edge, and after a lot of badgering she'd gotten Matilda to buy some clay pots and dirt and seeds so she could grow some flowers. While Prince Twiggly went on and on about his hunting prowess and being a man of the world, Rachel tried to figure out how one potted a bunny. Did you feed it? Water it? What if it wanted to hop?

Finally, Prince Twiggly said something that caught Rachel's attention. "What did you say?"

Prince Twiggly looked annoyed. "I said, you are my own true love, and I want you to come away with me."

Rachel sat back, pots and bunnies forgotten. Away. To walk in the sunlight and pick wildflowers. To sit next to a stream and dangle her bare feet in the cool water. To travel with her beloved and see all kinds of things and talk to all kinds of people.

"You and I and Fuzzy Four-Foot would go away? Together?"

"I would ride Fuzzy—I mean, I would ride the horse," Prince Twiggly said. "You would ride in a closed carriage."

"Why? I could learn to ride the horse."

"It doesn't matter if you could or not. Princesses don't do that. Besides, it wouldn't be proper for you to ride horseback. All the commoners would be able to see you."

"But if I ride in the carriage where they won't be able to see me, *I* won't be able to see anything either!" Rachel protested.

Prince Twiggly waved his hand, dismissing her objection. "Your life will be much better once we're married. Now, let's see. Mother has the east tower because she likes the morning light, and Aunt Mary has the north tower because she likes to paint. But you could have the south or west tower. The south tower has a lovely view of the lake. And there would be afternoon walks in the ladies' garden. And when I came back from state visits, I'd tell you all about them. And, of course, there would be our evenings together." He giggled.

Rachel's eyes narrowed. "You mean you're going to take me from this tower and put me in another one?"

"It's a much nicer tower," Prince Twiggly huffed. "Lots more room. Lots more windows too."

"And I'm never going to ride Fuzzy Four-Foot or travel with you when you visit the Twelve Kingdoms?"

"Of course not! Princesses don't *do* that."

Rachel looked mulish.

Prince Twiggly thought she looked cute.

"Well," Rachel said after a long while, "since my braid is the only way into or out of the tower, I can't leave today. And you have to get that closed carriage," she added when he started to pout. "Tell you what. You come back tomorrow and bring a skein of silk with you. I'll start weaving a ladder with it, and as soon as it's finished, we'll be able to go away." She smiled. "Just the two of us."

Eager to experience wedded bliss, Prince Twiggly didn't object when he was hustled out the window and lowered to the ground.

Rachel smiled and waved as she watched Prince Twiggly climb into Fuzzy Four-Foot's little leather chair and ride away.

That afternoon, Matilda was delighted with Rachel's preoccupation. The girl was so in love, instead of putting the sugar lumps in her tea, she slipped them into her pocket and never noticed the difference.

Tomorrow, Matilda decided, she would arrive early, catch the young lovers together, and act so outraged, the poor prince wouldn't be able to do anything but agree to have Rapunzel's lifelong companion accompany them. Too excited to hide her glee, Matilda hurried back to her cottage to celebrate the success of her Plan.

Rachel, too, had plans. As soon as she felt confident Matilda wouldn't return that evening, she packed some clothes, a sewing kit, and a couple of books she'd actually enjoyed into two pillowcases. When that was done, she picked up her little embroidery scissors and, eventually, cut off her braid. She tied the end with twine so the braid wouldn't unravel, secured it to the hook in the wall below the window, and went to sleep.

The next morning, Rachel was awake and waiting for hours before Prince Twiggly and Fuzzy Four-Foot trotted toward the tower. When she heard, "Rapunzel, Rapunzel, let down your hair," she tossed the braid out the window and waited.

She let him climb three-quarters of the way up before she gave him a hand. Wheezing, he tumbled through the window. Happily, Rachel conked him on the head with an empty chamber pot.

Five minutes later, the pillowcases were on the ground, the sugar lumps were tucked in a pocket, and Rachel, now wearing Prince Twiggly's tunic and tights, was quickly climbing down the braid.

She spent a few minutes talking to Fuzzy Four-Foot while she petted his nose and fed him sugar lumps. Since he had no objections to her plans, she opened the large bags tied behind the little leather chair and found another set of clothes, two flasks, some bread and cheese, and a small bag of gold. Satisfied, she stuffed what she could into the bags, left the rest, and climbed into the little leather chair.

Then she and her beloved headed into the forest and the world beyond.

Half an hour later, Matilda crept up to the tower. She saw the braid hanging down. She saw the pillowcases. She didn't see a horse. She scampered up the braid and tumbled through the window, right on top of Prince Twiggly, who was sitting on the floor, holding his head and wearing nothing but his underwear.

Matilda looked at the chamber pot. She looked at Prince Twiggly. She looked at the braid tied to the hook. She opened a hidden cupboard, removed two full bottles of home brew, handed one to Prince Twiggly, and then slumped against the wall.

They spent the rest of that morning and most of the afternoon commiserating with each other about how Rachel, despite Matilda's best efforts, simply was not Proper Princess Material. Together they came up with Suitable Criteria for a Proper Princess. They decided she had to be blond (not necessarily natural), big-bosomed (definitely natural), and have the IQ and disposition of an eggplant.

Pleased to find someone so sympathetic and understanding, Prince Twiggly hired Matilda on the spot to be his Official Princess Selector.

By the time they decided to leave, Matilda was too tipsy to remember the secret staircase, so she and Prince Twiggly suffered a hair-raising climb down the gold braid before Matilda teetered off to her cottage to pack her things and Prince Twiggly, dressed in a sheet, tottered off through the forest to try to find his host's house.

As for Rachel . . . Well, she and Fuzzy Four-Foot spent a few years having misadventures and causing havoc throughout the Twelve Kingdoms. Eventually she settled down in a small village by the sea and married a man who was the human equivalent of her beloved Fuzzy Four-Foot.

But that's another story.

THE WEAPON

SERGEANT FERGUSON STOOD AT THE EDGE OF the campfire light, nervously clearing his throat and pulling at his frayed shirt collar.

"James?" he called quietly, straining to see into the trees on the other side of the fire. "You there, James? I got recruits to stand picket duty with you. Lieutenant's orders. James?"

"Why don't you announce to the whole damn Reb army that you're standing there, Ferguson?" a deep voice in the trees asked with friendly malice.

A shadow solidified into a man casually turning a large hunting knife over and over again in his hands.

Ferguson jerked a thumb toward the two young men with him, a smile twitching across his face. "Got recruits."

"Got dog meat," the man replied, returning the smile, his eyes never leaving Ferguson's sweating face. He eased himself down onto a tree stump by the fire, repositioning the smoking wood with the tip of his knife. "But you might as well leave them here. They can get themselves shot here as well as anywhere, I guess." He looked at the two young men. "Though not necessarily by the enemy." He let out a fierce, barking laugh that quit almost before it began. "Sure, Ferguson, leave them here. I'll look after them."

"Good," Ferguson said, stumbling, retreating. "Good." And then he was gone.

The recruits watched the man silently poke at the fire. He was an older man, in his early forties, with a face deeply lined from weather and years, and black roughly cut hair that was beginning to gray at the temples. His dark eyes caught and held them as they shifted nervously from side to side. He watched them, and his lips pulled back in a wolf's grin to reveal teeth too white against the deeply tanned skin.

"You planning to spend the night on your feet?" he asked. "No? Then park your asses."

They sat across the fire from him, letting backpacks and rifles slide to the ground.

James slipped the knife into the sheath on his belt, pulled a bottle of whiskey from his pack, and offered it to the first boy, a small, wiry youth with red hair cut military short and heavy black eyebrows that gave his face an angry, troubled look.

"Welcome to the Civil War," James said, "where old-fashioned weapons are reproduced with the most up-to-date technology, where generals use shortwave radios to relay orders but still send messengers to ride along the lines so they can get their balls shot off, and where you actually have the privilege some of the time of knowing the man you're killing." The laugh burst out, staccato sharp. "But at least the crappers are modern. They don't make you use leaves on your baby-skin asses." He smiled at the boy, his nostrils flaring as if he'd run a long way. "What's your name, strawfoot?"

"Jim Harrison."

"Jim Harrison," James said. The wolf's grin froze, hungry and sharp.

"My father was Henry Harrison. Did you know him?"

James nodded his head slowly. "I knew a Harrison, a long time ago."

"Is he still . . . ?"

James shook his head, still smiling. "That would have been remiss of him. Hell, boy, these are economic wars we're fighting for the consumption of goods and civilian job security—and the consumption of flesh and blood. It wouldn't do not to have the battlefield quotas filled." He pointed to the whiskey bottle. "You going to drink it or sleep with it?"

Harrison unscrewed the cap and put the bottle to his lips.

"Harris, my son, we can try to be civilized. You should have a cup in your pack."

Harrison flushed. He pulled the cup out of his pack and poured a fingerful of whiskey into it before handing the bottle to his friend.

The other boy was still struggling to get his cup out of his pack. He had a round, jelly body and a moon face freckled with blackheads.

By all the dogs of war, James thought, *that one's walking carrion.*

"And your name, strawfoot?" James asked as the boy finally freed the cup and poured himself some whiskey.

"Ezekiel Franklin," he said, handing the bottle to James, "but my friends call me Ben."

James let out that barking laugh. "This is the Civil War, Ben Franklin. You should be in Boston dumping tea." James splashed some whiskey into his cup and set the bottle beside him. "Or wouldn't being an assistant assistant's assistant in a war office somewhere qualify you for a high enough civil service ranking to keep Daddy happy once you did your tour of duty?"

Franklin studied his shoes; Harrison watched the fire. James's grin became fierce.

Finally, Harrison said, "You didn't tell us your name."

"You're right; I didn't," James replied. He watched the boy's lips tighten, the skin around the mouth turning white. "Henry James."

"Was he a famous general?"

"He was a writer."

Harrison snorted, tried to sneer. "You were named for a writer?"

"Indeed I was, strawfoot. My mother's passion was books, not men, and as she was a rather frail woman, I suppose she found his volumes more courteous companions than whiskeyed, sweating bodies that would sometimes grope for her in the dark. I think she'd hoped the name would help me become a civilized man of letters." He laughed. "Shit, I almost killed her coming out"—he spread his arms wide, an embrace across the fire—"and look what I've done with my life since."

"You're old to be a soldier," Harrison said, wondering nervously if he was being disrespectful and almost hoping that he was.

"True. I've been looking—waiting—for something. But I think this will be my last battle. My enlistment's up in three days. I guess it's time to settle down." James refilled his cup and handed the bottle to Franklin, who looked up from his shoes, startled. "Where do you hail from?" James asked him.

"Batavia, New York," Franklin said.

James nodded and smiled, watched the whiskey bottle pass to Harrison. "And you?"

"Sharon, Pennsylvania," Harrison replied. "Say . . ." He handed the bottle back to James. "Isn't it illegal to be drinking while on picket duty?"

"Harris, my son, we're doing picket duty on the edge of a battlefield in the middle of a war that makes a mockery of the war it's imitating except in its ability to slaughter young men. Shit, boy, nothing is illegal here."

They were silent. James threw more wood on the fire. Beyond them was the low hum of men quietly talking around other campfires and someone picking out the melody of "Amazing Grace" on a harmonica. It was a sad, sweet sound.

Harrison watched a deep sadness, a weariness, settle over James's face. What could be so important that a man would wait so many years in places like this for it to come? And why the pain, why the sadness? Harrison leaned forward toward the unseeing older man, one hand tentatively reaching to touch him, to try to understand.

"Do you think we'll go into battle soon?" Franklin asked, breaking the spell.

Harrison jerked his hand away.

The wolf's grin was back. "In the morning," James said cheerfully, "if we don't get a downpour like we had today."

Harrison studied the whiskey in his cup while Franklin kept lifting his cup to his lips, then lowering it again without drinking.

James watched them. *False courage—wasn't that what they once called it? Well, take what courage you can anywhere you can get it. All the bullshit rhetoric in boot camp can't dull the truth once you're here: they have sent you here to die, strawfoot. A century ago, some jackass bureaucrat figured out war would eliminate surplus population and unemployment in one step. If you weren't working in a service industry to supply the people who worked in the factories making the weapons and materials to supply the men who were fighting the wars, and if you had tits instead of balls, you did your patriotic duty by lying on your back with your legs spread to produce the next crop for the war machine. But only with soldiers. That was the morality catch they wrote in so that all the men with guns in their hands would shoot at one another instead of at the prickasses back home who were banging everything they could get their hands on.*

"Cheer up, men," he said as he poured himself more whiskey. "After tomorrow's battle, you'll be heroes, and when you go home on leave, you can whisper to your girl about your brush with death while you're warming your meat in her oven. And if you really do well, maybe you'll even get a cert to stand stud."

"Harrison got his certificate in boot camp," Franklin boasted.

Harrison blushed and punched Franklin in the arm. After a moment, he took a snapshot from his shirt pocket and handed it to James. "Her name's Margie."

The snapshot was blurred but showed a plain, broad-faced girl standing in front of a white farmhouse, proudly displaying her swollen belly for the camera.

"A hometown girl?"

"Nah. She's from Marstown. Her dad's got a farm outside of town."

"Right near boot camp," James said softly. "How convenient." He handed the snapshot back to Harrison. "How'd you get a cert before active duty?"

Harrison shrugged. "Had something to do with the tests, I guess. They gave me these tests over and over—must have been a hundred times. Never said what for. But General Armstrong himself got me a cert and assigned me to work weekends for

Margie's dad, and I'd stay over Saturday nights. She wasn't keen on me at first. Didn't want a noncom around. But General Armstrong talked to her dad, and the next weekend—"

"She couldn't keep her hands off him," Franklin crowed.

Harrison shrugged and smiled at James, one man to another. James didn't smile back.

Harrison looked at the snapshot. "She got big fast, and they wouldn't let her—you know—after they confirmed she was pregnant."

"She your first one?" James asked, looking at the fire.

Harrison blushed. "I really like Margie," he said defensively. "We're getting married when I finish my tour of duty."

James poked at the fire. "She looks big. You sure it's yours?" he asked quietly while he pulled his knife slowly from its sheath.

Harrison blushed again. "Of course I'm sure!" he said angrily. "I was the first one, and I was the only one."

A giant wood beetle crawled around James's foot. The knife flashed and pinned the insect to the ground. James twisted the blade round and round and round as the insect's shell crunched and broke. When there was nothing left but pulp on the ground, James cleaned the blade on his pant leg and slipped the knife into its sheath. He poured himself more whiskey and this time didn't offer the bottle to the other two.

Slowly, eyes still on the pulp near James's foot, Franklin asked, gulping, "Have you ever killed a man with that?"

James took a large swallow of whiskey. "I've slit a few throats with it."

Harrison jumped up and disappeared into the trees.

"Don't go too far, strawfoot, or a Reb picket will take a bead on your pecker." James poured himself more whiskey. "What's with him?"

Franklin licked his lips and cleared his throat several times. "His mother was murdered when he was four. Someone slit her throat. He was already in a government school. He didn't find out for a long time what—"

Harrison sprang out of the trees. "You got no right!" he screamed as he lunged at Franklin. "You got no right telling him about that. You got no right!"

"Settle down, Harrison," James snarled, hauling him off the other boy. "I said settle down." He shoved Harrison to the ground and kept shoving him until he stayed down.

Franklin cowered by his pack, gingerly fingering his split and already swelling lip.

"I didn't mean nothing, Jim. Honest, I—"

"Shut up," James snapped, "or you'll get us all killed. There are Reb pickets on the other side of the stream just beyond these trees."

They quieted and realized how still the camp had become. Everyone listened, waited, but no one approached the campfire. After a long while, the hum of voices began again, the harmonica playing the "Battle Hymn of the Republic."

James sat down and kicked at the fire with the toe of his boot. Franklin dabbed at his lip, sniffling to himself, while Harrison sat with knees drawn tight to his chest and stared at the smoke rising out of the wet wood.

The silence settled tightly around them.

James opened a pack of cigarettes, tapped it on his knee, held it out. Both boys took one and held it, waiting.

Franklin looked at Harrison and elbowed the air. "Go ahead—show him. Go ahead."

Harrison scowled at the other boy. He looked at James. "All right," he said, sitting up straight and pulling his shoulders back. He took a small box of wooden matches from his shirt pocket, took out one match, and held it up. James leaned forward, elbows resting on knees, and waited.

Harrison held the match tightly between thumb and forefinger. He concentrated on the match head. Droplets of sweat appeared above his lip. He concentrated and concentrated. His hand began to shake. Suddenly the match caught fire.

"Zzizzzz," Franklin said, laughing and rocking until he fell backward.

Harrison lit his cigarette. Smiling, he cupped his hand around the match and leaned forward. Smiling, James lit his cigarette on the match and blew it out.

"Good trick," he said.

"I know a few," Harrison replied, still smiling and feeling more grown-up than he had all evening.

"Why are you here, strawfoot?"

There was a brisk sound. Harrison crinkled his nose. Waving his hand in front of his face, he said, "Jesus, Franklin."

"Um," Franklin said, looking around nervously.

James laughed and jerked his chin toward the center of the camp. "The modern conveniences are that way or"—he grinned at the boy—"there's always nature, if you're careful where you stand."

Franklin took off for the center of camp.

James poked at the fire. "Your friend shouldn't be here."

"He's a good guy," Harrison said.

"He's walking carrion. How'd he get out of boot camp?"

Harrison scuffed the ground with his foot. "He went through the training twice."

"And someone made a present to someone else, and he was passed through. They didn't do him any favors."

"He's got a good job lined up, but he has to have a tour of duty in order to qualify for it."

"The only way he'll survive tomorrow is if you accidentally shoot him tonight so that he's in a field hospital when we march." James threw his cigarette into the fire. "But you never said."

"Said what?"

"Why you're here."

"Oh. For Zazu." Harrison grinned. "I'm supposed to be in Europe right now. I've got a friend who works in assignment. He switched my tour of duty at the last minute so nobody'd catch on for a while."

The teeth gleamed from the wolf's grin. "Well, like you say, Margie's too big to—you know."

The scowl returned to Harrison's face. "Zazu's my sister. We're twins. That's why Margie's so big, you know. She's carrying twins." He watched the firewood shift and settle. His scowl softened. "They sent Zazu to a special school when we were little. Even before Mom . . . I get to visit her a couple times a year. We don't get much time together, and she's always . . ." A smile twitched his lips. "She can do the match trick like nothing." He looked at the fire, thoughtful. "Anyway, she says they're always listening to her, watching her. They offered her a cert that had been decorated for valor, but she wouldn't have him. Caused quite a stink, I guess. I don't think she's happy in that place. She talks a lot about having a garden, making things grow that are beautiful and good. I saw her just before I went to boot camp, and all she did was cry. They were going to give her a test soon, and after that she was going to have three certs attending her until she . . ." Harrison wiped his eyes on his shirt cuff. "That's why I didn't go to Europe. I didn't want her to be alone."

"And did she pass the test?"

"Not yet. She'll be taking it any day now."

James rubbed a hand over his eyes. "Mary used to love her garden," he said softly to himself.

Harrison's head snapped up. He was about to speak when they heard a metal pot being kicked and "Sorry, oops, sorry, sorry, oops, sorry." Franklin had returned to them.

"Shoot him, strawfoot," James said quietly, looking away. "If you're his friend, shoot him."

Franklin settled by the fire, grinning, wiping an arm across his brow. "Whew," he said.

"Now you're ready for battle," James said, pouring himself another whiskey.

Harrison reached out his hand for the bottle. James looked at him for a long while before handing it to him.

"How many battles you been in, James?" Franklin asked, watching the bottle pass between the two men and wondering what else was passing between them.

"Too damn many," James replied sharply. He stared into the fire. He looked older, more tired, beaten. "Doesn't matter which war you're drafted into," he said softly. "They fight them all using the old battle plans so men can keep on dying at Iwo Jima and on the Dunkirk beaches, and at Gettysburg." He sipped the whiskey. "Still, you can't be sure who'll win or lose. They use the same plans, but they aren't the same men. Men who are supposed to retreat stay and fight and win while men who were supposed to win a skirmish turn tail and run. Some things don't change, though. Pickett's Charge never changes."

"You fought at Gettysburg?" Harrison asked quietly.

"Three times. Twice on this side, once on the other. Sides don't matter. The dying—that's what matters." The barking laugh. James raised the little finger of his left hand. Half of it was missing. "Left that as a souvenir the last time." He grinned at them, but it faded quickly, leaving his face careworn and weary. "Grist for the mill, boys. That's what we are. We become broken-down and maimed and old here."

Someone whistled in the trees behind them, two short, one long. Harrison grabbed his rifle.

"Rebs!"

"Put the rifle down or I'll shoot you myself." James opened his pack and pulled out a tin of coffee. "What've you got to trade?" he asked Franklin.

"Trade?" Franklin blinked at him.

James squatted by Franklin's pack, examining the contents. He took out two thick bars of chocolate, studied Franklin's worried face, and put one back.

The whistle came again. This time James answered, one long, two short.

"What are you doing?" Harrison was sweeping the trees with the rifle.

"Keeping up a Civil War tradition of barter and trade." James stepped into the woods.

"But they're the enemy."

"Put the rifle down, strawfoot. Tomorrow they're the enemy. Tonight?" He shrugged, took his canteen, and disappeared into the trees.

A man was waiting on the other side of a fast-running stream.

"What was all the fuss, Yank? You got officers prowling around?"

"Worse. I got recruits doing picket duty with me."

The man laughed. "Shit. Well, I guess you need to get target practice on something. What've you got?"

James held his hands out. "Chocolate and coffee—and not that cowshit you call coffee."

The man whistled softly. "You been robbing the boot camp cradle, Yank?"

James grinned. "It was a donation for the war effort."

The man laughed. "I'm sure it was. The devil himself would donate his right arm if you were around to persuade him."

"What have you got?"

"Whiskey and tobacco—and not that cowshit you call tobacco. Trade?"

"Trade."

They met in the middle of the stream, each cursing the slick rocks underfoot. After the exchange, they paused before turning back.

"There's a lot of brass in camp tonight," the man said.

"Why's that?" James asked, friendly and unconcerned.

The man hesitated. "You the one that bullets don't touch?"

"Sometimes I'm just lucky."

"Hope your luck holds out, Yank. Rumor's going around camp that they're going to try out a new weapon tomorrow."

"Oh? What kind of weapon?"

"Don't know. A carful of generals drove in before sunset, hush-hush, with a convoy kept under heavy guard." The man grinned. "Took half the camp to push those vehicles out of the mud. Should have known better than to drive on a dirt road after all the rain today. Anyway, the guards got a bit distracted by a little staged entertainment, but the only thing in the trucks was enough food for a first-class blow—champagne, caviar."

"Maybe you're going to invite us all to dinner and poison us with Reb cuisine." The white teeth flashed in the dark.

"Anything—" The smile suddenly vanished. "Anyone else arrive with the generals?"

"Yeah. A scrawny little bitch with a pinched face and red hair. Not the sort you'd expect officers to find amusing, but she must do something right the way they're all around her. Doesn't figure, does it?"

James looked up at the sky. "It's going to be clear tomorrow. Probably be hot as hell. Well, it'll give us all a chance to get used to the weather there."

"You figure most of you will end up there tomorrow?"

James nodded. "And most of you, Reb." He turned and made his way back to the bank. He looked back at the man still standing in the stream. "Keep your head down tomorrow."

"You too, Yank. If you get a chance, shoot a general."

"One of yours or one of mine?"

"Doesn't much matter, does it?"

James returned to camp. For the rest of the night, he stared at the fire and drank his whiskey, never saying a word to the boys on the other side of the fire.

"COME WITH ME," James said the next morning, pulling Harrison toward the trees.

"But we're ready to move out," Harrison protested, trying to free his arm from a grip that was becoming painful.

James released his arm. "You really intend to see that girl again? Then come with me."

"What about Ben?"

"Let him have the chance to feel like a soldier."

James turned away, quickly disappearing into the trees. Reluctantly, Harrison followed.

"Aren't we going to fight?"

"Of course we are. We aren't going to be stupid is all." James watched the troops begin to move out. "It's going to be bad," he said softly. "If what that Reb told me last night is even half true, it's going to be real bad." His hand fell gently on Harrison's shoulder, and then his fingers tightened until the boy flinched. "Listen to me, strawfoot. You know the feeling you get when you do the match trick? I want you to concentrate on that feeling until it's all around you, until you're inside it. When I give the signal, you run like hell for that enemy ridge, screaming a battle cry that'll chill blood, and if anything touches that feeling around you, you smash it, smash it hard. You understand? We have to get to that ridge, boy. We have to reach the enemy. You understand?"

"Yes," Harrison said hoarsely, chilled by the look in James's eyes. "Yes, I understand."

James patted the boy's cheek. "Good. Good. Get yourself ready. There isn't much time."

They waited. It wasn't long before the cannons began firing, and then, in the still morning air, they could hear the sounds of men fighting, hear the screams of men dying.

And then there was something else.

It was a hum, a vibration that Harrison knew came from within himself.

James shook him. "Fight it, boy. Fight it!"

Harrison thought of the match, concentrated on the match. The hum made him angry, made him want to strike out.

"Now," James snarled softly. "Now let's see about your damn weapon. Come on, Harrison."

James was running, his rifle in one hand, his knife in the other. He screamed as he ran, a hoarse, angry battle cry. All through the battlefield the hum was louder. Around them, men exploded like firecrackers.

Lungs burning, vision blurred, Harrison ran after James. He slipped and almost fell, never seeing what was left of Franklin, never seeing anything but black swirled with red. That was where the humming came from. He thought of the match. He thought of fire. Running, screaming, he caught up to James. And then there was white fire, so hot with rage it burned cold. *White, white, white, white, white.* In the center was the black match with the red head. *Light the match; light the match; light the match; light . . .*

Harrison stumbled and fell. He tried to get up, but his trembling arms and legs wouldn't support him. His cheek pressed into the mud, he gasped for breath, waiting for the pain in his head to ease. His nose bled freely; he didn't try to stop it.

"You can rest now, strawfoot. It's over."

Harrison raised his head. James stood a few feet from him. Harrison pushed himself into a sitting position, dabbing at his nose with his sleeve, and looked back the way they had come.

His mind refused to understand the carnage, refused to believe that what lay in the field had once been men. He turned away, but the Reb camp was full of the same torn, twisted bodies. Something caught his eye, and he cried out. On hands and knees, he scrambled toward the body of a red-haired girl dressed in a long black robe.

"Zazu! Zazu!"

The girl lay on her back in the trampled mud, her eyes closed. Harrison flung himself down beside her and shook her as he began to sob. His head sank until it rested on her chest while he continued to cry and call her name.

James picked up a revolver lying beside a general's uniform.

"It's better this way, Harris, my son. Much better for her. She wanted to grow flowers, not death. She would have been too dangerous to keep once she realized what they wanted her for." He looked around at the exploded bodies lying twisted in the mud. "They're running out of ways to make war, strawfoot," he said sadly. "The fossil fuels are almost gone. We don't even have enough metal anymore to wage modern warfare, to build planes and tanks. Upper-class civilians want what gasoline supplies are left, what metal is left. That's all we're here for, to maintain someone else's prosperity. So you see, they had to do something before we were fighting with stones and clubs, before too many of us realized how futile, how insane it is. They had to find a new weapon, a new resource. And they found it, by unlucky chance, about twenty years ago. We've always been grist for the mill, but we cannot, must not, become the mill, too, or we'll never be able to end this slaughter. Do you understand, Harris, my son?"

James squatted down and gently squeezed the boy's shoulder. "After my Mary, my sweet Mary, asked me, begged me, made me promise that I wouldn't let what we'd created out of love be used to create death, they tried to hunt me down. Once they found her body, they knew I'd try to stop them. It was simple, really—there were so many bodies that day—to find one that was similar in coloring and build. I even knew him—a likeable, quiet man named Harold James. So we traded dog tags—he didn't need his anymore—and I faded away, one of the dead. It was so easy. We're just numbers, not men. I waited here among the thousands. I waited here for you, Jim, for you, because I promised her I'd take care of you the way I took care of her. Do you understand? I promised her."

Harrison was still quietly sobbing when James put the gun

to the back of the boy's head and pulled the trigger. He looked at the girl, gently brushed the hair from her face.

She opened her eyes.

She has Mary's eyes, James thought, feeling the years-old pain of loss.

"You promised," she whispered. Her lips twitched into a little smile. She closed her eyes, trusting.

Before he could think, before he lost courage, James put the gun to her forehead and pulled the trigger twice.

The gun slipped from his hands into the mud. He never noticed. Gingerly, as if not to disturb them, he shifted Harrison's body until he could remove the photo from the boy's shirt pocket.

Somewhere in the camp, a man cried out. A few men staggered over the battlefield, looking for survivors.

James straightened up. He slipped the photograph into his shirt pocket, pulled out a cigarette, patted his pockets for a match, and found none. Looking around, he saw a torn field map lying in the mud. Tearing off a corner, he twisted it into a thin cylinder and held it loosely between his thumb and index finger. A moment later, it became a cheerful little flame.

James lit the cigarette and trampled the map into the ground before setting out for a white farmhouse to fulfill the last part of his promise.

HOTTING FUGGAM AND THE DRAGON

HOTTING FUGGAM CAME TO OUR VILLAGE ON A sunny summer afternoon—and demoralized everybody. He tipped his derby to the old men sunning themselves in the square and said, "A perfect day, gentlemen. You're truly blessed with glorious weather."

And they said . . .

"Hot. Too hot."

"Fields are drying up."

"Hasn't been this hot since—when was the last time?"

"Nigh on twenty year."

"That's right. That's right."

"Goin' to have to find me a bit of shade."

"Hot?" said Hotting Fuggam. "But this is delightful weather. Why, three months ago I was visiting a tribe who lives deep in the Vara Desert. It gets so hot there in the summer, they never need a fire. They just set a griddle on the sand and cook their meals on that."

Well, the old men looked at Hotting Fuggam. They squinted at the cloudless sky. One said, "Goin' ta rain." Another said,

"Feel the damp in my bones." And with that, they shuffled off toward their houses.

He met the ladies at the general store and told them how becoming their dresses were. Then he told them about ladies who lived way south of here who dressed up in colors like Yelping Yellow, Outrageous Orange, and Passion Purple—sometimes all at once—and how restful it was to the eye to see ladies showing restraint in their choice of colors.

The ladies looked at their bright summer dresses and felt dull.

He told the village fiddler about a man he'd met who could play a whole symphony on a single fiddle string, and the fiddler immediately said that his bow needed to be rehaired, and it was a poor time of year to be taking the horse's tail, and he didn't think he could possibly play anything, oh, at least till autumn.

He told the children about this wonderful ball that children played with in a distant land beyond the sea. It was a smoky white globe that was tied to a string, and you dipped it in water and spun it over your head, and as you spun it, the ball would change colors, and if you spun it fast enough, you'd have a rainbow.

The children put down their hoops and their plain rubber balls, sat on the doorsteps, and moped.

It was very depressing.

Since my mother ran the only boardinghouse in the village, I saw more of Hotting Fuggam than anyone else—mostly because they had the advantage of running into their own houses and hiding behind locked doors. Still, by the end of that first day, I was feeling a bit sorry for the round little man who had a smile for everyone and stories that would take the wind out of the biggest blowhard's sails.

Until he began to talk about cooking. Now, Mother is what they call a good country cook. That means the meals are simple, the food identifiable, and there's plenty of it. That first night, Mother served her special pork chops. They're thick, juicy, and so tender you can cut them with a fork. However, a pork chop is just a pork chop. It is not suckling pig marinated in a plum wine sauce. And baby carrots sautéed in butter, no matter how sweet they are, are not caramelized carrots. And Mother's biscuits—a recipe that's been handed down for generations—are not twenty-seven thin layers of pastry with layers of honey and chopped nuts in between. I tried to explain that the comparison was a compliment—of sorts—but Mother took it so hard, she served porridge at every meal for the next three days, and with each serving, the porridge got colder and the lumps got bigger. When Hotting Fuggam told Mother about a king he'd visited who commanded his chef to make lumps as big as dumplings, it was time to do something drastic.

I figured there had to be something around here that was big enough and drastic enough to eclipse Hotting Fuggam's stories and send him on his way. And then I realized we had just the thing. So, armed with clean towels, I thumped up the stairs right after dinner, waited a minute for my porridge-laden stomach to catch up, and knocked briskly on Hotting's door.

His gold-toothed smile almost blinded me as he hustled me into the room, reassuring me all the while that this was the quaintest, most comfortable room he'd ever had the privilege of sleeping in, and it was such a cozy little bed, and it was wonderful to lie down on clean cotton sheets—why, the last place he'd visited, the bed was so big you could stretch your arms and stretch your legs and you still couldn't touch the sides, and the sheets were satin and never let a man feel like he had a grip on the mattress—and he couldn't want for anything, but wasn't it kind of me to think of bringing him extra towels.

I almost felt bad about being so deceitful, but those satin sheets and the thought of breakfast made me go through with it.

"Have you ever seen a dragon?" I asked as I fiercely fluffed the pillow.

"A dragon? Yes, I have. In fact—"

"Really? Then perhaps you could help us get rid of ours."

"Yours?" He looked a bit like a baby owl, sitting there blinking at me.

"Why, yes," I said. "It lives on Demon Ridge, about ten miles east of here, and it's ever so fierce. It flies in every few weeks and burns our crops and steals our livestock. Last time, it made off with a full-grown cow—a good milker, too—and had a one-dragon barbecue. We'd be ever so grateful if you could coax that dragon into the next county—or farther."

Hotting Fuggam sat there for a long, long minute, pulling on his lower lip and frowning at the floor. "Yes," he said finally, pulling back his shoulders and clearing his throat. "Yes. Well." With the courtliest of manners, he ushered me through the door. "Let me think on it, and I'll see what I can do."

And that, I thought gleefully as I thumped down the stairs, was that.

You see, I truly didn't expect Hotting Fuggam to go after that monster on Demon Ridge. I expected him to pack his bag and slip quietly away well before sunup. And I was perfectly willing to settle his tab out of my own wages in order to sit down to a bowl of Mother's stew accompanied by a basket of fluffy biscuits. So I was more than a little dismayed when I bounced into his room early the next morning to find him in front of the mirror, settling his derby on his head just so.

"Wh-what are you doing?"

He turned to me with a smile. "I'm going to solve your dragon problem, my dear."

"Bu-bu-but . . ."

He patted my shoulder and led me from the room. "No need to worry. No need at all. But do ask your dear mother to reserve the room until I return."

Well, I felt so bad I went down to the kitchen and fixed him a nice basket of fruit and cheese—the only edible things in the house that didn't require cooking. I figured if his last meal couldn't be elegant, at least it could be substantial. So I packed the basket to the brim and watched him strut briskly toward the east, toward Demon Ridge, toward his last cookout.

By noon, everyone knew where Hotting Fuggam had gone. While we all agreed that he was crazy, we also felt guilty about not being better company during his last days.

By midafternoon, the smoke started rising above Demon Ridge. Great, black, belching, flame-flickering clouds of it. Everyone watched, horrified, until it got so late we couldn't tell the smoke from the night sky. I watched, too, and began to feel very, very guilty.

The next morning, the smoke cloud was thicker than ever, and it grew and grew and grew throughout the day. And the next day. And the day after that.

Four days after he had left, Hotting Fuggam returned to our village. His coat was dulled by ash and smoke, there were scorch marks on his trousers, and his shoes flap-flopped on his feet since the lacings must have become too heat-brittle to tie. But the most amazing thing was the creature that hop-flapped beside him, belching a little ball of smoke each time it landed, squawking in protest each time Hotting tugged on the belt-turned-leash.

We poured into the village square and formed a wary circle around Hotting Fuggam and the creature. He ignored everyone else, but he gave me a formal little bow and handed me his end of the leather belt.

"Your dragon, my dear."

Well. It certainly looked like a dragon, but this little critter would be doing well to make off with a piglet or a chicken. It would only annoy a full-grown cow.

"That's not our dragon," I sputtered.

"There wasn't another one," Hotting Fuggam replied.

"But . . ."

"Hot air," he said, puffing out his chest a bit. "It's all that hot air that puffs them up and makes them so big. Fills them up and makes them cranky. I just let the air out is all."

Everyone began jabbering then. How did he do it? What did he do?

As if they didn't know.

"One other thing," Hotting said, still looking at me. He pointed to the dragon, who already seemed a little more puffed up. "You have to keep using the fire, or he'll just get bigger again."

"Use the fire?" I said cautiously.

Hotting leaned over and tickled the dragon's belly. At first only smoke came out, but after a moment, there was a steady, six-inch flame coming out of the dragon's mouth. The dragon continued to huff and flame until Hotting stopped tickling. Then it flopped on its belly with a last belch of smoke and, letting out a little whimper, promptly fell asleep.

Now, Mother may have her faults, but she's no slow-top. "Think of the cooking fuel it will save," she muttered as she promptly grabbed the leash and dragged Smoky toward the back of our house to try him out.

The other folks dribbled away, and in a minute, the only people in the square were Hotting Fuggam and I. I almost said, "Thank you," but then I caught the gleam of truth in the little man's eyes, so I said, "Did you have a nice chat?"

Hotting Fuggam blushed.

"You know," I said, "it really wasn't fair of you, telling poor Smoky about all the things other dragons do in distant lands. After all, he's just a country dragon doing what country dragons do."

The little man smiled. "So are they all, my dear. So are they all. But unless one is very wise, what is familiar can never compete with what is not."

And with that, Hotting Fuggam gave me a courtly little bow and strutted off toward the boardinghouse.

TUNNEL

HER HAND SLIPPED ON THE SWEAT-GREASED steering wheel as she groped for the headlights switch. Her last thought was that it looked like a giant's open mouth displaying large stone teeth and an endless asphalt tongue.

Then the tunnel swallowed her.

Black. Silent except for the hum of rubber on asphalt. Full of savage red eyes in front of her, round white eyes in back. The car directly in front of her was an old model, the taillights, cat-eye slits in the fins, staring at her above a gleaming bumper grin. The Cheshire cat gone mad.

She concentrated on the lights, on the movement, grateful to be surrounded by cars on three sides. To her left there was only the darkness, the unforgiving stone. She wiped her hands on her jeans, one at a time, and concentrated on that still-unseen pin-prick of light at the far, far end. Concentrated on the promise of fresh air, daylight, a world expanding outward. Hope.

Chasing the cat-eye taillights, her hands tight on the wheel, she remembered a drawing class she'd once taken, remembered horizon lines and vanishing points. A trick of the eye. A matter of perception.

She flicked a glance to her right and suppressed a whimper. Only half a lane there, empty of cars. Empty of everything except encroaching stone. She took blind comfort in the glaring headlights behind her as she stepped on the accelerator, trying to close the distance between herself and the cat-eyed car in front. But the Cheshire cat sped along the asphalt thread until, with a last glowing wink of its eyes, it disappeared.

Only one pair of headlights behind her now. One where there had been so many.

There! For a moment she saw it, the pinprick of light up ahead. Hope surged through too-tense muscles, and she smiled just before a flash of light made her squeeze her eyes shut for a second. Nothing behind her now except the unrelenting dark.

She swerved to the right when stone scraped on metal, slowed a little to retain control, straddled a solid white line that divided nothing.

Stone scraped metal again, this time to the right. She slowed a little more, a little more, making fine adjustments with the steering wheel, her eyes steady, determined, fixed on the unwavering pinprick up ahead.

She slowed to a crawl, refusing to stop, while the stone scraped one side and then the other. Finally, when she heard both sides scrape, she stopped and tried to reverse . . . but the walls had narrowed. The scream of metal twisted by stone ended any thought of going back.

Her labored breathing filled the car as she opened the glove box, and her hand closed on the small flashlight. She flicked it on for a moment, comforted by the weak yellow circle. Slipping her head and one arm through the long strap of her purse, she put the flashlight inside the purse, rolled down the window, and squeezed through the narrow opening. She slid across the car's hood, finally resting against the grille, safe in the fading circle of the dying headlights.

Still ahead was the pinprick, the promise.

She took one step toward it and was surrounded by the dark. Reaching back, she couldn't feel the car, not even a trace of heat. She dug in her purse until she found the flashlight. Flicking the switch, she wasn't surprised to watch the glow fade a minute later. Still, it represented safety, so she held on to it as she took step by cautious step toward the pinprick of light.

THE FAIRY TALES

"Match Girl" was my first professional sale and is among the darkest stories I've ever written.

If I was going to boil down the message in these first three retellings, it would be that we can't wait for the prince; we must be our own champions.

The fourth fairy tale? I had circled around a retelling of "Snow White" for several months, trying different points of view that fizzled out after a few sentences—or before I wrote even that much. Then one evening, the first paragraph of this version came to me. I had intended to write those sentences and then make dinner. Hours later, food forgotten, I looked at the story and thought, *Where did you come from?* My only answer is that I dance with the Muse and follow where she leads.

Warning: "Match Girl" contains physical and
sexual violence as well as torture.

MATCH GIRL

I STUMBLED BEHIND THE WAGON AS IT STARTED across the bridge to Brimstone Spere. Even with rags wrapped around my torn boots, my feet were frozen past feeling, and I kept falling farther and farther behind. I'd been walking since sunup because Da said the horse couldn't pull the extra weight. Da always drove the wagon. Moll insisted she was too old to walk, and William, their grown son, was too delicate to brave the cold.

That left me.

No point thinking about that. As Moll always said, a stray picked up by the side of the road could earn her keep or stay by the side of the road. I'd seen too many girls lying in roadside ditches, frozen and crow-picked, not to know that, no matter how bad living with Da, Moll, and William made me feel, it could be worse.

Besides, there was no place to go, no promise of something better. Oh, travelers said there was a place of fire and magic on the other side of the mountains, a place full of dream-spinners and spell-weavers, but that was just camp talk. No one had ever found a road leading to the mountains, and no one had ever found a way over them.

Still, to have warmth and kindness, to have a roof and walls, to stay in one place and watch the seasons fade one into another until the cycle started again, to cup a handful of sun-warmed earth as if it were holy . . . What would I be willing to do to find such a place?

While I longed for that wishful flutter of warmth, my numb feet slipped in a rut, and I fell, turning my ankle as I hit the frozen ground.

The wagon continued across the bridge.

Blinking back tears and biting my lip, I staggered to the bridge and clung to the railing. No point crying out. They'd never look back to see if I was all right. They wouldn't help if I wasn't. If I fell by the roadside, they'd pick up the next likely stray, and the cycle would start over.

Half-blind from fatigue and the waning light, I kept my stiff hands on the railing and shuffled over the bridge's badly mended planks.

Once we made camp, there'd be a chance to rest. Once I fetched the water and firewood, I'd be able to pull off my wet boots and, hopefully, rub some feeling back into my feet.

The thought of fire pushed me into a limping run as I followed the fading wagon over the bridge and down the narrow road.

Despite my best efforts, the horse was already unhitched by the time I reached camp, and Moll was waiting for me. Her lips were a sharp line, and her eyes held that bright, brittle look that always meant pain.

"Dawdling again, you lazy slut?" Moll swung her arm.

The heavy hand slammed my shoulder into the wagon. I cried out, loud enough to satisfy Moll, muffled enough so Da and William could ignore it.

Moll looked me over. "You're a worthless piece of trash."

"Yes, ma'am," I whispered. My shoulder throbbed, but I didn't dare rub it.

Moll stepped closer. "Don't go speaking under your breath at me, girly."

"Yes, ma'am," I said louder.

"Yes, ma'am, what?"

My ribs squeezed my heart. "I'm a worthless piece of trash."

Moll's eyes glittered with satisfaction. "Don't forget it again." She sniffed and pulled her shawls closed. "The cold's brought out the ache in Da's back, and William's chest is rumbling again, so you'd best get the fire started before filling the buckets at the well. It's just a bit of a way down that path." With a last sniff, she left to assure Da and William that their needs would be met shortly.

I stayed behind for a minute, furiously blinking away tears. "My name's Phoenix," I whispered, swallowing the sobs that would earn me a strapping. "Phoenix, not 'girly.' And I am not trash. No matter what they say, I am not trash."

It was full dark before the chores were done and the precious ham bone simmered in the pot. Da and William sat by the fire on two of the three wooden crates we used for chairs. Moll fussed by the wagon.

Sighing, I stretched my hands toward the fire.

Three pairs of eyes stared at me.

Moll pulled a drawstring purse from the wagon and thrust it into my hands. "A penny a piece. Bring back bread for supper and a jug of wine for Da and William."

Confused, I opened the purse and stared at the matches. "Where do I sell them?"

Da hawked and spat. "Stupid as well as shiftless."

Moll shoved me away from the fire. "Town's on the other side of the trees. If you weren't always dreaming, you'd have seen the fires when you went to the well."

I turned away, not daring to glance at the fire or the pot that hung above it. I was just out of the fire's light when Moll grabbed my arm and pinched hard.

"I don't want any selfish, whining excuses outta you," Moll hissed. "You get that bread and jug of wine if it takes all night, you hear?"

"Yes, ma'am."

"I've left better than you in the ditches, girly. Just remember that."

I closed my eyes. The frozen, crow-picked girls didn't go away. "Yes, ma'am."

She let me go with a shove to help me on my way.

The path curved past the well and widened as I reached the town. The moon was the only light in the soot-black sky, but it looked smeared, as if a hand had tried to clean it but had left a layer of dirt. I wished it were brighter because I'd already tripped twice, and my hands and knees were raw from landing on the hard ground. When I saw the town, I wished the moon gone.

Brimstone Spere was a burned-out soul captured in a rotting shell. On both sides of the wide main street, crumbling buildings leaned over dark, narrow alleys that, despite the biting cold, stank of excrement and rot. Piles of garbage supported broken stairs. Shattered windows were covered with oiled paper that didn't keep out the cold. No smoke rose from the chimney stumps.

The town's residents seemed to live around the small bonfires in the center of the main street. At least the men did. They sat on wooden crates that circled the fires, passing around jugs of whiskey, laughing and gambling, filling the night with harsh words and dark intentions. Between the bonfires, merchant carts sold everything from bread and withered vegetables to whiskey and wine to remade clothes and boots to things made of brass and leather I was glad I couldn't name.

I thought I was too cold to be scared, but Brimstone Spere produced a shiver deep inside me. I wasn't sure if I was afraid of the danger I could see or the danger I could only feel.

I crept from building to building, staying in the shadows and hoping the men wouldn't notice me. I had to sell the matches, but only a fool would approach that many wine-flushed men who had that hard, hungry look in their eyes. Were there any women around the bonfires farther up the street, or were they all huddled inside the crumbling buildings? I'd already passed the wine seller and the bread cart. Neither had much left to sell. If I didn't hurry, I wouldn't get the supplies, and if Da and William became angry because they didn't get their wine, Moll would tie me to the wagon wheel and strap me again. Besides, there was a bowl of ham soup waiting for me.

With the threat of the strap and the promise of a bowl of hot soup spinning in my mind, I flitted past two more bonfires before pausing near an alley half-hidden by garbage. I pulled a fistful of matches from the drawstring purse I'd tied to my belt.

A hand grabbed my shoulder and spun me around.

He was a big, raggedly dressed man with a dark, greasy beard. His breath smelled of garlic and whiskey. The rest of him just stank.

Greasy-Beard grinned at me in a way that loosened my guts. "You're a bit skinny, tart."

I took shallow breaths through my mouth. "I'm not a tart, sir," I said politely, hoping politeness wouldn't get me hurt. "I'm a match girl."

Greasy-Beard's eyes glittered. "Well, match girl, I've got a candle that needs to be lit. How much?"

My hand shook as I wiggled one match out of my frozen fist. "A penny, sir." I held up the match.

He laughed. "A fair enough price." His fingers dug into my shoulder as he shoved me to my knees and fumbled with his clothes.

I flailed wildly, hitting his thighs and trying to break his grip because I knew what he was going to do, and his fingers hurt the shoulder that was already bruised.

He yelped in surprise and let go, but before I could scramble away, he pulled me up by my hair and slapped me twice. "Hit me again and I'll break your hands," he snarled. He yanked back on my hair, forcing my mouth open.

I choked and gagged while he used me. When he finished, he pushed my face against his groin and grunted with pleasure. "That's the only way a woman should use her mouth."

Finally, he pushed me away and slapped me again when I turned to spit. The blow sent me flying into the pile of garbage. I threw my hands out to protect my face, the matches scattering on the wet cobblestones in front of me. I felt a tickling shiver as a broken bottle sliced through the meaty part of my left hand. A moment later my body recovered from the shock, and the tickle became a throb of pain. I sat there, numb, staring at the blood pouring onto the cobblestones from the deep, jagged cut.

Laughing, Greasy-Beard dropped a penny in my lap and returned to the bonfire.

I don't know how long I sat there, whimpering and watching the blood run, before I regained enough sense to pull the rags off my boots and wrap them around my hand. My skirt was soaked with slush and blood, and my legs ached from sitting on the wet cobblestones. I needed warmth and a place to hide.

Light-headed, I giggled. I could hide in the alley, and I had all those nice little matches to keep me warm. Not all of them, no. Just one. Just for a little warmth. First, I had to pick up all the ones I'd dropped. They were wet and probably useless, but I'd never be able to explain losing that many, and Moll would think I'd used them and strap me.

Cradling my left hand against my belly, I got to my knees and reached for the dropped matches.

They were wet and red, floating in a pool of moonlight. As I stared at them, the wooden sticks changed to soot black and the match heads became tiny moons.

I picked one up. My fingers tingled as if they could already feel the warmth.

I gathered the matches and crawled into the alley, ignoring the smell and the rustling and squeaks. Dropping the white-headed matches into my lap, I held one up and stared at it.

It flared and burned.

Within that white halo was part of a clean, simple, cozy room. In the back corner, an iron stove stuffed with firewood sent out waves of heat. A large loom filled the front corner, positioned to catch the light from the side and front windows. Below the windows were shelves stuffed with woven baskets holding skeins of wool neatly sorted by color. There was a large throw rug in front of the stove and a rocking chair, still moving as if someone had just left.

I longed to sit at the loom, to hold those skeins of wool, to pick out colors in the winter light and create something beautiful as well as useful. I longed for that as much as I longed for the stove and the rocking chair. I imagined I was the one who'd left the chair rocking and would return in a minute. Drawn by the warmth from the stove, I leaned forward and . . . the match went out.

I quickly lit another white-headed match and waited impatiently for the room to reappear. Instead, there was only the smeared moon and an ancient, ageless voice.

There's the fire that burns from without and the fire that burns from within. One consumes; the other cleanses.

I stared at the burned-out match, puzzled by how a voice I'd never heard before could sound so familiar.

The cold burned my legs. I ignored it as I fumbled with the drawstrings and made sure the purse had an inside pocket. After placing the white-headed matches into the pocket, I staggered into the street.

Other men approached me, but I ran from them, afraid they wanted more than matches.

I found the women at the far end of the street. Gray in color, gray in spirit, they shuffled silently around their pitiful fires.

As I approached, an old woman, sitting alone, looked up and beckoned.

"Come, child," she said, smiling. "Come and warm yourself."

I hesitated, frightened by the twisted body wrapped in black rags. One of the crone's eyes was half-hidden by a scar-thickened lid, but there was intelligence in the other hazel eye and kindness in the wrinkled, scarred face.

"Thank you, ma'am." I sat on a wooden crate and held my hands toward the fire.

"Name's Nix. Tch! What happened to your hand, child?"

"I cut it."

"Let me see." Nix unwrapped the dirty rags and shook her head. "Tch. Has to be cleaned or it'll never heal. See?" She held up her left hand. There was a thick, jagged scar on the meaty part of her palm. "Thumb's not good for much because of that." She pulled a cloth sack into her lap, fumbling and muttering, finally pulling out a large bottle. "Hold still."

I bit my lip and cried silently while the liquid from the bottle burned and bubbled in the cut.

"Hurts fierce," Nix said, wrapping my hand in clean rags, "but it'll heal now if you take care." She fumbled in the bag once more, pulling out pinches of herbs and dropping them into a tea ball, which she lowered into a pot. "A medicinal tea. My own recipe. It'll help the healing."

"Thank you, ma'am." I closed my eyes and tucked my left hand against my belly. It hurt, but it was a clean hurt.

Nix poured the tea into two tin cups. "Why are you here, child?" she asked gently, handing me a cup.

I sipped the tea, pleasantly surprised by its taste. "Da and Moll wanted to come to Brimstone Spere to rest before going back out on the road, so I had to come too."

"Why?"

The scuffled footsteps of the other women seemed far away. If I closed my eyes, I could almost imagine the warmth from the fire coming from an iron stove. I shook my head. That place didn't exist. No point in dreaming. "I've got no choice."

Nix snorted. "There's always a choice, if you've courage enough to make it."

Unable to think of a reply, I looked away straight into the misery-filled eyes of a woman standing near another fire, wearing an iron cage around her head.

"Scold's bridle," Nix said quietly. "Her man slapped her because he didn't like the food on his plate, and she spoke sharply to him. That's her punishment. It was a first offense, so her tongue is spooned instead of spiked."

Horrified, I couldn't look away. "I don't understand."

"I hope by all that's sacred you never do, child."

The woman in the scold's bridle moaned.

Ashamed of staring at someone else's pain, I turned toward the fire. "I have to go." I set the empty cup on the ground. "Thank you for the tea, ma'am."

Nix studied the fire. "Tell me, child. Do you really believe you're selling matches in Brimstone Spere?"

I wondered uneasily if she could tell somehow what Greasy-Beard had done. "What else would I be selling?"

The haunted understanding in Nix's eye chilled me. "Perhaps little bits of your soul? Small sparks that, dribbled away, mean nothing but together could create a glorious blaze?"

I studied Nix's scarred face. "Do I know you?" I asked hesitantly. "Your face seems familiar, but . . ."

Nix's soft laugh was full of gentle bitterness. "Does it, now? Dreams seen in the fire can become real, you know, if you've courage enough to embrace the fire."

I glanced at the bonfire.

Nix shook her head. "There's more than one kind of fire, child."

I shivered. How could Nix know about the room in the white-headed match or what the voice had said? "Who are you?"

Nix pulled a few coins from her sack and pressed them into my good hand. "Here. That should be enough."

"I can't," I protested. "You'll need them for yourself."

"Will I?" she asked softly.

Mumbling my thanks, I hurried down the street.

Nix's voice followed me. "Remember, Phoenix. There are two kinds of fire. Which are you going to sell?"

I whirled around.

There was no one, and nothing, there.

The soup was gone by the time I returned to camp, but Moll grudgingly gave me a piece of fried bread and a cup of water while Da and William passed the wine jug between them.

Moll cuffed me for not being able to clean the dishes properly, but no one asked about my bandaged hand. When the dishes were finally put away, Moll said tightly, "Turn in."

There was only one reason I was allowed to turn in this early. I wasn't sure I could stand William shoving his thing inside me tonight. "I—I haven't finished the chores."

Moll's voice was flat and hard. "Turn in."

Not daring to argue, I climbed into the wagon, unrolled the two thin mattresses, and spread the blankets. I'd just managed to pull off my wet boots when William stumbled up the wagon's steps and fell heavily beside me. I tried to set the boots in a corner so the blankets and mattress wouldn't get wet, but William was already pushing me down, pulling at my clothes.

"Not tonight, William," I pleaded, pushing at his shoulders, hoping, just once, he might listen.

He tossed the boots aside and rammed his knee between my legs.

"Please, William, please. Not tonight."

He stared at me through narrowed eyes. "Why?" he asked, his voice slurred. He grabbed a fistful of my hair and pulled. "You been giving it out tonight? That why you don't want to do your duty?"

Tears leaked from my eyes. "No."

Grunting, William thrust into me. I whimpered.

"Tell me." There was a queer note in his voice. "Tell me what you did." His hand clamped on my breast and squeezed.

I told him what I'd been forced to do.

He rode me hard but finished quickly. When he rolled off me, he said, "Maybe we've got you selling the wrong thing."

I LEFT THE wagon before sunup, got the fire started, and had fetched one bucket of water from the well before Moll climbed down from the wagon. William had used me again last night and had roused Da from his wine-soaked sleep enough to demand woman's duty from Moll. Now she watched with bitter eyes as I tried to pour the water into the holding barrel.

"Slut," Moll hissed, yanking the bucket out of my hand. "Can't control yourself enough to let a decent woman get some rest."

No point telling her I wanted William's attentions even less than she wanted Da's.

She grabbed my bandaged hand and squeezed. I floated on the pain.

"If you're too delicate to earn your keep here, you can earn it in the alleys." Moll sniffed and closed her shawls. "Should've known something like you wouldn't try to do respectable work. Now git." She shoved me against the water barrel. "We need a slab of bacon and some bread for breakfast."

I cradled my bleeding hand. "I—I don't think there's enough coins left."

Moll's lips tightened. "I expect you'll find a way to earn them."

The sun was well up by the time I reached Brimstone Spere. The town looked worse in daylight. Except for a few starving mongrels nosing around the garbage piles, the wide main street was empty. Still, the merchant carts had to be somewhere, so I trudged up the street, slush seeping into my torn boots and freezing feet, which still hurt from yesterday. My hand throbbed. I pressed it against my belly, savoring the fever heat.

It took most of the morning to find the hog man and buy his last bit of bacon. It was mostly fat with a sliver of meat in the middle, but it was all he had and all I could afford. The bread cart had fresh bread already dusted with soot.

I sold a few matches to the women scurrying from cart to cart before scurrying back into the buildings. The rats were bolder than the women in Brimstone Spere. Since I had enough coins, I bought a half jug of wine for Da and William, hoping Moll would be pleased.

Moll wasn't pleased. She sported a fresh bruise on her cheek, Da's reaction to waking with a wicked head and a sore back and finding no food waiting for him. Moll said nothing as she took the supplies from me, but her eyes promised that the punishment would be worse because it was delayed.

No point asking if I'd get any of the food.

As soon as Moll started preparing the meal, I bolted for the trees, hoping I wouldn't stumble over Da or William. Moll wouldn't yell and call attention to herself today, and she wouldn't come after me if I got far enough away fast enough. It would give me a few hours before having to face the pain. A few hours of being wet, cold, and hungry.

The second time I tripped over a root, I gave up and crawled behind a tree, hoping it would shield me from anyone coming down the path. With my back pressed against the trunk, I pulled out a white-headed match and stared at it.

The match burned.

A different room, but part of the same place. Another iron stove, much larger than the first one. A well-scrubbed pine table sprinkled with woven mats of woodland browns and greens. Two places were set. Two thick slices of fresh bread lay on a cutting board with the rest of the loaf, waiting for the creamy butter. In the center of the table steamed a pot filled with thick chunks of meat, potatoes, carrots, and onions. Beside each plate was a mug of fresh milk.

I leaned forward and breathed deeply, my mouth watering. I couldn't imagine why there were two places set or why I'd want anyone living in my house, but I imagined it was my table, my plates, my food. I reached to pull out a chair and sit down.

The match went out.

I cried out in disappointment, hurriedly dug out another white-headed match, and then hesitated. Last time, the picture didn't come back. Last time, there'd been that ageless, ancient voice.

I licked my lips and stared at the match.

There's more than one kind of hunger.

I dropped the match and slowly got to my feet. There might be more than one kind of hunger, but if I didn't get some food and warmth soon, the other kinds wouldn't matter.

I spent the rest of the day on the edge of Brimstone Spere, my mind as numb as my body. When night fell, I once again crept along the wide main street.

The bonfires promised warmth to my sluggish body. The men circling the fires promised something else. A few of them bought matches from me, satisfied with a quick grope before letting me go. A couple thought I owed them more than a match for the penny price, but something made them nervous enough to step away after a few obscene gestures and suggestions.

Shivering and exhausted, I stepped into an alley, leaned against the wall, and raised my right hand to my face. It was the only way I could tell if I was still holding the matches.

So cold, I stared at the bonfires. If I threw myself on top of one, would there be a moment of warmth and comfort before the pain? If I sold my body to those men, would they let me stay by the fire? Would they give me something to eat?

I pushed away from the wall.

"There's more than one kind of hunger, child." Nix's voice floated from the alley's depths. "There's more than one kind of cold. You can warm the body and still freeze to death."

"Doesn't matter," I said through chattering teeth.

"You think not?" A twisted hand pointed past my shoulder.

I looked where the finger pointed. A woman lurched down the street, her lower legs encased in wood.

"Leg presses," Nix said softly. "The screws are tightened every few hours. The bones are crushed by now. The wood's the only thing keeping her up."

"Why's she trying to walk, then?" I whispered, feeling sick.

"Punishment. She tried to run away, tried to get out of Brimstone Spere. Now she has to walk from one end of the street to the other. When her master finally removes the presses, she won't be able to run from anyone or anything. More than bone is crushed in that wood, child."

I turned. "How do you know . . . ?"

I stared at the empty alley. Cold, exhaustion, hunger. I knew they were real because they hurt. But Nix? Maybe Nix was nothing more than a dream dressed in hunger and cold, no more real than the place that existed in the white-headed matches.

At least that dream place held a measure of peace.

I fumbled with the purse's strings, trying to open it without dropping the matches already clutched in my hand. My left hand was almost useless, but it was so numbed by the cold it no longer hurt. I was concentrating on the purse so hard I didn't hear the approaching footsteps or realize anyone was there until two hands pressed me against the wall.

"I've been looking for you, match girl," the man said.

He was the first man I'd seen in Brimstone Spere who had clean, unpatched clothes and didn't stink. Because of that, he scared me more than the rest of them put together.

"You want to buy a match, sir?" I raised my hand timidly.

The man's soft laugh held a cruel note. Gripping my chin, he turned my head from side to side. "You'd be passably pretty if you were clean and fed." He pulled aside my ragged shirt, cupped my breasts, and smiled, satisfied, as my nipples stiffened beneath his thumbs.

I shivered. No point saying my body was reacting to the cold and not his touch.

He continued to cup one breast and tease the nipple while he reached beneath my skirt and thrust his rough fingers into me.

He released my breast to muffle my scream, pressing my head against the wall while I twitched and jerked like a puppet.

Then he pulled out his fingers and thrust his thing into me, scraping my back and buttocks against the stone wall.

When he was done, he squeezed my shoulders and smiled. "You're tight enough, but too dry to give much pleasure." He laughed and ground his hips against me. "That's no problem. I've got medicines that can change that quick enough. You'll like being one of my women, match girl. You won't have to sell little fire sticks when you've got something hotter to sell." His fingers dug into my shoulders. "I take good care of my women as long as they treat me right." He stepped away from me and arranged his clothes. "I'm sure your master and I can reach an agreement."

I waited until his footsteps faded before peering around the corner.

The street looked different. The bonfires weren't in the same place. A woman wearing a wool cape over a velvet dress wearily climbed the steps of the building I leaned against. She looked feverish and drunk in a strange kind of way and, despite the warm clothes, I could tell she was frozen.

"Phoebe!" The man who'd just left the alley strode up the street, his teeth bared and his hands clenched.

The woman turned toward him. "Master Colton," she said in a dead voice.

Colton reached the stairs and gripped the rail. "Damn you, Phoebe! Stop acting like a dried-up bitch and get your ass in there."

Phoebe's lifeless hazel eyes stared at him a moment before she climbed the rest of the stairs and went into the building.

Shaken, I stepped farther into the alley. William didn't own me, but he'd sell me fast enough for the price of a few jugs of wine. Moll would complain bitterly about having to do all the work, but they'd pick up another bewildered, starving child once they started traveling again. That was the world, the only world I'd ever known except for that place in the dreamscape.

I pulled out a white-headed match.

It was late spring, maybe early summer. A soft ivory shawl slipped off my shoulders as I followed the sun-dappled path up a gentle slope, brushing aside low-hanging branches with an easy hand. Birds flitted through the trees around me. Out of sight but nearby, water sang over stone. I was in no hurry, simply walking to enjoy the afternoon warmth and the smell of rich earth.

As I neared the top of the slope, I reached for a handhold to help me up the last few feet.

A man's hand reached down.

Startled, I jerked back, almost losing my balance. The hand remained still, silently offering its strength. There was kindness and understanding in the man's face, and his eyes held respect as well as desire.

I smiled shyly and reached for his hand.

The match went out.

I held up another white-headed match.

If you have the courage.

I stared at the match for a long time. The courage to do what?

I knew. Just as I knew that the place in the matches was real, or could be. Just as I knew that the stories about dream-spinners and spell-weavers living on the other side of the mountains were more than camp talk. I knew . . . but I didn't have the courage.

I DRIFTED THROUGH the next day, stumbling from one chore to the next. The wind had picked up, and I froze despite my exertions. I couldn't feel my legs below my knees, and my fingers were too stiff to bend. It didn't matter. Soon I'd be nothing more than a burned-out soul captured in a rotting shell.

I was too numb to wonder why William tensed every time I left camp for water or firewood, or why, as the afternoon waned, he watched me so anxiously. I was too numb to remember there was a reason to be afraid.

Night fell early that last day. Da had already gone into Brimstone Spere for the cockfights, so it was just the three of us gathered around the fire. Bitterly silent, Moll filled tin cups with soup. William pressed a cup into my hands, smiling queerly. The hot tin burned my hands. I didn't feel it.

I was half-finished when William took the cup from me and pulled me to my feet. "Time to go," he said, still smiling. He grabbed a blanket from the wagon and threw it over his shoulders before gripping my arm and heading up the path to Brimstone Spere.

"We've got a big night ahead of us. Don't want you to fall and hurt yourself," he said cheerfully, tugging me along, never noticing that I couldn't keep up with his longer stride.

Colton waited for us by the largest bonfire, his smile cruel and knowing.

That was when I remembered the danger. Something inside me snapped.

I jerked out of William's grasp, struggling to keep my balance. Scowling, William grabbed for me. I knocked his hand away.

"Don't give me any trouble, you selfish bitch," William snarled.

A spark of anger burned in my belly. I spat the words like venom. "You spineless, grubby little prick. You don't own me. Nobody owns me. I won't be sold so you can fill your belly with wine."

"Bitch!" William lunged at me, screaming.

I dodged him and tried to run, but suddenly there were men all around me, grabbing my arms and legs while I bit, kicked, scratched, screamed, did everything I could think of to get free. Pinned, I watched William's fist come toward my face, but Colton grabbed him.

"If she's damaged, the deal's off," Colton snapped.

William hesitated, then stepped back, pouting. "Bitch."

Colton smiled and clapped William's shoulder. "A couple of hours bridled and saddled will take the fight out of her."

I kicked and screamed as the men dragged me toward an unlit bonfire. While one man started the fire, others dragged a piece of canvas off a wooden device. The front of it looked like the stocks I'd seen in other towns, but low to the ground. The rest was a terrifying triangle of wood and leather straps.

Greasy-Beard came up the street carrying two head cages. "Spooned or spiked?" he asked Colton respectfully.

"Spooned," Colton replied. "I don't want her mouth damaged permanently."

Greasy-Beard dropped one cage, opened the other, and held it over my face. The spoon was a piece of nubbed metal shaped like William's thing. "Open wide," he said with a leering grin. "You know how to do that."

I clamped my teeth together.

Undisturbed by my small rebellion, Colton pulled my shirt open and pinched my nipple until I screamed. Laughing, Greasy-Beard thrust the spoon into my mouth. The nubs scoured my tongue. Once the metal cage was locked around my head, Colton released my nipple after a final squeeze.

I moaned. I couldn't help it. The nubs scraped my raw

tongue, and the cage forced my mouth closed so that the metal cut my lips.

Greasy-Beard locked my head and hands into the stocks while William and Colton forced my legs apart and strapped them to the saddle. When they were done, Colton threw my skirt over my back and thrust his rough fingers into me. I squealed and struggled, but the straps held me tight.

Colton laughed and gave my ass a hard slap. "Who wants to ride the fidgets out of my new mare?"

Men laughed. Coins clinked as they changed hands. Then hands squeezed my breasts as the first rider mounted.

After the third man, William squatted in front of me and smiled. "Tell me you're sorry, and I'll let you go."

I tried desperately, but I couldn't form words.

William shook his head. "Not ready yet? Just as well." He patted the front of the cage. The spoon scraped my tongue until it bled.

I screamed while William drank and Colton laughed and man after man rode me hard. When I couldn't scream anymore, they let me go.

I sat on the wet cobblestones until Colton hauled me to my feet. I stared dumbly at him as he removed the scold's bridle. Blood dribbled from my mouth.

Colton smiled. "After this, you'll appreciate having something softer in your mouth, even if it's just as hard."

Men slapped their thighs and laughed. William staggered by, grinning obscenely.

"Don't try to run away, match girl," Colton said with soft menace. He pointed to a woman crawling toward a bonfire, dragging what was left of her legs, and shook his head. "A damn shame she tried to run away. She was a good tart. Made a decent profit for me."

Colton sauntered to the largest bonfire, whistling confidently as he swung the scold's bridle from his fingers.

My mind started working again. Run? Oh, I was going to run. Even if my body never left this place, I was going to run farther than he'd ever imagine. Better to freeze in the warmth of a dream than live another day in Brimstone Spere.

But I was still scared.

Struggling to stay upright, I turned away from the men and hobbled up the street. I looked back once. Colton watched me, smiling, sure I couldn't escape. Keeping to the shadows, I passed the last bonfire crowded with bent, gray women and slipped into the alley.

I braced my back against the wall. I didn't dare sit down because I wasn't sure I could get up again. It took both hands and my teeth to open the drawstring purse. I pulled out a white-headed match.

I ran through the large garden behind the cottage, searching desperately. I rushed past vegetable beds that would have held me spellbound a few hours ago. I ignored the magical pull of the herbs. I was blind to the glorious flowers. I cried as I ran, sure the match would go out before I saw her.

When I finally found her, she was kneeling beside a flower bed, cupping a handful of sun-warmed earth as if it were holy. There were moon-silver streaks in her shining black hair, and her hazel eyes were shadowed with old pain and shining with hard-earned wisdom.

"Choose, Phoenix," she said in a voice that was ancient, ageless, and as familiar as my own.

I dropped the burned-out match and pulled three more from

the purse. Bracing my arm against the wall, I faced the front of the alley and held the matches up to the full moon.

Nix studied me from the white fire of the first match. Phoebe stared at me from the second. Phoenix watched with haunted understanding from the third.

New life rises from the ashes of the old, child, Nix whispered.

The match burned out, and she vanished.

Phoebe flinched, said nothing, and vanished.

You know what to do, Phoenix urged as she began to fade.

"Will it hurt?" I asked, knowing it was a child's question but too scared to care.

Of course. But you already knew that.

Yes, I did. I pulled out the last white-headed match.

"Phoenix!"

Startled, I dropped the match. William blocked the exit.

"What are you doing in here? Colton wants you." He stepped into the alley.

I grabbed the match and scrambled backward. "No," I whispered, wondering if I was too late, wondering if he could stop what would happen once it began. "No."

"Don't give me any sass," he snarled, pushing me farther and farther back.

One more step and I'd lose the moon.

Shaking, I held up the match.

William raised his fist.

The match flared bloodred before turning a cold, burning white. I tipped my head back and dropped the match down my throat.

My soul caught fire and shattered my life. I burst into flames.

William screamed and ran.

Pain blazed through me as nerves sizzled, flesh melted, bone charred, skin crackled and split. My hair stood on end as fire leaped from my skull. The last thing I saw before my eyes exploded was the moon riding full and clean in the soot-black sky.

I OPENED MY new eyes. They were hazel, the color of the woodland.

I took a deep breath. The sweet, steady Fire burning inside me tingled. I studied the thin, clean scar on my moon-white hand and smiled as I brushed shining black hair from my shoulders. My gown was a soft, midnight rainbow. When I raised my arms, the sleeves lifted like wings.

I was Dream-Spinner, Spell-Weaver, Woman.

The people of Brimstone Spere would call me other things. It didn't matter. Beyond the mountains were other women like me and men with the strength and courage to embrace a woman of fire.

I left the alley and glided down the street.

I passed Colton. He made a sign against evil and fled. As I passed Greasy-Beard, he picked up a chunk of wood. Fire spat from my fingertips. The wood burst into flames, and he screamed.

Da and William stared openmouthed for a moment before stumbling after me, calling to me, telling me to remember everything they'd done for me.

I passed the well and followed the path to the camp.

Moll stared at me with bitter eyes. "I could have been like you." Her expression softened, and she reached out. "Stay, girl. Stay and help Moll."

I shook my head. She didn't want to embrace the Fire; she

only wanted to use mine, and Fire is too sacred to be given away to those who will not cherish it.

Moll cursed me when I turned away and followed the narrow road to the bridge. As I crossed the gray, rotting wood, curls of smoke rose from my footsteps. A path opened before me. Never looking back, I walked toward the mountains and the life beyond while the bridge to Brimstone Spere burned to ash.

RAPUNZEL

'VE ALWAYS CRAVED WHAT I COULDN'T HAVE. AT first, I craved the blacksmith's son because, in our village, a good blacksmith was a respected man. Then I craved the miller's son because he was handsome, and his father was prosperous. Then I craved the merchant's son because he was educated, and his father was wealthy.

Instead, I got Amery, because after the others had gotten what they craved from me, they had continued to speak flowery words of love but never spoke of marriage.

A simple, hardworking man, Amery knew—after the wedding night, anyway—that he hadn't been my first choice, but he did everything in his power to show me how much he loved me.

When I craved the fancy lace and expensive silk some of the ladies in the village wore, Amery worked extra hours for weeks to buy them for me. He even paid the village seamstress to make the dress so that I would have one fine garment to wear on special occasions, one fancy dress that wasn't put together with my indifferent stitches.

I wore it twice before I became ashamed of it.

When I craved a garden like the other women had, bright with flowers and bursting with fresh vegetables, Amery got up early for a full week and prepared the soil. When the ground remained empty, he paid good money for seedlings instead of buying seeds and planted the garden on his rest day while I was out visiting.

I was delighted to see my young garden appear like magic, but I lost interest in a week or two when the weeding and watering became a chore. After that, Amery cared for it whenever he had time.

There were so many things I craved, so many things that always seemed just out of reach, but what I craved most of all was a child. It shamed me to stand on the outside of the circle of women who would gather on market days and exchange stories and boasts and sorrows about their children. It shamed me that I had neither helpful hints to pass along nor reason to ask the older women's advice about childhood troubles. I was never in the center of that circle, being praised or soothed for no more reason than being a mother.

Amery failed me for years, but finally, miraculously, the day came when I knew I carried a child.

Overjoyed, Amery couldn't do enough for me. He worked harder than ever, more hours than ever to put aside a little money for whatever the child would need. On his rest days, he built a fine, sturdy cradle. He bought special brews and herb bags from the village granny to ease my sickness. If I felt too ill or weak to do my housework, he would do it when he got home. If I hadn't done any cooking or baking, he would heat the soup, set out the day-old bread, then encourage me to eat, waiting until I'd had my fill before easing his own hunger with whatever was left.

Best of all, I was now part of the inner circle when the women gathered on market day. I was the one being given soothing advice and gently ribald teasing. I was the one who received the sympathetic tongue-clucking when I hesitantly admitted to feeling so tired by the time I finished the housework.

For the first time in my life, I had everything I craved.

And then I went up into the cottage loft and saw Gothel's garden.

I don't remember why I was up in the loft. I never went up there because I didn't like the narrow stairs. Maybe I wanted to see if it would make a suitable room for the child. All I clearly remember is looking out the small window and realizing that, for the first time, I could see over the high stone wall that separated Gothel's land from our little piece of ground, could see the lush, vibrant garden that made every other garden in the village look pale and withered. Most of all, I could see the bed of fresh, green Rapunzel lettuce.

I stood there in that hot, dusty little loft with my mouth watering because I could almost taste that lettuce and with tears streaming down my face because I knew I'd never get any. The village granny knew a bit about herbs and charms, but Gothel was a witch full and true, and that stone wall wasn't so high just to keep out the deer and rabbits.

Shaking, I managed to climb down the loft stairs. By then the craving was so intense it made me dizzy and weak, so I lay down on the bed. I was still there when Amery came home and found me.

It took him an hour of coaxing before, sighing and sniffling, I told him about the lettuce I so desperately craved.

His eyes went blank with shock. He rubbed my hands. "But,

Hedwig, dearest, that's Gothel's land. Besides, we have lettuce in our own garden. I'll pick some and then—"

"Not like that lettuce," I snapped, pulling my hands from his and hiding them under my apron. My lower lip quivered. "No one else has lettuce like that. *No one.*"

"Hedwig." His voice trembled with an unspoken plea.

Knowing better than to act sullen, I gave him a brave little smile and said, "You're right, Amery. Of course you're right. Lettuce is lettuce. Pick some from our garden, and I'll make a nice salad."

And I did, all the while apologizing for silly women's cravings.

Amery's relief faded during the meal as I nibbled the salad and kept saying how good it was so he'd know how hard I was trying to pretend these scrawny, wilted leaves tasted the same as the fresh, green ones I'd seen over the garden wall.

For a few days, I made sure there was a hot meal waiting for Amery when he got home, a hot meal I'd only pick at despite his coaxing. A couple of days after that, he came home one evening and handed me a square of cloth filled with large, fresh, beautiful green leaves.

"Amery," I said breathlessly, hugging the bundle. I knew exactly how they would taste, exactly how it would feel to chew and swallow those fresh, green leaves. "Amery, did you really . . . ?"

He wouldn't look at me. And I knew. Just as I knew I wouldn't be able to taste anything with so much bitterness filling my mouth.

"Mistress Olinda has the finest garden in the village," Amery mumbled. "I thought . . ."

"Not the finest." I opened my arms and let the bundle fall to the unswept kitchen floor. "Not *the* finest." I went behind the blanket that separated our bed from the rest of the room and lay down.

Amery apologized, coaxed, and pleaded for an hour, sounding as if his heart would break. Weary of him, I got up, fixed the salad, and tried to eat it to prove to him that I wasn't being stubborn.

As the days passed, I did less and less. Every morning I climbed the narrow stairs up to the loft and stared out the window at that bed of fresh, green Rapunzel lettuce that I would never taste. When the dust and heat became too much, I'd go back to the kitchen and sit there, doing nothing, feeling nothing. I couldn't even rouse myself to meet the other women on market day.

Finally, one evening when Amery came home, I held out my hand to him and said quietly, "Amery, I'm not trying to be stubborn. Truly I'm not. But I want you to know . . . Amery, I will die if I don't taste the lettuce growing in Gothel's garden."

I saw the anguish in his eyes, and the fear. He stood still and silent for a moment before he sighed and left the cottage. A while later, he rushed back inside, breathing hard. He fumbled inside his shirt and pulled out a thick handful of green leaves.

Tears filled my eyes as I hugged him. I wasn't sure if I was laughing or crying the whole time I carefully washed each of those leaves. I quickly made a salad and ate every bit of it, sighing contentedly between each mouthful.

By the next day, however, the craving was three times worse because now I knew, *really* knew, how good that lettuce tasted. When Amery came home that evening and listened to my stumbling, tearful words, he just nodded and went out again.

He was gone much longer the second time. When he came back, he was shaking terribly and his skin was sickly gray.

"She caught me," he gasped, collapsing against the kitchen table. "Gothel caught me as I was leaving."

I pressed my hand against my mouth, feeling sick with relief when I saw that he still had both of his big, callused hands. Weaving slightly, I fetched the bottle of spirits we kept for special occasions and poured a calming glass for both of us.

Minutes passed. Amery sipped his drink and stared at the kitchen table. I could see a little bit of green poking through his shirt ties. Finally, my patience snapped. I wanted to know what happened. I wanted him to hand over the Rapunzel so that I could make my salad. "So Gothel caught you. What did she say? What did *you* say?"

"What could I say, Hedwig?" Amery asked, sounding beaten. "Thief she called me and thief I am. I tried to explain about your need. I offered to do work for her to pay for what I'd taken. I even offered her the bit of money we'd saved up."

I choked back my resentment. I'd counted on that money to buy some things for the child so that when the other women offered clothes their children had outgrown, they would understand I was accepting out of neighborly practicality rather than needing their charity.

"She took all of it?" I finally asked. "*All* of it?"

"No." Amery's voice shook. "She wouldn't accept money in exchange for what was taken." He tugged the leaves out of his shirt and laid them on the table between us. He tried to smile. "She said that, being a woman, she understood about these little cravings, and that you could have as much Rapunzel as you desired."

"Well, then." Annoyed that he had frightened me by making such a fuss but willing to overlook it, I reached for the fresh, green leaves.

As Amery watched me gather the leaves, a terrible *something* filled his eyes. I thought about what he'd said. My hands wouldn't move.

"If she didn't accept the money . . ." Amery said nothing, forcing me to ask outright. "What does she want in exchange?"

Amery refilled his glass and took a big swallow before answering. "She wants the child."

"*No!*" I flung the leaves at him and wrapped my arms over my belly. "I don't want it. Give it back to her. What were you thinking to make such a bargain?"

"I had no say in this bargain, Hedwig. I had no say." He flicked a finger at the leaves scattered on the table. "And it makes no difference if I give these back. These, and all the other helpings to come, are a gift. The child is payment for what was already taken." He pushed away from the table but stayed long enough to rest a hand on my shoulder, as if that would comfort me. "I'm going to sit outside for a bit. Fix your salad, Hedwig. You don't want the cravings to make you ill again."

I couldn't stomach those fresh, green leaves, not that night or any night after. I never asked for Rapunzel again, hoping Gothel might forget the bargain in the months remaining before the child was born. I never asked, but every morning there was a handful of fresh, green leaves tied with a bloodred ribbon waiting for me on the front step.

It rained the night I sweated and wept and screamed my daughter into the world. I remember because the sound soothed me and helped me rest whenever I could. I remember because the morning stayed dark long after the sun should have risen. I remember because I haven't seen a bright morning since then.

Amery stood beside the bed, crying silently, smiling bravely. When it was over, the midwife let him hold the babe while she fussed and soothed and tended me. Too soon, I was back in the freshened bed, washed and wearing a clean nightgown, and the midwife was gone.

I held out my arms. "Give her to me."

Just as Amery laid the babe in my arms, another voice said, "Give her to me."

Gothel stood beside the bed. Tall, thin Gothel with her witch-wild black hair and eyes so light they looked more silver than gray.

"Give her to me," Gothel said again, reaching for the child.

I couldn't speak. I couldn't move. I couldn't look away from those silver eyes.

And then she was gone, and my arms were empty.

Amery patted my shoulder. "Rest, Hedwig," he said in a broken voice. "Rest."

Alone, I lay listening to the sounds that came from behind the blanket that separated our bed from the rest of the room. I heard the scrape of a kitchen chair being pulled away from the table. I heard the heart-tearing, muffled sobs.

I listened and grew angry. What was I supposed to tell the other women when they came to see the babe? The midwife knew the child had been alive and well when she'd left. How could I say it died and not have a body to show? Even if I managed to keep them all away, how would I explain never bringing the child when I went out on market day? How would I explain that Gothel, the witch, had my child?

How would I explain?

Anger pushed me out of bed. I shuffled to the blanket, pulled it aside, and stared at Amery, his head pillowed on his arms as he sobbed.

"This is your fault." I leaned against the wall to steady myself.

Amery wiped his face with his sleeve and looked at me. "What was I to do, Hedwig? What was I to do?" He raised his big, callused hands. "If I'd lost my hands for thieving, how would we have lived? How would we have provided for the child?"

"Then you shouldn't have done it!"

"But you would have died."

He looked so bewildered I couldn't stand it. "Don't be such a fool," I said with all the contempt I felt for him at that moment. "Who ever heard of a woman dying from a little craving?"

He stared at me. Stared and stared. Then his face changed. It took a long time for me to realize that what I had seen was his love for me trickling away when he finally understood.

Saying nothing, Amery went to the chest at the foot of our bed and pulled out the cloth traveling bag he used whenever he had to work away from the village for a few days. He packed his other change of clothes, packed his shaving mug and razor, packed everything he could call his own.

It all fit in that one bag.

Still saying nothing, he brushed past me and picked up the wooden box that held the tools that had been handed down to him from his father and his grandfather.

Then he walked out the door.

The last thing I said to him, the last thing I screamed at him as he walked down the road and out of my life, was "You sold my daughter for *lettuce*!"

MEN ARE THIEVES.

You put your heart and magic into something to make it beautiful; you build walls to keep it untainted by the world; you nurture it for the pleasure it will bring you, and they'll sniff it out, no matter how high the walls, and taint the pleasure, sully the beauty.

Like that thief spoiled my lovely garden.

Like that prince spoiled my Rapunzel.

I thought I'd kept her well hidden in the high tower in the heart of a forest. Not so. The princeling sniffed her out even there.

I remember the day her betrayal of my affection could no longer be hidden. I remember how she held her head up even though she trembled with fear. I'd given her everything she needed: good food and fine clothes, needlework and music to keep her occupied, my company when I visited the tower. And do you know what that ungrateful girl said when I discovered her deceit? "He loves me."

"Loves you?" I screamed. I grabbed her golden braid and began pulling it toward me, hand over hand. "Of course he loves you. Why wouldn't he love a beautiful girl so innocent and untouched by the world? But what kind of love does he feel for you, my sweet Rapunzel? Hmm? What kind of love? I'll tell you what kind. Passion's love. The body's love. The kind that fades with the dawn and returns with the twilight. You think not? Then why didn't he take you away?"

Her lips quivered, but she didn't cry. "He *is* going to take me away. I'm weaving a ladder from the skeins of silk he brings each evening. When it's finished, we'll go far away from here."

I laughed and drew more of the braid through my hands. "Skeins of silk? Weave a ladder? You're such a fool, Rapunzel. If he truly wanted to love you anywhere but the bed, why didn't he bring a rope? Better yet, why didn't he free you from *this* golden rope?"

She hesitated, didn't answer. I could see in her eyes that she'd wondered the same thing, but, having no knowledge of the world and its thieves, she didn't understand.

"I'll tell you." Nothing but a few feet of taut braid between us. "Because this is a fine leash, sweet Rapunzel. A fine, golden leash. No other woman could cover his bed with such a curtain of gold. Out there, in the world, a woman would be chained by hair like this. But he didn't mention that, did he? Of course not. Do you want to know what would have really happened? Your prince would have continued to come each evening, bringing you silk so that you would spend your time weaving a useless ladder. It's a high tower. How many rungs of this ladder do you get from a skein of silk? Long before the ladder was finished, you would become too big, too awkward, for your prince to enjoy. The night would come when he'd have to sit and talk with you instead of showing you how much he *loves* you. He'd kiss you before he left, but he wouldn't come the next night. Or the night after that. He wouldn't return, Rapunzel, because you would no longer be the girl he craved, and you never would be again. But he would remember and love you forever—whenever he thought of you at all."

I jerked the braid. When she stumbled against me, I grabbed the hair at the back of her neck. "And I'm to care for his spoiled leavings while he goes away with sweet memories? I think not, Rapunzel. I think not."

I slapped her. Slapped her and slapped her. When she fell and tried to protect her face and belly, I pounded her with my fists. Pounded and pounded as if that would change anything.

It didn't. Nothing would change her back into what she'd been.

When I left the village all those years ago, I blighted the

garden so that no one else would enjoy its bounty. Between one breath and the next, the flowers withered and the vegetables began to rot.

Nothing so quick for my sweet Rapunzel.

I dragged her across the floor until I reached her needlework basket. Then I snatched up the shears and cut off her braid.

She trembled when I put my arms around her.

She shuddered when I smiled at her.

Swifter than a fleeing shadow, I took her away from the tower and brought her to a desolate place. Oh, she could survive there, if she knew how to work, how to scratch a living from harsh land.

I took a sharp stone and drew a circle around her, a circle as large as the tower. "Here's your new home, sweet Rapunzel," I spat at her. "Here's the bounty your deceit deserves."

She looked around, her eyes dulled by pain as she struggled to understand. Finally, she looked at me and made an effort to stand straight and tall.

I wouldn't tolerate her pride, so I told her about her parents, about how she'd come to be in my possession. I told her *everything*. When I was done, she had no pride. She slumped to the ground, as beaten in spirit as she was in body. What was left of her hair hung limply around a face already swollen and discolored by bruises. Sitting there, she no longer looked like my Rapunzel.

And I was glad.

I returned to the tower before nightfall and prepared my magic. I didn't have to wait long before I heard him call out, "Rapunzel, Rapunzel, let down your hair." I secured the braid to the window and let it tumble down to meet him.

Such a fine, handsome boy, so eager for his love.

He wasn't eager to finish the climb when I leaned out the window, the shears in my hand, and smiled at him.

"A pleasant evening for love, wouldn't you say, princeling? But sweet Rapunzel has gone away. Far, far away. So far away, *your* desire will never find her. Nothing to say, princeling? Nothing to say? I thought not."

I swiped at him with the shears. He wasn't in reach, but he jumped back just the same, losing his grip on the golden braid.

As he fell, the thorns of my anger sprouted and grew. Grew and grew as he fell, screaming. They pierced his eyes, his ears, his heart. Then they melted away.

Shaken and bruised but otherwise unharmed, he looked up at me.

"Justice tempered with mercy, princeling. Another thief asked that of me, many years ago. This is my justice. Your heart will never forget her. Whenever you look upon another woman, you will also see the innocent beauty no woman touched by the world can match. Whenever a woman speaks to you, you will also hear the voice no other can match in sweetness. She'll be with you always and never with you, and she'll become more lovely with each passing year because you will grow older, but she will always be sweet Rapunzel."

I watched him stumble away, already grieving even though it would take some time for him to realize he'd just begun to grieve.

I pulled up the braid and coiled it in the center of the bed.

My sweet, deceitful Rapunzel. She'll spend the rest of her miserable life locked in a tower she'll never escape. When it comes to building walls, words can be stronger than stones.

Because the last thing I said to her, the last thing I screamed at her before I left her in that desolate place, was "I bought you for a handful of *lettuce*!"

A STONE WALL surrounds my garden, high enough to keep the village dogs and other small animals out and low enough that neighbors can rest their arms on the top stones while they tell me the day's news. Everyone says I have the finest garden in the village. Ethelde says it's because there's magic in me, that the Lady of the Land, She of Many Names, claims me as a daughter, and any land I work with my own hands becomes fertile ground.

Who am I to argue with the wisewoman, the witch, my mentor?

I sometimes wonder if Gothel thought she was working magic when she left me in that desolate place. Did she think a circle scratched into the ground would hold me in the same way as a tower of stone? Or had affection warred with pride at the very end, and that circle was the only way she knew how to set me free without admitting it?

For a long time, I neither knew nor cared, but now that strands of silver weave themselves through my golden hair and my eldest daughter swiftly approaches the time when the women in the village will celebrate her first rite of passage between girl and woman, I find myself thinking about all of them: the parents I never knew, Gothel, my handsome young prince.

I don't remember much about the journey from that desolate place to this village. I remember I stayed within that circle the first night, too numb, too frightened, to move. And then the sun rose, and some promise carried on the wind sang within me.

With my feet planted firmly in the earth, I raised my arms to the sun and wind in an ancient, instinctive greeting.

I stood there for a long time. Then I said to She of Many Names, "No more towers," and stepped out of the circle. After that, grief and fear clouded my mind and shadowed my thoughts so fiercely the world slipped away from me. Or I slipped away from it.

But I kept following the promise carried on the wind.

Eventually it brought me to Ethelde.

For the first few days, I ate the broths and bread she set before me. I slept through the nights and most of the daylight hours as well. I walked in her garden, blind to the glory all around me. I saw the plants as strangers I didn't care to know, so I didn't ask their names, and Ethelde didn't offer to tell me.

But as the weeks passed and my belly swelled, as I watched Ethelde's garden grow and bloom, as my body learned what my mind was not yet ready to embrace, I began to change. I began following Ethelde around the cottage and garden as she went about her work. She welcomed my company but never explained her tasks. She sang while she worked, and the songs always fit the rhythm of the task.

After a while, I began to sing with her.

She just smiled at me and said nothing.

After a while, since my fingers had come to know the feel of every plant in the garden, I no longer saw them as strangers but as friends. So I asked their names. And she told me.

Gothel's words had been a vicious flood that had cut deep into the soul's landscape, leaving destruction in its wake. Ethelde's words were soft rain, quietly sinking in and nourishing parched land.

It wasn't until the day I went into the village with her and listened to the respectful way the men spoke to her and saw the way the women deferred to her that I fully understood that Ethelde was a witch as powerful as Gothel and that the choice I had made when I stepped out of the circle was to become one. I hadn't realized because Ethelde is everything Gothel was, and everything Gothel wasn't.

After the twins were born, the young men in the village began to come courting. The blacksmith's son, the miller's son, and the merchant's son brought little gifts when they invited me out for a walk. They came with charming manners and flowery words of love. But they always wanted to end the walks in one of the quiet hollows where the village girls offered their bodies for love and the young men took their bodies for pleasure. And after the flowery words, there was always the question, "Will you, Rapunzel? Will you?"

Since my answer never changed, they eventually stopped calling.

All except Imre, a simple, hardworking man who had no flowery words, who never invited me for a walk without inviting Ethelde to go with us, who never brought gilt trinkets, and who never failed to do some small chore around the cottage whenever he called. Imre, who, when he finally took me for a private walk and asked, "Will you, Rapunzel?" didn't bring me to one of the hollows but to a fine cottage he'd built with his own hands. It had a separate room for him and his wife and a divided loft that would easily hold two children or more. It had a workroom with its own small hearth. It had a small private bathing area. It looked out on a large plot of empty, carefully turned land enclosed by a stone wall.

Imre said nothing while I explored each room. He said nothing when I stood in the workroom doorway that opened onto the garden.

Finally, he said in his quiet, deep voice, "Will you, Rapunzel?"

Imre had no flowery words, but I felt his love in every stone. So I said yes.

In all the years since, I've never regretted my answer.

That first spring, Ethelde helped me plant my garden. "Don't try to fill all the land all at once," she told me as we planted the herb, vegetable, and flower beds. "I'll harvest more than I can use, and you're welcome to it. Leave yourself room to grow."

That first summer, Imre teased me when he saw the vegetable bed. "You've planted enough of your namesake to feed the village." When he saw the look in Ethelde's eyes and the way she nodded her head in understanding, he didn't tease me about it again. By the end of that summer, he, too, understood the truth of his words.

At first, the men came to me directly, but as the years have passed and they've come to realize that, when Ethelde finally returns to the land, I will stand in her place, they've become a little shy with me. The women will come to me and ask, but if the men have to come, they'll wait until evening when Imre is home. They'll come up to him while he's leaning against the stone wall, smoking his pipe, and murmur their request. He'll bring me the net bag they gave him and say with a solemn voice and twinkling eyes, "Master So-and-So's wife has a bit of a craving." I'll fill the bag with fresh, green leaves from my Rapunzel, and together we'll return to the stone wall and our anxious neighbor.

"A gift," I tell them every time because, sometimes, they aren't sure if they should offer something.

They would never understand what I get in return.

In the summer, after the children are asleep, Imre and I sit outside on the bench he built for me. I sit with my feet on the end of the bench and my knees up. He straddles the bench and sits behind me, his strong arms holding me close. Most of the time we talk about small things when we choose to talk at all. But sometimes Imre will press his face against my neck and say, "Are you content, Rapunzel?"

I always tell him, "I'm content. More than content."

Which is true.

He always goes in first to give me some quiet time alone to listen to the wind's music, to listen to the earth's wisdom. Some nights, when I finally come to bed, he just holds me, his big, callused hands stroking the silvered gold hair that I never allow to grow past my breasts. On other nights, we give each other another kind of pleasure.

I think about them sometimes, when I'm sitting alone: the parents I never knew, Gothel, my handsome young prince. I think about the twins who look like him and the son and daughter Imre and I made together. I think about Imre and the difference between the fire of a boy's passion and the strength of a man's love.

I chose well, and my life is rich because of it.

I think about them, and I'll tell you this. My daughters will never crave what belongs to another because they'll know they can have what they want most if they give it their hearts and their hands. And my sons will never be so blinded by passion that they cannot see the other textures of love because they'll know that love, too, has its seasons. They'll know these things because Imre and I will show them.

Sometimes my neighbors talk about misery or desolation,

but they don't understand what they're really talking about. No one, not even Ethelde, understands misery and desolation as well as I.

Misery is a heart that can never be content with what it has and, by always craving something more, brings about its own destruction. And desolation is a heart so fearful of losing what it hoards that it never knows the richness that comes from being able to give.

In her anger, Gothel wished me a miserable, desolate life.

But I learned the lessons well, and mine is the stronger magic.

THE WILD HEART

NOTHING HOBBLES A GOOD STORY AS MUCH AS the truth.

So I saved my breath to cool the bowl of stew and swallowed the words along with the ale. Besides, I've heard this story in every village I've passed through.

Satisfied that she'd have an audience at least until the bowl was empty, the plump wife of the tavern owner wiped one end of my table with a damp, dirty rag.

"There was this magical frog," said the tavern wife, "and he jumped right out of the pond where the queen was doing her washing up, and he told her she'd be having a babe right quick. Well, the king and queen were that happy because they'd wanted a babe for ever so long."

I finished my stew while she told me about the fairy's curse and how the princess fell into a deep sleep after she pricked herself with a spindle, and how a briar hedge grew up suddenly and surrounded the old tower that stands next to the castle. When she told me the terrible fate of the brave, handsome princes who had come to rescue the princess, she dabbed at her eyes with an apron that was as dirty as the rag she'd used to wipe the table.

"So the princess still sleeps in the tower?" I asked, straightening the leather cap that covered my head from crown to neck.

She nodded. "It's been fifteen . . . ah, no, it's been ten years now." She smiled slyly. "I remember because that was the year all the young men were courting me."

I drained the tankard and opened my coin pouch.

All business now, the woman looked me over more carefully. My clothes were worn, but the quality was as good as her husband might buy. And I'm sure mine were much cleaner.

"What brings you to these parts?" she asked.

I smiled at her. "You tell the tale well, but I've heard it before. I thought I'd see if I could wake the sleeping beauty."

She laughed so hard she almost fell over. "You?" she gasped, clutching her sides. "You? You're not a prince."

My smile faded.

Her laughter died.

I carefully laid the coins on the table. "No, I'm not."

THE CASTLE'S JUST over the next rise. To pass the time, let me tell you a story.

Once upon a time, there was a lovely queen who was married to a king almost twice her age. One day, while bathing in a secluded pool near the castle, she was joined by a companion who promised her a child. Only the queen knows for sure, but it's doubtful her companion was a talking frog. Which might explain why, a few years later when a guest at the castle teasingly remarked that the little princess must have a bit of foreign blood from a neighboring land, the king looked furious and the queen looked very pale.

Despite what you may have heard, the princess wasn't beautiful, and she wasn't plain. Like most people, she was somewhere in between. But what made people notice her was the inner light burning so brightly she seemed to glow. She embraced life joyously. Yes, she was polite. Yes, she was kind. Yes, she was gentle and caring. She also had curiosity and courage and an adventurous spirit. She laughed and jumped and ran. She skinned her elbows and skinned her knees. She climbed the trees in the orchard better than the boys. If her eyes swam in tears when she was scolded for tearing her gowns, it didn't stop her from embracing the next adventure, the next challenge.

Twelve of the nurses responsible for the princess's care would cluck their tongues, shake their heads, and talk among themselves about this stubborn, unladylike streak in their otherwise delightful charge. The thirteenth nurse, who, it was rumored, had a few drops of foreign blood and had been hired by the queen despite the king's objections, merely smiled and said only gentleness could tame the wild heart.

The other nurses didn't like the foreign nurse, probably because the princess liked her best. She was the only one willing to take long rambles or go riding. She was the only one willing to hitch up her skirts and wade in a stream. She was the only one who understood that the Wild Heart and the Gentle Heart were two halves of a whole, and both were as necessary as air and water, food and sleep.

Sometimes the other nurses would talk as they stitched and mended. Sometimes, if the princess was working quietly on the other side of the room, they would talk woman talk, forgetting how well voices can carry.

"The kitchen maid's belly is swelling," one of them would say, sniffing in disapproval. "She pricked herself with a spindle."

That's what they said when one of the lower serving girls was dismissed. "She pricked herself with a spindle."

But sometimes, when one of *them* came to the sewing room looking smugly pleased, the others would just as smugly tease, "Oh, did you sit on a spindle last night? Was it a *big* spindle?" And they'd laugh.

"Why would anyone want to sit on a spindle?" the princess asked the foreign nurse one time. "Wouldn't it hurt?"

The foreign nurse's lips tightened. She looked nervously at the other women. "There are spindles and there are spindles. Now hush. I've already said too much."

Not enough, not nearly enough, but still too much, because the next day there were only twelve nurses looking after the princess.

The day the princess turned fifteen, a great feast was planned. Since the king was out for the day doing something kingly, the princess went up to the queen's rooms to visit. The queen wasn't in her sitting room, but a handsome stranger was. Believing he was a guest who had come for the feast, she brushed off her manners and greeted him as a proper young lady should.

Instead of conversing politely, he circled around her, blocking the door. "Do you like spinning?" he asked.

"Not really," she said, backing away from him.

He licked his lips. "Maybe you haven't used the right spindle."

She didn't like the strange look in his eyes. She didn't like the way he kept smiling as he walked toward her.

She ran for the queen's bedchamber, hoping her mother was there, hoping she could reach the door and lock him out.

Her legs tangled in her skirt.

Do I need to tell you what happened next? Let's just say that she fought with all her strength and courage, but it wasn't enough. Not nearly enough.

After he left the room, she heard voices murmuring, then turning harsh. When the queen flew into the bedchamber, she drew some courage from her mother's fury until the first hard slap.

"You little bitch," the queen hissed. "You've ruined everything. *Everything.* How dare you come here, to *my* rooms, and tease him, entice him, spread your legs for him in *my* bed. He was *my* lover. *Mine!* You think this makes up for all the other ways you don't act like a proper woman? You think your husband's not going to know what a little slut you are when he mounts you on your wedding night? And your father's going to blame *me* for this when your noble bridegroom complains." She raked her hands through her hair. "And if your belly swells . . . Isn't it enough that you ruined the pleasure I've been looking forward to for *weeks* without me having to worry about that too?" Her eyes glittered. She bared her teeth. "Damn your wild ways. Damn your wild heart. I've endured enough from you. No more, do you hear me? *No more.*"

The queen swept out of the room, locking the door behind her.

Caged by the Gentle Heart's fear, the Wild Heart raged in silence.

A short while later, the queen swept into the room again. She set a basin of warm water and a sponge on the wash table, and dropped a towel and an old skirt and top on the chest at the end of the bed. Yanking the torn gown and undergarments off the princess, she snapped, "Wash yourself, and do a good job."

While the queen bundled up the bloody sheets and ruined

clothes, the princess washed herself. And washed herself. And washed.

Even though it, too, was afraid, the Wild Heart howled to be free to move, to act. But the Gentle Heart clung to it desperately.

Things blurred after that. The basin with the sponge and blood-tinted water disappeared. So did the dirty towel. The queen helped the princess dress. With one hand wrapped around the girl's wrist and the other arm hugging a lidded clay pot, the queen hurried them through the servants' corridors and out of the castle to the old tower.

They climbed the narrow, winding staircase until they reached the room at the top. Inside were a bed, a piece of polished metal that was used as a mirror, a small table with uneven legs, a candleholder with a partially burned candle, and steel and flint.

"We have to hurry," the queen muttered. "The king will be back soon, and this must be done before he returns." She took the lid off the clay pot, which was filled with earth. She lit the candle and tried to smile. "In a way, what happened today was partly my fault. I should have done this sooner. Right after the first time you bled. That's when my mother did it to me. For me. It hurts a little, but it's better this way. In a few days, you won't even notice. Now, more than ever, it's important for you to act like a modest young woman. You'll never do it while the wildness is in your heart."

Too frightened to move, the princess watched while the queen mumbled strange words and moved her hands over the clay pot.

The princess felt a queer tugging inside her, as if something were being pulled out of her and into the strange words and patterns the queen was forming. As her inner light grew weaker and weaker, her right hand felt heavier and heavier. It pulsed.

The Wild Heart howled in fierce desperation.

"It's ready," the queen said. Taking a little knife out of her skirt pocket, she pulled the princess's right hand over the clay pot, jabbed the girl's fingers several times, and then squeezed to draw the blood. "This will get the wildness out. All it takes is a few drops of blood on the spelled earth and the wildness will be trapped inside the pot." She smiled grimly. "Don't worry. Some of it has to remain with you. Otherwise, you'll give your husband no pleasure when he comes to your bed."

The princess shivered. A husband. A bed. Another man wanting to use his spindle like the stranger had. And the Wild Heart gone.

It's hard to say whether it was fear or rage that reacted when the first drops of blood fell onto the earth in the clay pot.

The princess yanked her hand out of the queen's grasp. Unbalanced, she hit the table as she fell. The uneven legs rocked hard enough to pitch the clay pot onto the floor, shattering it.

Blood dripped from her fingers.

Air claimed some drops.

Her tears claimed some.

The candle flame claimed a few before it went out.

The earth, freed of both pot and spell, claimed more.

And from those things, an older, wilder magic gave birth.

Thunder shook the tower. When it faded, there were three people in the room where there had been two.

The third, with its savage eyes and bared teeth . . . it was more than a shadow and less than a soul.

It was the Wild Heart, unchained.

"Go," the princess whispered as she struggled to sit up. "Go before she finds a way to trap you."

It didn't question, didn't hesitate. It was out the door and down the stairs before the queen could gather her wits.

When it left the tower and ran into the woods, the princess collapsed, still living but no longer alive.

Once the queen realized she couldn't wake the girl, she dragged her over to the bed. Then, weeping hysterically, she made her way back to the castle just as the king returned.

The queen wept out a pathetic story about the foreign nurse returning and casting a wicked spell on their precious daughter, and how she, realizing the princess was missing and seeing the woman sneaking out of the old tower, had rushed to her daughter's defense while one of the guests—did the king see the scratches on the poor man's face?—had chased the woman, catching her long enough to discover that the spell could be broken by a prince's kiss. But she had used more of her wicked magic and escaped into the woods.

As you can imagine, the castle was in an uproar. So it was easy for the Wild Heart to sneak back in and steal clothing from the male servants' quarters.

The Wild Heart knew two things: it had to grow older and stronger before it returned to the Gentle Heart, and the Gentle Heart had to be protected until that time.

It waited long into the night, until everyone had wearily gone to bed. Then it called the old magic that had given it birth, and crying softly for the one who lay within, it circled the tower three times.

By the time it finished the third circle, the briar hedge had begun to grow. By the time the sun rose, a thick, tangled, thorny mass surrounded the tower.

Before the first servant stirred, the Wild Heart was gone.

You wonder about the princes? Oh, they came, and they did look splendid as they rode to the castle on their fine horses. But they didn't come out of love. They came for the prize hidden in the old tower. They came for a chance to rule a kingdom.

They didn't understand the nature of the briar hedge.

So they drew their swords and battled the thorns that were as long and as sharp as daggers. They hacked and slashed, slashed and hacked, and the more they cut, the faster and thicker and more tangled the briar hedge grew. Sometimes it grew so fast it surrounded one of them between one sword stroke and the next.

But they didn't remain caught there. As long as no one tried to push forward into the tower, a prince's companions were always able to cut away enough of the hedge to pull him free.

There were a couple of them who almost understood the magic. They kept their swords sheathed and used poetry and songs for their weapons. Moving gently, speaking softly, they coaxed their way through the thorns and tangles, all the way up to the room at the top of the tower. Once there, they discovered that the hedge had broken through the shutters of the window near the bed and filled half the room, arching over the bed like a canopy.

Being able to see the prize, they became frustrated and drew their swords to slash and hack their way through those final few feet. Violated so close to the Gentle Heart, the thorns retaliated.

They did cut. They did wound. But even then, they didn't kill.

Finally admitting defeat, the princes who had understood enough to reach the room but not enough to win the prize were allowed to pass back through the hedge and rejoin their companions.

After a while, they all decided the prize wasn't worth the pain, and they returned home.

Nothing died among the thorns except greed and ambition.

Ah, there's the castle. That dark, tangled mass beside it is the old tower.

The princess is still up there, living but not alive.

The king died a few years ago. After the year of mourning ended, the queen married one of the handsome princes who had come to claim the prize. She lives in another castle now, a long way from here, but when the royal procession passes through this part of the land, she and her prince-husband spend a few days at the castle.

No one talks about the tower or the one who lies within. No one tries to understand the nature of the briar hedge.

The princess is neither mourned nor missed by anyone except the Wild Heart.

It's better that way.

You like the other tale better?

Well, nothing hobbles a good story as much as the truth.

I LEFT MY traveling pack at the edge of the woods and walked toward the old tower, wondering if I would be welcome.

It was easy to find the starting point. The briar hedge was thicker and more tangled near the tower door.

I pricked my finger on one of the thorns. Let it taste me. It quivered. Inside the tower, something else stirred.

I slowly circled the tower, walking widdershins to unmake what had been made. As I walked, I touched the hedge gently, sang to it softly.

By the time I completed the first circle, the hedge was covered with green leaves. By the time I completed the second, buds were swelling. By the time I completed the last circle, the tower was covered with beautiful, bloodred flowers nestled among the thorns.

I stood before the hedge, waiting.

It stirred, untangled, formed an archway leading straight to the tower door.

I climbed the narrow, winding staircase and entered the room. The hedge parted. I walked into the thorny, blooming bower, leaned over the bed, and gently kissed her lips.

She sighed, stirred, opened her eyes.

"It's time to go," I said softly.

I helped her stand, supported her as we passed through the hedge. By the time we reached the other side of the room, she was able to stand on her own.

I stepped back and studied her while I waited.

Protected by the thorns, she, too, had grown in her own way.

She took a deep breath. Took another.

I pulled off the leather cap that covered my head from crown to neck. My hair tumbled down my back.

"I've missed you," I said quietly. "I've needed you."

She stared at me. "You're—"

"More than a shadow and less than a soul."

Her eyes filled with tears, but she smiled. "I've dreamed of you."

"And I of you."

We studied each other for another minute before shyly opening our arms and stepping into an embrace.

The wind sighed. The hedge stirred.

When the sounds faded, there was one person hugging herself where there had been two.

We wore my leather jerkin and shirt over her skirt. We wore my boots instead of her slippers.

We made a neat bundle of the leftover clothes and left the tower.

Stopping just beyond the hedge, she broke off one of the thorns and slipped it into our skirt pocket. I picked one of the flowers and tucked it into the jerkin's ties.

We wanted to jump and run. We wanted to cry healing tears.

Instead, we sneaked into the kitchen, snitched a carry sack, and filled it with bread, cheese, and joints of cooked meat. Finding a litter of newly weaned kittens in one of the storage rooms, we were tempted to take one.

Nuzzling the small bundle of fur, I offered to find a quiet village where we could settle down.

Gently returning the kitten to its littermates, she said she wanted to see a bit of the world first.

We had to slip out of the kitchen quick before our muffled laughter woke the servants.

Picking up our traveling pack on the way, we stopped at the orchard, climbed a tree, and picked all the apples we could carry.

Laughing quietly, we feasted on our stolen bounty. Alive and once more whole, we slept in the orchard for a little while.

By the time the sun rose and the servants began to stir, the briar hedge was sinking back into the earth, and the Gentle Heart and the Wild Heart were gone.

THE FAIREST
ONE OF ALL

MIRROR, MIRROR ON THE WALL, WHO IS THE fairest one of all?"

"You, my queen, are fair, 'tis true, but Snow White is more fair than you."

THEY SAY THE old queen laughed while she danced to her death. They say her eyes never left the prince and his bride while his men fastened the red-hot iron slippers to her feet and forced her to stand and dance. Oh, the laughter sounded more like screams toward the end, but with her last breath, the old queen had said to the fair princess, "Don't tuck these away too far, my dear. In a few short years, they'll be needed again, and they'll fit you as well as they fit me."

That sounds like a cruel thing to say to a young bride, doesn't it? No one will deny that the old queen had a cold heart, but she had understood the world she lived in. Beauty is power, but only as long as beauty lasts. And beauty, as seen in the reflection of a mirror or a handsome prince's eyes, flees with the seasons.

But there is something you must understand: mirrors lie. So do handsome princes. It is not their fault. Not really. They're just made that way, able to reflect only one kind of truth, which is, in a way, a lie.

So the old queen asked a question, and I gave her the only answer I was capable of giving. I am just silvered glass and magic. What else could I do? She asked. I answered.

And she laughed while she danced to her death.

"MIRROR, MIRROR ON the wall, who is the fairest one of all?"

"You, my queen, are fair, 'tis true, but Snow White is more fair than you."

Her pained cry is the color of sepia. "But I *am* Snow White!"

And so she was, once. But no more. There are faint lines in the pretty face and frost in the raven hair. The gentle, pretty girl faded into a sad woman when her prince-who-is-now-king began to make excuses about why he couldn't walk in the gardens with her, why he couldn't dine with her, why he no longer came to her bed or welcomed her in his.

So she asks the question, and I answer without quite answering because she doesn't understand that the name doesn't matter, never matters. There will always be the next Snow White.

Always.

"MIRROR, MIRROR ON the wall, who is the fairest one of all?"

Why do you ask? Why can't you see? This is what I would ask him if I were capable of asking questions. But I can only answer.

"The maiden is a prize most fair, but your lady is beyond compare."

There. That should satisfy the young prince.

Of course, it doesn't. He's already savored his lady's kisses, already spoken honeyed words of undying love in order to explore the mystery between her thighs. Now he wants a new challenge, a new mystery. He wants the fever of the chase, a name to pursue.

He comes back, this prince-who-will-be-king. A day later? A week later? What does it matter? He comes back and asks the question.

This time I do not answer. I'm tired of telling truths that are a kind of lie.

So he looks for the answer in another kind of mirror. He looks for the answer in the eyes of the other young noblemen.

And there he finds the answer he wants.

"MIRROR, MIRROR ON the wall, who is the fairest one of all?".

She weeps while she asks the question. Her life is in tatters. With one whispered slur, she has been changed from an admired prize to be won into tarnished prey.

I do not answer. The prince's cold civility is answer enough.

"I loved him," she cries. "I *believed* him."

That was her first mistake. Not understanding the essential nature of princes—and mirrors—was her last.

"I WANT TO know what part you played in this tragedy!" the king roars while he waves a crumpled letter. "Did you profess your love and then abandon her as she claims? Are you the reason her father is dragging the lake for her body?"

"No," the prince says. "No! I made no excessive compliments. I made no promises, no offers of marriage. It is not my fault!"

The king retreats, duty satisfied. The prince sighs in relief.

THE SEASONS CHANGE before the prince stands before me again. The tragedy is forgotten—or, at least, no longer mentioned. He is, after all, the king's son.

Smiling, he smooths his hair and straightens his garments.

"Mirror, mirror on the wall, who is the fairest one of all?"

This time I answer. I give him a name.

Later that evening, when the king slips into the room and asks the same question, I give the same answer.

A KING DEAD. A prince dying. A kingdom in tatters.

Murderers, like suicides, are not buried in consecrated ground. Will that be true of the king and prince as well?

I will answer no more questions. My silvered glass darkens, darkens, darkens until it reflects nothing at all.

BLACK JEWELS

Many Black Jewels fans like to know where the shorter stories fit into the timeline of the novels. For the three stories here . . .

"By the Time the Witchblood Blooms" takes place between the end of *Daughter of the Blood* and the beginning of *Queen of the Darkness*.

"The Khaldharon Run" was a deleted scene from *Heir to the Shadows* and takes place between sections one and two of chapter 10.

"The Price" takes place between the story "Kaeleer's Heart" in *Dreams Made Flesh* and *Tangled Webs*.

BY THE TIME THE WITCHBLOOD BLOOMS

I T WAS A PERFECT PLACE FOR MY LINE OF WORK. FOR both of my professions, actually, but I was there for only one of them.

The dining house catered to Blood aristos, so it exuded quality and comfort. The sunken main room had a rough-stoned fountain in the center that looked so natural you would swear they had built the room around it. Tables were scattered around the room with plenty of space between them—a sensible precaution, all things considered. The Blood's social structure is such a complicated dance, juggling caste, social rank, and Jewel rank, that an inadvertent nudge could turn into a violent confrontation in the space of a heartbeat.

Not that I would mind, unless something nasty landed on my plate. I enjoy carnage, especially when it's an aristo male being torn into little pieces. Unfortunately, I'm too much of a professional to indulge in things like that very often.

On either side of the sunken main room were large, comfortable booths, discreetly shielded from the tables below by a wall óf ferns and lightly spelled so that conversations remained private.

When I'd arrived that afternoon to look the place over, I'd chosen one of the booths for tonight's little game. The owner of the dining house graciously closed this section of the room so that I and my companion would have it all to ourselves. That wasn't difficult since this was a late dinner even for the Blood, and the few people left in the main room were lingering over drinks by the time my companion arrived.

We settled into the booth, and the game began.

My companion was a Purple-Dusk-Jeweled Warlord from an aristo family. That gave him some power. His serving one of the stronger Queens in this Territory gave him more. Enough so that he felt he could do anything to anyone as long as they didn't wear darker Jewels than his, didn't come from an aristo family, and didn't serve in a Queen's court.

Which was true. He *could* do anything to anyone, and no one could touch him—unless, of course, they hired someone like me.

According to our most ancient legends, the Blood were given their power, their Craft, in order to be the caretakers of the Realms. The Jewels some of us wore not only acted as a reservoir for our power but also indicated how deep—and dark—that power was.

There are many words that could describe what the Blood have become. "Caretaker" isn't one of them.

Which is why, for me, business is so good.

My companion was a handsome-enough man, if you found pigs erotic. Then again, whores don't choose clients based on how they look.

Neither do assassins.

"So, was I your first?" he said, dipping his fingers into the bowl of stained shrimp.

Idiot. I'm half-breed Hayllian, who are a *long*-lived race. My eyes have too much green in them to be pure Hayllian gold, but the light brown skin and black hair came from the son of a whoring bitch who had sired me.

I daintily cut one of my stuffed-mushroom appetizers. "Ah, no, sugar. Not *my* first." I laughed, soft and husky, and flashed him a look from beneath my lashes. "Your great-great-grandfather perhaps."

He grunted, ate another stained shrimp, and licked the sauce from his fingers in a way, I'm sure, he thought was erotically suggestive. "Might have been old Jozef. I'm a lot like him, you know."

I didn't doubt that for a moment.

He finished the last stained shrimp. The sweet-hot sauce produced beads of sweat on his forehead. Patting his face with his napkin, he shrugged and said, "They make it too mild here." His eyes wandered back down to my décolletage. "I like things really hot."

Ah, Warlord, I thought as I smiled at him, *soon enough you'll have all the fire you want.*

While we waited for the next course, I rested my elbows lightly on the table, tucked my chin in my laced fingers, and leaned forward to give him a better look at my breasts, which were barely covered by the silk of my dress. It was good he'd eaten all the stained shrimp. I would have hated for a serving boy to snitch the last one and suffer for it.

He patted his forehead with his napkin again. The look he gave me said the heat wasn't just from the stained shrimp.

"So now you're a tenant at a Red Moon house here?" He

tried not to sound too eager, but his eyes wandered to my delicately pointed ears, the only physical evidence of my mother's mysterious race.

My ears make me unique, which means expensive, and I *do* have a reputation for being the best of the best. When I choose to settle at a Red Moon house for a while, appointments are made weeks in advance, which is something no other whore can claim. Only half of what I do in bedrooms has anything to do with sex, but it's such *easy* bait.

"No, I'm not a tenant," I said. "This is a pleasure trip. I'm just passing through." Which I had told him when I invited him to dinner.

He still looked sulky and disappointed—because, of course, he hadn't believed it. His kind never does. Then a sly, calculating look came into his eyes. "But you won't be leaving until morning, will you, Sorrel?"

"Surreal," I said, correcting him. The bastard knew perfectly well what my name was. He was just trying to goad me into thinking I was too insignificant to remember so that I would be willing to prove I'm everything *my* reputation says I am.

That was fine with me. I was willing to let him play out his game since it fit in with my own.

I smiled at the serving boy who brought the prime ribs. He placed my dish in front of me, the sharp blade of the knife carefully tucked beneath the meat. I glanced at the knife to confirm there was a small white enamel spot in the handle. My companion's knife had a small red spot.

Perfect.

Giving the boy a flicker of a warning smile, I picked up the knife and began to eat.

The Warlord grunted. "If the owner's going to have a dining house without rooms upstairs, the least he could do is have serving boys who aren't surly." He gave me a leering grin. "Or serving girls."

I gave him a saucy smile in return. "If you want to fill your belly, you come to a dining house. If you want to fill something else, you go to a Red Moon house. Besides, who wants to play with amateurs?"

A vicious light filled his pale eyes. "Playing with amateurs can be quite entertaining."

I just stared at him. He probably thought the vicious light in my own eyes was due to jealousy.

Fool.

I used Craft to chill the air around me, indicating my displeasure, and ate my dinner.

He chafed at the quiet censure, and his expression changed to thwarted-little-boy-turned-mean before he remembered that, if a man wanted to be accommodated by a whore of my skill and reputation, part of the price was the illusion of courtesy.

Hiding his temper, he picked up his fork and wiggled it against the meat. "Meat's good. You can cut it with a fork."

I made a moue when meat juice splashed on the linen tablecloth. Finally realizing I wasn't impressed by his vigorous wrist action, he picked up the knife.

I flashed him a wanton smile of approval and settled down to eat.

His conversation was boring, being centered entirely on himself, but I didn't allow my attention to wander. Who knew what interesting tidbits he might let drop as he bragged about his connections.

I was admiring the bloodred, black-edged flower tucked into

the fern pot opposite our booth when my companion noticed my gaze wasn't fastened on him.

"What's that?" he grunted, tearing a roll apart and dunking a piece into the butter bowl.

I looked away from the flower and shrugged. If he didn't know witchblood when he saw it, I wasn't about to tell him.

"Pretty," he said, probably thinking it would please me.

I almost laughed.

The meal, thank the Darkness, finally ended. After the brandy was served, he returned to his hoped-for agenda. "Listen," he said, leaning forward so he could stroke my wrist with his fingers. "Since you say you don't have a room and this place is lacking in the finer points of service, I know a place—"

"Regrettably, Warlord, the hour is late, I'm expected elsewhere tomorrow, and my Coach leaves shortly."

His face immediately changed from leering soft to cruel hard. Despite my youthful looks, I'm not a girl easily frightened into submission. I'm far more of a witch than he ever was a Warlord, and he was just a prick-ass who enjoyed hurting women, especially young women.

I dropped my right hand into my lap and used Craft to call in my favorite stiletto. It would have been a shame to gut him publicly, particularly after I'd gone to such trouble to do the thing so neatly, but he was going to be dead either way, and that was the point.

"What's this?" he growled. "*You* approached *me*. You think you can get me to spend good marks to fill your belly and then just—"

"As you say, *I* invited *you* for dinner." I leaned forward, looking at him with wide-eyed earnestness. "I wanted to meet you. You've a reputation among the ladies. In fact, one girl was left speechless after a night with you. Can you wonder why I'd want to meet you?"

"Since I changed my plans for this evening in order to come here, I expected something more than just dinner."

Of course he did. And he *was* going to get more than dinner. Just not what he expected.

When he finally believed that I wasn't going to go anywhere with him, he started getting nasty, so I cut off his words. There were plenty of other things I wanted to cut off, but I restrained myself. "Since I invited you, it will be my privilege to pay for the meal in exchange for your company and conversation. Besides, I told you this was a pleasure trip, and I don't mix business with pleasure."

Making one more try to get what he had come for, he looked at my mouth and suggested that the booth was private enough for me to give him some small comfort. On any other night, those words alone would have earned him a knife in the gut, but tonight I simply declined. Mumbling something about my reputation having gone to my head to think I could waste a Warlord's time and not be accommodating, he left to find a Red Moon house with more compliant game.

When I was sure he'd gone, I slid out of the booth, plucked the flower from the pot, tucked it into my water glass, and settled back into the booth. While I waited, I called in a pen and the second of my little black books, and made careful notations about what I had done. Since the ingredients could be found almost anywhere in the Realm of Terreille, this would be another of my closely guarded little recipes for death.

I vanished the book just as the owner of the dining house approached, a snifter of brandy in each hand. He set one in front of me before gingerly slipping into the booth.

It was always like this. Before, my clients are eager for the deed to be accomplished, and I'm treated with the deference due my skill. After . . . after, they begin to wonder if they might not one day be on the receiving end.

I stroked the witchblood petals and waited.

"It's done?" His voice shook a little.

"It's done." I continued to stroke the petals. "Legend says that the reason witchblood can't be destroyed once it's planted is that its roots grow so deep they're nourished in the Dark Realm."

"A plant from Hell?" He swallowed the brandy. "I want no ghosts or demons here."

Of course he wouldn't. "How is your daughter?"

"The same." He wiped his mouth with the back of his hand. "Always the same since that . . . since he . . ."

"How old is she?"

His mouth quivered with the effort to speak. "A child," he finally replied in a broken whisper. "A girl just beginning to be a woman."

Yes. I was twelve the first time I was thrown on my back, but the man was only strong enough to take my virginity. When he was done, I still had my Craft, still wore the Green Jewel that was my birthright. I came away from that bloody bed still a witch, not just a Blood female. I've been paying men back in their own coin ever since.

The owner pushed a carefully folded napkin across the table. I lifted one edge, quickly counted the gold marks. As a whore, even with the fees I charge, it would take almost a month to earn this much. As a first-rate assassin, it was a pittance of my usual fee. But even I, at times, do charity work.

I vanished half the marks and pushed the napkin back across

the table. The owner looked troubled—and a little frightened. I sipped my brandy. "Use the rest for the girl," I said with a gentleness harshened by my own memories. "A Black Widow is the only kind of witch who can heal what's left of your daughter's mind and possibly give her back some semblance of a life. One with that much skill will expect to be paid well for her services."

"That has nothing to do with your fee," he protested.

I studied the witchblood. The plant will grow anywhere a witch's blood has been spilled in violence or where a witch violently killed has been buried. It's true that once it takes root over such a place, nothing can destroy it.

It's also true that if the petals are properly dried, it's a sweet-tasting, unforgiving poison that slowly blossoms into unrelenting pain. It is virulent and undetectable until it's far, far too late.

At this point, the Warlord would be feeling nothing more than a bit of a bellyache, and if, as I suspected, he was already entangled with a young whore, he wouldn't even notice.

The owner cleared his throat nervously. His son, who had insisted on being the serving boy tonight, placed two more snifters of brandy on the table, then shifted from foot to foot. Glancing from his father to me, he said, "What should I do with the knife?"

"Cleanse it as I showed you," I said, "and then bury it deep."

The youth hurried away.

Actually, there'd been nothing on the knife the Warlord had used but a glaze made from roots and herbs that would cause the mild bellyache. But they had wanted to see death being made, and since I wasn't about to tell them about the powdered witchblood I'd slipped into the bowl of stained shrimp, the mess I'd created in the kitchen that afternoon while I concocted the glaze had sufficiently impressed them. The Warlord will associate the bellyache with overindulgence and then forget it. By the time the witchblood blooms, no one will think of this place . . . or me.

I turned my attention back to the owner. "As for my fee, I'm keeping enough for expenses. I don't want the rest."

"But—"

"Hush." I smiled at him as I raised the brandy snifter in a small salute. "I was on a pleasure trip when you approached me, and"—I laughed, truly delighted—"as I told my arrogant dinner companion, I don't mix business with pleasure."

THE KHALDHARON RUN

AAAAAAH! DOWN—PUT—STOP THAT! LUCIVAR, put me down!"

"Can't. You're dizzy. If I put you down, you'll fall on your face and hurt your little snout."

"I wouldn't be dizzy if you'd stop spinning us around!"

"Too bad."

"Put me down or I'll do you an injury!"

Lucivar stopped spinning and propped Jaenelle up when her feet finally touched the ground. That she needed to hold on to him to keep her balance did everything for his mood and nothing at all for hers.

"You're a grumpy little cat," he said, grinning at her.

She bared her teeth. "Sit down. I want to look at your back."

Lucivar spread his wings and lifted his arms to the sky. "My back's fine. My back's wonderful. We did it, Cat. We did it!"

"Not yet, we haven't," she muttered. "Now sit down."

"I don't want to sit. I want to soar. We should—"

"Sit down!"

Three kindred wolves froze in mid-sniff and sat down.

After estimating how much physical damage she might be willing to do to him if he ignored That Look, Lucivar meekly sat on a flat rock and spread his wings for her inspection.

"I feel good," he offered over his shoulder.

"I could fix that," she muttered at his spine.

After a few minutes of silent prodding, he felt like doing a bit of prodding of his own.

"Well?"

"The healing's coming along nicely. Two and a half more weeks should do it."

Lucivar turned to look at her. She moved with him, continuing to examine his back and wings. "Two and a half weeks for what? You said the healing would be done when I made the Run, and I just made the Blood Run—and I made it as well as I ever did. Even better."

He felt her eyes rise until she focused on the back of his head. A shiver ran down his spine. The back of his neck prickled in warning.

When she came around to face him, the butterfly caress of her fingers along his wing terrified and excited him.

He looked at her subtly altered face. His mouth went dry and, for a moment, he could have sworn there had been a tiny spiral horn in the center of her forehead.

"You made the Blood Run," Witch said, annoyed amusement filling her ancient sapphire eyes. "If you were anyone else, I'd say you had done very well and the healing was complete. But you're not anyone else. You're Lucivar Yaslana, an Ebon-gray Eyrien Warlord Prince, and I know what you're capable of doing. So the healing will be complete in two and a half weeks."

"What happens then?" he asked warily.

Witch smiled. "We make the Khaldharon Run."

WITH HIS EYES unfocused, Lucivar could almost see the colors of the darker Winds as they braided, fanned out, and twisted down the Khaldharon Run.

He blinked, focused his eyes, and studied the physical canyon below him. The river ran slow and deep through the center. Dwarfed trees hugged the banks. Late-summer and early-autumn wildflowers provided splashes of color, a vibrant counterpoint to the dried grass that, in the late-morning light, looked like stone breathing.

Nothing grew twenty feet above the river. Scoured clean by the forces that claimed the canyon, stone walls rose to meet the sky.

In Terreille, it took an Eyrien warrior decades to prepare for this. It took a few short minutes for a man to live or die, or be crippled, or maimed beyond recognition. Out of all of the hunting camps, a double handful of the best warriors came each year to test their strength against the Khaldharon Run.

Jaenelle had warned him that the Khaldharon was stronger in Kaeleer because the Shadow Realm lived closer to the Darkness and the source of the Winds. The Winds were stronger, faster here than in Terreille. He wondered if she understood what that meant. He wondered if the fools in Terreille understood that there were shades of power, and power that blazed in Terreille might become a feeble glow in Kaeleer.

Lucivar smiled. He had a feeling he and the males in the Shadow Realm would have quite a few things in common.

"Ready?"

Lucivar glanced at Jaenelle as she fussed with the strange cape attached to the rest of what she was wearing—or not wearing. He rubbed the back of his neck. Were older brothers allowed to express opinions about their kid sisters' clothes? True, the black spidersilk bodysuit covered her from wrist to neck and from neck to ankles, but even her skin didn't hug her bones that tight. She must have used Craft to get into the thing. And those black leather slipper-socks were useless for walking over rough ground. The only thing he approved of was the silver half circle she wore across her brow. A small Black Jewel rested in the middle of the filigree, a splendid blend of delicacy and power.

"Ready?" Jaenelle asked again. She raised her arms.

Lucivar choked on his heart.

Black iridescent wings were raised toward the sun. Black that held all the colors of the Jewels. Why was she wearing black wings?

He looked at the Khaldharon Run and broke into a cold sweat. "If you're going to glide to the meeting place, you'd better get started."

She smiled at him. Cats probably smiled at mice that way. "You're not going to say anything stupid, are you, Lucivar?"

Lucivar swallowed hard and hoped he looked calmly arrogant. "No. And you're not going to do anything stupid. The Khaldharon isn't a game, Cat. I can't watch out for you in there."

The temperature around them dropped ten degrees.

"I can take care of myself," she said too softly. Then her voice rose. "I can fly as well as you can, and I don't need another arrogant Eyrien male telling me what I can or can't do."

"It has nothing to do with being arrogant or Eyrien or male," he snapped. What did she mean by "another"? "Hell's fire, Cat, just because someone can fly doesn't mean she—or he—can make the Khaldharon." He held out his hand. She didn't take it. "Look. If you want to try a Run, I'll work with you—"

"Don't patronize me," she snarled.

Being reasonable was getting him nowhere, so he tried undiluted arrogance. "I forbid you to make the Khaldharon Run."

She dove into the canyon.

Free fall. Hawk fall. He reveled in the speed and the anticipated pleasure he'd have when his prey was safely wrapped in his arms and he could wallop her ass until his hand hurt.

Damn! He was larger, heavier. He should have caught her by now. They were too close to the starting edge. If she turned in and caught one of the Winds, he'd have to catch her and pull them under the Run. At these speeds, twenty feet wasn't much to work with. Damn her stubbornness. Damn, damn, *damn*.

She opened the black spidersilk wings, caught the Sapphire thread, and took off down the Khaldharon Run.

Lucivar opened his wings, sharpened his angle, and caught the Red, trying to outrun her.

She danced on the Winds to a song of her own making, dropping from one Wind and catching another, never more than four body lengths ahead of him and never within reach. He followed her, the Khaldharon forgotten as he focused on the dance, learning her physical language, waiting for the opening to overtake her.

The Gray thread ran straight above her for several hundred yards. He caught the Gray and shot forward.

She dropped to the Green and fell back, laughing as she shouted at him, "Your turn."

Suddenly he was leading the dance, probing ahead to untangle the Winds and choose the threads that would keep them relatively safe in the center of the canyon. He couldn't look back, couldn't divide his concentration. It didn't matter. He felt her behind him, her wild joy a lifeline between them.

He surrendered to that joy, surrendered to the Khaldharon, and felt subtle, invisible chains snapping all around him, torn apart by fierce pleasure. Any leash he submitted to now would be of his own choosing.

Lucivar bared his teeth in a smile. Almost to the Sleeping Dragons. Almost to the end of the . . .

She flashed under him, running on the edge of the Ebongray, physically so close her hair swept over his belly and chest as she passed him. She waited until the last second before breaking free of the Winds and rising up and over the Sleeping Dragons.

Seconds later, he shot over the Sleeping Dragons. That last bit of precision flying gave him one more reason to wallop her. He partially closed his wings for a controlled dive and caught her as she glided serenely toward the grass where Smoke, the younger wolves, and a full picnic basket waited to celebrate the successful completion of the Run.

Jarring both of them with a rough landing, he spun her around, grabbed her upper arms, and lifted her until she could look him straight in the eyes and see how furious she had made him.

Unimpressed, she smashed her forearms against his, trying to break his hold. "Lucivar! What in the name of Hell is wrong with you?"

"Wrong with me?" He couldn't think of any response to that except to shake her, so he did. "Wrong with me? You dive into the canyon, take off down the Khaldharon like it's nothing more than a dance in a meadow, and you wonder what's wrong with *me*?"

Jaenelle glared at him. "You said you weren't a hysterical male."

"I'm not hysterical," he shouted, giving her another shake for good measure. "I'm terrified. You could've been killed!"

"So could you." Her voice warned him that was still a possibility.

He bared his teeth. "At least I knew what I was getting into."

"Don't be such a conceited ass," she snapped. "You're not the only one who's made the Khaldharon Run before."

He dragged her close enough for their noses to touch. "You've made the Run before?" He was so furious he actually sounded reasonable.

"Of course. Lots of times."

He roared. He swore. He shook her.

She hauled back and kicked him in the shin. Hard.

Howling, he dropped her and clutched his throbbing leg. As he hopped around on the other leg, he dredged up the nastiest things he'd ever heard in the Eyrien hunting camps and flung them all at her. When she snapped back at him, he yelled, "If you're going to swear at me, at least do it in a language I understand."

It wasn't the smartest suggestion he'd ever made.

She had stamina and imagination. He had volume.

"*You could have told me!*" he roared, even more furious because roaring was less effective when a man was still hopping on one leg. "How was I supposed to know you could fly like that?"

"You knew I could fly!"

Lucivar tested the kicked leg. Sore, but it would hold him. "I knew you could fly, but I figured if you had learned from the same idiot who taught you to fight with the sticks, I was going to have to break you of a lot of bad habits before teaching you how to do it right."

She hissed. She spat. She puffed.

She looked cute when she was dangerous.

"What's wrong with the way I use the sticks?"

He watched her eyes, his nerves tingling. "Nothing at all if you were an Eyrien boy. Since you're not, quite a bit."

He ducked, felt the sizzle of unleashed power as it passed over his left shoulder, heard a solid thump behind him.

The large boulder held its shape for ten dry-mouthed heart-beats before it crumbled into little pebbles.

He straightened up and gave her a small but respectful bow. "I was wrong about the flying, but not about the sticks." Then he grinned. "If I'd known you could do that kind of precision flying, we could have been working on aerial dances during the past couple of weeks."

Jaenelle gave him a sour look. "I've done a couple of aerial dances. They're boring flutters for weak-winged women."

"With your skill, I can see why you would be bored with the simplest ones, but the real aerial dances are a combination of grace and precision that requires fire and courage. Of course, there haven't been witches who could do those dances since Andulvar Yaslana's time, so your instructor probably didn't even think about showing you."

Now, what had he said that could put that much hurt in her eyes?

He approached her cautiously. When she didn't snarl at him, he drew her into a gentle hug. "The man who taught you," he said quietly. "He knew you before you were"—he forced the word out—"hurt?"

She nodded.

"And he waited with your father for you to get better?" He waited for her confirming nod and sighed. Would he have been any less protective, any less fearful of having her hurt or lost again after coming so close once? *Yes,* he answered fiercely. The risks would have been calculated, encouraged in areas where her interests and his strengths met. He would have let her take the small hurts so she would learn how to prevent the large ones. *Yes?* he asked with rueful honesty, remembering that he'd forbidden her to make the Khaldharon Run. All right, he was entitled to a few mistakes in judgment. After all, he'd never been an older brother before.

When she wrapped her arms around his waist, he rested his cheek on her head. "Men who get scared to the marrow can become overprotective and not even be aware of it."

She sniffed.

"We're not all overprotective."

"Yes, you are," she muttered. "You can't help it, though. It's part of what you are."

Lucivar shook his head, thinking of the Eyriens he knew. "Not all Eyrien males are protective of females, let alone overprotective."

"No, but all Warlord Princes are." She sounded exasperated. "Doesn't matter what species you are, either. All Warlord Princes are like that—arrogant, aggressive, dominating, territorial, overprotective, possessive bullies."

"I am not a bully," he said heatedly. "I won't argue with the rest of it, but I'm not a bully."

Jaenelle glared at him. "Who used Craft to freeze my chair in place until I'd eaten all the snap beans?"

"You need to eat your vegetables."

"You put too many on my plate. And I don't like snap beans."

"That makes me a bully?"

"Yes!"

Lucivar chuckled. "I wonder why you put up with us, then."

"You have some good qualities," Jaenelle grumbled. "I can't remember what they are at the moment, but I'm sure you have some."

Giving her a final squeeze, Lucivar stepped back. "Next time you plan to do something that will make me hysterical or terrify me, tell me first, all right?"

"Why?" she asked warily. "So you can talk me out of it?"

"I won't talk you out of it as long as I'm invited to come along."

She looked stunned. Then she grinned. Then her silvery, velvet-coated laugh filled the air.

The wolves came out of hiding and sent polite but pointed thoughts that all centered on the picnic basket.

"You really think I can improve with the sticks?"

Lucivar gave her his lazy, arrogant smile. "Getting tired of being knocked on your ass?"

"Yes!"

"Once we've adapted the standard moves into a fighting style that suits you, you'll be able to hold your own with just about anyone. Not me, of course." Grinning at her snarled "Of course," he opened the picnic basket and started handing out food, making sure the wolves got the plain beef sandwiches. Wolves, he'd been told with a growl, didn't like mustard. He unwrapped a sandwich for himself. "Cheer up, Cat. There isn't anyone else who can take me either."

"I'll try to remember that when I'm sitting in the dirt." Jaenelle looked at the four males stuffing their faces and lunged for the picnic basket. "Hey! Where's mine?"

"Help yourself," Lucivar said magnanimously, careful not to wave his sandwich or his hand too close to her teeth.

Even the wolves agreed that, when hungry, Jaenelle wasn't a force to be played with.

SATED BY FOOD and sun, Lucivar watched Jaenelle amble up from the river. She'd changed into knee-length trousers and a gauzy, tie-string blouse, and had pulled her hair back in that loose, careless braid he found maidenly and charming. He wondered if she'd finally worked herself up to telling him whatever had been on her mind since they'd finished eating.

Jaenelle sat beside him, plucking grass. "Lucivar," she said with quiet care, her eyes fixed on her hand. "I did a little research on the Eyrien traditions about making the Khaldharon Run. I know a man is supposed to receive a reward if he's successful."

The food solidified in his stomach. The traditional reward for an Eyrien warrior making the Run was the woman of his choice for a night. The thought of Jaenelle offering herself or offering to obtain another woman to . . .

Don't offer it. Please, don't suggest it.

She swallowed hard. "The traditional reward would have been . . . a bit difficult, and from some of the things you've said, I didn't think you would consider it much of a reward." She glanced at him anxiously and chewed her lower lip.

He melted in relief. "No, I wouldn't have."

"So I thought, maybe, if you wanted to, we could go to the Fyreborn Islands tomorrow, spend the day there, and return the following morning." She nervously plucked grass.

Lucivar tucked his wings in and rolled onto his side. "The Fyreborn Islands? Where the dragons live?" When she nodded, he surged to his feet, dragging her up with him. "Come on. If we're leaving early tomorrow, you need to get some sleep."

"Sleep? It's still afternoon! Are you figuring on getting up at three in the morning?"

He narrowed his eyes and gave her a considering look. "You think we can get up that late and still have you fully awake by dawn?"

She hissed. She spat.

Should he pet to soothe or . . . "You know it always takes you a few hours to wake up fully after you grumble out of bed, and until you've had some coffee, you're really not fit to talk to, let alone do anything else."

She puffed.

Ignoring her detailed threats to various parts of his anatomy, Lucivar vanished the picnic basket, whistled for the wolves, and tossed Jaenelle over his shoulder. "Come on, Cat. Let's go meet some dragons."

THE PRICE

"ELL, SHIT, SUGAR. SOMEONE HAD A PARTY and didn't invite me." And it was the kind of party I used to like. Nasty.

And yet, as I stood in the doorway, looking at what had been a nicely decorated sitting room, I felt edgy, uneasy. There's no law against murder among the Blood, and if I'd come upon a room like this when I lived in the Realm of Terreille, I wouldn't have thought twice about it. But in the Realm of Kaeleer, the Blood still live by the Old Ways, and the whole dance of Protocol and power usually works to keep confrontations from becoming fatal.

So what happened last night that ended with three men being hacked to pieces, resulting in a room now redecorated in a blood-and-gore motif?

And why did I think *hacked*? Using Craft and the power that makes the Blood who and what we are, a person could do just as much damage to a human body. But something in the room whispered to me that this was . . . not personal, exactly, but definitely a hands-on killing. There was a lingering sense of fury and hatred here.

I know those feelings well, and my past contained rooms just as messy. But there was something else here that I almost recognized but couldn't quite name.

Of course, that could have been nothing more than annoyance with myself for being at the scene. If I'd stayed home this morning, I would have been tucking into breakfast right now. But I'd gone for a walk and ended up at this establishment because they serve a fine breakfast—and because this place was the closest thing to a Red Moon house in Kaeleer. So I'd come here to take a look at my past, which had contributed to my recently failed romance.

The Blood have a saying: Everything has a price. The price for my first attempt at a physical relationship with a man where money didn't change hands was a bruised heart. Funny how the heart gets bruised when someone tells you you're not what he wants—even when you already know he's not what you want either.

But there's nothing like a bit of slaughter to take a person's mind off her own problems.

Using Craft, I stepped up on air so that I was standing a handspan above the carpet. I walked into the room. Three male bodies were splattered over the carpet, the walls, the furniture, and the painted screen that turned one corner of the room into a private area. I assumed there were only three because I found three left hands—and I found other body parts in triplicate.

"Lady Surreal?"

As I turned toward the doorway, I lowered my right hand and called in my favorite stiletto, using Craft to keep it sight shielded so it wouldn't be obvious I had a weapon ready. A moment later, when I recognized the man in the doorway, I vanished the stiletto.

"Prince Rainier."

Rainier was an Opal-Jeweled Warlord Prince from Dharo, another Territory in Kaeleer. I'd seen him a few weeks ago at a party here in Amdarh and, more recently, enjoyed dancing with him at a family wedding. I'd also noticed him in the dining room this morning, reading a book while he ate breakfast. A fine-looking man with a dancer's build, fair skin, dreamy green eyes, and a mane of brown hair, he stood out in Dhemlan's capital city, where the residents had the common coloring of light brown skin, black hair, and gold eyes. Which was, actually, the common coloring of all three of the long-lived races.

Being half-Hayllian, I had the black hair and light brown skin, but my eyes were gold-green and my ears came to delicate points—the legacy of my mother's people. I was also a Gray-Jeweled witch, so my power was darker and deeper than his. That didn't mean I could afford to be careless. Warlord Princes were natural predators and also very protective. That should have been a contradiction, but it wasn't; it just made them extremely lethal.

"Why did they ask you to see this?" Rainier said as he looked behind the painted screen. He paled, and I didn't imagine his breakfast was sitting well, but when he moved away from the screen, he studied the room with a hunter's eye.

"Maybe because I wear the Gray," I replied, shrugging. Or maybe because the owners of this place had heard a few things about me and wanted my professional opinion. "And you?"

Grief tightened his face. "I had an appointment here after breakfast."

Here. Not just in this establishment, but *here*. "You knew them."

"If these are the same young men who reserved this room, then, yes, I knew them."

"What were they doing here?"

"A weekly lesson. I was hired as a secondary instructor."

It was better not to ask about that while I was still in this room.

"They didn't deserve this," Rainier said quietly.

"Are you sure?"

"Yes, I'm sure." His voice sharpened. Everything about him sharpened.

I nodded and looked around again. He knew these men; I didn't. "So. Three men were killed for no apparent reason. If there wasn't a reason, there wasn't a payment. Which means no one hired a professional to get rid of them."

"A professional? You mean an assassin? How do you know it wasn't?"

"Because I am a professional. Was a professional." I shrugged. "There's not much call for assassins in Kaeleer."

"I'd heard—" He fumbled, seeming to remember belatedly that I was related to the most powerful Warlord Princes in the Realm of Kaeleer.

"That I was a whore? I was that too. You could say one career led to the other."

Wariness in his eyes now.

"I didn't kill them," I said. "If I had, I would have done a better job of it. Let's go. There's nothing more to do here."

He was under no obligation to go with me, but he followed me out of the room, stayed with me while I talked to the owners, and made suggestions about whom they should talk to in the Queen of Amdarh's court to report this incident.

When I left the building, he went with me, walking on my left—a signal to everyone who saw us that I was the dominant party. As a Warlord Prince, he belonged to a higher caste than did I, a mere witch. But my Gray Jewels outranked his Opal. In the knife-edged game of power the Blood play on a daily basis, which of us held the high card in terms of authority could change in the blink of an eye.

I turned a corner, heading away from the theater district with its playhouses and music halls. Those streets would be quiet at this time of day. I wanted the bustle of people and the distraction of shops.

Even this early in the morning, there were plenty of people in the shopping district, plenty of faces. . . .

"We didn't find their heads."

"They were behind the screen," Rainier replied grimly.

"Damn. It might have helped to see what they looked like." Might have given me a clue about why this had happened. Of course, I could have used a clue about why I was still chewing over this. I'd made a good living killing men. I should have been able to shrug these deaths off. I couldn't—because something just wasn't right about the kills.

"It wouldn't have helped," Rainier said. "Their faces were burned past recognition." He paused, then added, "Witchfire."

Knowing how fiercely witchfire can burn, I swallowed hard, glad I hadn't managed to get breakfast. Did make me reassess my companion's nerves, though. He'd looked at those faces and had kept *his* breakfast down.

"So, what kind of lessons were they getting?" Maybe knowing why the men had been in that room would help me figure out why they died.

"Sex," Rainier replied.

I stopped walking. People flowed around us. "How many women?" I could feel my blood chilling, feel the old rage rising.

He looked puzzled. "One."

Some of those messy rooms in my past had occurred when the males had thought the odds were in their favor for rough sex without the female's consent. They learned how deep and pure female rage can be. Of course, they died learning it, so the lesson didn't do them much good.

Rainier shook his head. "It's instruction, Surreal. Frank discussion about what a woman wants from a lover. Some demonstration."

"Demonstration." Maybe the little bastards had gotten exactly what they deserved.

Rainier took my left hand in his right and lifted it, his eyes never leaving mine. His lips, warm and soft, surrounded one knuckle. The tip of his tongue stroked my skin.

A sweet, unexpected feeling flowed through me, banishing anger.

He released my hand, and said quietly, "Demonstration."

Hell's fire, Mother Night, and may the Darkness be merciful. He must have been a dedicated student when he'd been learning those lessons. I had to clear my throat in order to get my voice back. "So." I couldn't think of anything else to say.

His smile was pure male as he took my arm and started walking again.

"Understanding what pleases is just as important in a man's personal life as it is if he serves in a court," Rainier said.

Hard to argue, since that little demonstration made me feel deliciously female and desirable. But it also plucked at the edgy, uneasy feeling I'd had in the room, so I looked for something else to talk about—and stopped walking half a block from a corner.

"What's he doing?" The boy was shepherding females from one side of the street to the other. That was obvious. Why he was doing it wasn't.

"Who?" Rainier looked around, then grinned. "Oh. He's training. Since there are two boys about the same age at the other corners, their instructor is probably sitting in that coffee shop across the street, keeping an eye on them."

Things were different in Kaeleer, but . . . "You *train* males to be a pain in the ass?"

"We train them to serve."

"That's what I said." My comment annoyed him. I didn't care. If he spent one day on the receiving end of that kind of stubborn attention, he'd have a totally different opinion about a male's right to serve.

Then my stomach growled.

Rainier studied me. "Would you like to go to the coffee shop? They don't serve meals there, but they do have baked goods."

"Fine." I stepped away from him. "I'll meet you there."

"Surreal."

I heard the warning in his voice, but I ignored it and walked to the corner. I'd noticed the boy stepped aside if a woman already had a male escort, and I was curious.

A cute puppy, all bright-eyed and eager. A little Yellow-Jeweled Warlord. A miniature man. His eyes widened when he saw my Gray Jewel, but he took a deep breath and smiled.

"May I be of service, Lady?" he asked.

Protocol. Specific phrases that had specific answers. Protocol balanced power, giving the weaker among the Blood a safe way to deal with the stronger.

"I'm going to the coffee shop across the street," I replied.

"Then I will escort you, if it pleases you."

I held out my left hand. He slipped his right hand beneath it, checked the street to make sure no horse-drawn carriages or Craft-driven coaches were approaching the crossing, then led me across the street.

"Thank you, Warlord," I said when I had been safely delivered to the door of the coffee shop.

"It was my pleasure, Lady."

And it was. I could see it in his eyes. There would be bitches who would bruise his ego, dim the pleasure in those eyes. There would be many, many more witches who would gently reinforce his training, confirming his place in the world as a man worthy of courtesy and consideration, a man valued for who and what he was.

While I waited for Rainier to join me, I watched the boy escort two young witches across the side street. He continued up the street with them past three shops before one of the women murmured something—obviously a reminder that his duty was completed, since he stopped and turned back. As he passed the alley between two of the buildings, he hesitated, took a step closer toward that shadowy place that would put him out of sight.

Edgy. Uneasy.

He was almost at the mouth of the alley.

Something wrong.

Using Craft to enhance my voice, I bellowed, "Warlord! Here! *Now!*"

As I ran across the street, I began to appreciate the value of training. The boy didn't hesitate. He spun at the sound of my voice and ran away from the alley just as *something* reached out to grab him. Something sight shielded. I couldn't *see* it, and yet I *could* see it, like an afterimage that remains on your eyelids after you close your eyes. A robed arm. A gloved hand. Reaching for the boy.

As he ran past me, I grabbed a fistful of his shirt and swung him behind me, throwing a Gray shield around both of us at the same time I called in a hunting knife—a big knife with a wickedly honed blade. I probed the alley with my psychic senses. No one there anymore, but I picked up a hint of the same fury and hatred that I'd sensed in that room.

"Stay here." I released the boy but kept a Gray shield around him as I moved toward the alley. Into the alley.

Female. I was certain of that now. Definitely a witch skilled in her Craft.

"Everything has a price, bitch," I said softly, even though I knew she was gone. "Maybe you had a reason to go after the men—or thought you did. But not the boy. Not a child. Everything has a price—and when I catch up to you, and I will, I'll show you how to paint the walls in blood."

"Surreal?"

A light psychic touch, full of strength and temper. Rainier at the mouth of the alley, guarding my back.

I backed out of the alley, staying alert in case the bitch was skilled enough to hide her presence. I didn't turn away until Rainier's fingers brushed my shoulder. As I turned to face the street, I got my next lesson in how well Blood males are trained in Kaeleer.

There were hard-eyed, grim-faced men everywhere. A female had yelled on a public street. It didn't matter that it had been a command and not a cry of fear or distress. A female had yelled—and they'd responded. They'd poured out of the shops, out of the carriages and coaches. Whatever had upset the female was going to be fixed. *Now.*

Which explained why assassins weren't needed in Kaeleer.

Protocol was the only tool I had—especially since the Warlord Prince standing beside me had risen to the killing edge to become a living weapon.

Using Craft again to enhance my voice, I said, "Thank you for your attention, gentlemen. There is nothing more to be done here." I raised the hunting knife, so the men who could see me couldn't fail to notice it. Then I vanished it and lowered my hand.

I waited, hardly daring to breathe until I saw the men in front of me relax. Communication on psychic threads rippled over the street. Men returned to their carriages and coaches, to the shops or interrupted meals.

I heard Rainier release a slow breath as he worked to step back from the killing edge.

When the boy's instructor joined us, I released the Gray shield I had put around the little Warlord. The puppy couldn't tell us more than that a lady had called to him, asking for help. He'd hesitated because he couldn't see her, and she'd sounded . . . strange.

She hadn't been able to mask her hatred. It must have bled into her voice. And it was going to piss her off that her prey had escaped. Which meant another man was going to die.

After the instructor bundled his students into a carriage and drove away, Rainier wrapped a hand around my arm.

"You need something to eat," he growled.

I did, but I heard "I'm going to fuss over you" in that growl, and I really didn't want to be fussed over. "Don't worry about it, sugar. I can—"

His fingers tightened. "Lady, let me serve or point me toward something I can kill."

Shit shit shit. Warlord Princes rose to the killing edge in a heartbeat, but they couldn't always come back from it on their own. You either pointed them to a killing field or gave them something else to focus on—which usually meant a female they could fuss over and look after for a while.

"I could use a meal." I shook off his hand, saw the temper in his eyes chill, and immediately linked my arm through his to give him the contact he needed. We walked for several minutes before he chose a dining house that had a small courtyard in the back for guests who wanted to eat outdoors.

I don't know what passed between Rainier and the Warlord waiting on the tables in the courtyard. We weren't asked what we wanted to eat—I wasn't anyway—but I'd barely settled in my chair when coffee, glasses of red wine, and a basket of bread appeared on the table. That was swiftly followed by bowls of greens that were delicately dressed, thick steaks, vegetables, and some kind of casserole made of potatoes, onions, and sausage. The meal lasted long enough for the wild look to fade in Rainier's eyes—and for me to reach a few conclusions.

I leaned back in my chair. "There's a killer out there." Which pretty much described anyone who was Blood, but I was making a distinction between the potential in all of us and someone using that potential.

Temper flared in Rainier's eyes. "There was no reason to go for that boy."

"Sugar, I don't think reason has much to do with this."

He frowned. "You think this killer is a witch who has slipped into the Twisted Kingdom?"

I didn't think she was insane in the way he meant, but hate can be its own kind of madness.

He sighed. "Then we have to find her and give her what help we can."

"No, we have to find her and kill her."

"But—"

"No." I studied him. "You didn't sense anything in that room or in the alley, did you?"

He shook his head.

"I did. Maybe it's because I'm . . . familiar . . . with what I felt that I was able to sense it at all."

Rainier swirled the wine left in his glass. "What kind of men did you kill, Surreal?"

"The ones who broke witches, killed witches, tortured witches, shattered their lives." I drained my glass. "The ones who preyed on children."

"You became an assassin to pay them back for . . . ?"

"My mother. And for me." I set my glass on the table. "Are you coming with me, Rainier?"

"Where are you going?"

"Hunting."

He studied me for a long moment before he nodded. "I'm with you."

I COLLAPSED ON a bench in one of the little parks that were sprinkled throughout Amdarh. Even in the city's busy shopping district, you couldn't go more than two blocks without finding a plot of green that provided shade or a dazzle of color from flowers or the soothing trickle of a fountain.

"The bitch is good; I'll give her that," I said when Rainier joined me on the bench. We'd been hunting for two days—and two more men had died. One was an old man tending a shop for a friend who was ill. The other was a young Warlord who had shielded himself long enough to send a warning on a psychic thread. Despite men converging on the spot from all directions, the witch had still managed to slip past them.

"Here." Rainier gave me a glass bowl and a spoon he'd gotten from a food stand nestled in one corner of the park.

"What is it?" I poked the spoon into the shaved ice in my bowl.

"Flavored ice," he said as he dug into his own bowl.

I tried some. The ice, flavored with berry juice, was just the refreshment I needed after hours of prowling the streets. Halfway through, I started poking at the treat, my pleasure in it gone. Edgy. Uneasy. Worried about something I didn't want to put into words.

I sighed. "We've been hunting for two days, and we don't know any more than we did when this started."

"You know more than you think," said a deep voice—heavy silk with a husky undertone of sex.

Rainier tensed, instantly wary. I looked over at the black-haired, golden-eyed man standing near the bench. I hadn't seen him approach, hadn't heard him, hadn't sensed his presence until he wanted it felt.

If you wanted to look at a prime example of a beautiful predator, Daemon Sadi was it. If you wanted to survive the encounter, looking was all you did.

Daemon settled on the bench with the feline grace that, combined with that body and face, made a woman's pulse spike—even when the woman knew what could happen to her if the Sadist became annoyed. He was a Black-Jeweled Warlord

Prince, the most powerful male in Kaeleer. He was also, may the Darkness help me, family.

"You're supposed to be on your honeymoon," I said.

"We are. Jaenelle and I came back to Amdarh for a day to visit the bookshops and pick up a few supplies before going to the cottage in Ebon Rih." He paused, and his eyes got that sleepy look that always scared the shit out of me. "That was the intention anyway." He looked at Rainier. "Surreal and I have a few things to discuss. Why don't you take a walk?"

"Lady Surreal and I are working together," Rainier replied.

I could have smacked Rainier for the subtle challenge in his voice. He knew better than that.

"Fine," Daemon said—and he smiled.

Rainier paled. He excused himself and retreated. Not far. That Warlord Prince temperament wouldn't let him back down all the way. So he settled on another bench where he could keep me in sight.

"Are you going to share that?" Daemon asked.

I handed over the bowl and spoon. "I thought you liked Rainier."

"I do. What does that have to do with anything?" Daemon took a spoonful of flavored ice before handing it back to me. "Mm. That is good."

"We *are* working together."

"Whatever you tell him is your business." He studied the park and waited.

"All right," I finally said. "What do we know? There's no reason for the killings."

"Just because you don't know what it is doesn't mean there isn't one," Daemon said, his tone a mild scold. "Consider the predator instead of the prey. She's an opportunistic killer. She's not hunting for a particular man or a particular kind of man. She strikes when she can, where she can. She attacks males who wear lighter Jewels, so the odds are she wears at least the Opal Jewel."

"But not a Jewel that's close in strength to the Gray," I murmured. "Her sight shield couldn't hide her from me completely the one time I spotted her."

Daemon nodded. "So you know you can take her without getting hurt unless you're careless. She also chooses males who aren't prepared to defend themselves, which indicates she wants the thrill of spilling blood without the risk of their fighting back."

I huffed in frustration. "You arrived in Amdarh today. How did you figure all this out so fast?"

He laughed softly. "I've been playing this game a lot longer than you have. Besides, Lady Zhara and I had a chat this morning before I came looking for you, and she gave me all the information she had about the killings."

A few weeks ago, the witches in Amdarh got their first taste of what it's like to dance with the Sadist. After that unfortunate incident, I bet Zhara, the Queen of Amdarh, was thrilled to have a chat with Daemon.

Then he looked at me. "Are you worried that you'll find a mirror when you find her?"

Damn him. He knew.

"She's not a mirror, Surreal. You never made a kill that wasn't deserved. You took pleasure from the killing, but you never killed for pleasure. There's a difference."

"You don't know all the kills were deserved."

He just looked at me.

We've known each other for centuries. I was a child when I

met him, when he helped my mother and me. I'll never know how closely he kept track of me after I began my career with a knife, but now I had no doubt, none at all, that if I'd become a killer in the same way the witch we hunted was, I wouldn't be sitting here. He would have destroyed me long ago. I shouldn't have felt relieved knowing that, but I did.

"How do we find this bitch, Sadi?"

"If you can't find the predator, give the predator a reason to find you. Provide irresistible bait." His smile was gentle and vicious. "The prey that seems the sweetest is always the one that got away."

I CROUCHED IN front of the little Yellow-Jeweled Warlord. The miniature man. My irresistible bait. "You know what to do?"

"Yes, Lady," he said, his voice so subdued I could barely hear him.

"I'll be close by."

He nodded. "If she cuts me, will it hurt?"

I looked toward the table tucked in the back corner of the coffee shop. Jaenelle Angelline looked back at me, her sapphire eyes full of something feral and dark.

"Yes," Jaenelle said gently, "it will hurt." She pointed to the wooden frame that held the web of illusions she'd created to play out this game. "By itself, the illusion I've made of you will fool the eye, but in order to fool the hand when someone touches it, it has to be linked to you. While nothing will actually happen to *you,* you will feel whatever happens to it."

The little Warlord looked into those sapphire eyes. Whatever he found there gave him what he needed. "I will serve to the best of my ability."

Jaenelle smiled. "I know."

I gave the little Warlord one last, long look. He had a loose button on his jacket. It hadn't been loose yesterday evening when the boy and his instructor came to the family town house so that Jaenelle could build the web of illusions.

Some of the tension inside me eased. It was such a little detail, but I'd be able to use it to tell when the switch was made and the illusion took the boy's place out on the street.

We took our positions. Daemon stayed in the coffee shop with Jaenelle. The boy's instructor took his usual place at a window table. Rainier and I sight shielded before leaving the shop. He crossed the main street to tuck into a doorway near that corner. I crossed the side street, settling into a doorway just beyond the alley. The boy went to the corner to perform escort duties, leading ladies across the street.

We watched, waited. So far, all the killings had taken place in this part of the city, but there was no guarantee the bitch wouldn't start hunting somewhere else, no guarantee she'd come close enough to spot the bait.

An hour passed. We watched. Waited. I tensed every time a lone female approached the corner, every time the boy offered his hand as an escort—and breathed a sigh of relief every time he stepped into the coffee shop to receive advice from his instructor. But every time the small figure left the coffee shop, it was still wearing a jacket with a loose button.

I gritted my teeth. I trusted Jaenelle, and I could understand her delaying as long as possible before making the switch in case someone *could* recognize the illusion for what it was. But, Hell's fire, why was she waiting so long?

We were coming up on the two-hour mark, which would end the training session, when something drifted toward me on the air. Something that made me edgy, uneasy. I scanned the people going about their business, cursing when I lost sight of the boy as a carriage passed by. Then I saw him again. And I saw her. She came from Dhemlan, so there was nothing about her looks that would attract attention, but I knew it was her.

They crossed the side street on the opposite side from me. I held my breath and hoped Jaenelle could still make the switch from boy to illusion before the rest of this game was played out.

The witch said something to him that made him smile, brought out that bright-eyed puppy eagerness to please.

They crossed the main street. He stayed at the corner. She continued up the street, toward the alley. Toward me.

She glanced at the alley, then stopped and cried out, "He's hurt! Mother Night, he's hurt!" She looked around frantically. "Help me, Warlord. Help me. He's hurt!" She darted into the alley.

The boy stayed true to his training. A female had cried for help. He ran into the alley after her.

And I saw the loose button on his jacket.

I heard his panicked cry as I rushed into the alley.

"Let him go, bitch," I snarled, calling in the hunting knife.

She whirled to face me, the boy held against her, a knife as mean as mine pressed against his neck.

Her eyes danced with the glee of the kill. The smile she gave me was malignant.

"Let him go," I said again. I saw terror in the boy's gold eyes, but I had to play out the game—and hope.

"There's no law against murder." She pressed the blade against the boy's neck hard enough to cut the skin. Blood trick-led from the wound.

"True. But it's also not condoned when there's no reason."

"He's male. That's reason enough." She pouted. "You're female. You should be on my side."

When the sun shines in Hell, bitch. "Let him go."

"All right."

She ripped the knife across the boy's neck and throat. Blood sprayed the alley walls. Sprayed her. Sprayed me.

I just stood there, frozen by the feel of warm blood on my face. *We failed.*

"Why?" Before I finished with her, I was going to get an answer. "Tell me why you killed those men, killed this boy."

The alley was suddenly filled with hatred, with fury . . . and bitter hurt. *That* was the other thing I'd sensed in that first room but couldn't quite recognize.

I knew that feeling too. Didn't matter. Not with that boy's blood on me. "What happened, sugar? Did your lover walk away after taking all he could stomach from you?"

Her fury drowned out the bitter hurt. "He didn't walk far." She pouted. "But the males in the village were so angry about him dying like that, my aunt commanded that I stay in Amdarh for a while. They exiled me, a Queen's niece, from my own village because of that bastard."

"That doesn't explain killing the men here." Something wasn't right. Broken heart or not, something wasn't right.

"They're all the same!" she shouted. "They make you feel special until the contract ends; then they walk away."

"The man you killed was a consort under contract?" No wonder the men in the village were pissed off. If he'd fulfilled his contract, a consort had the right to walk away without repercussions.

"He was better than the other ones I've had, and I wanted to renew the contract. But he refused. The bastard started packing his things a minute after the contract ended."

"Guess he just didn't want to spend another year in bed with a snotty little bitch." I studied her. She wasn't nursing a bruised heart. A bruised ego, maybe, but not a bruised heart.

That malicious gleam filled her eyes again. At that moment, I hated her with everything in me.

"I can do anything I want with a male," she said. "No male is going to make me feel special, then walk away. Never again. And there's nothing you can do about it."

"Now, that's where you're wrong." I smiled. "As you pointed out, there's no law against murder."

Before she even thought to run, I created a Gray shield bubble around her, trapping her.

"Everything has a price," I said softly. "I'm calling in the debt for the men you killed here in Amdarh—and the boy." Especially the boy. "You like splattering the walls with blood and gore, sugar? Well, now's your chance."

I gave her one moment to realize what was going to happen. Then I fed all of my own fury into my Gray Jewels as I unleashed their stored power and slammed it into her. Her body exploded, a storm of red mist and white bits of bone swirling in a Gray bubble. I thrust a rapier of Gray into the mind I could still sense in that mist, breaking her power, finishing the kill. There would be no ghost or demon-dead to haunt this alley.

Then it was done. Debt paid. But the price for stopping that bitch was much, much too high.

"Surreal."

Grief tightened my throat, but I obeyed the command in that

deep voice and walked to the mouth of the alley . . . where Daemon waited.

"You played the game well," he said. "Why didn't you splatter her over the walls? You wanted to."

"After what she'd done, it didn't seem fair to have men spend a couple of days scrubbing her off the bricks."

He looked into the alley. "Leave the bubble. I'll take care of it later."

I nodded, feeling heartsick. "All of this because males are trained to serve, to please."

"Hardly," Daemon replied dryly. "That was her excuse. I've seen her kind too many times over the years. She liked inflicting pain, and she liked having control over the person while she did it. She didn't kill any of those men because they were trained to serve; she killed them because they had the right to walk away from someone who wanted to hurt them."

He was right. I knew he was right, but . . . "I guess I should—" I looked down at my clothes.

No blood.

I turned and looked into the alley. No blood sprayed on the walls. No small body.

"No one can create an illusion the way Jaenelle can," Daemon said softly.

No small body in the alley. "When . . . ?"

"She made the switch the first time the boy came back into the coffee shop for instructions. She needed him on the street just long enough to hone the details in the illusion."

Jaenelle would pay attention to the details—right down to a loose button on a jacket. Which meant I'd watched an illusion for most of those two hours and never known the difference.

Relief made me dizzy, weak. Daemon put his arm around my shoulders and led me to the coffee shop. Rainier entered the shop just behind us.

The little Warlord sat on a chair at the back of the shop. He looked shaken, but he was safe. Whole. Alive.

"Hmm," Jaenelle said as she gently probed the boy's neck. "Swallow now. Does that feel sore?"

"A little," the boy replied.

Caught by those sapphire eyes, he didn't look shaken anymore. A bit dazzled, but not shaken. Jaenelle had that effect on males.

"Hmm," Jaenelle said again. "There's no damage, no injury. But I think a bit of medicinal care is still required."

The boy's eyes widened. "Medicine?"

I guess bravery only goes so far.

"Mm. A dish of flavored ice twice a day for the next three days will take care of the soreness." Jaenelle's eyes sparkled with laughter. "Can you handle that?"

The boy grinned. "Yes, Lady." He bounced off the chair and came over to stand next to Rainier and me.

"Now," Daemon said, slipping a hand around Jaenelle's arm to coax her to her feet. "Since everything is settled, my Lady and I will take care of our shopping and resume our honeymoon."

"Daemon is going to teach me how to cook," Jaenelle said, smiling at him.

"Oh, how"—*brave of Daemon*—"nice," I replied.

Everything has a price. I wasn't sure who was paying whom with the kiss that followed, but it was certainly a demonstration.

After watching for a few seconds, the boy tugged on Rainier's sleeve. "Am I going to learn how to do that?"

Rainier grinned. I closed my eyes.

Daemon broke the kiss and chuckled as he led his Lady out of the coffee shop.

Within a few minutes, the boy and his instructor were gone as well.

"Well," Rainier said. "It's been interesting, Lady Surreal."

"That it has, Prince Rainier."

He hesitated. "What are you doing this evening?"

Soaking in a deep tub of hot water. Sleeping. "Why?"

"Would you like to go dancing?"

We would never be lovers. Just then, that was a point in his favor, since I wasn't ready to spend time with a man who wanted to be a lover. But maybe we could have some fun together as friends.

I smiled at him. "Yes," I said, "I'd love to go dancing."

THE LANDSCAPES OF EPHEMERA

"They called her the Voice because she had none."

That sentence haunted me for years. Who was "she" and why didn't she have a voice? The other thing that haunted me was a question: What happens to our bodies when we pack down negative feelings instead of giving them a safe outlet—instead of giving *them* a voice? Eventually the opening sentence and the question led me to the city of Vision, where they came together and became a story.

THE VOICE

1

THEY CALLED HER THE VOICE BECAUSE SHE HAD none. Fat, mute, and dimwitted, she was an orphan the village supported, providing her with a house and caretakers. And she was always included in village life. Oh, she wasn't invited into people's homes—everyone went to the Voice's house when a visit was required—but every time someone had a "moody day," as my mother called them, every time something happened that was less than pleasant, a special little cake was made. The "moody" person took the treat to the Voice's house, waited until she took her special seat in the visitors' room, then handed her the food.

She never refused a moody cake. Never. She would smile at the children when they handed her the treats, and sometimes she smiled at the adults. She never smiled at the village Elders, but she also never refused their offerings when they came to visit. You always knew that she didn't refuse because that was part of the ritual—you stayed and watched her eat what you had brought, and when you left, you felt better. The moody day was gone, and you went back to your ordinary life.

I never considered the oddity of an orphan having a visitors' room that bore a resemblance to the audience chamber in the Elders' Hall. I never wondered why having a moody day required making a treat that was given away. And I never wondered why an adult provided escort and oversaw the visit until a child was considered trustworthy enough to take the treat to the Voice and not eat it herself. I never felt anything but a smug pity for the girl—and being just ten years older than me, she was barely more than a girl at the time—who always wore these loose, strange hoods that covered her head and neck and was provided with simple smocks and trousers as covering for her body because, despite being young, there was no need for her to dress in pretty clothes that would attract a male eye, as the other girls were doing.

So I lived quite happily—and innocently—in the village that supported the Voice until the summer I turned ten years old. That was when I had my first glimpse of the truth.

IT HAD BEEN a hot summer, and there had been little rain. Men were wearing their summer garb—sleeveless tunics and lightweight pants that were hemmed above the knee. Some of the younger men—the bachelors in the village who were looking for a wife—were even bold enough to cut off their trousers to midthigh length, which delighted the older women; mortified the older, knobby-kneed men; and scandalized the village Elders. It wasn't until women began fainting on a daily basis while doing housework in the heat that the Elders were forced to revise their strict dress code for our female population and permit short sleeves on the tunics and trousers that were hemmed just below the knee. The Elders reasoned that it was simply too hot for strenuous activity, so the sight of female limbs would not excite male flesh.

The number of women who became pregnant during that summer—and the number of bachelors who were required to make a hasty contract of marriage—showed everyone how embarrassingly incorrect the Elders' reasoning had been. And, according to the whispers of a few sharp tongues, it also proved how old the Elders really were.

But those were insignificant things to a ten-year-old girl who was relishing the feel of air on her arms and legs when she was outside playing with friends.

That was where we were when I had the first glimpse of the truth—outside in the shade of a big tree, lazily tossing a ball between the three of us: Kobbi (who was Named Kobrah), Tahnee, and me, Nalah. Then the Voice plodded by, her tunic sleeves and trousers full-length, of course, since the sight of her fat limbs would offend the eye. And then the boys came, with a glint in their eyes that made the three of us huddle together like sheep scenting a pack of wild dogs and instinctively knowing that separation from the flock meant death.

The boys weren't interested in teasing us that day, not when the Voice, looking back and recognizing danger, began lumbering toward the nearest house, no doubt hoping to be rescued.

They moved too fast, surrounded her too quickly.

"Aren't you hot?" they taunted the Voice. "Aren't you hot, hot, hot? We'll help you cool off."

They grabbed at her, pushed at her, and she kept turning,

kept trying to move, no different from some poor, dumb beast. Until one of them grabbed her hood and pulled it off, exposing her neck for the first time in our young memories.

The boys scrambled away from her, silent and staring. Then she turned and looked at us girls. Looked into my eyes.

I didn't see a poor, dumb beast. There was intelligence in those eyes, as maimed as her body. And there was anger in those eyes, now unsheathed for everyone to see.

Some adults finally noticed us and realized something was wrong. The murmur of concerned voices changed into a hornets' buzz of anger when the adults realized what we had seen—and why. The Voice was solicitously returned to her house; the boys were marched to the Elders' Hall to have their punishment decided; and we three girls were escorted to our homes, where our escorts held whispered conversations with our mothers.

I spent the rest of that afternoon in solitude, keeping my mind carefully blank while I watched the play of light and shadow on my bedroom wall. But my mind would not remain blank. Thoughts seeped up and got tangled in the shifting patterns of leaves on the white plaster wall.

The Voice had not been born mute. Had the injuries that had healed into those horrific scars happened at the same time she lost her parents? Was there a time when she had been called by another name? Even if her voice had been damaged and could not be repaired, the healers could sew better than the best seamstress and took pride in the health of the whole village. Why had they patched her up so badly?

The pattern on the wall changed, and another thought drifted through my mind as the words spoken by the teachers each school day seemed to swell until I could think of nothing else—until I could hear the threat under the words that were intended as thanksgiving: *Honor your parents. Give thanks for them every day. Without them, you are orphaned, and an orphan's life is one of sorrow.*

The Voice was cared for by the whole village. She had a house.

But it's one of the oldest houses in the village. Is she the first who lived there? If you ask your mother or grandmother, will they admit that another mute orphan lived there before?

Everyone brought her food and treats; even little children, helped by parents, presented her with treats.

Does she ever truly want them?

Why does she have those scars?

I didn't have an answer. Didn't want an answer. I hurt for myself, and I hurt for the Voice.

An hour before dinner, I emerged from my room. My mother studied my face carefully, then said, "I'll make you a moody cake. You take it to the Voice. You'll feel better."

"No," I said, my voice rough, as if something were eating away at my throat. "I'll make it."

Mother studied me a little longer, then nodded. "Very well. You're old enough."

So I made the little moody cake while Mother went into the garden and made no comment about her dinner preparations being delayed (it was considered bad luck to prepare other food while a moody cake was being made). And if a few tears fell into the mixture, I didn't think it would spoil the taste.

As soon as it was cool enough to be placed on the little plate that was always—and only—used for food presented to the Voice, I left the house. The fact that neither of my parents commented or demanded that I wait until after our evening meal told me how concerned they were for me.

She was in the visitors' room, sitting in the oddly proportioned chair that looked as if it had been specially made for a much fatter person. Since she was already there, I was not her first visitor. Probably Kobbi and Tahnee had already been there with their mothers. She was alone, which wasn't unusual. There was always a caretaker in the house, but visitors usually meant the caretaker had a little time for herself.

I approached the chair until I was standing at the correct, polite distance. But I didn't extend the plate. Even though she had been bathed and carefully dressed and a new hood covered her head and neck, I looked into her eyes and remembered those horrific scars.

Tears filled my eyes as I touched my own neck and whispered, "I'm sorry."

To my amazement, since she never showed emotion beyond a simple smile, her eyes filled with tears too. Then she smiled—a true, warm, compassionate, loving smile—and reached out, took my little moody cake, and ate it.

Feeling so much better, I wiped the tears from my face and smiled in return. "I have to go now."

She didn't respond in any way when I turned to leave. She never did.

Before I reached the door, ready to skip home to my family and dinner, the boys who had taunted the Voice entered the room, followed by stern-looking fathers and nervous mothers. I jumped out of the way and pressed myself against the wall to avoid notice, but no one was going to notice me at that point.

And considering what happened, no one even remembered I had been there.

The first boy stepped up to the chair and extended the plate with its little offering.

The Voice picked up the offering and threw it on the floor.

There were shocked gasps from all the adults in the room, and the boy's father hurried to the doorway that led to the rest of the house, calling for the caretaker.

The second boy made his offering. She mashed it in her fist, then smeared it on her clothes. But the third boy, the one who had pulled off her hood, revealing a secret, exposing her pain . . .

She moved so fast no one could stop her. One moment she was sitting, just staring at the boy; the next, she lunged at him, grabbing the cake in one hand and his head in the other. As he started to yell, she shoved the cake into his mouth, forcing him to swallow or choke. So he swallowed—and the look in her eyes haunted my thoughts for years afterward.

Shortly after that, the boy contracted Black Pustules. These were painful boils that developed deep beneath the skin. Sometimes it took weeks before they reached the point where they could be lanced. And a single lancing never cleaned out a pustule, no matter what the healers tried. The pain of healing was endured over and over while new eruptions developed and needed to be lanced. It took several sessions before the hard nugget that was the core of the pustule could be extracted and the body finally healed.

But no matter how carefully the healers dealt with their patients, the final extraction left scars.

It always left scars.

In the weeks that followed, I didn't see the Voice walking around the village, but I'd heard my parents whispering to friends that the Voice had been refusing all offerings, and the Elders and healers had accepted the necessity of taking measures—for the health of the village.

My curiosity got the better of me and, pretending to have a moody day, I prepared a little cake and took it to the Voice.

No child should know so cruel a truth as what I saw that day.

She was no longer left unattended, and one of her caretakers was a burly young man. She was dressed in a robe with a matching hood. The design of the robe's sleeves was clever but didn't quite disguise that her arms were bound to the chair. The fact that she no longer had even the illusion of freedom was bad enough, but . . .

They had done something to her so that the caretaker, applying pressure on a dowel of wood attached to something inside her mouth, could force her mouth open enough for the offering to be pushed inside. Then her mouth was forcibly closed so she couldn't spit out the treat.

They had taken away all her choices. She would consume what the villagers wanted her to consume.

She looked at me, and I felt as if I had betrayed her by coming here and forcing her to take something she didn't want. But I couldn't tell her it wasn't a real moody cake, not with the caretaker standing right there, listening. And I couldn't say I had changed my mind and the Voice didn't need to accept my offering. That wasn't done, ever. So, in the end, I watched the male caretaker force her mouth open, shove in my little cake, and seal her mouth shut again.

I didn't cry until I was safely home. Then I hid in a sheltered spot in my mother's garden and cried until I made myself sick.

I avoided the Voice's house as much as I could. Oh, I still made the moody cakes when some telltale sign warned my mother that I was not in harmony with the world. I was still trusted to go by myself, so my parents didn't know that once I was safely out of sight, I found a hiding place . . . and ate the moody cake.

There was nothing in the making of it, nothing in the ingredients that could explain the sour, gelatinous, grape-size lump that I discovered was in the center of every moody cake. Break it open and you'd find nothing, but put it in your mouth and you could feel that lump growing in the center of the cake. And yet you couldn't spit it out. You could spit out the cake, but then the lump remained with nothing to sweeten it.

The first time I ate the moody cake, I was sick for a day, but my mother concluded that I had eaten something that didn't agree with me and, fortunately, didn't press me to find out what it was.

The second time I ate a moody cake, a Black Pustule developed on my belly. It was painful and frightening, but I was more afraid to tell my parents and admit I hadn't been taking my moody cakes to the Voice, so I dealt with it in silence, learning that a warm, wet cloth brought the pustule to a head quicker and a sewing needle was a sufficient lance. Extracting the core is something I do not care to describe, but the substance was a harder, thicker version of the gelatinous lump in the moody cake.

Perhaps if I had been older, I would have understood. As it was, seven more years passed before I reached that moment of understanding.

2

"YOU REALLY DID IT?"

It was the disbelief and admiration in my older brother Dariden's voice that had me creeping a little closer to his open window. I was seventeen; I knew better than to eavesdrop on my brother's conversations with friends. I found out too many things about him that diminished my feelings for him and gave me no liking for his friends. Especially Chayne, who had recently married Kobbi and was now one of the Voice's caretakers—or guards, as I thought of the people who controlled her.

"Wasn't easy, since Vision is such an unnatural city, but I managed to slip away from my father for an evening and find a particular shop."

"And the stuff works?" Dariden asked.

Chayne laughed softly. "She's pretty to look at, but when you spread Kobrah's legs, she's a cold piece. So I put three drops of this drug in her wine, and she falls into a sensual haze. I can do almost anything to her. She's passive on the drug, but her body is so hot and willing, it doesn't matter that her brain isn't in the bed."

"A wife only needs enough brains to know when to spread 'em," Dariden said with a smirk in his voice.

I didn't dare move. Hardly dared to breathe. If Dariden found out I had overheard this, he would make my life a misery. Or more of a misery than it was.

"Will she do . . . *that* . . . when you give her the drug?" Dariden asked.

"No," Chayne replied, sounding disgusted. "Even with an extra drop of it—which is all I dare give her, because I was warned that too much will make a woman's brains go funny permanently—I can't make her do *that*. But it doesn't matter because . . ."

Chayne lowered his voice, so I leaned a little closer to the window, still not daring to move my feet.

"I put three drops on *her* tongue, give her a glob of that mixture we feed her when we aren't stuffing her with the offerings, then close her up and wait a bit. Once the drug is working, I can spend hours in her mouth, with her tongue lapping and licking. And I know just how far to open the lever for the right tightness."

"And then she does *that*?" Dariden asked, sounding breathless.

Chayne laughed softly. It was such a cruel sound. "Well, swallowing is what she does, isn't it?"

They left Dariden's room, and I said a hasty prayer to every goddess and god I could think of that they wouldn't come around to the back of the house and realize I had heard them. My prayer must have been answered, because they left the house through the front door, and I was able to slip in through the kitchen door and reach my room undetected.

My father was a good man. I was sure of it. How could he have raised a son who would think such horrible things were exciting?

Is your father truly a good man? some part of me asked. *He goes to the Voice's house with moody cakes when he's unhappy about something. Does he really not know what he's forcing her to eat?*

He couldn't know. Couldn't. But if he did know, that might explain the worry I had seen in his eyes over the past year.

I had kept my secret for five years, dutifully making the moody cakes when my mother felt I needed to visit the Voice, and just as rebelliously eating the cakes myself. During those years, I learned that eating pieces of regular cakes and breads that we made at home and gobbling the pastries I bought at the bakery with my spending money absorbed the worst of the effects of the Black Pustules. I still got them whenever I ate a moody cake, but they weren't as big or as painful. On the other hand, I had plumped to what my father had initially, and teasingly, called a wifely figure—meaning my fat-softened body was not the sleek shape a man looked for in a bride but accepted in a wife after the babies started arriving. After all, a man had to make some sacrifices in order to have children.

Then Tahnee blundered one evening when she told my mother she hadn't seen me at the Voice's house at a time when I should have been there. Realizing her error and believing that I must have been sneaking out to meet a boy and had used the Voice as an excuse, Tahnee did her best to deny her own words, but her suddenly vague memory about where she had been on a particular evening didn't fool my mother, who then saw my days of being slightly ill in a totally different way.

After that, I had an escort for each visit to the Voice's house, and when I watched the caretaker feed her the moody cake, I felt sick inside—because I felt better. But until I was seventeen and made the trip to Vision, I still didn't know why.

3

DARIDEN WAS WILD TO GO TO THAT PLACE THAT WAS considered an unnatural city and something even more, even stranger. In the end, I was the one who went to Vision with Tahnee and her parents.

Despite my mother's efforts to control what I could eat when I was in the house and despite the bakery, in an effort to help me regain my maidenly figure, agreeing not to sell me anything unless I had a note from one of my parents (which I never was given), my body remained stubbornly plump. My father, in an effort to be helpful, had taken to whispering to me whenever he escorted me to visit the Voice, "If you don't stop your foolish eating, you'll end up looking like that."

She was huge. When her mouth was forced open to receive an offering, her eyes disappeared within the folds of fat. It hurt me to see her and know I was adding to her pain. It hurt me to hear my father say something so cruel to the daughter he professed to love.

But on the particular day that led to my going to Vision, Chayne was the caretaker on duty when my father whispered his encouragement—and I had what the healers described as a mild emotional breakdown.

I screamed. I wailed. I wept. I sat on the floor and howled with a pain that filled the visitors' room and frightened all the grumpy-faced children who wanted to feed a moody cake to the Voice so they could leave and be happy, happy, happy while she . . . while she . . .

In the end, I went with Tahnee and her parents because they had already planned a week's stay in Vision and I could share a room with Tahnee—and also because when my brother offered to escort me, I started screaming that he fornicated with barnyard animals and molested small children, and every time my father got near me, I began making guttural noises that, as my mother told me when I was calmer, sounded like they were coming from a savage animal.

My mother was correct about that. Something was building inside me, and I didn't know why. All I truly knew was that I hated the village I lived in and hated participating in something that not only violated another person, but violated something in myself as well.

I needed to escape, but I didn't know how.

Sometimes all it takes is a change of vision.

4

THE JOURNEY TO VISION TOOK TWO DAYS OF STEADY travel, the only breaks being those required to rest the team of horses. At times the hills were so steep we had to get out and walk, because it was all the horses could do to pull the weight of the coach and our luggage up the incline. But when we reached the crest of the last, gentler hill, we looked down on the strange glory that was Vision.

It was a patchwork city that spread out across a vast plain, backed by old, rounded mountains cloaked in the restful green of living things. Some parts of the city dazzled the eye, while others seemed lost in shadow—and still other places must have been farmland and pastures. Not one city, but many. And so much more than I could have imagined the first time I saw it.

So we descended the hill, passing the last crossroad that would lead to other places. After that, there was no destination but the city, which was reached by a bridge that had a peculiar but carefully made sign posted a coach's length before the bridge itself: ASK YOUR HEART ITS DESTINATION.

Upon seeing the sign, Tahnee's father muttered about the need to avoid the "peculiar" folks that inhabited the city. Then, in a heartier voice, he reassured his three ladies that we would not be visiting any of the peculiar places.

But I looked at the sign and, even though I thought it was foolish, shaped my answer as the horses stepped onto the bridge: *Escape. Freedom. Answers.* If my heart had a destination, it was shaped by those three words.

At the other end of the bridge was another peculiar sign:

WELCOME TO VISION. YOU CAN FIND ONLY WHAT
YOU CAN SEE.

As I read the sign, the sun went behind a bank of clouds, and
everything turned dark and chilling. Then the sun returned,
and the world looked fresh and dazzling—and not quite the
same.

Since I was on this journey because of my lack of mental
health, I didn't ask if any of my companions had witnessed
those same moments of dark and light. I just watched the city,
barely listening to the comments of the other people in the
coach. And while we journeyed, I considered the significance of
the words if that sign meant exactly what it said.

THE FIRST TWO days, I found nothing of interest and tried
not to resent the hearty comments that came too often about
how a change of scenery could do a person good. I *wanted* a
change of scenery. I had been searching for that change for two
days.

And I almost missed it when it finally appeared on the third
afternoon of our visit.

The bazaar in the center of the city took up entire blocks,
almost ending on the doorstep of the rooming house where we
were staying. Having tramped through it with us the first two
days, Tahnee's parents left us on our own that third afternoon,
convinced that two girls from a small village would come to no
harm despite the cacophony of sights and sounds. And no harm
would come to us, because the white-robed Shamans walked
the crowded streets. Their pace steady, their faces serene, they
walked among the buyers and sellers, sometimes stopping to

accept a slice of fruit or a cup of cool water. They seldom spoke to the people around them, but when they smiled and said, "Travel lightly," it always sounded like a blessing.

On the afternoon that changed so many things, Tahnee was cheerfully haggling with the son of a merchant, more to have a reason to remain close to the handsome boy than because she was seriously interested in whatever she had found to haggle over that day. I wandered down the row of booths just for something to do while I waited. Then I saw a flash of white disappearing between two booths. No, more than that. In a place that was crowded and where every merchant jealously guarded his allotted space down to the last finger length, there shouldn't have been a space that would have easily fit four booths.

That was the moment I realized I had passed that gap in the booths more than once each day without really seeing it—or wondering about it.

I stepped into that gap and saw something else that had eluded my eyes during those first two days.

The bazaar backed up against a white wall. The gap in the booths matched the width of the archway leading into . . .

The streets, gardens, courtyards, and buildings might have been another world. For all I know, they were. The place was white and clean, and with every breath I breathed in peace. And with every step I took, a pain grew inside me, as if a Black Pustule had formed deep within my body and was festering.

Still within sight of the archway, I stopped moving. Then I looked up, and something shivered through me, as if I were a bell that had been struck and somehow retuned to match the resonance of the building in front of me.

THE TEMPLE OF SORROW

I walked up the steps and pulled the rope beside the door. Heard the bell calling, calling.

A Shaman opened the door. His hair was grizzled, his face unlined. I have never seen anything before or since that matched the beauty of his eyes.

He smiled and stood aside to let me enter.

"Is this your first visit?" he asked.

I just nodded, struck dumb by the odd sensation of feeling too gaudy and too plain at the same time. It was my first experience with having a crush on a man, and I didn't know what to do or say.

Then I remembered I was wifely plump rather than maidenly sleek, and there was something festering inside me.

"I see," he said softly, and I was terrified that, somehow, he had. Then he said, "This way," and led me to a pair of doors on the left side of the building.

He opened the doors, and the sound . . .

"No," I gasped. "No. I can't. That is—" *Obscene. A violation.*

Something that sang in my limbs.

He closed the doors. "That is sorrow." His voice was quiet, gentle. "That is why this temple is here. To give it voice. To set it free. Sorrow should not be swallowed. It will linger in the body, cleave to the flesh, long after the mind and heart have forgotten the cause."

Each word was a delicate blow, a butterfly tap that reverberated through my heart.

"What do I do?" I asked.

He opened the doors again, and we stepped into the room.

It sounded like the entire city was in that room, but in truth, there was no more than a double handful of people, and the room could have held twice that many. Some were wearing a hooded robe that had a veil over the face, which allowed them to see and breathe but obscured their identity. Others sat with their faces exposed to the world.

The sound in the room rose and fell, sometimes barely a hum and other times crescendoing to be the voice of sky and earth and all living things.

In one of the quieter moments, the Shaman whispered, "The gongs provide a tone. If the first one you try does not fit the voice you need today, try another."

"Then what do I do?"

His hand rested on my shoulder for a moment, the warmth of it a staggering comfort. He smiled and said, "Then you release sorrow."

Too self-conscious to really try the available gongs to test their sound, I chose one based on the pleasing simplicity of the frame that held it. It did not produce a sound quite as deep as what I wanted, but having timidly struck it once, I wasn't about to get up and move to another place in the room.

I kept my eyes fixed on the floor just in front of my cushions, sure that it would be terribly rude to look at the other people in the room. I hummed, fearful of being heard, while something inside me swelled and swelled until it was ready to burst.

The voices around me rose and fell. Sometimes a gong would sound, and one voice would be raised in a wordless cry. Other times each gong was rung, and the accompanying voices filled the room. Over and over until, at last, there was only one voice still keening, only one heart not yet purged of sorrow.

Mine.

But I, too, fell silent, too exhausted and hollowed out to go on. I had lanced my well of sorrow, but I had not extracted the core.

One by one, the other people stood up and left. I was the last person in the room, and by the time I reached the door, the Shaman stood there, a question in his beautiful eyes.

"If you need us, we are always here," he said. Then he escorted me to the outer door and added, "Travel lightly."

"Oh, my friends and I are staying in the city for a few more days," I said, wondering if that was considered flirting or too bold—and wondering if Shamans even had such interests in the flesh.

His eyes smiled, though his expression remained serious. "Some journeys can be made without setting a foot outside your own room." He paused. "If you need us, we are here. Remember that."

It wasn't until I returned to the friendly cacophony of the bazaar that I noticed the sign above the archway. It said, THE TEMPLES, as if nothing more were required in identifying that island of peace.

"Nalah!" Tahnee rushed up to me. "Where have you been? I almost went back to the rooming house without you, but . . ."

The day before, I might have stammered something or become defensive because I was unwilling to tell anyone where I had been. But that day, I saw something in Tahnee's face, in her eyes.

"We've spent the afternoon wandering around the bazaar, looking at so many things."

"Yes," Tahnee said, wary but willing to hear me out. "We have. But . . . you haven't bought anything."

"I don't have as much spending money as you, so—"

"Oh, I can give you some if—"

"I'm looking very carefully before deciding what gifts to purchase for my parents and brother as a way of thanking them for allowing me to see Vision."

"Oh." Tahnee nibbled her lower lip. "It would be better if we both came to the bazaar, don't you think? Safer that way. Ah . . . how much longer will you need to decide on your purchases?"

"There is still so much to see; I think it will take at least another day or two," I said, linking arms with Tahnee as we headed in the direction of the rooming house.

She gave me a sidelong look. "You are all right, though, aren't you?"

"Yes," I replied honestly. "I feel better than I've felt in a very long time. Perhaps the best ever."

"I feel the same."

I didn't think we had the same reason for the feeling, but I was glad to hear her say it. And, for me, it was true. I felt better. Much better.

I felt the same way I used to feel after making a moody cake and bringing it to the Voice. But that was something I didn't want to think about. Not yet. So Tahnee and I returned to the rooming house and endured a mild scold from her mother about almost being late for the evening meal. But her father looked at us and said with a wink, "Had a little adventure, did you? Nothing wrong with a little adventure—as long as it doesn't go too far."

Too far? I thought about what the Shaman had said about making a journey without leaving your room and realized I already had gone too far—because now there was no going back.

THE NEXT TWO days were deceptions tacitly permitted by Tahnee's father, since he knew we were up to something but figured that, being together, neither of us would go too far in our little adventures. And there was a tacit agreement between me and Tahnee that neither of us *would* go too far and put the other's "little adventure" at risk.

I don't know where she went, but I guessed that a handsome young man had been given some time off from work in his father's booth. I went to the Temple of Sorrow.

The gongs reverberated in the air. Voices rose and fell. And the sounds and the tears lanced a pain deep inside me that had been growing and festering since the first time I had eaten a moody cake and had gained an inkling of what it meant to be the Voice.

I lanced the pain, knowing there would be scars. But I wasn't able to extract the core of that pain until later in the evening when Tahnee and I were in our room, not saying much as each of us contemplated how to spend our last day in the city.

"The boys at home," Tahnee said, curling up on the bed and fixing her gaze on the wall rather than look at me. "I mean no criticism of your brother. He seems nice enough, although it will be years yet before he is considered of marrying age. The ones who *are* of marrying age . . . they're all like Chayne, and I don't want to live with a man like Chayne. Kobbi . . ." Tahnee licked her lips, a nervous gesture. "Kobbi thinks Chayne is doing something to her when he wants to do the marriage thing. You know. In bed."

Since she seemed to expect it, I nodded to indicate I understood.

"She's not sure, and it isn't every time they . . . do things. But sometimes she doesn't feel right in the head the next day. Chayne was real worried the day she had a bad spell after one of those nights, and that was when she began thinking that maybe he was doing something. Before she could get up the nerve to tell her father, Chayne began making cutting little remarks, especially around her father, saying that a good wife would not begrudge giving her husband little pleasures when he had to work hard to provide her with a home and clothes and food. So when Kobbi finally got scared enough to tell her father . . ."

"What did he say?" I whispered, feeling as if the world itself held its breath while waiting for the answer.

"He hit her." Tahnee's face had a bewildered expression, as if everything she had known and trusted had changed suddenly and betrayed her. "He said she shamed him by being a poor wife, and he would denounce her as his daughter if Chayne continued to have cause to complain."

In the silence, I heard the patter of rain. I looked out the window and watched the sky weep. Lulled by the sound, Tahnee fell asleep. I stayed awake much longer, letting thoughts drift and form patterns.

Honor your parents. Give thanks for them every day. Because an orphan's life is one of sorrow.

There was no ingredient used in the moody cakes that wasn't used in other foods. So what made the cakes a vessel for feelings we didn't want? And who had decided that one person would be sacrificed for the health of the village? Who had decided that the people in my village would not have to carry the weight of their own sorrows?

Maybe there was no one left to blame. Maybe no one truly knew anymore.

But the Elders continue it, my heart whispered. *They see her; others care for her. Are there Black Pustules festering all over her body, always hidden because she had been trained to keep her body covered? Someone stripped a child of the ability to speak and scarred her so she would be ashamed to reveal the reason for her silence. The people who did this still live in the village.*

We all did this. Day after day, year after year, we handed someone a plate of sorrow disguised as a treat and expected her to swallow it so that we could feel better instead of carrying the weight—and the scars—ourselves.

Welcome to Vision. You can find only what you can see.

As something inside me continued shifting and forming new patterns, I wondered if I had changed enough to see what I needed to find.

THE FOLLOWING AFTERNOON, I turned a corner. It was that easy.

The Apothecary was on a street that is one of Vision's shadow places—neither Dark nor Light, since it is a street that can be reached by hearts that resonate with either.

On another day, the looks of the man standing behind the counter at the back of the shop would have scared me enough to abandon my plan. That day, I studied him in what light came in through his grimy windows and decided if looks were a measure of a man, this one could do what I needed.

I told him what I wanted, and I paid him what he asked, relieved I had enough coins for the purchase and a little left over so that Tahnee would not end up paying for my family gifts completely out of her own pocket.

"Enough for three people, you said?" he asked when he returned from the curtained back room and handed me a small bottle.

"Yes, three." I was almost sure that there was only one caretaker in the later hours, but I had to be certain I could deal with whoever was there. Because there would be only one chance.

"I am curious," he said as I turned to leave. "Do you seek revenge?"

I slipped the bottle into my pocket and carefully buttoned the pocket flap. Then I looked at him. "I seek another's freedom."

He studied me a moment longer, then raised his hand and scribed a sign in the air. I didn't know if it was a blessing or black magic—and I didn't care.

The next day, we began the journey back to our village. Tahnee and I gave each other sly looks and pokes in the ribs that were followed by giggles, which confirmed to her parents that we had gotten up to some mischief. It also made them relax, confident that nothing much had happened during our visit.

My parents, too, were relieved by the sly looks and the giggling. I was once again the daughter they knew.

Only my brother noticed something different. Or maybe it was just envy trying to bare its fangs.

"You look good, Nalah," he said. "Rested. Almost like a different person."

I just smiled. I didn't tell him he was right. I *was* a different person.

Now I was dangerous.

5

I COULD NO LONGER LIVE IN THIS VILLAGE AND PAR-ticipate in the cruelty of destroying someone else in order to keep myself clean of all but the "good" feelings, and I was afraid of what might happen to me if the Elders decided I was no longer in harmony with the rest of our community. There must have been others before me who had seen and understood what we had done by not having to live with the weight of our own sorrows. What had happened to those others? Had they tried to change the heart of a village, or had they slipped away one day to escape what they could not change and could not endure?

Or did they lie beneath the blank markers that festered in the thorny, weed-choked part of our burial ground that was set aside for the Un-Named—the ones who had done something so offensive their names were "forgotten" in the village records and family trees.

Alone, I could escape, could vanish into the vastness of the world—or, at least, vanish into the streets of Vision. I was certain of that. But if I tried to help the Voice and was caught . . . I would suffer a tragic—and fatal—accident and be buried under one of those blank markers, just one more of the Un-Named. I was certain of that too.

Knowing what was at stake, I spent a week watching, looking, seeing. And the more I focused on the need to leave this village, the more things subtly changed.

An Elder, claiming his cart horse had turned vicious and had deliberately knocked him down into a pile of manure, had taken to leaving the poor animal tied up to the hitching rail behind the Elders' Hall, still harnessed to the cart without a handful of grain or a sip of water. Anyone who looked could see the horse was mistreated, but everyone averted their eyes and didn't disagree with the Elder's right to discipline his own animal, even though I'd heard my father mutter that, most likely, the poor beast had been doing nothing more than trying to get to its feed bucket when it had knocked the Elder down.

The men muttered; the women made moody cakes; and everyone pretended they couldn't see the horse and, therefore, couldn't see its misery.

I saw the misery. I also saw a horse and cart that would be easy to steal.

Then there was the blank marker stone that suddenly appeared behind the Voice's house, far enough from the kitchen door not to be a nuisance and close enough that it could be used as a step up into the cart.

Every day I watched the village and the people. Every day I tucked a few more things into the traveling bag that looked like a small trunk made of cloth stretched over a wooden frame. I had bought it at the bazaar, using my purchases as the excuse to acquire it. Dariden laughed at me when he saw it, saying the cloth could be torn so easily, I might as well not use anything at all. True, the cloth wasn't as sturdy as a wooden trunk, but it had one important advantage: I could carry it by myself.

By the time everything was ready, my biggest worry was Tahnee. She tried to act as if nothing had changed, but I could tell by the leashed desperation in her eyes that *everything* had changed—and I realized that she, too, had been waiting for something to happen—and had been growing more and more anxious with each passing day.

I could not wish her scheme to fail because, like me, she was no longer in harmony with the village and staying would only do her harm. But I did wish with all my heart that her scheme was delayed just a few days longer, even though I knew my own disappearance would make her escape all but impossible.

Which was when things began going wrong. Just little things. Just enough things for me to realize how easy it had been for me to move forward with this plan.

"Nalah, what are you doing with that skirt?" Mother asked, catching me as I tried to sneak out of the storage cupboard that held our out-of-season clothes.

"I—" My father's mother had made it for me two years ago, before she got funny in the head and died in her sleep one night. The dark green material was of good quality, which Mother had declared a waste, since it couldn't be worn in decent company, and the needlework was exquisite. My grandmother had kept all the beads, spangles, and tiny mirrors that had decorated her own wedding dress and had gifted them to me on a skirt.

When Mother protested, my father's only comment was that it was more practical to have the beads on the front of the skirt than on the part I sat on. Which proved that the male part of my father's brain had been asleep when he looked at the skirt, because the beaded vines and mirrored flowers were intended to draw the eye to the untouched flower between my thighs. It was a skirt a girl wore when she was ready to attract a husband.

I had been too young to wear it when my grandmother had made it for me, and there was no one in this village whose attention I wanted to attract. But I wanted to take the skirt with me. I wanted the hope that I would wear it someday.

"I was going to take it over to Tahnee's tonight, along with a few other things," I said, suddenly inspired. "We're going to try on clothes, see what we still like. Maybe trade." I said this last bit in a low mumble, which made Mother sigh but also made her shoulders relax.

"The three of you used to trade so often, half the time I wasn't sure if I was washing your clothes or theirs," she said.

I nodded, then looked around to be sure I wouldn't be overheard, even though I knew Mother and I were alone in the house. "Tahnee's a little unhappy about the way Kobbi has been acting lately. I guess married life changes a girl?"

Mother's face softened with understanding as she put an arm around my shoulders. "It can be a difficult adjustment for some girls." She hesitated, then added, "Maybe you should make a moody cake."

I shivered and knew she felt that shiver, but I wrinkled my nose and said, "I'd rather try on clothes."

"You're my daughter, Nalah, and I do care about you. You know that?"

I looked into her eyes and felt the pain of love. She did care. And that was why she couldn't afford to see. And why I would stop looking if I stayed. If I held a little daughter in my arms, would I let her flesh carry the weight of sorrow? Would I let the Black Pustules form and listen to her scream in pain when they were lanced—and see the scars that would mark her when the hard cores were extracted? Or would I make a moody cake and teach that little girl the proper way to present it to the person whose sole purpose in our village was to swallow such offerings?

I kissed her cheek. "I don't need a moody cake."

I hurried to my room to pack the skirt, then hurried out to find Tahnee and let her know my mother thought I would be at her house tonight. But when I found her sitting under the big tree where she, Kobbi, and I used to play on hot summer days, everything changed again.

"Kobbi's father denounced her," Tahnee said in a hushed, tearful voice. "She tried to tell her mother that Chayne was doing something bad to her, something that made her head feel funny. Her father overheard her and dragged her to the Elders' Hall. He denounced her and demanded that her name be struck from the family record."

My chest felt so tight I could hardly breathe. "She's an orphan?"

Tahnee nodded. "And I heard that Chayne is so shamed because she's an orphan by unnatural means that *he* may denounce her as his wife, since he'll no longer receive the other two parts of the dowry."

"She can't inherit because she no longer exists in the eyes of her family." And I could see Kobbi's fate if I went ahead with my plan—because an orphan's life is one of sorrow.

"Listen," I said, grabbing hold of Tahnee's arm. "I'm coming over to your house with a bag of clothes. That's what I told my mother."

"Oh, I don't—"

"You're going to pack a bag of clothes—basics and the things too dear to leave behind. But don't pack a bag that's so heavy you can't carry it. You're going to tell your mother that you and I are going over to Kobbi's house. We're going to try on clothes like we used to do when we were girls, and we're going to make moody cakes to help Kobbi feel better because she's our friend. After a denouncement, a man has three days to change his mind if he spoke in haste or out of anger, so if Kobbi comes to her senses, her father might restore her to the family. That's what you're going to tell your mother."

Tahnee wiped the tears off her face and gave me a long look. "What are we really going to be doing?"

"Escaping. We're going back to Vision."

Her breath caught, and for a moment I wondered if I had been wrong to tell her. Then the fire of hope filled her eyes.

"The three of us?" she asked.

I hesitated, and felt as if the world itself waited for my answer. "Four of us."

AT DINNER THAT night, even Dariden was subdued, although he rallied once when he heard I was going over to Kobbi's house with Tahnee.

"You shouldn't be friends with the likes of her," he told me, glancing at our father for approval of such a manly opinion.

"What happened to Kobbi could happen to anyone," I said, helping myself to another spoonful of rice. Then I looked my brother in the eyes. "If I had ended up married to someone like Chayne, it could have happened to me."

My father made a tongue-cluck sound of disapproval for my criticism of Chayne, but Dariden paled as he realized I knew what Chayne had been doing to Kobbi. And as he stared into my eyes, he understood that, with the least provocation, Tahnee and I would spread that information to every female in the village, and any standing Chayne had in our community would be crushed under the rumors that he drugged his young wife in order to do unnatural things in the marriage bed.

"You're looking pale, Dariden," I said, putting enough concern in my voice to draw Mother's attention. "Perhaps you should stay in tonight."

"You're not feeling well?" Mother asked him.

Cornered, Dariden just stared at his plate. "Been working hard," he mumbled. "Guess I should turn in early tonight."

So I was free to leave the house, secure in the knowledge that Dariden and I wouldn't cross paths tonight. Even if he retreated to his room, he wouldn't be able to sneak out the window, because Mother always checked on us at regular intervals when we weren't feeling well. Dariden had learned this the hard way as a boy when he had lied to Mother about feeling ill in order to sneak out with his friends, and had found our father waiting for him when he snuck back in.

I left the house with my travel bag and stopped just long enough to slip into our little barn and take a small bag of feed and an old round pan that could hold water. I didn't have a waterskin, and that was a worry. It turned out to be a foolish worry, because Tahnee had bought a waterskin at the bazaar and hidden it under her other purchases.

We didn't see many people on the way to Kobbi's house, and those who saw us looked away when they noticed the bags of clothes and realized where we were going.

The woman who opened the door . . .

Tahnee and I stood there, too numbed to speak. Our friend Kobbi was gone, and in that moment when my eyes met the crazed wildness in Kobrah's, I knew that even if we got her away from Chayne and the village, we had lost her forever. But we would still try to save her.

"I was going to burn down the house," Kobrah said, as if that were the most ordinary thing to say. "But it can wait until later. Maybe I should wait until Chayne is home and sound asleep. Yes. That would be better."

She stepped aside to let us in. We slipped into the house and closed the door before daring to say anything.

"We're leaving," I said hurriedly. "We're running away to Vision. You can come with us."

She'll destroy us, I thought as I waited for her answer. *Chayne has burned out the goodness in her, and if she comes with us, she'll destroy us.*

But I didn't take back the offer. I just waited for her answer.

"Yes," she finally said, softly. "Yes." She turned and went into the kitchen.

Leaving our bags by the door, we hurried after her. "We didn't dare take any food from home . . . ," I began.

"I have food," Kobrah replied. She pulled out her market basket. "I boiled eggs this afternoon, after I got back from the Elders' Hall. Chayne doesn't like hard-boiled eggs. Maybe that's why I made them."

Her voice sounded dreamy—and insane. But she moved swiftly, storing the eggs, wrapping up the cheeses, taking all the fresh fruit.

Then Tahnee, in an effort to help, reached for a loaf of bread still cooling on the counter.

"No!" Kobrah snarled. "*That* is for Chayne."

Tahnee stepped away from the counter, white with fear. She looked at me, her thoughts clear on her face: *Do we dare eat anything that comes from this house?*

Kobrah smiled bitterly. "The rest of the food is safe." She went into the bedroom, and we listened to her opening drawers and slamming them shut, followed by a cry of triumph and the rattle of coins in a tin box.

Kobrah was packed in no time, and even after we told her about having a cart, she refused to add anything to the small travel pack she used to carry when we spent the night at each other's houses. After the second time we urged her to bring more clothes or at least a few sentimental trinkets, she said, "I want no reminders of this place."

The hours crawled by until, finally, we had reached that in-between hour when all the family men were dutifully tucked in with their wives and children and the younger men were still at the drinking parlor or carousing elsewhere with friends.

We crept out of Kobrah's house, lugging our traveling bags and other supplies, always watchful, always fearful of discovery. But something watched over us that night, because whenever we passed a house with a dog, the wind shifted to favor us, and the dog, never catching our scent, remained quiet.

We made it to the tree where we used to play and where, in many ways, this journey had begun seven years before on the day we had seen the Voice's scars. Kobrah and Tahnee remained there with the bags while I went on to the Elders' Hall, now carrying nothing more than the old pan, a waterskin, and the small bag of feed. If caught, I could truthfully say I had felt sorry for the horse and had snuck out to give it some food and water.

But there were no lights shining in the hall except for a lamp in the caretaker's room, and that provided me with just enough light to make my way to where the horse watched me.

"Easy, boy," I whispered when he began making noises. He was hungry and thirsty, and I was holding what he wanted. He would be making a lot of noise soon if he didn't get some.

Staying just out of reach and keeping one eye on the lighted window, just in case the caretaker looked out to see why the horse was fussing, I poured water into the pan, then held it out for the horse. He drank it down and looked for more, but I scooped out a double handful of feed and gave that to him next. Another pan of water and another handful of feed. Not much for a big horse, but all I could do for now. I put the waterskin and bag of feed in the back of the cart, but I held on to the pan, afraid it would rattle and draw attention.

"Come on, boy," I whispered as I untied the horse from the hitching rail. "Come on. You're going to help all of us get to freedom."

He came with me without noise or fuss, and when we were far enough away from the hall that the *clip-clop* of hooves and rattle of the cart wheels wouldn't draw anyone's attention, I began taking full breaths again.

We paused at the tree just long enough to haul the traveling bags and supplies into the cart and have Kobrah and Tahnee hide in the back. One person leading a horse and cart might go unremarked. All three of us out at this time of night with this particular horse and cart . . .

Our luck held. We got to the back of the Voice's house and got the cart positioned so the blank stone marker could be used as a step. Now the rest of the plan was up to me, and if I failed one of us, I failed all of us.

It didn't occur to me until much later that Kobrah and Tahnee never once suggested abandoning this part of the plan. I suppose that, more than anything, proved none of us belonged in the village where we had been born.

The plan was simple. I would go in on the pretense of consoling Chayne on the loss of the dowry and the embarrassment of Kobrah's behavior. I would slip a third of the drug I had bought into a drink, avoid any amorous advances Chayne might think to make before he drank down the drug, and then get the Voice out of the house and into the cart so we could be far down the road before anyone realized we were gone.

I just didn't know how to do any of that. So I prayed hard and with all my heart, because five lives were at stake now. The horse had become a conspirator with us, and even though he was a poor, dumb beast, I was sure the Elder would blame him for following the girl who had offered him food.

Tahnee held the horse, petting him to keep him quiet. Kobrah remained in the cart. I went around to the front and rang the visitors' bell, still wondering what to say to get myself inside at this hour.

That wasn't a worry. Chayne answered the door, looking sleepy, rumpled, and surly, and I suspected he had been drinking, even though he wasn't supposed to when he was on duty. Then another expression slithered into his eyes as he looked at me, and I felt a thread of pure fear roll down my spine when I realized I wasn't the only one who had a drug that had been purchased in some shadow place. Chayne had *his* bottle with him, because he used it on the Voice as well as Kobrah.

And he intended to use it on me. I looked into his eyes and knew it.

"I heard what happened this afternoon," I said, sounding a little breathless. "I thought . . . maybe . . . you would want to talk to someone."

"Talk?" He laughed softly, and I heard the sound of a heart turning evil. He stepped aside to let me enter. "Sure, we can talk. Come back to the kitchen. I was having a bite to eat."

There was bread and cheese on the table, as well as a half-full bottle of wine. Looking at Chayne's flushed face, I had a feeling that wasn't the first bottle he'd opened tonight. Which explained why he hadn't paid attention to the sound of a horse and cart.

"Let me get you some wine," he said, picking up the bottle and taking it with him to the cupboard that held the glasses.

Watching him to make sure he wasn't paying close attention

to me, I slipped a hand into my skirt pocket and took out the vial of potion. I worked the cork with my thumb, loosening it while I glanced at Chayne's glass of wine and then back at him. He would see me if I reached across the table, and if he saw my hand over his glass . . .

Then he turned toward the kitchen window, and I thought my heart would stop. Had he heard a noise? I was almost certain he wouldn't see the horse and cart unless he went right up to the window and looked out, but I couldn't take that chance. And I couldn't waste the opportunity he provided by turning his back on me. I pulled the cork off the vial and dumped some of the drug into Chayne's glass, heedless of how much I was using.

"Is there anyone else here tonight?" I asked, tucking my shaking hands in my lap while I worked the cork back into the top of the vial.

He stopped moving toward the window, but he still kept his back to me.

He hadn't heard a noise. He wasn't interested in looking out the window. That was just the excuse he had used for turning away from me while he slipped his drug into my glass of wine.

He came back to the table, set the wineglass in front of me, and smiled the kind of smile women instinctively fear. "No, there's no one else here tonight. Except the Voice. She's the perfect chaperone."

I would have been a fool to come here alone. I hadn't been a friend to Kobrah when I had kept silent after overhearing Chayne tell Dariden about the drug. Now all our fates came down to whether I could avoid drinking from my glass without arousing Chayne's suspicion.

"Drink up," Chayne said, raising his glass in a salute as he watched me.

He knew I knew about the drug—and he didn't care. He was between me and the door. We were alone. He wasn't so drunk that I could get away from him.

Then a door slammed, making us both jump. A moment later, Kobrah stood in the kitchen doorway, breathing like a bellows, looking as if she'd run here all the way from her house.

"Are you going to poison Nalah too?" Kobrah asked. "Isn't it enough that you ruined me?"

"Go home," Chayne said coldly, turning his back on her to look straight at me. "Go back home while you still have one. And if you say anything else that causes trouble, I'll be looking for a new wife, and you'll be grateful for any place that will take you in. You know what they say about an orphan's life."

He didn't see the rage on her face, but he smirked when I, trembling, whispered, "An orphan's life is one of sorrow."

Looking pleased, Chayne said, "That's right," and drank down all the wine in his glass.

The Apothecary had assured me the drug would work fast. Even so, agonizing hours filled the space between each heartbeat before Chayne staggered, grabbed at the table to keep his balance, then collapsed on the floor.

I caught Chayne's wineglass before it rolled off the table, righted the bottle before the rest of the wine spilled out, then got around the table in time to stand between Chayne and Kobrah.

"I was going to kick his face until it was all smashed and broken," Kobrah said in that dreamy, insane voice. "He deserves to have his face smashed. You don't know all the things he's done."

I held up a hand to stop her, then crouched beside Chayne. His eyes were open, but his mind was swimming in some dream world, and his limbs wouldn't work for a few hours.

"You," he said, drawing out the word.

Inspired, I stared at him. "Us," I said, raising a hand to draw his attention to Kobrah, who was standing behind me. "We are the goddesses of justice and vengeance. Tonight we wore the faces of women you know in order to test you, human. And you failed."

Kobrah laughed, a chilling sound.

"When the sun rises tomorrow, you will stand in front of the Elders' Hall and tell everyone about the drug you gave your wife. You will confess every harm you have ever done to any living thing. If you do not, we will come back every night for the rest of your life. We will come back in a dream, night after night, and peel the skin off your face so that everyone will see who you really are."

I stood up and walked out of the kitchen. Kobrah followed me.

"If he doesn't confess all the things he's done, will he really have that dream?" she asked.

"Yes." When I bought the drug, I had emphasized the need to hide the memory of my presence and had been assured that, in the first minute or two after the drug was taken, the person would believe anything he was told.

Kobrah smiled. "That's better than kicking him in the face, because he'll never tell the Elders *everything* he's done. He would end up among the Un-Named."

We opened doors, searched rooms. Most people never went beyond the visitors' room, never saw this part of the house. Judging by what could be seen by moonlight, the rooms set aside for the caretakers were better furnished and had more luxuries than any of them knew in their own homes. But there were two rooms that had basic furniture of bed, chair, and dresser. No rug on the floor. No sketches on the walls. Not one pretty bauble to delight the heart.

There was no need for such things when a person had been silenced and could not voice her pain, when she had been kept uneducated so she could not give shape to her thoughts. When she was caged within her own flesh so that she couldn't escape other kinds of cages.

The first of those sparse rooms was empty, and Kobrah stared at it for a long time, shuddering, as we both realized that room had been readied for a new occupant.

In the second sparsely furnished room, we found the Voice.

"It's me," I said, hurrying to the side of the bed. "It's Nalah."

The wheezing, labored breathing eased a little, and the reason squeezed my heart until it hurt.

Hearing someone at the door, she had expected Chayne to come in and do things to her after he'd given her the drug.

But seeing her in the bed, I realized how big she was—and I also realized the flaw in my plan.

I didn't know if she was capable of walking far enough to reach the cart. And if she wasn't able to climb in by herself, even the three of us weren't strong enough to lift her.

"We're running away," I said. "You can come with us. I know a place that can help you. You'll be safe there." I swallowed hard to say what had to be said. "We have a cart behind the house. You can ride in the back of it. But if you want to get away from here, you have to walk to the cart; you have to climb in the back. If you can't do that . . ."

She struggled, flailed. I grabbed a wrist and pulled to help her sit up. When that wasn't quite enough, Kobrah wrapped her arms around my waist and leaned back, adding her strength to the effort.

We got the Voice on her feet. Got her walking. By the time we left the bedroom, she was wheezing. By the time we got to the back door, her lungs sounded like damaged bellows, and I wondered if she would collapse before she reached the cart. She couldn't open her mouth, so she sucked in air through her teeth.

How much time had passed? How much did we have left before someone noticed the horse was gone? Since we hadn't come home by now, and knowing Chayne would be working tonight, Tahnee's mother and mine would assume we had stayed with Kobrah and wouldn't be expecting to see us until after breakfast. The second stage of the potion I bought was supposed to produce lethargy, so hopefully Chayne would fall asleep and not wake up until the daytime caretakers arrived.

Desperate, determined, the Voice took one step after another. I stayed beside her, having no idea what I would do if she fell, while Tahnee held the horse and Kobrah ran back into the house. She returned with a bundle, which she tossed into the back of the cart.

"Clothes," she said.

Up to the blank marker stone that provided the Voice with the step needed to get into the cart. She grasped the sides of the cart and pulled. Kobrah and I pushed. Tahnee held the horse steady.

Then the Voice was in the cart, on hands and knees, panting from the effort.

"Lie down," I told her while Kobrah ran back into the house a last time to fetch a blanket to cover the Voice until we were out of the village.

I took my place at the horse's head and sent up one more prayer to whoever would listen to me. *Please, let the cart be strong enough to hold her. Let the horse be strong enough to pull the load. Please.*

The horse leaned into the harness, straining to take that first step. But he did take that first step. And the next one. The cart moved. The axles didn't break.

"Good boy," I whispered. "You're a brave, strong boy. Step along. That's it. Good boy."

Clip-clop. Clip-clop. That was the only sound besides the rattle of the cart's wheels. No other sounds disturbed our village's silence.

Two days' journey to Vision in a coach with a team of horses that could maintain a trot for miles at a time. How many days with a half-starved horse who could do no better than a steady walk?

We had gotten out of the village, had left the last house behind us, and I was just starting to breathe easy when we heard *clip-clop, clip-clop, clip-clop* coming toward us.

I kept walking, kept up my whispered encouragement to the horse. Kobrah darted to the far side of the cart and hunched over to avoid being seen, while Tahnee remained near the back of the cart.

The man rode toward us, leading another horse. He seemed vaguely familiar, but it wasn't until Tahnee let out a stifled cry of joy that I recognized him as the young man at the bazaar whom Tahnee had haggled with and flirted with.

And fallen in love with?

I doubt he knew who I was—or cared. He dismounted, shoved the reins into my open hand, and leaped at Tahnee, snatching her off her feet as he held her tight.

"I'm sorry," he said. "I'm sorry. You must have thought I

failed you, that I wasn't coming. The world . . . There were delays. I . . ."

Kobrah came around the side of the cart, her eyes on the horses.

"Do you need both horses?" she asked, and there was something in her voice, something in the way she moved that made us all tense.

"I . . ." He looked back at his horses, then looked at Kobrah—and then tried to shift Tahnee behind him without being too obvious about what he was doing . . . or why.

We've lost her, I thought. *If we don't let her go, she'll destroy us.*

I think Tahnee realized that, too, because she looked at her lover and asked, "Could we ride double?"

We didn't know what we were asking of him, didn't know what the loss of a horse would mean to him or his family. But he knew, and he still went back to his horses, untied the second one, and walked it over to where Kobrah waited. Handing her the reins, he said, "Take the horse."

After she mounted, she looked down at him and said, "May the gods and goddesses of fate and fortune shower your life with golden days."

Then she rode back to the village. I didn't know what she intended to do, but I knew the rest of us needed to get as far away as we could.

"You two go on ahead," I said. "Tahnee's travel bag is too big to carry on horseback. If I bring it to your family's booth at the bazaar, will it get to her?"

"It will." He looked in the direction of the village. "But that will leave you—"

"We got this far by working together," I said, cutting him

off. "Now we have to separate." Thinking about the sign before the bridge leading to Vision, I looked at Tahnee. "Now we have to let our hearts choose our destination."

Tahnee hugged me. Her lover studied my face, as if memorizing it, then said, "Travel lightly."

He mounted his horse, pulled Tahnee up behind him, and the two of them cantered down the road, heading for Vision . . . and freedom.

I stood there, feeling so alone. More so because I wasn't alone. But I couldn't look at her just then, couldn't offer any promises or comfort. I would save us—or I would fail.

"Come on, boy," I said softly. "Come on. We've got a way to go."

The horse leaned into the harness, straining to take that first step.

One step. Another. And step by plodding step, we got a little closer to a dream.

6

I HAVE SINCE HEARD THAT EPHEMERA TAKES THE measure of a human heart and helps or hinders what that heart desires. I don't know if that is true or not. I do know the horse shouldn't have made it up the hills I remembered as being so steep. But he did make it. Sometimes I thought he'd break under the strain if he had to take another step up an incline, but somehow the hill always leveled out before that last step, and the descents were gentler than I recalled. I'm sure someone would tell me my mind had exaggerated some things on that first journey in order to make it a grander adventure.

I don't think I exaggerated anything. The world changed itself just enough to give us a chance. Just as I believe the world changed itself that first afternoon when I spotted riders in the distance and knew they were men from the village, looking for us. We kept walking, and my prayer became a chant: *Please don't let them find us.*

They should have found us, should have caught us. They never did.

Several days after leaving the village, in the hushed hour before the real dawn, I stopped the exhausted horse in front of the Temple of Sorrow. Standing on tiptoes, I peeked over the side of the cart, not wanting to stand at the back. The Voice looked at me, a question in her eyes.

"We made it," I said. "I'll get help."

She couldn't get out of the cart. For anything. I realized we had a problem the first time I smelled excrement. But when I went around to the back of the cart, dithering about what to do, the plea in her eyes was more eloquent than words. Every minute I spent caring for her was the minute that might make the difference between getting to Vision or getting caught. So I made my heart as hard and cold as I could make it, and I kept us moving until I saw the bridge and felt numbed by the knowledge that we had reached the city.

I hurried up the broad steps of the temple and rang the bell. Rang and rang and rang.

"There is someone on duty," a voice grumbled as the door opened. "You don't have to wake up the whole tem—"

The moment he saw me, the Shaman stopped his complaint.

"Please," I said, feeling the tears well up now that I didn't have to be hard and cold. "Please help us. She's in the cart. She can't . . . I can't . . . Please."

He touched my arm, giving the warmth of comfort. Then he went down the stairs. The sky had lightened enough that I could see his face go blank with shock when he looked inside the cart.

He ran back up the stairs and disappeared inside the temple, leaving me standing there while something savage raked its claws inside me until I thought I would bleed to death without anyone seeing a drop spilled.

Now that I wasn't hard and cold, I couldn't think, couldn't move, didn't know what to do.

The Shaman returned, rushing past me with six others in his wake, two of them women. One woman, the last out the door, stopped and touched my face gently.

"Do you know where to go?" she asked. "Which door leads to the room for sorrow?"

I nodded.

"Then go in. Find your place."

I felt sluggish, dull. I looked toward the cart. "Horse."

"We'll take care of him. Go in now."

Even at that early hour, there were five other people in the room. I chose a place that spared me from sitting next to anyone else. I smelled of horse and sweat and exhaustion. The cushions were soft, and the minute I sat down, my legs and feet began to throb. The last time I had rested had been unintentional. I had leaned against the horse, too tired to stand on my own, and woke up sometime later to discover the horse, too, had fallen asleep, his head resting on my shoulder.

Voices rose and fell. Gongs sounded and faded. I drifted.

Then the doors opened, and the Shamans walked in, leading the Voice. I thought they would take her to a room where she could be cleaned or at least change her out of the filth-encrusted clothes. They had done none of those things, just led her to a spot and helped her lower herself to the mound of cushions.

The voices of the other people in the room sputtered into shocked silence. All through the journey, I had seen without seeing. The Voice wasn't wearing her hood. The scars on her neck were clearly visible.

The Shaman picked up the mallet, struck the gong in front of the Voice, then slipped the mallet into her hand. The gong's deep sound filled the room. The Voice rocked back and forth, clearly in pain.

Then another gong sounded, and a male voice, low but clear, sounded a note. Another gong and another voice rose to fill the room. Another. Another. Another.

A sixth gong and a sixth voice, raw and keening.

Mine.

She had no voice, so we gave her ours, singing the sorrows until finally, in one of those moments when the sound was hushed and spent, the Shaman said, "That is enough for now."

Those five people stood up, looked at the Voice . . . and bowed. Then they left the room, and the Shamans came forward to help her stand.

After they led her away, one Shaman remained.

"You must be tired and hungry. If you want, I will show you to one of our guest rooms right now. But if you can wait a little while longer, I would like you to come with me."

I followed him to a room that, at first glance, contained little more than a small table and two chairs and yet felt so restful to heart and mind, there was no need for anything else.

On the table were a pot and two cups. We sat, and the Shaman poured the tea. I stared out the window, watching bright-colored birds flit around a tiny courtyard where miniature trees were growing in stone pots.

"Now," the Shaman said after a silence during which we had done nothing but watch the birds and drink tea. "Can you tell me how this happened?"

I told him about our village. I told him about the saying we learned in school. I told him about that awful day when I was ten and first began to understand the truth about the Voice. I told him everything, even the things I had done that shamed me. All through the telling, he kept his hands loosely wrapped around the teacup and his eyes on his hands.

I finished my story at the moment when I rang the bell that morning, looking for help.

Those beautiful eyes remained lowered for a moment longer. Then he looked at me.

He wasn't human. Not like me. He was the fury of storms and the laughter of a cool stream on a hot summer's day. He was flood and drought and slow, soft rains that woke up the crops and gave us an abundant harvest.

He was the voice of the world—and the world would do his bidding.

In that moment, I understood why the Shamans walked the streets of the city and why they were respected—and, sometimes, feared. In that moment, I feared for the people in the village I had left behind, especially my family.

"A strong will and loving heart," he said quietly. He pushed back his chair and stood. "Come. It is time for you to rest."

The luxury of a tub full of hot, scented water where I soaked and washed until I felt clean. The pleasure of a clean bed in a simply furnished room that made no demands on body or heart or mind. And if, in the moments before sleep, I found myself yearning for someone who wasn't quite a Shaman, there was no harm in that.

For the rest of that day, I floated among gentle dreams.

FOR TWO MORE days, I remained in the Temple of Sorrow. Sometimes I sat in the sorrows room to purge myself. Other times, I and the others who happened to be in the room would raise our voices on behalf of the Voice. Her pain was huge, and because I felt some responsibility for causing it, her pain was killing me.

I suppose that was why the Shaman was waiting for me when I came out of the sorrows room that last evening.

"You did a good thing bringing her here," he said. "Now you must take the next step in the journey."

"I don't understand."

"She needs to stay. You need to go. Tomorrow."

I hadn't thought beyond reaching here, hadn't considered what it would mean if I couldn't stay at the temple.

The Shaman smiled. "There is a community in the northern part of the city. It is a full day's journey from here, nestled in the foothills. Beautiful land. Good people. Artistic in many different ways. I have family up there. You will be welcomed."

"I could find work there?"

"I think that someone with your heart could find a great many things."

For a moment, I thought a blush stained his cheeks, but the sun was setting, so it must have been a trick of the light.

Which was how I ended up driving the cart, which had been scrubbed and freshly painted, to the northern part of Vision and the community of people who were not Shamans but understood more about the world than I had ever imagined.

7

FOR THE FIRST SIX MONTHS, NEWS ABOUT THE VIL-lage trickled in to me. After that, I never heard about the village or its people again.

The night we ran away, the Elders' Hall was set on fire, and while the caretaker managed to get out unharmed, the building itself burned to the ground. The other building that burned that night was Chayne's house.

As for Chayne, he screamed himself awake for a week. Then he stood in front of the ruins of the Elders' Hall and confessed his offenses against all living things. He disappeared shortly af-ter that, but Dariden claimed to have seen him behind the or-phan's house, looking bloated and hobbling around as if crippled while the caretakers watched him. Dariden also claimed Chayne must have been in a horrific accident that no one wanted to talk about, because in that moment before the caretakers noticed him and hurried to block his view, Dariden saw terrible scars on Chayne's neck.

Tahnee and her lover reached Vision. While his parents were not pleased to have a son make a hasty marriage to a girl who feared being found by her own family, they stood witness at the marriage and helped the young couple set up housekeeping.

I haven't seen Tahnee since the night we ran away. Despite having mutual friends, our paths never cross. Maybe we aren't meant to meet. At least, not yet.

I don't know what became of Kobrah. I don't know if she

reached Vision or even tried. The horse, however, was returned to the merchant's booth in the bazaar by a grateful young man who had needed a ride in order to reach the city. By all accounts, the horse had been handed over to several riders during those months, each person needing a mount for a little while—and each one promising to assist in getting the horse back to its owner in Vision.

I sent one letter to my parents, assuring them that I was safe and well but not telling them enough that they would be able to find me. I cannot change the customs of our village because our village does not want to change. Until the magic dies that allows one person to become the well of sorrow for so many, the village will look away while the Elders maim someone in order to make that person's flesh a vessel.

I cannot change the village. But I saved the people I could.

8

TWO YEARS TO THE DAY, I STOOD ON THE BOTTOM step of the Temple of Sorrow. I had a letter to deliver—and a teasing scold to deliver as well, if I had the courage. I now knew why the Shaman had blushed the day he told me about the community in the north. My lover's eyes are not quite as beautiful as his uncle's, and while he has a fine sense of the world, Kanzi is not a Shaman. Despite those "flaws," he is a talented artist and a good man.

Our marriage was arranged to take place at the end of harvest, and the letter I was delivering was a nephew's enthusiastic invitation and plea for his uncle to attend the wedding and stand as a witness.

So I stood on the steps, wondering if it was a Shaman or an uncle who had been playing matchmaker the day he sent me north, when the sound of finger cymbals caught my attention and I wandered over to a temple that was a little farther down the street.

A woman, dressed in the wheat-colored robes of a Shaman's apprentice, was playing the finger cymbals in a happy little rhythm while a dozen children stood on the steps below, swaying to the rhythm and then freezing when the cymbals stopped.

A game, I decided, smiling as I moved closer, because there was something about the woman . . .

She turned and looked at me. I didn't recognize her face, but I knew her eyes. She wore a hood that covered the hideous scars on her neck, but the robes covered a slimmer body that no longer carried sorrow.

She looked at me and smiled. And in her eyes, I saw warmth, compassion, gratitude. Love.

Raising my hand in a small salute, I walked back to the Temple of Sorrow. A moment later, the finger cymbals picked up their rhythm.

I rang the bell, and he answered. His look of delight faded when he saw my face.

"What's wrong?" he asked, stepping back to let me enter. "What's happened?"

"I need . . ." What did I need? I hurt so much, but I didn't know why. "She's . . ."

Understanding. "She's not here anymore," he said gently.

"I know. I s-saw . . ."

"I see." His warm hand cupped my elbow as he led me toward the sorrows room.

"No," I said, pulling back. "Wrong . . . sound." I knew that much.

He closed his eyes for a moment. When he opened them, they were shiny from tears. "Of course. I understand now."

He led me to a room on the other side of the building. It was set up the same way as the room of sorrows, but instead of gongs set before each placement of cushions, there was a wind chime hanging from a stand.

The Shaman stepped out of the room and closed the door.

I stepped over to the nearest wind chime and jostled it. Bright notes filled the room. Bright notes . . . like the radiant face that had been hidden for so many years.

Stepping into the center of the room, I brushed a finger against each wind chime, moving from place to place, faster and faster, until the room was awash in sparkling sound that squeezed my heart until the tears flowed, faster and faster. Until I collapsed on the floor in the center of that room and shed tears that were a bright, sharp, cleansing pain.

They were the last tears I ever shed for the Voice, and they were not tears of sorrow. They were tears of joy.

THE WORLD OF THE OTHERS

Holiday stories are sentimental and fun—or frustrating if you're a Wolf trying to celebrate the Winter Solstice in the human way for the first time.

"Home for the Howlidays" is a Meg and Simon story that takes place a few months after the events in *Etched in Bone*.

As for "The Dark Ship" . . .

For years, I had a picture of a ghost ship sailing under a full moon. Tattered sails. Skull and crossbones. The physical picture disappeared at some point, but the image remained, and I would wonder about it from time to time.

Many years later, that image collided with a chance to see some sailing ships and a visit to an environmental booth that included a tank full of sea lampreys. From there, a story formed about pirates and vampires and Elders, oh my.

HOME FOR THE HOWLIDAYS

1

DORMENTE 17

SIMON WOLFGARD STUDIED TWYLA MONTGOMERY, who stood on the other side of the book cart and gave him a look that clearly indicated there was only one correct response to what she'd just said, and if he wanted to keep all the fur on his tail, that was the response he would give her. The trouble was . . .

"Roo-roo? Roo-roo!"

. . . standing outside the back door of Howling Good Reads, waiting for the Wolfgard pack's human grandma.

"The other children are going over to Eve Denby's house to decorate cookies," Twyla said. "That includes Sam, so that means including Skippy. It would break that boy's heart to be left behind."

He knew that. He did. Skippy had been trying so hard to shift to a human form in order to do things with the human children who played with Sam. But . . . "Skippy can't pass for human."

"No, he can't," Twyla agreed. "But he's managed a between form that's balanced."

Meaning from the waist down Skippy looked like a Wolf standing on his hind legs, and from the waist up he looked like an adolescent human male who needed a good meal.

"Roo-roo?"

Any minute Skippy would start his yodeling arroo and alert the rest of the human female pack that something was going on in HGR's stock room. As much as he liked the females individually—most of the time—he was wary of them when they approached him as a pack because the female pack always had *ideas* that even human males barely understood and usually made no sense at all to the *terra indigene*.

"He doesn't know how to decorate cookies," Simon said.

"Neither does Sam," Twyla replied. "Neither does Frances, for that matter. Her folks weren't much for holiday traditions that children might enjoy."

She looked sad. Frances's sire, Cyrus "Jimmy" Montgomery, had been one of Twyla's grown pups and a very bad human—and had been responsible for doing so much damage to Simon's mate, Meg.

"Skippy can go over to Eve's house in his Wolf form and then shift to his between form when he's inside," Twyla said. "I've got a flannel shirt for him to wear that will keep him warm and is long enough to cover the boy bits that the girls don't need to see. Then when he and Sam are ready to go home, Skippy can shift back to Wolf."

"The cookies won't be pretty." He'd seen some of the decorated cookies that Nadine Fallacaro had made for Tess to sell at

A Little Bite and didn't think any of the pups would make anything close to that good.

Twyla huffed. "Pretty is not the point. The children are going to have fun decorating cookies for their families. No one expects fancy or perfect. Not from children that age."

Meg would be thrilled to receive a decorated cookie from Sam—and from Skippy. But Simon tried one more time to do his job as the Lakeside Courtyard's leader and protect the skippy-brained Wolf. "The human children will laugh at him."

"They will not."

Simon leaned away from the cart. Did Miss Twyla just growl at him?

"Do you really think I'll stand by and let that happen?" Twyla asked.

No, but words could be like a trap hidden under leaves. The damage was done before you knew the trap was there.

"Besides," Twyla added, "it's the children from families already connected to the Courtyard who will be there. Children that Skippy plays with every day. Anyone who uses sharp words will be sent to their room or sent home."

Simon gave in. Miss Twyla was not only an older female and Lieutenant Montgomery's mother; she was also a member of Simon's pack—by her choice. "Okay."

Twyla nodded. "Doesn't matter what those cookies look like; you will praise the effort."

That growl was aimed right at him. "Okay." Before she could turn away, he said, "Miss Twyla?" Would she understand how hard this was for him to ask?

"Yes, Mr. Simon?"

"The *cassandra sangue* who were kept in those compounds and cut to reveal prophecies. They never had a chance to participate in human holidays. This will be Meg's first Winter Solstice celebration, and humans give gifts to other humans. To special humans. But when I asked her what she wanted for a present, she said she didn't need anything."

He swallowed the whine of frustration. How could he help Meg celebrate if she wouldn't cooperate?

Twyla shook her head and smiled. "My husband, James, used to get the same look on his face when he'd ask me that question, because I gave him the same answer that Miss Meg gave you. Gifts don't always have to be things, Mr. Simon. Sometimes it's being able to do something special that would make a person happy." She looked at him, and her smile warmed. "I'll do a bit of gift sleuthing for you and see what I can find out."

Gift sleuthing. He liked the sound of that.

"Roo-roo!"

"I'd better get these children over to Eve Denby's so we can start decorating cookies," Twyla said.

"And I'd better get this cart of books out front and restock the display tables before Vlad bites me," Simon replied.

"Mr. Vlad is up in the office. It's Miss Merri working the front of the store today."

Great. He'd rather deal with his Sanguinati comanager than the exploding fluffball who was now the bookstore's assistant manager. At least he knew when he was about to rile Vlad. With a human female? What had her snapping at you one day wasn't the tiniest bit of bother the next.

When he reached the front part of the store, Merri gave him a disapproving, narrow-eyed look before she tried to grab the cart and haul it over to the checkout counter instead of letting him take it to the displays that needed to be restocked. It took snarling at her to win the tussle for the cart. She still grabbed an armful of books off the cart's top shelf and reassured the customer on the phone that they did have those particular authors and titles in stock and she would hold them under the counter for forty-eight hours.

It wasn't *his* fault it had taken so long to bring the stock to the front of the store, but he was certain it would end up being his fault if he said anything. So he growled softly to himself and refilled the displays with sentimental stories by human authors and grisly thrillers by *terra indigene* authors—and wondered what it said about humans buying gifts for other humans that the fang-and-claw thrillers were selling as strongly as the sentimental stories.

BODIES TRAPPED IN twisted metal, trapped underwater. Thick ice covering metal, becoming a grave.

"Meg?"

Snarling monster with shining eyes slamming into its prey until the prey, crushed and helpless, slid down the bank toward the river.

"Meg?"

Men wearing official black coats. Memorial garden. Ash and earth.

Men in police dress uniforms standing at attention. Ash and earth.

Weeping. Grieving.

"Meg!"

Sam? What . . . ? *Sam?*

Meg Corbyn blinked, gasped, swayed.

"Roo?" Nathan Wolfgard's rumble of inquiry—or warning—coming from the front room of the Liaison's Office.

Meg blinked again and focused on Sam and Skippy, who were standing in the sorting room, watching her.

"We brought you some cookies," Sam said in a small voice. "Miss Nadine and Miss Eve made the cookies, but we decorated them."

The images faded, as if she'd awakened from a bad dream, and all that was left were the feelings of grief.

Then she looked at the container Sam held out, and the grief faded, replaced by shadowed delight. "You decorated cookies for me?"

"You and Uncle Simon," Sam replied.

Meg took the container and opened it, aware that Nathan, the office's watch Wolf, had vaulted over the front counter to find out what was going on in the sorting room. Since he was in human form, she hoped he'd taken a moment to pull on the flannel pajama bottoms he kept handy since, naked, Nathan was considered to be a nicely built male. She found the outraged squeals of women suddenly confronted by a naked man unnerving. Nathan said the appreciative sounds other human women made while they eyed him were similar to how a Wolf sounded right before a trapped bunny became the lunch bunny—a sound he found equally unnerving when it was directed at him.

"Problem?" Nathan asked.

"Cookies." Meg slapped the lid on the container and growled, "Mine. Specially decorated for me."

Sam nodded. Skippy wagged his tail.

Nathan gave her a look that said she could have her special cookies, but she'd better have a container of Wolf cookies in the office that were just for him.

Of course she did.

After lifting the lid and admiring all the cookies, she promised to save them until she got home so that Simon could see all of them before any were eaten.

Sam and Skippy went out the office's back door. Nathan returned to the front room and shifted back to his Wolf form.

Meg stepped to one side of the room where she couldn't be seen by anyone in the front of the office and rubbed the scars on her upper right arm. She must have had another episode.

When a blood prophet spoke prophecy after her skin was cut, she didn't remember what she said. But she'd been sorting the mail. She hadn't made a cut. This speaking without any preparation was the continued result of the cuts Cyrus Montgomery had made when he'd abducted her a few months ago. He hadn't known how to do the cutting properly, and now she was left with a collision of sights, sounds, and images from overlapping visions that overwhelmed her without warning, blinding her to the tangible world around her and taking away some of the freedom she'd fought so hard to have when she had escaped from the compound where she'd been kept as property.

She had stumbled into the Lakeside Courtyard almost a year ago, seeking shelter from a snowstorm and searching for work— and a place to hide from her owner. Until the abduction, she had been building a life in the Courtyard. *Had been*. Lately it felt like she was looking through a window, watching what other people could do. Simple, ordinary things that were out of her reach now.

Meg shuddered. The images were gone. All that was left was a feeling that one of her friends was going to die soon.

"VLAD?"

Vladimir Sanguinati leaned on HGR's checkout counter and smiled at the boy and the adolescent Wolf. "Sam?"

Hard to believe that a year ago Sam had been a frightened, traumatized pup who had been unable—or unwilling—to shift out of his Wolf form after seeing his mother killed by hunters. Now he played with other pups in his Wolf form and played with his human friends in his human form. Most of the time.

Today he and Skippy had been doing some holiday thing at the Denby residence. Shouldn't the pup look happier?

"Could I have a piece of paper and a pencil?" Sam asked. "I need to write something down for Uncle Simon. For you too."

Vlad tore a couple of sheets off the memo pad that was kept near the register and gave them to Sam, along with a pencil. "Why don't you go into A Little Bite to write your message? I'll join you in a few minutes."

"Okay."

Vlad watched Sam and Skippy walk through the archway that connected the coffee shop and the bookstore. Sam looked subdued. Fearful? Had something happened at the Denby house? Or had something happened . . . ?

<I need you over here,> Vlad said when he spotted Blair Wolfgard.

Blair walked over to the counter. <I came in for a book.>

<Right now, I need you to stand behind the counter and not bite the customers unless they don't give you money for the books they're holding.>

Since Blair was the Courtyard's enforcer and had an attitude of "Bite first, ask questions later—or never," it was necessary to be specific about certain aspects of customer relations.

<Problem?> Blair asked after a moment.

<Maybe. It shouldn't take long for me to find out.>

At least it's not the lunchtime rush, Vlad thought as he

walked into A Little Bite. *Our enforcer shouldn't scare off too many customers.*

Two human women sat at a table enjoying coffee and sandwiches—and enjoying what the female pack called eye candy. Meaning him. If he'd just wandered in to take a break from HGR's customers, he might have flirted a little—and been tempted to feed while he flirted. But Tess, the Harvester who ran the coffee shop, sipped a little life energy from every customer, so he and Tess had an understanding. He didn't feed in the coffee shop, and she didn't feed in the bookstore.

He approached the counter, maintaining the fiction that a Sanguinati would order a coffee and treats and wasn't the least bit scary. And he *wasn't* scary compared to Tess, but most humans who knew about her kind of *terra indigene* and crossed her path didn't survive long enough to tell anyone, so she was just the woman with the strange hair who ran the coffee shop.

When she was calm, Tess's hair was brown and straight. Today it was green with threads of brown, and it was starting to curl—trouble signs.

"Here." Tess set a mug on the counter next to a plate that contained several types of cookies. "Sam is waiting for you, and he doesn't look happy. Find out why and fix it." She turned toward the woman coming up on Vlad's right. "Would you like more coffee?" Her voice warned that the woman had better not be coming up to the counter looking for anything else.

Vlad set the plate of cookies in the middle of the small table where Sam waited for him. Then he settled in the other chair. Not seeing Skippy, he hoped the Wolf had gone outside instead of trying to sneak into the room that was now Nadine's Bakery. The last time Skippy had done that and tried to make off with some kind of pie that was part of the lunch specials, Nadine had

chased the Wolf around the coffee shop and through the bookstore, doing an impressive imitation of a Bear roar while waving
a rolling pin over her head.

"Something you want to tell me?" Vlad asked.

Sam pushed a piece of paper across the table.

Monster. Shiny eyes.
Ice. Metal.
Ash and earth.
Police dresses.
Weeping. Greeving.

"Meg had one of her episodes?" Vlad asked, struggling to
sound matter-of-fact. Sam was upset enough as it was.

Sam nodded. "She said more words, but that's all I can remember."

"It's enough, pup. It's enough."

"You'll tell Uncle Simon?"

"I'll tell him." No smile would look sincere right now, so
Vlad didn't even try. "You'd better find Skippy before he gets
into trouble. You're done playing at the Denby house? You'll be
staying in the Courtyard for the rest of the day?"

Sam nodded, slid out of his chair, and headed for the back
door of the coffee shop.

Meg's recurring episodes were an ongoing sorrow for all her
friends, human and *terra indigene* alike. Simon felt that sorrow
more than the rest of them because he was Meg's mate—and he
was the leader who'd had to tell the Courtyard's human liaison
that she could no longer go out alone in the BOW, the small
box-on-wheels vehicle that she used to drive around the Courtyard to deliver packages. The second time she'd had an episode

while driving and come too close to crashing into a tree, Simon, backed by *all* of Meg's friends, had insisted that she no longer drive until the episodes were under control. Unfortunately, there was no way to tell if that would ever happen.

Besides being the watch Wolf in the Liaison's Office, Nathan Wolfgard was now Meg's designated driver when she made her afternoon deliveries. Clipping her independence made them all sad, but better that than a broken body.

Simon walked in and sat down in Sam's place. "Trouble?"

Vlad turned the paper around so Simon could read it. "There could be."

SIMON WATCHED CAPTAIN Douglas Burke study the short list of images that Sam had given to Vlad.

"This is disturbing," Burke said, tapping one item on the list. "To me it indicates the death of a police officer."

Officers Karl Kowalski and Michael Debany. Lieutenant Crispin James Montgomery. They were Meg's friends and lived in apartments owned by the Lakeside Courtyard. They shopped in the Courtyard's stores. Kowalski's and Debany's mates worked in the Courtyard, and Lieutenant Montgomery's pups played with Sam.

"Sometimes Meg sees something that happened in the past," Simon said.

"To give context to something that is about to happen," Burke countered. He stared at the list. "Lots of people traveling around the holiday to spend time with family. Lots of people going to parties or having a meal with friends. Weather predictions are calling for several inches of snow blanketing the entire Northeast Region right before the Solstice. Lots of fender benders happen during weather like that, and then there are drivers who hit a patch of ice and slide off the road. It's a busy time for cops."

Something else, Simon thought as he caught a hint of worry in Burke's voice. *Something more.* "A busy time for cops and . . . ?"

"I've been hearing about men who were part of the Humans First and Last movement forming gangs with the intention of destroying property or even attacking people who believe we should work with the *terra indigene.* Some officers answering a call for assistance have been attacked. Have been shot. Killed."

"Not in Lakeside." The Sanguinati paid attention to the stories in the local newspaper and the news reports on TV. If this was happening in Lakeside, they would have said something.

"No, not in Lakeside. And no trouble reported in Ferryman's Landing or in the River Road Community. Not yet, anyway." Burke stood. "If anything comes across my desk that sounds related to the images Ms. Corbyn saw, I'll let you know."

Simon escorted Burke out of HGR's office, then left the patrol captain browsing the display tables while he joined Vlad behind the counter.

<He's worried about the list?> Vlad asked, using the *terra indigene* form of communication.

<Yes,> Simon replied. <He's worried.>

2

DORMENTE 18

"GOOD AFTERNOON, MR. WOLFGARD." RUTHIE STUART gestured to the books she'd set on the counter. "Could you check the gift lists? I want to make sure I'm not buying a dupli-cate book."

"What gift lists?" Simon thought it was a reasonable ques-tion, so Ruthie's suddenly looking like a wide-eyed trapped bunny excited all of his hunting instincts.

It took effort, but he resisted the urge to leap over the coun-ter and pounce on her since she was Karl Kowalski's mate as well as being a member of the female pack and one of the Court-yard's employees.

"Where are the lists?" He smiled—and maybe his fangs were a *little* more Wolfy than human as a way to encourage her to talk.

"B-behind the counter," Ruthie stammered. "In a folder with snowflake stickers on the front." She looked toward the archway that led into A Little Bite. "I'm sorry. I thought he knew."

Merri Lee approached the counter, eyeing him.

"What is wrong with the two of you?" Having the exploding fluffballs turning into bunnies was confusing and could not be good. It meant they were up to something.

Merri eased closer to him in order to reach under the coun-ter and grab the folder. "We—"

"Meaning the female pack?" he interrupted.

"Okay." Merri hesitated. "Are you including Nyx Sanguinati and Tess in the female pack? And Jenni and Starr Crowgard?"

He growled at her.

"Okay, okay. We decided that, rather than try to buy pres-ents for all our friends, we would draw two names out of a hat and give a small gift to those two people."

"Like a secret Santa Claus," Ruthie chimed in.

Simon cocked his head. This sounded interesting. "Santa has claws?"

"Ahhh . . ." Ruthie was back to looking at him with bunny eyes.

He knew about what humans called the Winter Solstice and the *terra indigene* called Longest Night. Instead of sensibly finding a warm place to sleep with your mate or your whole pack, humans ran around with shopping bags full of things. Last year, he'd been aware of the flurry of shoppers on the day before Longest Night—and aware of needing help to shove the last few shoppers out the door at the early closing time—and he'd been aware of TV commercials that featured the large, white-bearded male who dressed in a red coat and pants and stood in front of some stores and boomed ho-ho-ho to everyone. But last year there hadn't been humans around whom he trusted, and being aware was different from understanding.

How many of these Santas were there? Had a pack of them slipped into Lakeside? They seemed to be in a lot of places.

"Problem?" Vlad asked as he joined them at the counter.

"Did you know these Santa creatures have claws?" Simon asked. He remembered something he'd heard about them. "Do you think the Santas are a kind of Sanguinati?"

"What?" Ruthie squeaked.

"Wait!" Merri said. "That's not—"

"The Sanguinati have fangs, not claws," Vlad pointed out.

"But the Santas can go down chimneys to deliver presents," Simon argued. "Sanguinati could shift to their smoke form and go down chimneys."

"Wearing that suit of clothes?" Vlad grimaced. "There is no shadow of Sanguinati that would wear *those* clothes."

"Maybe the Santas wear red clothes to hide the bloodstains when they eat the naughty children."

"No!" Merri banged her hand on the counter. "No, no, no!

Santa does not have claws, and he doesn't eat children. He's a jolly, magical human who brings gifts to good boys and girls all over the world."

"What does he bring the naughty children?" Vlad asked.

Ruthie had that bunny look again. Merri's nostrils were flaring, and since she was standing on the same side of the counter as Simon, he wondered if she was going to try to bite him.

"Maybe the Sanguinati should think about participating in this ritual," Vlad said. "A little discreet feeding during the night could turn hyperactive children into calm children who would let their parents sleep past sunrise. Parents might consider that a gift."

Merri growled at Vlad. She poked a finger at Simon. "You two will *never* discuss Santa with any of the children connected to the Courtyard. You'll terrify them."

Simon stared at her. He was a Wolf. He knew how to wait for the optimum moment to give chase. "We might forget about Santa if *someone* explained about these gift lists—especially if one of the lists has Meg's name on it."

Merri flipped through the papers in the folder and pulled out one that had Meg's name at the top.

"Books?" That made no sense. The books listed were in stock. They were also in the Courtyard's library. "Meg can't buy books for herself?"

"None of us have bought books for ourselves this month," Ruthie said. "We've written down the books that we're interested in as a way to give someone ideas for shopping."

"The items with checkmarks?" Vlad asked.

"Already purchased," Ruthie replied.

"There is no indication of who purchased which book."

"Exactly. Even if we see the list and know which books were purchased, when we receive them, it will still be a surprise."

Vlad looked bewildered. Simon felt relieved. At least he wasn't the only one stuck in the mud of human female logic.

"It's not a book, so it's not on the list, but Jenni told us that she and Starr are giving Meg a geode," Merri said, wagging a finger to indicate that Ruthie was the other human who had been told.

Rocks. Meg seemed fascinated with certain kinds of rocks.

"Jenni also mentioned that Meg doesn't own any wearable shinies, and there were a couple of pendants at Sparkles and Junk that she might like," Ruthie said. "Males often give their mates a wearable shiny."

They smiled at him.

Right. No biting the gift-sleuthing helpers. He'd go over to Sparkles and Junk and talk to Jenni as soon as Nathan and Meg went out to make afternoon deliveries.

"Well, I'm glad that's settled." Vlad took a step away from the counter.

"What's settled?" Simon asked.

Vlad ignored the question and took another step back—a not-surprising reaction when dealing with Merri and Ruthie. "I'm going up to the office to check e-mail."

"You just came down from the office," Simon protested.

Vlad made a hasty retreat, leaving Simon with the exploding bunny fluffballs.

"Good job," he said. "Well done. Now move so I can go and check our stock."

Merri and Ruthie got out of the way.

Simon stood in HGR's back room and wondered how long he could pretend to check the stock he'd already checked earlier that morning to avoid further interaction with his employees.

And he wondered what sort of shiny Meg might like.

3

DORMENTE 20

OFFICER KARL KOWALSKI HELD OUT A SLIP OF PAPER. "Message for you, Lieutenant."

Lieutenant Crispin James Montgomery—Monty to his friends—took the slip and frowned at the message. "Steve Ferryman needs to see me urgently?" The message actually said the *mayor* of Ferryman's Landing needed to see the officer who worked with the Lakeside Courtyard. Did Steve phrase it that way, or did the person who took the message write it that way?

"Weather reports indicate we're going to get several inches of snow today, and it's already starting to come down," Kowalski said. "River Road only leads to Ferryman's Landing and Talulah Falls, so it isn't a priority road anymore—at least not the half of it that Lakeside is responsible for plowing," Kowalski said.

Meaning if he had to get to Ferryman's Landing, he and Kowalski needed to leave now.

"It's Solstice Eve. Let's see if we really need to go." Monty picked up his phone. He tried the mayor's office in Ferryman's Landing and got the answering machine message that the office was closed for the holidays. He tried Steve's mobile phone and got the man's voice mail.

The longer he delayed by trying to reach Steve on the phone, the harder the drive would be.

Captain Burke wasn't in his office, so Monty left a note with time of departure and destination so that Burke would know he and Kowalski weren't available for a while. If anything came up that involved the *terra indigene*, Burke or Officer Debany would have to handle it.

"Let's go," Monty said.

"MEG?" SIMON CAUTIOUSLY approached his mate. He glanced at Nathan, who had summoned him and Vlad to the Liaison's Office. Then he absorbed the grim expression on Vlad's face. Finally, he focused fully on Meg, who didn't seem to know he was there. She just gripped her right arm as tears ran down her face. "Meg?"

Prophecy cards were spread out on the big sorting table. Three cards were image side up, revealing at least part of the vision that had Meg in its grip. The first card had an ambulance, a fire truck, and a police car. The second had a front-end loader, a dump truck, and a snowplow. The third card was a hooded figure holding a scythe.

He didn't know if it was the warmth of his hand over hers or just being touched, but Meg sucked in a breath, blinked, and finally looked at him.

"What can I do?" he asked.

She sniffled. Vlad set a box of tissues on the table.

After wiping her eyes and nose, she said, "You asked me what I would like as a present. What I'd really like is for all my friends to get home safely so that tomorrow's celebration of the Winter Solstice is a happy time." She looked at the cards and added softly, "But I don't think that's going to be possible."

"Put the prophecy cards away now and close up the office," Simon said. "The snow is falling fast. You won't be able to get home in the BOW if you wait much longer."

"I have some shopping to do, including picking up soup and

sandwiches from Meat-n-Greens for tonight's meal," she replied. "Jester called a little while ago and said he and one of the ponies will be bringing the small sled to take me home."

"You head out, then. We'll lock up."

Meg gathered her prophecy cards and put them in the box Henry Beargard had made for her. Vlad fetched her purse from one of the cupboards and gently herded her to the back room for her coat and boots.

Simon waited until he heard the back door close before going to the front counter and calling the Chestnut Street police station. While he waited to be put through to Captain Burke, he asked Nathan, "What about you? You can stay with us until the storm passes."

<I will stay around here,> Nathan replied. <I can get food at Meat-n-Greens like Meg is doing and then stay in one of the efficiency apartments tonight. Besides, if Miss Twyla comes back to her den after playing with the pups, she would be alone in this part of the Courtyard. Safer for her if one of us is nearby.>

Several police officers lived in apartments across the street from the Courtyard, including Lieutenant Montgomery, but sometimes even being across the street could be too far.

Simon nodded his agreement to Nathan's plan as Burke came on the line. "Captain? Are any of our police friends out on the roads?" He growled softly as he listened. "Understood. If you need a place to stay tonight that is closer than your home den, you can stay here."

He hung up and looked at Nathan. "Lieutenant Montgomery and Officer Kowalski went to Ferryman's Landing. The snow will make it hard for them to get home."

<Then Meg has a reason to be afraid for her friends,> Nathan said.

"Yes." After locking up the Liaison's Office, Simon headed for Howling Good Reads, while Nathan trotted to the Courtyard's Market Square.

"LOOKS LIKE ALL the stores are closing early," Monty said. "You would think they would be staying open a little longer for last-minute shoppers."

"This is an Intuit village," Kowalski countered. "Weather reports have been predicting several inches of snow for days now. I bet people here finished their shopping well before today."

"There's Steve Ferryman." Monty pointed at a figure that left a store and hurried toward the river.

Kowalski *bloop*ed the siren, making enough sound to have Ferryman turning in their direction—and then hurrying toward them.

"Gods above and below," Steve said when Monty stepped out of the car. "What are you doing here?"

"You called the station and said you needed to see me," Monty replied. "You said it was urgent."

Steve stared at him. "I didn't ask for you, Lieutenant. In fact, I just got off the phone with Captain Burke to warn him that a massive paralyzing blizzard is about to hit us. This isn't the snow the weather reports have been predicting. This is more and worse. It started on the western edge of Lake Superior, where some Intuits and *terra indigene* shifters were killed by HFL renegades, and has been screaming across the Great Lakes. We're not talking about inches of snow; we're talking about getting buried under several *feet* of snow as well as dealing with high winds and subzero windchills. This is a killing storm driven by Elders and Elementals. Even our plows are heading in while the crews can still see the roads."

"Steve!" someone shouted. "Last ferry is ready to leave! Let's go!"

Steve turned and shouted, "I'll be there in a minute." Then he pointed to the sky. "See that black wall? That's the storm's leading edge. My family has a feeling we have enough time to get across the river and secure the ferry before the storm hits this side of Great Island. And then no one is going anywhere for the days it will take to dig out." He looked at Monty. "I wouldn't have called you. Not with that coming."

Monty felt a chill that had nothing to do with the outside temperature. "It was a trap."

Steve nodded. "Probably. We've been hearing about those kinds of traps. Cars being run off the road and the people either deliberately trapped inside their vehicles or just left to endure the storm—and often die. Look, I have to go or I'll be putting everyone else on that ferry at risk. You're welcome to join me on the island. Or there are a couple of places over here where you can get a room. Folks on this side of the river will be happy to help you. But if you're hoping to get back to Lakeside, you need to go now. From what we were told by Intuits living around the shores of Lake Honan, this storm is going to sweep in faster than you can safely drive."

"We'll go," Monty said. "Let us know how you fare."

"If the phones still work, I will." Steve jogged toward the man waiting for him, and the two of them hurried toward the river and the waiting ferry.

Monty got in the car and buckled his seat belt. "Get us home, Karl."

"Yes, sir." Kowalski made a U-turn and headed south toward Lakeside while Monty told him about the Elemental-assisted storm that was sweeping over the Great Lakes.

After a few tense minutes, Kowalski said, "The snow is filling in the road faster than I expected. If this isn't the storm yet, we could be in trouble."

"This will be Lizzy's first Solstice without her mother," Monty said quietly. "I'd like to be there for her."

Kowalski kept glancing in the rearview mirror. "I appreciate that, Lieutenant. I'd like to get home to Ruthie. But I think we need to consider taking shelter at the River Road Community—if we can make it that far."

Before Monty could turn his head to look behind them, the storm hit, the wind slapping the back of the police car into a skid.

No traction, Monty thought as Kowalski worked to straighten the car and keep them on the road. *No visibility.*

Kowalski turned on the flashing lights. "If there are any other fools on the road, they might see the lights before they run into us."

"Whoever sent the message to lure us out here will also be able to see us."

"If they're out here, they're driving in this too," Kowalski said, glancing at the car's odometer. "And if they're leaving it to chance that we'll get stuck too far from help, we might still get close enough to the River Road Community to make it the rest of the way there on foot."

Walking in the teeth of a blizzard? They didn't stand much of a chance.

Not something he would say to his partner, since Kowalski knew that too.

"I'll call Roger Czerneda and let him know we're out here. He lives in the community now."

It turned out that the lone human police officer who worked in Ferryman's Landing hadn't gotten out of the mainland side of the village before the storm hit and was sheltering there. But he promised to alert other residents of the community to keep a lookout for the Lakeside officers and assured Monty that there would be a place for them to stay.

The call to Captain Burke wasn't reassuring.

"I must have been on the phone with Steve Ferryman about the time you reached the village. He didn't make that call asking for you."

"I know," Monty replied. "We saw him just before he caught the last ferry to the island side of the village." He hesitated. "Kowalski thinks we can reach the River Road Community and shelter there."

"Wise decision." A pause so long Monty wondered if they had been cut off. "Lieutenant, watch your back. HFL renegades have been targeting cops who are answering calls for help. The renegades in some areas got their hands on dump trucks or snowplows, and they've rammed police cars, pushing them off the road and burying them in the snow."

"Were the officers rescued?" Monty asked.

Burke didn't answer. Finally, he said, "Get to the community—and watch your back."

"Not good?" Kowalski asked when Monty ended the call.

"Not good."

Kowalski glanced at the odometer. "I estimate that we're less than a quarter mile from the River Road Community now." He flinched as headlights suddenly appeared behind them. "Looks like one of the plows is still on the road. The driver might be heading for the community too." A moment later, his voice rose. "What the . . . ? Hang on!"

An engine roared. The lights got closer. Then . . .

WHEN SIMON WALKED through HGR's back door, he heard so much noise coming from the front of the store, he wondered if they were under attack. If they were, it seemed strange that Michael Debany, dressed in his police uniform, would be gutting the stock room shelves of all the books for youngsters and piling them onto a cart.

"What are you doing?"

"Practicing domestic harmony," Debany replied as he continued to grab books. "We're going to get whacked with some heavy snow tonight. It's already starting."

"Books will not stop the snow," Simon pointed out. That should be obvious, even to a human, but Debany was mated to Merri Lee, so Simon wasn't sure anything was obvious.

"One of the female pack mentioned a custom in a land on the other side of the Atlantik Ocean where everyone receives a book as a holiday gift, and they all spend part of the Solstice reading and eating treats." Debany paused for a moment. "I think half the residents of the Courtyard are in the store right now buying enough books so that everyone in their gard will have a book tomorrow. Apparently, Jester is arranging to have everything delivered by sled or sleigh or something that's pulled by horses since Blair Wolfgard said the BOWS are 'stabled' until the ponies clear the roads in the Courtyard. The rest of your customers are people in the neighborhood who realized this is the only place they can walk to in order to pick up a few last-minute gifts." He pushed the cart toward Simon. "Can you take this cart to the front? I'll get started on the thriller-and-fangs cart."

"Aren't you supposed to be working?" Simon asked as he pulled the cart out of the way.

"I am working."

"I meant police working."

"I am. I just came inside to warm up for a few minutes and ended up helping out back here. As soon as I fill this cart, I'll go back out and keep an eye on the traffic. Henry Beargard is out there now and said he'll help push cars that get stuck when they stop at the traffic light on Crowfield Avenue, and the juvenile Wolves are with him to help dig out cars that are parked in your customer lot. Officer Hilborn is out there too, providing human police presence so that people in the cars don't have a heart attack when they're suddenly surrounded by Wolves."

Police presence. Sleigh. Reminded of his task, Simon maneuvered the cart through the crowded aisles. Snarling at Others and humans alike who tried to grab books off the cart as he passed, he reached the counter, followed by the book mob.

Maybe it was the addition of the human pack introducing their customs for this holiday that made things different this year, but Simon didn't remember this kind of buying frenzy in previous years.

He pushed the cart up to the counter—and up to Blair Wolfgard, who was acting as security guard along with two Sanguinati standing on either side of the front door. Merri was working the register while Miss Twyla packed the books into shiny festive bags and Ruthie helped human customers. Vlad was helping the *terra indigene*—or, more likely, making sure the Others had a chance to reach the register and purchase their books without needing to shed human blood.

As one woman reached out to grab a Wolf Team book from the cart, Blair slapped a furry hand on top of the cart and growled, "If you want to keep your fingers, keep your paws off the books and wait your turn."

Leaving customer relations to the Courtyard's enforcer—and hoping no one ended up being eaten—Simon pushed his way into A Little Bite, then pushed his way to the counter.

"I have to see the girls at the lake," he told Tess. "I'll be back as soon as I can."

Tess had an office upstairs, but he'd already spent too much time getting through HGR, so he ducked into the back room, which was now officially Nadine's Bakery. Ignoring Nadine's sputtered protest, he stripped out of his clothes, leaving them as far from her baking as he could, then stepped into the back hallway and opened the back door, ignoring the gasp of the human who had just walked out of the coffee shop's restroom.

As soon as he was outside, Simon shifted to his Wolf form and ran toward the small lake that was the Elementals' domain in the Courtyard.

He found Winter and Air skating on the frozen lake. When Meg had first met her, Winter had looked like a young girl. Now she looked like a mature female—but she still wore the scarf that Meg had given to her.

"Wolf?" Winter glided to the edge of the lake. "A storm is coming. You should all go to your homes soon."

"We know about the snow, but—"

"More than snow. A *storm* is coming, driven by the Five Sisters and the rest of our kin."

Meaning the Elementals who ruled the Great Lakes and all the other Elementals who lived around those lakes.

"Why?"

"The bad humans are killing again. The storm traps them, making them easy for the Elders to find. That storm will be here soon and will rage until it reaches our kin on the shores of the Atlantik."

Simon thought about the prophecy cards Meg had turned over that afternoon. Would Montgomery and Kowalski be killed by HFL renegades or by the storm if driving on the roads became impossible before the men could find shelter?

<Tomorrow is Longest Night. It's a time when humans give gifts to other humans who are special to them. I'd like your help to give Meg a special gift—from all of us.>

"What gift?" Air asked.

<She has seen images that indicate the death of a police friend. Lieutenant Montgomery and Officer Kowalski are on River Road now, driving back from Ferryman's Landing.>

"They won't outrun the storm," Winter said.

<I know. Can you help me find them and bring them home as a gift for Meg?>

They said nothing. Then they nodded, and Winter said, "For Meg."

<Vlad? Get to the pony barn as fast as you can. We're going with Winter and Air to rescue Lieutenant Montgomery and Officer Kowalski.>

<On my way.>

Snow fell while they waited for Jester Coyotegard to harness two of the Elementals' steeds to the sleigh. Winter and Air decided that Simon should stay in Wolf form since a human form would be more vulnerable to the storm's bite.

He didn't argue.

The big sleigh arrived, pulled by Twister and Tornado. The floor of the sleigh was covered with blankets—the ponies' contribution to Meg's gift so that Montgomery and Kowalski wouldn't freeze to death before getting home. Simon in Wolf form and Vlad in his smoke form snuggled into the blankets. As soon as they were settled, the sleigh raced out of the Courtyard and over the city streets.

Simon closed his eyes. He really didn't want to see the sleigh—and Twister and Tornado—deal with any traffic that foolishly got in the way.

MUST HAVE BLACKED *out,* Monty thought as pain washed through him. *How long . . . ?* "Karl?"

"I'm here," Kowalski replied, sounding rough. "Banged up some, but here."

Monty looked out the windshield, trying to judge where they'd landed after being rammed. The police car was at an angle, making it impossible for him to open his door. They were off the road but still a safe distance from the river. He hoped. It wasn't possible to see the river. He could barely see beyond the hood of the car.

Hurt or not, if they could climb out of the car from the driver's side, they could alert Captain Burke about their location and then head for the River Road Community.

In fact, he should try to reach his mobile phone now and contact the captain, or . . .

Monty struggled to think as pain stabbed him when he tried to move his arm. Or they could use the police radio to contact the station.

"Karl, can you . . . ?"

The rumble of a big vehicle—a plow clearing a street of snow.

Then a sound shook the car.

No. This was more than a sound.

"Gods above and below," Kowalski said. "They're burying us under the snow." He tried to open his door, pushing as hard as he could—and only succeeded in creating a gap that let in snow. He shut off the engine and sat back, panting. "Might be able to break the windshield and get out that way—if those bastards out there leave that much of the car exposed."

Monty saw movement—a figure barely visible pushing through thigh-deep snow to reach the front of the car. A figure that raised a shotgun and aimed it at them. No way their killer would miss, not with the length of the car's hood between them.

"Lizzy," he whispered. His mother would take care of his little girl. So would the *terra indigene* in their own way. But he wouldn't be there for her. He wouldn't . . .

Snow suddenly splattered the windshield and froze instantly. Red snow.

Monty glanced at Karl, who seemed to be barely breathing.

No shotgun blast. No sound except . . . screaming. Even above the howl of the wind, he heard someone screaming. And then they weren't screaming.

A few minutes later, something cleared the packed snow away from the back of the car. Scraped away the snow until its claws scraped metal.

Something gripped the back wheel wells and dragged the car up to the edge of the road, leaving it beside the silent plow.

"Karl?" Monty touched the younger man's arm. "Can you move?"

"Give me a minute, Lieutenant. I need a minute before facing what's out there."

Yes. Kowalski wasn't just talking about the *terra indigene* who might still be out there in the storm. He was talking about . . .

There had been screaming. And then the screaming had stopped, and the snowplow was silent.

There was red snow frozen on the windshield of the patrol car.

Gritting his teeth against the pain, Monty released his seat belt and fumbled his mobile phone out of his pocket, surprised that his hands weren't working quite right. Then he sighed. "No signal."

"I guess we'd better head for the River Road Community." Kowalski sounded . . . blank . . . and Monty wondered if his partner was in shock.

They pushed the car doors open and stepped into a storm that sucked the warmth from a man's bones and stole his breath. Even that wasn't enough to distract him from what he could see in the cab of the snowplow. It wasn't enough to avoid seeing that whoever had hauled the police car out of the snow had used the sleeves of one of the HFL renegades' winter coats as padding against the wheel wells—and hadn't removed the arms that were in the sleeves.

"Lieutenant!"

Monty watched a snow tornado moving toward them at the speed of a galloping horse. Before he could shout, pray, even think, the tornado stopped and the snow fell to either side of the road, revealing two elegant steeds pulling a large sleigh driven by two females who were terrifyingly familiar.

"Arroo!" A Wolf leaped out of the back of the sleigh and ran toward them, followed by a column of smoke.

"Lieutenant!" Vlad shouted as he shifted to human form. "Karl! Meg will be so happy to see you!"

Something Monty couldn't see stirred nearby.

"We're okay," Kowalski said. "Banged up but okay."

"Not okay." Vlad stared at them. "You carry the scent of wounded prey." He turned toward the Elementals. "The lieutenant and Kowalski need to go to the human hospital before we can take them home."

"We will take them," Winter replied.

Simon's teeth gently closed on Monty's wrist and tugged him toward the sleigh while Vlad helped Kowalski, who was favoring one leg.

When the four males were bundled under blankets in the back of the sleigh, Air turned and looked at Simon. "You will tell our Meg how the Elders helped rescue her human friends?"

"Arroo," Simon agreed.

"Tornado," Winter said. "Twister. We need to clear the roads to the human hospital. It will make our Meg happy."

The Elementals' steeds turned the sleigh around and headed back to Lakeside, creating a whirling tunnel as they galloped through the storm.

4

DORMENTE 20

MEG WAITED AND WAITED WHILE HEAVY SNOW turned into a brutal storm.

Simon was out in that storm, trying to rescue Lieutenant Montgomery and Karl Kowalski. So was Vlad. All because she had wished that all her friends would make it home safely.

Ruthie had called, worried because Karl and Lieutenant

Montgomery had gone out to answer a call and hadn't reported in once the storm hit.

What if Simon was caught in this storm while looking for her human friends? What if *Simon* was the one who couldn't make it home safely? What if . . . ?

She couldn't think of that. *Wouldn't* think of that. Sam and Skippy were in the living room with coloring books and crayons. Showing the boys how to color had been a distraction for a while since she'd never done it herself, only seen images of children doing artsy activities.

She hoped they wouldn't get bored with coloring the pages that were meant to be colored and test the crayons on walls or furniture. Well, if they did, she'd ask Eve Denby, who had two children, how to clean whatever had been . . . decorated.

Jester had called to tell her that the last deliveries to the Courtyard's various complexes had been delivered, and he was going to wait at the pony barn for a while since Twister and Tornado were still out somewhere.

Somewhere. With Simon and Vlad and . . . Who was driving the sleigh? Would Winter keep Meg's mate and friend safe? *Could* Winter do that in the face of this storm?

Meg wandered from window to window, watching and waiting—and hoping.

"Arroo!"

"Simon," Meg whispered. She rushed to the front door and pulled it open. "Simon!"

The Wolf bounded up the snow-covered steps, then paused on the porch to give himself a good shake before nudging Meg away from the open door.

Vlad, in partial smoke form, followed Simon, his hands

gripping the handles of two large carry bags. "Get inside, Meg. It's freezing out here."

She backed up enough to let them all get inside. Then she dropped to her knees and hugged Simon breathless. "You silly Wolf! What were you thinking, going out in that storm?" She looked at Vlad. "And you too!"

"We were with Winter and Air in their sleigh," Vlad said. "That's as safe as you can be out there."

"Well," Meg huffed, unable to think of anything to say that wouldn't imply that Winter and Air couldn't handle themselves in any kind of weather. In fact, the last time the city had been hit with this kind of storm, Winter and Air had *created* it. "Well."

"Simon and I have some news, if you can let him go long enough for him to shift and put some clothes on." Vlad smiled and looked toward the living room. "Go with Simon. I'll put this food away and keep an eye on the pups."

As soon as they reached the bedroom, Simon shifted to his human form. Meg threw herself into his arms.

"I'm fine, Meg." He sighed—a happy sound. "We're fine. We found Lieutenant Montgomery and Kowalski. They were hurt, so we took them to the hospital and waited while the doctors did whatever they did. Then we took them home. They're home, Meg. And Vlad and I are home."

He shivered.

Meg stepped back. "You're cold!"

"I'm not wearing fur, and I'm not wearing clothes."

She growled at him. "Well, put some clothes on before you catch pneumonia." Before he could respond, she sat on the floor and began to cry.

Showing Wolfish practicality, Simon let her cry for a minute while he pulled on warm clothes. Then he sat on the floor with her and held her until she cried herself out.

"I'll tell you all of it later, when the boys are asleep," Simon said. "For now, just know your friends are home and safe. All your friends."

All her friends. That was the best gift she could have received.

MONTY SETTLED IN the recliner and gave his daughter a weak smile. "I won't lie and say I'm fine, Lizzy girl, but the doctors looked me over real good and said I didn't have to stay in the hospital, said I was okay to come home so that we could celebrate the Winter Solstice together."

That wasn't exactly what the doctors had said, but being faced with a Wolf and a vampire who had brought in two injured police officers, and remembering the last time the *terra indigene* had brought an injured human to the ER during a violent winter storm, the doctors were thorough in their examinations but also eager to send him and Kowalski home—especially after Vlad mentioned that a nurse practitioner was a neighbor and could do the official checking of whatever needed checking.

Monty left the hospital, wearing a soft neck brace, one arm in a sling. Kowalski had some kind of brace around his left knee, as well as a neck brace. What kind of injuries? The doctors had told him. He just hadn't been able to hang on to the words. Vlad and Simon would know. They had listened to everything the doctors had said. Vlad had taken the prescriptions for pain medicines to the hospital's pharmacy and gotten them filled while Simon stood guard.

"Crispin?" A quiet voice full of worry underneath firm love.

"Mama?"

"Captain Burke is here," Twyla said. "He'd like a minute of your time if you feel up to talking."

"I can—" Monty tried to get out of the recliner and discovered he couldn't manage it.

"You can sit right there. I'll fetch Captain Burke."

Monty looked around as best he could without turning his head. "Lizzy?"

"Lizzy and Frances are in their room, playing a game."

He must have drifted for a minute, because the next thing he knew, Douglas Burke was crouched next to his chair.

"I am relieved to see you, Lieutenant," Burke said.

"I'm relieved to be here," Monty replied. "Kowalski?"

"I'm stopping at his place next to check on him. I'm staying with Debany and Ms. Lee tonight. An extra hand where it's needed." Burke's fierce-friendly smile was softer than usual. "You're home to spend the holiday with your family."

"Same can't be said for the men who ran us off the road. Their families will be wondering tonight, grieving tomorrow."

"Yes. Those families won't be the only ones. We do what we can to keep things smooth, but there is nothing we can do when humans choose to go up against the Elders and Elementals."

"Except survive."

Burke nodded. "Except survive." He stood. "Get some rest, Lieutenant. Your mother can reach me if you need anything."

"Yes, sir."

Monty didn't remember Burke leaving the room, but his thoughts settled on one truth: in a violent conflict, not everyone survives, and he was grateful that he was one of the survivors this time.

Still, when he was well enough to visit the Universal Temple, he would say a prayer for the families of the people who wouldn't be coming home.

5

DORMENTE 24

A FEW DAYS AFTER THE SOLSTICE, SIMON DROVE ONE of the Courtyard's sturdier vehicles to the River Road Community. Meg sat beside him. Vlad sat in the back seat, claiming to be the protector of the treats, but really there to help protect Meg if there were any HFL humans still around.

River Road had been cleared of snow in a way that had nothing to do with snowplows used by humans. Simon wasn't sure what the humans who lived in the area thought about that, but they were sensible, for the most part.

The turn into the community would be reached before the site of the attack. The police car had been towed back to Lakeside. The snowplow had been taken . . . somewhere. When Douglas Burke met with Steve Ferryman and Roger Czerneda to decide what to do with the snowplow, they found wallets, keys, mobile phones, and clothes belonging to two men.

They didn't find any bodies. They never would. Burke would send the families a Deceased, Location Unknown form since the attack had been aimed at his men. He would mail the personal effects to the addresses found in the wallets.

Simon didn't ask what the men had decided to do with the snowplow.

He drove up the plowed road that served the community and

stopped near the house occupied by several Sanguinati juveniles.

Roger Czerneda came out of one of the other houses and raised a hand in greeting.

"I'll give Officer Czerneda an update on Kowalski and Montgomery," Vlad said. He got out of the vehicle and headed for the human.

Simon looked at Meg. "Ready?"

She nodded.

They hefted the two large containers of treats out of the back seat and headed for the Sanguinati's house. Vlad must have been in touch before they left the Lakeside Courtyard because the garage door was open and there was a makeshift table of sawhorses and wood boards.

Meg remained in the open, which made Simon nervous since she was holding one of the containers, and there was no guarantee that the Elders who had helped Montgomery and Kowalski would be polite.

"Hello?" Meg called. She waited a moment. "Hello? Arroo? It's Meg. Broomstick Girl. The howling not-Wolf. We brought you some cookies to thank you for helping save our friends. We'll leave them in the Sanguinati's garage so they don't get wet."

As soon as they set the containers on the makeshift table, Simon hustled Meg into the vehicle and waited for Vlad to join them. What he was driving wasn't big enough to prevent an Elder from crushing it—and them—but he didn't think they would harm Meg.

No tracks he could see. No sign of a large being pushing through deep snow to reach the garage. But when he looked in the rearview mirror as they drove away, he noticed that the containers of cookies were already gone.

6

DORMENTE 25

WONDERING WHY HE'D BEEN SUMMONED TO THE LI-aison's Office when it looked like the whole female pack—including Miss Twyla—was crowded into the sorting room, Simon stood next to Vlad and Michael Debany and eyed the large box on the table.

"With the storm and everything else, we didn't work out all the details to share this with you on Longest Night," Meg said.

"And we needed help from those with the skills to do some of the work," Ruthie added, nodding to Eve Denby and Miss Twyla.

"You already gave me a present," Simon said. The winter coat Meg had given him wasn't like anything she would have found in the Courtyard, but he'd noticed Debany and Kowalski had been given the same kind of coat—something that would keep a human body warm during a Lakeside winter—so Ruthie and Merri must have helped Meg buy it.

Merri nudged Meg. "Time to open it."

Meg opened the box and handed out . . . fur?

Right color for Wolf fur but wrong smell.

Then Meg, Merri, and Ruthie put the fur on their heads, and suddenly they were wearing furry hats that completely covered their heads—and had Wolf ears.

Meg looked at him, her eyes bright with happiness, and began to sing . . .

"Happy Howlidays!"

"Arroo-ee-oo-ee-oo!" sang Merri and Ruthie.

"Happy Howlidays!"

"Arroo-ee-oo-ee-oo!"

"Happy Howlidays, dear Simon. Happy Howlidays to you!"

"Arroo!"

Vlad and Debany applauded. Simon wasn't sure what to say because he was busy resisting the urge to reach out and fondle Meg's Wolf ears. Then he glanced at Miss Twyla, who smiled at him—and he understood.

His present wasn't the furry hats or the song. His present . . . There were no shadows in Meg's eyes. She was laughing with her friends, delighted to be with all of them. To be with him, sharing a silly song.

His Meg was happy, and that was the best present of all.

THE DARK SHIP

L AST NIGHT I DREAMED ABOUT THE DARK SHIP.
People say it's bad luck to be on the water when the full moon rises, because that's when the dark ship goes hunting, its tattered black sails catching a fast wind that touches no other ship. People say it is crewed by monstrous beings that capture hardworking fishermen and honest sailors, and its captain drinks the captives' blood before giving the bodies to his crew, who devour the flesh and suck the marrow from the bones.

People say that if your vessel is suddenly becalmed and a fog rolls in without warning, look to the horizon, and if you see those black sails silhouetted against the moon, it is better to die by your own hand than to wait for the monsters to find you. Because they will find you. They always find you.

I LIVED IN Pyetra, a small fishing village on the coast of the Mediterran Sea. According to the grandmothers, it had been a prosperous village, and while the buildings near the water had been built out of the gray stone that had given Pyetra its name, the homes of the more affluent residents had been painted in soft pastels—yellow, rose, green, blue—so that, from the water, the village had looked like a bouquet of flowers set against the hills.

Then the Humans First and Last movement declared war on the *terra indigene*, and the Cel-Romano Alliance of Nations was torn apart by the Others' fury and power over the world. Instead of an alliance, nations were separated by veins of wild country, and anything human who stumbled into that land never came out.

Small villages like mine were untouched for the most part because the men who fished in the Mediterran or sailed that water to carry goods from one city to another—or sailed beyond our waters to trade—knew that the sea belonged to the *terra indigene,* and crews that were careful, and respectful, never saw the lethal terror that watched them but let them pass, and those were the men who returned home.

In a world torn apart by war, the vulnerable often fell victim to predators who waited for such opportunities to crack people's sense of right and wrong, using fear as a hammer.

In the end, it wasn't the Others who ruined Pyetra. It was a man called Captain Starr.

I SENSE THINGS about ships and the sea. I can't see the future like those prophet girls we'd heard about, but when I walk along the shore and watch the fishing boats heading out for the day, sometimes I know which boats will have a good catch and which ones will come back with an empty hold. Sometimes I can tell when the sea will be unforgiving and it's better not to stray too far from the harbor. I don't tell anyone what I know, except one or two of the canny old grandfathers, and even with them, I am careful. I was a child when it happened, but I remember the last woman in our village who had a feeling about the weather and the sea. She was publicly beaten to death for "ill wishing" because she had warned a captain of a storm on a day when the sea was calm and the sky was clear, and he ignored her. When the storm appeared like screaming fury, she was blamed for the loss of that ship and crew.

I sense things about ships and the sea. It was my misfortune that I had never been able to sense danger to myself.

I WOKE UP before dawn on the morning that was the beginning of the end. Too restless to go back to sleep and feeling a need I couldn't explain, even to myself, I dressed in my oldest shirt and skirt, put on my half boots, slipped a small folding knife into my skirt pocket, and went down to the water—down to the stretch of sandy beach protected by walls of rock that jutted into the sea. That beach had been turned into a baited trap that Captain Starr's men had set for whatever might leave the water and come ashore. Or for whatever—whoever—might be desperate enough to risk the trap to claim whatever bounty might be found.

That morning, I found one of the feral ponies, his front feet caught in the tangles of net. He had a barrel body and chubby legs, but it was his coloring that made me shiver and yet, at the same time, conjured fanciful thoughts. His body was the midnight blue of the sea in the darkest hours of the night, and his mane and tail looked like surf and moonlight.

He was just a feral pony, but I could imagine him being one

of the beautiful, deadly steeds that raced over the Mediterran Sea, harbingers of the dark ship's appearance.

I scolded myself as I made my way carefully down the path through the rocks to that stretch of beach. Wasting time imagining things could get both of us killed.

I paused when I reached the last rock and my feet touched sand. I'd have to step into the open in order to reach the pony, and I had a feeling there wasn't much time before Starr's men arrived with knives and clubs. If they found me here . . .

Hilda had been caught trying to free one of the village orphans who begged on the streets and was too hungry to resist the bait. The boy had tried to grab the thick piece of bread smeared with butter and honey—a barely remembered treat from the days before Captain Starr and his crew dropped anchor off our shore and became both terror and law for our village. The child was human, was known to us, had once had a family who lived in Pyetra. None of that had mattered. No one but the captain or his first mate decided the fate of anything caught in the trap, and to free something . . .

Captain Starr made some of us stand on the beach and watch as his men clubbed the boy to death. He made us watch. . . .

Hilda wasn't dead after Starr's men finished with her, but she was too broken to save herself when the tide came back in. We watched and listened as she drowned. Then we were allowed to return to our homes or businesses, mute accessories to murder because no one had dared speak out against that cruelty or had taken one step to save Hilda or the boy.

So I knew the risks when I approached the trap. Being here was foolish. Trying to save one feral pony wasn't worth my life. And yet, watching a sea eagle circle above the net before heading out to sea, I *knew* something bad would happen to our village if the pony died.

The wind shifted. The pony snorted, having caught my scent.

"Easy," I said quietly as I scurried toward him. "Easy. I'm here to help you."

The pony neighed and tried to rear, but his efforts to get free tangled his front feet even more.

"Shh!" Now I was sweating. If any of the men heard the pony, they would hurry down to the beach. "If you don't keep quiet, we'll both be clubbed to death!"

He quieted and stood still, allowing me to approach. I took out my folding knife and worked as quickly as I could to cut just enough of the net to free his feet—and tried not to startle and cut myself every time the pony lipped my hair and snuffled to breathe in my scent.

"There." I pushed the net away from his feet before reaching up and pressing a hand to his chest. "Back up. Back."

He backed away from the trap, but he didn't turn and run while I smoothed the sand and arranged the net so that it wouldn't look like someone had messed with it. There would be footprints in the sand—the pony's and mine—but there was nothing I could do about that. The men would know from the size of the print that an adult male hadn't been walking this way, but unless someone saw me, they wouldn't know I had been on this part of the beach.

"Go home now," I said. "Go home."

I ran back to the narrow path in the rocks. I had to get home before Mara noticed I was missing and told my father, who would use his belt on me. I had to get home and wash up and make myself as presentable as possible. But not too presentable.

I used to be pretty. I'm not pretty anymore. Father took care of that. He claimed it was for my own good, but afterward not even his friends believed that.

I ran—and the pony ran with me.

I stopped. He stopped.

"Listen to me."

He pricked his ears.

"You have to go home. If the men see you, they will kill you for the meat, for your hide. You need to go home so that you can stay free." I paused, then added under my breath, "One of us should be free."

He looked at me for a long time, and I could have sworn that something like sympathy filled his dark eyes.

He turned and galloped to the water's edge, running in the surf. A large wave rolled onto the beach, rolled right over him. I stared at the spot, expecting to see him struggling with a broken leg or something just as bad, but when the wave receded, the pony was gone. Just gone. And so were my footprints.

As I turned to climb the path up to the road, I saw a man standing on the nearest rock wall, watching me. He was tall and lean, dressed all in black, and he had black hair and olive skin. More than that I couldn't tell. If he was one of Captain Starr's men . . .

Keeping my face averted, I climbed the path as fast as I could, grabbing the rocks for balance and taking some skin off my palms in my haste. If I could get back to the dockside tavern my father owned, maybe I could get inside and disappear before the man had time to figure out who I was.

Panting, I dared to look back when I reached the road.

No man stood on the rock wall. All I saw was smoke drifting toward the sea.

When I was younger, the old grandfathers who hung around the docks and came to the tavern for their midday food and drink would tell me stories about the *terra indigene*, the earth natives who ruled so much of the world and viewed humans much the same way we viewed fish or deer. They told me about islands in the Mediterran—dangerous, secret places where the Others lived and where the dark ship lay anchored when its captain and crew weren't hunting human prey.

In some stories, the ship would appear out of the fog, a marauder that sank the ships of honest merchants who ferried a variety of goods among the Cel-Romano nations. In other stories, the ship was crewed by men the sea had never released. But when the moon was full, beings wearing the skins of those men would come ashore for a reckoning, and woe to those who had somehow escaped the justice of the living.

I heard birds overhead and jerked out of my musing. What was wrong with me? I had to get away from here!

I ran home and slipped up to my attic room unseen. I washed up and plaited my hair, but I didn't wash up enough to smell clean, and I didn't plait my hair to look that neat. I didn't want the men who came to drink in the tavern to see anything pleasing enough to make up for what my father had done to my face after a young man, who was in Pyetra to sell the olive oil produced by his family, wanted to marry me and take me back to his family's villa, depriving my father and his wife, Mara, of unpaid labor.

I used to be pretty before my father took a knife to one side of my face, before his fist damaged the sight in one eye.

I never saw the young man again. For a long time, I hoped he would come back and take me away, despite the damage to my face. But he never returned. Once I stopped feeling bitter about that, I wondered if something had happened to him and he couldn't return.

My father had wielded the knife, but it says something about my stepmother that the only gift she ever gave me after the bandages were removed was a gilt-edged mirror that my father hung over my dresser.

This is what you are now. As if I could ever forget while I was trapped within these walls, waiting on tables and cleaning up blood and puke after the men had their fun. But when I walked along the shore or stood on one of the rock walls and looked out to sea, I could dream of freedom. I could dream of being someone else, living somewhere else.

I had turned toward the bedroom door to go downstairs when I heard a sound at my open window, which reminded me to close it, despite how the heat would build in the attic during the day.

A seashell lay on the windowsill. A perfect, undamaged shell that looked like a white fan with a pearly peach interior.

A raven perched on the neighboring roof, watching me. I don't know how long we stared at each other before it flew away, but I had a feeling the bird was connected to the pony and to the man I had seen on the rock wall.

As I went about my work that day, I thought about the raven, and the gift of a perfect seashell. I thought about a midnight blue pony with a mane and tail the color of surf and moonlight. I thought about the man who had disappeared like smoke. And I wondered if the dark ship would appear in Pyetra's harbor.

But it wasn't the dark ship and its monstrous crew that docked in Pyetra the next day.

It was Captain Starr.

———

HIS NAME WAS Jonathan Brogan, but no one who wanted to keep their tongue called him anything but Captain Starr. A big barrel-chested man with thick, wheat-colored hair, a round face, and big square teeth that you couldn't help but notice since he laughed and smiled a lot. But his blue eyes were cold as a shark's, and what made him smile was often someone else's pain.

Before the war, he'd been a bully with a ship, a thug who strong-armed weaker men into paying protection money if they didn't want their merchant ships to mysteriously disappear or their fishing boats to be found adrift with the hold empty and no sign of the captain and crew. Now he was Pyetra's protector against the Others, Pyetra's hero who could murder a village girl for trying to free an orphan from a baited trap. Anything he or his men wanted, they took in exchange for escorting merchant ships past islands that Starr claimed were inhabited by beings that wanted nothing to do with Cel-Romano except when they came ashore to kill and destroy.

They say he was in a fight when he was young, receiving a terrible blow on the forehead that dented his skull in the shape of a star—a mark still visible and distinctive. They whispered that, perhaps, the damage had gone deeper than his skull, and that was what made him such a savage adversary.

Whatever the reason, everyone in Pyetra lived in fear from the moment his sails were sighted to the moment his ship sailed away, its hold carrying precious fuel for the engine that allowed him to maneuver even when there was no wind for the sails, as well as the best foods, ales, and wines from our shops.

That afternoon he walked into my father's tavern—and

everyone fell silent. Captain Starr's crew ate and drank here, but Starr and his first mate stayed at an inn far enough from the docks that the rooms didn't stink of fish, and fancy enough that the captain dressed like a gentleman when he met with the village leaders to discuss payments and accommodations.

Captain Starr sat down at a table Mara hurriedly wiped clean and smiled that toothy smile. "Enzo, my good man. A round of drinks for everyone, and your best ale and whiskey for me and my mate."

My father poured the drinks and brought them to the table. No one rushed to the bar to receive their free drink. I hid in the hallway that provided access to the storeroom and the door to the alley, overwhelmed by the feeling that something was going to happen.

Captain Starr sampled the ale and gave a nod of approval. My father relaxed. Everyone else in the tavern was smarter and waited to find out what Starr wanted before they believed they would be allowed to leave unharmed.

"I left two men here to keep an eye on the docks and the fishing boats and to take note of returning merchant ships," Starr said. "And to keep an eye on the baited trap since our enemies often come in by the sea. My men are nowhere to be found, and my first mate tells me the trap's net has been cut in a way that suggests someone freed whatever had been caught. Anyone here know anything about that?" He looked at my father. "Enzo?"

My father shook his head. "I've not been down to the water in days. Neither has my wife. Been too busy with running this place and putting up the supplies that came in the other day."

"What about that daughter of yours?" Starr still sounded friendly, but everyone knew there was nothing friendly about the question or what would happen if he didn't like the answer.

I eased back a little more. A couple of old grandfathers, sitting at the back table, saw me, then pointedly looked away—and said nothing.

"She must be about," my father said, "although she barely does enough work to deserve the food she eats."

"Find out where she was this morning," Starr said. "I don't think she fully appreciates that a daughter should be obedient in all things."

In other words, when he found me, my father would tie my hands to a spike he'd driven into the wall and beat me until I couldn't stand.

The tavern door opened, and something, some change in the air or in the room's silence, made me peer around the corner. The man I'd seen on the rock wall that morning walked up to the bar, set a gold coin on the wood, and said, "Whiskey."

The paper money that had been used in Cel-Romano was almost worthless now. Currency in a place like Pyetra was gold or silver or chits of credit that were traded among the residents, becoming a currency exclusive to the village.

After a glance at Starr, my father filled a glass to the brim with whiskey, took the gold coin, and, grudgingly, put two silver coins on the bar as change.

The man pocketed the coins and took a sip of whiskey.

"You're not a villager," Starr said, his blue eyes bright with malice—and suspicion.

"No, I'm not," the man agreed. He had a slight accent, like nothing I'd heard before.

"First time in Pyetra?" Starr asked.

"It is."

"Going to be here long?"

"I'm not sure."

"What's your name?"

"Captain Crow."

Starr's eyes narrowed. "I didn't see an unfamiliar ship moored at the docks or anchored in the harbor. Where is your ship, and what's your business here?"

Crow took another sip of whiskey. "What business is it of yours?"

"I look out for the people in this village. Their protector, you might say. So I'll ask again: Where is your ship, and what's your business?"

"My ship is nearby. As for my business . . ." Crow looked Starr right in the eyes, something no other man would do. "I hunt predators."

Starr's first mate snorted. "Like sharks?"

Crow continued to stare at Starr. "Something less honorable."

Everyone in the tavern held their breath. To call Starr dishonorable was courting death, especially for a man alone. He'd be lucky to get back to his ship without being knifed in an alley.

"There's no fuel for an unregistered ship," Starr said. "Fuel is strictly rationed since the war."

"My ship doesn't require anything but the wind," Crow replied.

A sailing ship without an engine? Fishing vessels relied on engines, but most had been refitted with sails to help the fuel last. And merchant ships ran before the wind with full sails except when coming into or leaving the harbor and docks. A sailing ship without an engine had to be ancient!

I shivered as a thought erased every other, like the incoming tide erases footprints on a beach.

An ancient ship—or an unnatural one.

"If you're here for supplies, spend your coin and be out of Pyetra by sundown," Starr snarled. "And don't come back."

Crow took another sip of whiskey, the level in the glass barely changed. He stepped away from the bar, then stopped. "I go where I please."

"Really? I've never heard of you."

"But I've heard of you, Captain Starr." Crow smiled a tight-lipped smile. "You should be careful about the cargo you carry when you're in Tethys's domain. The salt of tears has a different taste than salt water."

Who was Tethys? I waited for someone to ask the question. No one did.

I glanced at the old grandfathers, saw the way their hands shook.

They knew. And they feared this Tethys more than they feared Starr.

Crow left the tavern. Starr and his first mate walked out a minute later.

Starr and his men searched the docks, the warehouses, the shops, and the taverns, but no one had seen the mysterious man who claimed to be a ship's captain. No one reported sighting an unfamiliar ship near Pyetra.

But that night, when I finally went up to bed, I found Captain Crow sitting on my windowsill.

I stared at him, shocked, before I considered what kind of work Mara would have me doing in the alley behind the tavern if someone spotted him and told her a man had been in my room.

"Get away from there," I whispered fiercely. "You'll be seen!"

He stood, stepped to the side, then leaned against the wall. "Better?"

He sounded amused, and that amusement turned my fear into fury. If Mara came upstairs now . . . worse, if my father came upstairs to deliver the beating Starr had implied I deserved . . .

"How did you get up here?"

"The window was open."

"It wasn't." I was sure I had closed it.

"Open a crack," he amended. "It was enough. Why did you free the pony?"

"I don't know you." Couldn't trust him is what I meant. "Is Crow your real name?"

"It is when I captain the ship."

"And when you're not captaining the ship?"

"My name is Corvo Sanguinati."

Sanguinati. Blood drinker. One of the *terra indigene.*

It seemed there was some truth in the stories about the dark ship.

"What do you want from me?"

He regarded me calmly. "I want to know why you freed the pony."

"It was caught in the net. Starr's men would have killed it."

"They would have killed you, too, if they'd seen you." He paused. "'One of us should be free.' That's what you said."

He'd *heard* that?

"What's your name?" he asked.

"Vedette. But everyone calls me Dett." I smiled bitterly. "Mara always says I owe her and my father for letting me live. If she'd been able to have a child of her own, she would have

273

dragged me down to the sea on a moonless night and drowned me years ago."

"If you were free, what would you do? Where would you go?" Corvo asked.

I shrugged and attempted a sassy answer. "I would stow away on a dark ship that was headed anywhere but here."

"Dangerous to be a stowaway on any ship. Especially dangerous to stow away on that one. But paying for your passage? That might be possible."

No, it wasn't. I had no money and nothing to barter except my body, and I doubted Corvo Sanguinati would accept as payment what most other men would take—as long as they could turn one side of my face to the wall while they lifted my skirt.

Corvo rubbed his chin. "How did you know the pony would be on the beach?"

We were back to the pony?

I hesitated. Lying was the safe thing to do, but I had a feeling that Corvo was in my room for a reason, and it wasn't to hide from Captain Starr. If I lied to him now, I would never find out why he had come to see me.

"Sometimes I sense things about ships and the sea. I had a feeling I needed to go down to the beach this morning."

He nodded. "I wondered if you were an Intuit. I was surprised to see one of your kind living in a place like this instead of among your own."

"My kind?" People like me had a name besides ill-wisher?

No one would talk about my mother, and the few things that had been said were vague, but I'd had the impression that she hadn't been a local girl. Had she come here on a visit and stayed because she fell in love with my father? Or had she been forced into that marriage? I would never know about her, but learning there was a place where people like me were accepted was a gift—and a goal.

Corvo studied me. "The world gave humans the land that surrounded the Mediterran Sea as their territory, but the islands within the Mediterran have always belonged to the *terra indigene*. Intuits escaping persecution from other kinds of humans were allowed to settle on those islands, as long as they didn't fight with or interfere with us. They farm and fish—and teach us human skills."

"Like sailing a ship?" I asked.

"Like sailing a ship," he agreed.

He came to some decision. Pushing away from the wall, he reached into a pocket and pulled out two silver coins. Not looking at me, he placed the coins on the windowsill and rested one finger on top of them.

"This will buy one transaction with the *terra indigene*," he said. "You may ask any of us for one thing—including passage on a dark ship heading for an Intuit village."

My head spun with the enormity of what he offered. "But how can I contact you? The telephones don't work much beyond the neighboring villages anymore."

Another casualty of the war with the *terra indigene*. Humans no longer had quick communication over longer distances because telephone lines had been severed and couldn't be repaired in the veins of wild country that now broke apart the Alliance of Nations. Every attempt to restore the lines had ended in piles of human corpses. We were reduced to communicating as our grandparents had done, with letters sent overland or by ship.

"Set the coins where they can be seen and speak your intention clearly. Someone will hear you and relay the message."

How? I asked a different question. "Who is Tethys?"

Corvo smiled, showing a hint of fang. "She is an Elemental. She is the voice and heart and fury of the Mediterran Sea."

So the Elementals were real.

"Why would you help me?"

"You were willing to help someone who was different from yourself. I felt I should return the favor."

One moment he stood there, looking at me. The next moment, a column of smoke filled the same space before it flowed out the window, and Corvo, in his other form, disappeared into the night.

THE NEXT MORNING, men checking the baited trap found Captain Starr's missing men. Both had a round mark on their chests bigger than a man's hand—and holes that looked like they had been made by circles of curved teeth latching into flesh while something else had scraped the flesh away to reach the hearts and all that rich blood.

The men's legs had chunks of flesh ripped away, and those bite marks indicated a large shark had fed on the bodies after death. Maybe after death.

The shark bites disturbed the men who downed rough whiskey before going to work, but the round marks in the dead men's chests terrified all the men whose work brought them into contact with the sea.

As I served drinks and cleared tables, I listened to the grandfathers whisper about giant sea lampreys that were as long as a man is tall—lampreys that had a taste for warm-blooded prey. Human prey. And I heard another word whispered that day to explain a creature that shouldn't exist: *Others*.

Captain Starr's ship set sail a few days later with its hold full of provisions, along with the goods he had wrung from the village's merchants that he would sell for his own profit.

The morning after that, I ran errands for Mara, who claimed to be feeling poorly. I seldom had a chance to visit the shops on the main street, and almost never by myself. Mara didn't like to deprive herself of the enjoyment of seeing people flinch when they looked at my face.

Corvo hadn't flinched. I liked him for that.

That morning, I crossed paths with Lucy, who had been my friend before my father used his fist and a knife. We used to walk on the beach and talk about our hopes and dreams. I wasn't allowed to take those walks after my face healed because Mara decided that Lucy had given me ideas and that was why I'd thought I could get married and work anywhere but the tavern after she and my father had gone through the trouble of raising me.

Lucy came up beside me as I perused a cart of used books, standing where she could see the undamaged side of my face. She said nothing, just picked up a book and examined it, as if I were a stranger. As if I meant nothing at all and never had.

Then she said in a low voice, "Be careful, Dett. I heard things while Captain Starr was staying at the inn."

Lucy's family owned the inn that catered to ships' captains and well-to-do merchants.

"What things?" I pretended interest in a book that gave me a reason to turn slightly in her direction.

"That some captains are looking for a different kind of cargo these days," Lucy replied. "Apparently there are men in other parts of Cel-Romano who want to buy unspoiled goods." She returned the first book to the cart and picked up another.

"Starr asked my father if I was unspoiled goods. He asked if you were. And he wasn't just asking about girls."

My stomach rolled.

"There are cities around the Mediterran that are filled with supplies and hard-to-find goods that can be had just for the asking, but . . . things . . . are hunting in those cities now, so most people who go in to find the goods don't get out alive," Lucy said.

"Nimble orphan boys might be able to get in and out. A couple of times, anyway."

She nodded. "That's a possibility. But girls like us . . ." She shuddered.

It wasn't likely that Captain Starr was acting as a marriage broker.

"I'll buy this one so no one thinks to say anything about me standing here so long." Lucy held up the book. "I hope I like it."

She went into the shop to purchase the book. I hurried away and finished the errands for Mara.

That night I sat at the open window, clutching the silver coins. Fear of what might happen the next time Captain Starr's ship was spotted on the horizon filled me, leaving room for nothing else. I tried to convince myself that, at worst, it wasn't any different from Mara wanting to sell me for an alley hump, but it *was* different. What I couldn't sense was how it was different or why it felt dangerous.

I looked at the coins in my hand. One transaction with the *terra indigene*. One chance.

What did I truly want? To get away from Pyetra? Oh yes, I wanted that. But what about Lucy? What about the orphans the villagers would justify selling to Starr as cargo?

As I sat at my window, the wind brought the smell of the sea—and I had a feeling that it wasn't yet time to ask for the thing I wanted.

A WEEK AFTER Captain Starr's ship left Pyetra, other merchant vessels docked at the wharf or dropped anchor in the harbor. As the crews from those ships came ashore, so did the stories.

The dark ship had been sighted several times. Given that some of the ships had been sailing to Pyetra from the eastern side of the Mediterran while others had sailed from the west, I wondered if there was more than one dark ship. It seemed likely, but I was interested in only one.

Stories spoken quietly, fearfully, of spotting another ship that was suddenly engulfed in an unnatural fog. Seeing the flames as the ship burned. Hearing the screams of the men.

Or seeing a ship sail out of a bank of fog that dissipated in minutes. Finding what was left of the bodies of the crew—some drained of blood, some torn apart by a shark, and some with that queer round hole in their chests that looked similar to the mark a lamprey left on fish but so much bigger and so much worse when that mark was left on a man.

Or a wave rising out of nowhere, topping a ship's masts before the ship rolled, broke apart, and sank.

Or a whirlpool appearing in front of a ship, pulling it down—and men swearing they saw a giant steed galloping round and round the edge of the whirlpool until it, and the whirlpool, vanished.

They whispered about their own ships suddenly becalmed, leaving them helpless as a dark ship, its black sails full with an unnatural wind, caught up to them, drew up alongside—and then sailed past. And how the wind that had disappeared when the dark ship appeared on the horizon suddenly filled the sails again, allowing them to reach the next port.

Stories spoken quietly, fearfully, by men who'd had to sail past slaughter—and who wondered what cargo had provoked that kind of rage.

We found out what kind of cargo when Captain Starr returned to Pyetra.

I'D BARELY HAD an hour's sleep when Mara shook me awake.

"Get up," she said in a fierce whisper. "Get dressed and come downstairs. And be quick about it."

"But—"

"Be quick or you'll have nothing but your nighty."

The thought of wearing nothing but my nighty and being downstairs with men who had been to sea for a few weeks was enough to wake me up. My fingers shook as I pulled on my underwear and buttoned my shirt and skirt, put on my socks and half boots. I'd made a little pouch from a scrap of cloth in order to hide the silver coins and keep them with me—and hidden from Mara. I pinned the pouch to the back of the skirt's pocket, then slipped my folding knife into the pocket.

As I reached for the shawl I'd folded over the back of my chair, the door opened again.

"You won't need that." Mara grabbed my arm and dragged me down the stairs with such haste we came close to falling.

As she pulled me into the tavern's main room, I saw Captain Starr—and I knew.

"No." I tried to pull away from Mara. "No!"

A rag was stuffed in my mouth and secured with another piece of cloth. My hands were bound with rope.

Starr stared at my face and smiled. "I have a client who will pay well to have you for his new wife." He looked at my father. "You'll receive your portion of the sale price, as agreed."

Two of Starr's men dragged me out of the tavern and down to the dock and his ship. They pulled me up a gangplank. I fought them until they dunked my head in a barrel of water and held me down. When one of them pulled my head out of the water, the other said, "If you keep fighting, we'll hold you down longer next time."

Still struggling to breathe, I didn't resist when they hauled me to the ship's secure hold and left me there, bound and gagged.

But not alone.

There were younger girls, barely more than children, and some of the orphan boys who begged on the streets. None of them were tied up, but there were bruises on their faces, reason enough for them to huddle together now, silent and afraid.

I don't know how long it took them to load their living cargo. No adolescent boys, but several of the village girls who were old enough to be "wives" in a place where there was a shortage of expendable women.

It was still dark when men escorted Lucy into the hold, bound and gagged as I was. She sat next to me, shivering.

Soon after that, I felt the change in the ship's movement and knew Starr had given the order to cast off.

Unspoiled goods being taken to an unknown destination and a mean existence. Most of us wouldn't survive long after arriving at that destination, and those of us who did survive wouldn't want to.

We had one chance—if I could get free.

———

I HAD STARTED pulling on the gag when one of the boys looked at me and said, "Wait."

I might have resented the sharp command if I hadn't seen him watching the stairs down to the hold. Was he someone like me, who had feelings about things?

I slumped and waited, doing my best to look defeated, which wasn't hard.

A minute later, two men came down the stairs. One dropped a burlap sack on the floor; the other set down a small barrel and a tin cup.

"That's all there is until you're traded," the first one said. "Make it last."

They went up the stairs and secured the door.

The boy waited another minute, watching the stairs. Then he scurried over to Lucy and undid her gag.

"Dett too," Lucy said.

He hesitated, then did what she asked.

"One of Starr's men saw you giving us food," the boy told Lucy. "That's why he took you." He looked at the ropes binding our hands.

"I have a folding knife in my skirt pocket," I said.

I didn't feel his hand, but a moment later he held the knife. He freed Lucy first, then me. Folding the knife, he gave it back— and gave me an odd look, which made me wonder if he'd felt the coins.

Lucy rubbed her wrists while another boy, who looked to be the twin of the first, opened the sack and checked the barrel.

"Some food here," he reported. "Not much if it's meant for all of us. The barrel is half-full of water."

"We won't be here that long," I said, unbuttoning my skirt in order to reach the safety pin and little pouch. Retrieving the pouch, I held it tight.

"Dett . . . ," Lucy began.

"We're going to escape."

"How?"

I opened the pouch and showed her the two silver coins. "These will pay for one transaction with the *terra indigene*. The Others will help us get away from Starr and his men."

For a moment it seemed like nobody breathed.

"How?" Lucy asked again.

"You—all of you—need to get to the longboat, get it down to the water. Get into the boat and lower it down or cut the lines so it falls into the sea. It won't capsize. You'll be all right. And you'll be rescued quick enough." That much I sensed.

Lucy stared at me. "You mean *we'll* be rescued quick enough."

"Yes, of course," I lied, "but I need to set up the distraction that will make it possible for you to get away. Then I'll join you." I looked at the hold stairs and sighed. "But you have to get up on deck, and we're locked in."

The second boy smiled, fiddled with a seam in his trousers, and held up a thin piece of metal. "I can pick a lock."

WE REVIEWED THE plan and waited. Restless and bored, the children ate most of the food and water while we waited. While I waited. Then . . .

Orders shouted in anger. Responses shouted in fear.

I had a feeling the dark ship had appeared on the horizon and was bearing down on Starr's ship. If the stories had any truth, soon the fog would roll in, hopefully shrouding the deck enough to hide Lucy's and the children's movements as they made their way to the longboat.

The fog would roll in. The ship with its black sails and Sanguinati captain would attack. And the diversion I was about to purchase would ensure freedom for some of us.

I held out my folding knife to the boy who had freed Lucy and me. "It's time."

AS SOON AS the last child slipped out of the hold, I placed the two silver coins in the palm of my hand and held it out. "Corvo Sanguinati said these coins would buy one transaction with the *terra indigene*. I want to make that transaction now—with Fire."

I wasn't sure how this worked. If it took too long for the message to reach the Elemental I'd requested, then Lucy and the children would be caught, and this would be for nothing.

One moment I was alone. The next . . .

The female who appeared in front of me would never be mistaken for human, with her long red hair tipped in yellow and blue. She looked around, then looked at me.

"There are children making their way to the longboat to escape from these very bad men," I said. "We need a distraction, something the men will have to pay attention to instead of the children."

She studied me. "What do you want me to do?"

I took a breath and let it out slowly. "Burn this ship. Set the sails on fire and fill the cargo holds. This ship has weapons and supplies that will explode if touched by fire."

"You will not reach the small boat and escape."

"I know." But neither would Captain Starr. I'd make sure of that much.

I took a step forward, set the coins on the floor between us, then stepped back.

Fire pressed her hand against a wooden crate. The wood smoked. Then it began to burn.

She looked at me and said, "Run."

I scrambled out of the hold just as the sails burst into flames, as the masts ignited.

I hadn't paid attention to the location of the longboat. I hoped one of the boys had and could lead the rest to safety.

Fog blinded me. Smoke choked me. I felt a bitter satisfaction at hearing men shouting, scrambling.

The sea calmed. The wind died. Flames consumed the ship.

I reached the railing and clung to it, uncertain what to do. Then I looked toward the stern—and saw Starr and his first mate rushing toward the longboat that the boys were trying to lower into the sea.

I ran toward them, consumed by anger for Starr and men like him.

"No!" I shouted. "The captain goes down with his ship!"

Starr turned toward me. I grabbed his arm and held on, doing everything I could to stop him from getting into that longboat.

I heard the first mate cry out, glimpsed hands made of fire grabbing the longboat's ropes, burning through them. I heard the children scream as the longboat fell. Heard the splash.

Arms appeared out of two columns of smoke, grabbed the first mate, and threw him overboard.

"You bitch!" Starr roared. His free hand closed around my throat and squeezed.

That was when Fire reached the powder room—and the ship exploded.

I remember flying through the air, surrounded by debris. I remember something grabbing my arms and slowing my plunge into the sea, gently dropping me feetfirst away from the worst of the debris. I remember seeing the longboat moving swiftly, buoyed by water in the shape of a midnight blue steed with a mane the color of surf.

I remember one of Starr's men swimming toward me—and something large and sinuous swimming past. I remember the nightmarish sight of a round mouth full of curved teeth before the creature latched on to the man's chest.

The last thing I remember was hands closing around my arms again and Corvo Sanguinati saying, "You idiotic female. How did your species survive long enough to become such a nuisance?"

WHEN I CAME to, I was wrapped in a blanket and tucked into a bunk in . . .

"Captain's quarters," a voice said. "Captain Crow isn't pleased with you right now, but he insisted on your staying here while you recover."

I focused on the voice, on the face. A pleasant face that held kindness and humor.

"I'm Alano, ship's medic. Including myself, there are only four humans in the crew, and I take care of stitching them up if someone gets careless." He paused. "We don't usually get careless. And we're not usually reckless. You, however, have more than made up for that and have been the subject of great discussion, with the Others speculating about whether this is typical female behavior in humans or if it's just you."

"I didn't do anything."

Alano's eyebrows rose. "You blew up a ship. Well, you paid Fire to blow up a ship, but it amounts to the same thing."

"Doesn't," I said.

"It does," Corvo Sanguinati said.

I hadn't heard him come in, but I saw the humor wash out of Alano's face to be replaced with caution.

"Captain," Alano began, "she needs—"

"To answer a question," Corvo finished. "Why?"

We'd had this conversation before. Funny thing was, my answer was the same.

"You must have known you wouldn't have time to get off that ship, that *burning* ship," Corvo said. "If we hadn't been pursuing Starr's ship when you called on Fire, you would have died."

"Whether Starr reached port and sold us on or I burned the ship, I didn't expect to survive. At least this way, Lucy and the children will have a chance at a new life, a better life. Besides, I sense things about ships and the sea. I had a feeling you were nearby."

Corvo stared at me. So did Alano.

Then the Sanguinati turned to the medic. "Don't let her die."

When Corvo left the cabin, Alano said, "You won't die. You just need some rest."

As I drifted back to sleep, it occurred to me that Alano, like Corvo, had looked at the ruined side of my face and hadn't flinched.

THE FOLLOWING DAY, I was allowed to join Lucy and the children on deck. The girls were subdued, the boys excited. After all, we were on board the dark ship and headed for its home port.

In whispers, Lucy told me about the crew. There were a Hawk, an Eagle, an Owl, a Raven, a Shark, several Sanguinati, the four Intuits—and two males who could take a human form well enough to have arms and legs and perform tasks around the ship. They looked sinuous, especially when they moved, and the disturbing shape of their faces made me think of round mouths full of curved teeth. All Lucy had been told about them was that they were Elders and their form was ancient.

I didn't want to know more.

Alano and the other Intuit men expressed some concern about the children fitting in. All the towns on the islands in the Mediterran were inhabited by Intuits and Others, and I and the twin boys were the only ones with at least some Intuit blood. But word had traveled to those western islands, and by the time the dark ship dropped anchor and we were rowed ashore, there were families from several towns waiting at the docks to take in the children and give them new homes.

Once I was safely ashore, Corvo wished me well and said he was going home to spend time with his family. I wondered if that was his way of discouraging me from having any foolish romantic notions about him, but Alano confirmed that Captain Crow had a wife and children, and that the Sanguinati part of town was a protected, and private, place.

Lucy found work at an inn near the water and found love with Niklaus, one of the Intuit men who sailed with Corvo.

I went inland for a while and worked for a family who grew olives—and learned I was meant for water, not land. So I returned to the sea towns and learned to sail, and I studied to be a medic, and on the day Alano didn't return with the dark ship, having chosen a different kind of life on another island, I applied for the position—and was welcomed by Captain Crow.

I sense things about ships and the sea. That had value to a captain who hunted human predators. My face was valuable, too, when human leaders were required to come aboard to receive a warning. They looked at the ruined side of my face, and they looked at the table, which contained a silent warning to anyone who thought they could buy and sell humans and transport their cargo through the Others' domain.

The candleholders that were evenly spaced the length of the table were made of human skulls, some yellowed and old and some quite new. All had come from men who had escaped human justice.

I especially liked the skull that had a star-shaped indentation in its forehead.

NEW PLACES

Sometimes the Muse needs to find a new place where we can explore ideas with new characters. That's how I ended up meeting Cecily Blanque. Where does Cecily's part of the country fit on a map? I do not know, but I do know the water there makes life, and death, interesting.

FRIENDS AND CORPSES

1

MY NAME IS CECILY BLANQUE. I WORK FOR THE TOWN of Neuterville as a Deceased Reclamation officer—otherwise known as a corpse catcher.

Yes, I've heard all the jokes about our town's name, but you haven't heard the best joke. A couple of generations ago, our local government *voted* to change the town's and county's name to Neuterville from whatever it was in my great-grandparents' day. Maybe it was meant to be a warning so that the government couldn't be sued when some outsider moved into the county and figured out that they were limited to reproducing two children after drinking the water from Deuce Lake for a few years. Why two children? No one knows.

Since the water in other parts of the country is just plain old water, people love to speculate on why *our* water does what it does. Theories range from some kind of toxic weapon dumped here by a foreign power for reasons unknown to aliens from outer space who targeted our town and the surrounding area as the first step toward world domination. Pick a theory; it doesn't matter. Whatever the reason, that aspect of the water can't be filtered out or boiled out or any other thing that is supposed to make water safe to drink. And it *is* safe to drink. It's some of the purest water in the country. It just does what it does. (You want to grumble about a two-child limit? Try living in Bluelight County. The water supply there makes people glow in the dark.)

The other thing Neuterville's water sometimes does is confuse the recently deceased. Some people don't realize they should follow the Exit signs and leave the theater of the living. Some do realize but decide to stay for a few extra days and take in the second show. Either way, if they're alone when they die, they can go on for days—sometimes a couple of weeks—before someone realizes something isn't quite right about their neighbor or elderly aunt.

A congregation of flies is usually a dead giveaway.

That's where I, as a Deceased Reclamation officer, come in. Sometimes luring an animated dead person to the End of Days facility is easy—just gather up the top five books from the priority to-be-read stack and promise the person good lighting, a comfy chair in a refrigerated room, and plenty of quiet time to read. The person remains contained and happy until what kept them ticking takes that last tick—ideally when the person has reached the last sentence of the last book in the stack.

Sometimes one of the animated dead scampers off, unable—or unwilling—to accept gentle confinement during that last turn of the wheel, and a DR officer has to find them, capture them, and bring them to End of Days.

My mother wrinkles her nose whenever she sees me—and yes, even with the protection of the white coveralls DR officers wear on the job, my clothes can be a bit whiffy if I've had to wrestle a corpse into the back of the van—and she never tires of telling me that I have a dead-end job (and she says it with a straight face), despite the good pay and benefits.

Of course, part of her bias about the job might have been influenced by her own mother's refusal to go quietly when the time came. Grandma held off two DR officers for an hour with nothing but a rolling pin in one hand and a frying pan in the other while she shouted, "You'll never take me alive, coppers!"

She might have held them off longer if she hadn't slipped in some essence of Grandma and . . .

Well, the smell when she landed on her butt, splitting the intestines and skin, drove the officers out of her apartment. Temporarily, of course. They returned wearing gas masks and got her wrapped in heavy plastic and bundled into the van, but Grandma is the reason we all carry gas masks in our vehicles. And large sheets of heavy plastic.

Like I said, most of the animated dead don't cause many problems. Usually the team—there are three of us on Neuterville's payroll—only deals with a runaway once a week, if that. So I wasn't expecting any trouble when I reported for duty after a blissfully quiet, odor-free weekend.

Then "Aunt" Vera, my mother's bestest best friend, called the office.

2

VINCE SANTINO HELD OUT THE PHONE'S RECEIVER. "Cecily, that woman is calling again. She called several times over the weekend but insisted she couldn't talk to anyone but you."

I took the receiver from Vince, who stepped away from the desk to give me as much privacy as possible without leaving our small office. If Archie, the third member of the team, had taken the call, he would have had his head pressed against mine in an effort to hear what was said.

"This is Cecily Blanque. How can I help you?"

"Cecily? Thank goodness! Where have you been?"

I recognized the voice, although it wasn't usually this strident. "Aunt Vera?"

"Yes, yes! Now, listen. I'm at that old service station that's just off the main road before the turn into town. Do you know it?"

"Yes, I know it. What are you doing there?"

"I'll explain when you get here. Just get here as soon as you can. Where were you? Your mother says you're always working."

"I was off duty, but a member of the team is always on call," I explained.

"Trust Elvira to get it wrong," Vera muttered.

I hadn't told my mother I would be off duty, because I had wanted a weekend to read fun romances and watch the kind of thriller movies I enjoyed. Mother's idea of useful time off was doing activities that *she* wanted me to do instead of letting me spend the time doing things that I wanted to do.

She lost her ability to control any portion of my life when I moved out of the family home a few years ago, but she persists in thinking her harangues about my work, my friends, and everything else she can glean from my careful sharing of information will convince me to hand over my life for her to do with as she pleases.

Mother has a few issues.

Then again, so does Vera.

I heard an unladylike snort, as if someone had cleared their nose right into the phone. That was followed by a familiar buzzing that produced an uneasy feeling in my stomach. "Aunt Vera, are you . . . ?"

"Not over the phone! Just get here. And bring your van." She hung up.

"Problem?" Vince asked. He took the receiver out of my hand and set it back in its cradle.

"Maybe. Sounds like Vera is having some car trouble. I have to meet her."

Vince frowned. "Why didn't she say something before now? I could have called a tow truck for her. Did she end up spending the weekend in her car?"

"Don't know. I'll find out when I get there."

"Should I tell the boss you're taking a couple of hours of personal time?"

I hesitated. If Archie had been in the office, I might have fibbed. Archie was good at the apprehending part of our work, but he had no ability to keep anything to himself if a juicy detail or two might give him an audience for five minutes. Vince, on the other hand, was discreet.

"I don't know if this is personal or professional," I confessed.

"If you need help . . ." Vince left it at that because the phone rang again.

I hurried to the van and checked the supplies to make sure I had everything I might need, including the large locking container that *no one* referred to as a coffin because the next animated dead person you had to collect could be someone you knew.

The van's only identification was a small logo on the doors. Even so, parking the van anywhere tended to attract attention. Were you going into the diner to pick up sandwiches for the team or to give one of the patrons a lift to the End of Days facility? Or, worse, one of the staff?

Everyone remembers the diner's previous short-order cook. No one realized why he'd become more efficient (he'd stopped going out back for cigarette breaks) until some patrons found a few maggots in their salads. So our citizens were understandably interested in the whys and wherefores whenever they spotted our van.

That was the main reason I parked along the side of the service station instead of pulling up to the door of the convenience-store part of the building. I studied the hand-lettered *Closed for Inventory and Cleaning* sign on the door. Anyone who had ever been inside the place wouldn't believe the *Cleaning* part of the sign, so I hesitated a moment before trying the door. It wasn't locked. I went in and looked around.

"Barney?" I called. "You there?" Barney was the clerk who worked days. Since the door was open, he had to be around somewhere.

"Not here," a voice answered.

"Gus?"

Gus had worked the night shift at the service station for as long as I could remember. It was the sort of place that looked grungy even after it had been cleaned, and the snacks and canned goods that were sold, mostly to travelers, were always a day past their expiration date. But Gus was the guy you wanted working the counter if you weren't old enough to buy a six-pack of beer. He didn't care if you held up your driver's license or your library card. If it had your name on it and looked sufficiently official, that was good enough for him.

"Hey, Gus," I said as I walked toward the counter and cash register. "Have you seen . . ."

Hard to tell what Gus was seeing since he was on the floor, propped up against the spin rack of postcards that were yellow with age. (Who wanted to send an "I went to Neuterville!" post-card to their friends?) The floor around him was littered with empty bags of snacks that were now stuck to the floor, thanks to the congealed blood and other fluids.

Gus grinned and stuffed some corn chips—and a fly—into his mouth. He chewed and swallowed. "Don't have to worry about sodium anymore."

Or anything else. Except bursting. The buttons on his shirt had popped off, and the skin on Gus's belly looked like it was stretched over a basketball. I considered telling him that the normal in and out of food consumption didn't happen in ani-mated dead people, but there didn't seem to be much point. I would, however, suggest that he submit to being wrapped in plastic *before* he ate that one chip too many.

Ignoring the messy exit wound in his chest—evidence that he'd been shot in the back and probably hadn't seen his killer—I said, "A family friend called me from here. Have you seen her?"

"Vera? Sure. She went into the restroom to tidy up."

I walked over to the short corridor that held the restroom and the office. I noticed the blood on the floor, also congealed, leading to the restroom—a clue to what I would find when I knocked on the door.

"Aunt Vera? It's Cecily."

The restroom door opened. Vera frowned at me. "It's about time you got here."

She smelled like it was way past time for a DR officer to get here, but I couldn't say that to Vera.

"I brought the van," I said gently. "I can take you to the End of Days facility. You and Gus."

"You can't take me there yet. Not until we find the miscreant who did this and rescue his wife."

"Rescue his wife? What happened? Did someone run you off the road?" Vera often drove women from another county over to Neuterville for a "book club lunch"—which usually consisted of a dieter's sad salad and a pitcher or two of Neuterville water.

Filling up on food—or talking about books—wasn't the point of these lunches, although there was considerable debate about whether a weekly binge of our water had the same result as living here and being a daily consumer.

It was possible that a spouse who objected to these water-binging lunches had deliberately forced Vera's car off the road. The DR team wouldn't receive notification of a traffic accident if all the people involved were injured but not deceased. If there *had* been casualties but Vera had been the only animated dead person, and if she had scampered off before the police and ambulance arrived, no one would have known about her.

Which made me wonder where she had left her car.

"I was not in an accident, Cecily Blanque," Vera said in her most theatrical voice. She pulled open her coat to reveal a bloody blouse and a hole in her chest. "I was *murdered*."

3

"WHY WOULD SOMEONE MURDER YOU?" IT SEEMED like a reasonable question.

"Does it matter?" Vera countered, no longer meeting my eyes.

That evasion had alarm bells ringing in my head. Mom set great store by Vera Stanton, who had been her bestest best friend since high school, and anything perceived as criticism was met with vitriol. I had learned at a very young age to keep my thoughts and opinions about Vera to myself. That hadn't stopped me from recognizing that the woman was a manipulative liar who loved to slip in a verbal knife whenever she could.

She and Mom played a game I called Make Her Cry, sometimes with other people but mostly with each other. The game boiled down to making cutting remarks under the guise of "teasing" until one of them said something so cruel it made the other one cry. Then the winner would be sympathetic and apologetic about being "too truthful."

I wondered if Vera had played that game with someone who had snapped under the "teasing" and reacted with violence instead of tears.

"Yes," I said, "it does matter, since Gus is sitting out there with a hole in his chest, gobbling snacks." When she didn't say anything, I sighed. "I'll call in the team and the police."

"No police! No, Cecily. They'll side with those *brutes* who live in that hairy-chest county."

She meant the neighboring county to the west of Neuterville, where it was legal to buy booze but not birth control. However, as a kind of balance, the county to the east was a dry county that didn't have a single bar or liquor store but had as many family-planning centers as coffee shops.

"The smarmy body parts just want their fun and don't care what happens if a woman gets pregnant," Vera continued, waving away a persistent fly. "Well, women don't agree with that, and short of feeding rat poison to everything with a penis, they didn't know what to do until a friend—well, more of an acquaintance than a friend—contacted me."

All those helpless women just waiting for Vera to come to

the rescue. That sounded like a story I'd heard before. Unfortunately for Vera, I'd learned at an early age that her brand of hyperbole was spelled *l-i-e*.

"You know I've been doing house parties for a variety of products."

I nodded. Vera supplemented a modest inheritance by selling makeup and jewelry and containers that were supposed to make organizing your kitchen a snap. "And . . . ?" I had a good idea where this was going, considering the evidence around me.

Right off the darn cliff and into more trouble than being shot dead. Or almost dead. Sort of dead.

Vera snorted as the persistent fly tried to climb into her nose. "I started taking orders for bottles of water—much more lucrative than the makeup—and would bring them with me when I did these other house parties. Well, one of the women at the last few parties was *desperate* for my bottles of 'healthy water.'"

"Wait." I held up a hand. "You were selling Neuterville water to women outside this county? Did you fully disclose what *else* this water does if you drink it every day?"

"Well, *that* has never been confirmed, so I saw no reason to add to this woman's distress."

Never been confirmed? I was a Deceased Reclamation officer *because* it had been confirmed that people who drank Neuterville water might experience a delay in realizing they were dead. They were still dead, but the initial stages of the physical breakdown didn't happen as quickly from the neck up, thereby preserving the brain and its ability to continue things like thought, speech, and motor control—at least to some extent. Because of that, the timing of the final demise of animated dead people—or ADPs—could be . . . unfortunate.

Vera pulled her shoulders back, as if daring me to disagree

with her reason for leaving out that little detail about the water. It was hard to tell if the strain on her blouse buttons was due to her being rounder about the middle naturally or if she was starting to bloat. Which she shouldn't have been if this incident happened over the weekend.

Unfortunately, the timetable for the stages of decay wasn't as predictable with ADPs when they were active and out in the wild, so to speak, because the factors that slowed or accelerated decay were constantly changing as the ADP scampered around town.

"Anyway," Vera continued, "the woman's husband actually told her that he was *trying* to get her pregnant with another child, but he was also *trying* to get his mistress pregnant, and if the mistress got pregnant first, he was going to divorce the wife even if he'd gotten her pregnant too."

He didn't sound like he'd win any Good Husband awards, but . . . "So the wife started drinking the water to protect herself from an unwanted pregnancy?"

"Yes, but she didn't think that would be enough to solve her problems." Vera sounded indignant. "I *told* her not to give the water to anyone else. I *told* her."

"But . . . ?"

"She started using it in the coffee maker for the two cups of coffee her husband drank with his breakfast. And when he didn't get his mistress knocked up, he went to a doctor—a *doctor*, can you believe it?—who did some tests and told him he was shooting blanks."

That Neuterville water neutered after two children wasn't a secret. If the man had been drinking two cups of the stuff every day for several months and already had his quota of kids, that probably would have been enough for the shooting-blanks part.

But if he'd been drinking it longer than that, the other effect our water has on some people might have kicked in.

"He figured it out," I said, feeling an odd chill as a couple more flies settled on Vera's bloody shirt.

"He became *enraged*, and then he began chasing that poor woman all over their property, waving a gun and shouting that he wasn't going to be shooting blanks with *that*."

"He shot her?"

"No, he didn't shoot her." She hesitated. "Well, I don't think he shot her. He had a heart attack or something and dropped dead." She hesitated again. "She was *sure* he was dead. Then he started to twitch, and he was still holding the gun, and she didn't know what to do, so she got in her car and called me, and I was supposed to meet her here, but she didn't show up."

"But he did." Another chill went through me. "He showed up, recognized you from the house parties, and started shooting?"

"Yes!"

"But he doesn't know he's dead?"

"He might have figured it out by now," she muttered. "Stupid flies."

"So what we have here is a pissed-off animated dead man *with a gun*, a woman on the run who may have been shot . . ." And might also be a runaway ADP. "And you waited until I came back on duty to tell anyone?"

"The whole thing is delicate, Cecily. And your coworkers . . ."

"Are professionals." I pulled out my cell phone.

"What are you doing? You can't call anyone!" Vera tried to knock the phone out of my hand.

I twisted to avoid her hand and took a step away from her. "I have to call the team. For one thing, we need to transport Gus to the End of Days facility before he eats one corn chip too many. For another thing . . ." I looked over my shoulder at her. "What if this irate man with a gun shoots some innocent by-stander who looks vaguely similar to his wife?"

"Well . . ." She frowned. "Well . . ."

I walked out of the building. The animated dead still smelled dead.

I called the office. "Vince? We have a problem."

More than one, since I was pretty sure that everything Vera had just told me was a lie.

4

I ARRIVED AT THE END OF DAYS FACILITY WITH GUS and Vera. Vince was waiting for me. Archie was out on a call, which was worrying. I hadn't explained much—I was more in-terested in getting my two people to the facility as fast as I could since they had already been dead for a couple of days—or more—but I did emphasize that we might have an armed, angry ADP running around Neuterville.

It was possible that Vera was telling the truth about that. Unlikely, but possible since *someone* had gone to the service sta-tion and shot Gus.

Gus was easy. Once we gave him bags of his favorite snacks, promised he could munch his way to the very end, and gave him his choice of available rooms, he happily settled into the special area at the facility. It was a walled, open-air room that had a big drain in the floor and had raised beds with a variety of flowers, so it looked peaceful—and it provided ADPs with many ways to participate one last time in the circle of life.

The birds knew what it meant when someone settled into

the special area. They also knew there wasn't much time between the last moment of awareness and the facility's staff coming in to gather up the remains before hosing down the area, so
they perched on the walls or in nearby trees—or circled overhead, patiently waiting.

Gus took off his clothes and dropped them in the special
container just inside the door. He put the keys to the service station and his apartment in a small box. His wallet went into a
special bag since it contained all his identification and currency
cards—useful things for us to have now, because we needed
that information to contact next of kin and a person's attorney,
if they had one. Besides, Gus had already been dead long enough
for the contents of his wallet to absorb dead-guy smell. We
didn't need people losing their lunches when we returned Gus's
personal possessions.

Vera refused to sit anywhere but the waiting room because,
she said, she wasn't going to let some hairy chest lock her into a
room until she'd seen justice done. Having met Vera when she
was alive, Vince didn't argue with her. He just called William
Puget, Neuterville's commissioner of health and safety—also
known as our boss.

"Are you sure there's no insanity in your family?" Vince
asked after I told him everything—or at least as much as I'd
been told, which probably wasn't the whole story. It never was
with Vera. And I couldn't shake the feeling that we were being
told a whole bunch of lies so that Vera could carry out some
plan.

"We're not related. She's my mother's best friend from high
school, so she's an honorary aunt." I sounded defensive. Wonder why.

"This is a mess."

"Yep."

"We need a description of the man—and the woman."

"Vera insists that she can't describe him, but she'll know him when she sees him."

Vince stared at me. "What the fuck, Blanque? She would have been looking right at him when he shot her."

"Which doesn't mean she registered things like height or hair color or anything else except that he had a really big gun." I thought for a moment. "Which might be an exaggeration."

Vince shook his head. "Not our job to make the determination, but from what I saw of the exit wound when she removed her coat, I'd say really big gun was accurate."

That was just peachy.

5

WILLIAM PUGET, COMMISSIONER OF HEALTH AND safety, always wore a dark blue uniform and white shirt when he was on duty. He looked impressive. He looked like authority.

He looked madder than a bag of wet cats when he walked in and saw Vera.

"If visitors come to our town and drink our water, that is their choice," Puget said, staring at Vera. "Since many visitors come here for a long weekend every season or use their vacation time to stay a couple of weeks at one of the nearby spa ranches, usually there is only one consequence, if there are any consequences at all. However, *selling* Neuterville water to people outside this county and *not* disclosing *all* the potential consequences of drinking the water over an extended period of time is against the law *and* violates the agreements we have with our neighboring counties that we will not export our water and undermine their chosen way of life."

"Agreements between *men*," she said. "*Women* don't choose that way of life."

Puget hesitated, then resumed the mantle of authority. He had to. Animated dead people in a place where no one knew how to deal with them were no laughing matter, not to mention a health hazard to live people if the animation lasted through the bloat stage until the burst.

"Those who want what our town offers are free to come here," he said.

"Yes," Vera replied. "Those who come here for lunch with friends are met with a fist in the eye when they get home. Is that what you call free?"

"That is regrettable." Puget sounded like he did regret the picture Vera painted. I'd have to tell him about Vera's brand of hyperbole. "But bringing quantities of our water into towns that are unaware of—and unprepared to deal with—*all* the consequences is recklessly endangering the lives of others, and *that* we can't allow."

"Well, what are you going to do?" Vera snapped. "Kill me?"

She always took things a step too far.

Puget's voice turned hard and cold, stripped of all sympathy. "The animated dead person who shot you is now at large in this town, looking for his wife, who may or may not be alive. If she *is* still alive, and if this man kills her, you will be charged with accessory to murder and be secured in a specially designed coffin that allows the natural progression of decay to take place while ensuring that you have absolutely nothing to do until your brain dissolves and dribbles out your ears."

Vera gasped.

A fly flew into her mouth and down her throat.

It did not sound happy to be there. Like buzzing at a window that doesn't provide a way out.

"I really don't know what he looks like," Vera said. "It all happened so fast." Her voice vibrated a bit. Probably courtesy of the fly.

"What about the woman?" Puget asked. "You must have known her well enough to sell her the water. You must know her name, where she lives. You could provide *some* description so that our police can find her before her irate husband does."

"I'll talk to Cecily."

"You'll talk to Ms. Blanque *and* Mr. Santino to make sure you don't try to manipulate a personal connection with one of my officers."

"As if I would."

Commissioner Puget stared at Vera.

I noticed one of her eyes was starting to look cloudy.

Drinking Neuterville water doesn't mean an animated dead person stays animated forever. It just slows down some of the first stages of decay for a few days, allowing a person to remain active and aware while their innards are turning into gaseous goo.

Puget turned that stare on me. "If you and Mr. Santino determine that a drive-around will expedite finding this man, then I'll sanction that decision for twenty-four hours. However, full gear will be required for the ADP."

Vince and I exchanged a look. It would take both of us to get Vera into "full gear," and explaining some of that gear . . .

"Any questions?" Puget asked.

Not any I could ask the man who was my boss. "No, sir."

"Good. Then get this sorted while you have the chance. I'll

talk to our police liaison to make sure everyone is on board to find this individual as quickly as possible."

The Deceased Reclamation department was loosely connected to the police department, but we seldom required a joint effort to apprehend someone. Most of the Neuterville citizens who became animated spent their extra days doing the things they most enjoyed—although residents usually avoided doing things like kneading dough once the skin started to slip. Very conscientious ADPs set out the necessary legal papers in a place that would be easy for their loved ones to find before they puttered their way through their final days.

6

A LOT OF THINGS BOTHERED ME ABOUT VERA'S STORY. Mom once said that Vera never told the whole story about any of her "pranks" unless she was cornered and *had* to tell everything. And that got me thinking about my mother and her best friend.

Shortly after I'd moved into my own place, Sally Small, who is my closest friend, and I had been invited to my mother's house for afternoon coffee and cake—deliberately timed to happen when Vera was staying over for a few days to help Mom deal with empty-nest syndrome. Mom and Vera spent that excruciating hour making their "It's all in fun" cutting remarks about my job and making fun of Sally's last name, even though the Smalls ran one of the best spa ranches in the county and were very well off financially—which was something neither Mom nor Vera could claim and probably a big reason why they never passed up an opportunity to criticize anyone in the Small family.

When Sally and I said goodbye and escaped that afternoon, my friend, who reads psychology books for fun, said, "They have a toxic relationship founded on rivalry and one-upmanship. You know that, right?"

At the time, I'd just shrugged, because I was so conditioned not to say—or think—anything negative about Vera. Sally dropped the subject because she is my friend and doesn't believe in creating unnecessary conflicts between people.

Unlike my mother and Vera.

Yes, I'd shrugged off the comment at the time, too embarrassed by Mom's and Vera's meanness to acknowledge what Sally was trying to tell me. Now I thought hard about a friendship that was more like an addiction and a sharp rivalry driven by a need to win at any cost than a connection between two people who liked each other. I thought about how Vera relished digging up the dirt about someone—which was how Mom learned that Dad had gotten two girls pregnant while he'd been away at university, and how Dad had learned that Mom had "done the deed" with someone else in order to have me since he had already filled his two-child limit.

I thought about how every time Mom or Vera met someone and was giddy as a teenage girl who finally got to date the hot guy, that relationship soured bit by bit as the guy stopped calling for a date, or just stopped calling, and whichever one of them hadn't been dumped hurried over with ice cream, baked goods, and triumphant sympathy.

Husband, wife, mistress. That much of Vera's story was probably true, even if the details were pure fiction.

And if I added a toxic friend into the mix?

Yeah. A lot of things bothered me about Vera's story.

7

AFTER LEADING VERA TO AN INTERVIEW ROOM—
which conveniently doubled as a containment room when
necessary—I walked to the far end of the corridor and used
Vince as a shield since he was taller than me. With his back to
Vera, she couldn't see the expressions on our faces.

"Things aren't adding up."

"Ya think?" Vince replied.

If I made an accusation and was wrong, my mother would be
furious, and I would have to deal with the fallout for a long time.
Problem was, I was pretty sure I might not be totally right, but I
also wasn't wrong. "We need to send Archie and a police officer
to the service station to find Vera's car and look in the trunk."

"For . . . ?"

"Barney, the day clerk. Gus worked nights. Has for years. If
this happened over the weekend, where is Barney, who should
have shown up for work and noticed something was wrong? If
nothing else, he should have noticed Gus sitting there dead,
stuffing himself with corn chips."

"Fuck," Vince said quietly. "Did you see her car when you
drove into the service station?"

"No, but I glimpsed a car in a service bay on the garage side
of the building. It could be Vera's."

"Let's get Vera's statement since it's supposed to be a team
effort. But first, I'll contact Archie and inform Commissioner
Puget that additional police assistance may be required at the
service station. Anything else?"

"Just follow my lead."

"Oh, I'll be right behind you, Blanque."

Chivalry wasn't dead. It just knew when to use someone else as a shield.

"A DIAPER?" VERA sounded outraged. "You expect me to wear an adult diaper? Why would I agree to that?"

"Leakage," I snapped. "If you're going to ride in the front of the van with me in order to find this guy, you have to be properly suited up, and that includes an adult diaper, because hitting a bump in the road at your stage of dead could get messy."

That was another thing that bothered me. If whoever killed Vera also killed Gus, why weren't they at the same stage of decay on the ADP timeline? And if Vera had been killed before she drove to the service station to contact me, then who shot Gus?

"There is the alternative," Vince said, sounding so conciliatory I wanted to smack him.

"What alternative?" Vera jumped on the suggestion.

I just wanted to jump on something. Like Vince's head. "Yeah, Vince. What alternative?"

"Vera could write a check to the Deceased Reclamation office for five thousand dollars to cover the cost of thoroughly cleaning the inside of the van if she does experience leakage— or a burst." He looked sympathetic. "It's very expensive to do a thorough cleaning after . . . you know. It's not just steam-cleaning the seats and carpets; it's taking apart the vents and everything else that might end up with tiny particles of biohazardous material. So you write us a check. I'll take it down to the bank and deposit it, and as soon as it clears, you and Cecily can ride around looking for your friend—and her deceased, on-the-lam husband." Vince smiled as if relieved he could offer this solution.

So we were playing good corpse catcher, bad corpse catcher? Clearly Vince had called dibs on being the good guy.

"I don't have that kind of money just sitting around!" Vera protested. Then she switched to being huffy. "Besides, I don't have my checkbook with me."

"I could fetch it for you," I offered. "But even after we cash the check, you'll still have to be fully suited up—including the adult diaper." Before she could start playing the "if I'd had a daughter" mind games that she often aimed at me, I pulled out a small notebook and mini pen from my coveralls pocket and said, "While you're deciding, I need information. What's the name of your friend? Where does she live?"

"What does it matter? She's not there *now*."

"We don't go anywhere until we have her name." I stared at Vera. "She's your friend—or a business acquaintance at the very least. You sold her lots of bottles of Neuterville water while doing your other parties. You have to know the woman's name and her address."

"The makeup parties weren't at her house."

"Then you held them at the house of someone else in the same town, and that person might know your friend's address. What's the name of the town?"

"I don't remember." Vera delicately touched her temple. "I think I have some memory loss."

I noticed the way the skin moved on her fingers, as if she were wearing a loose protective glove.

"You said her husband, the man you claim shot you and is now running around Neuterville armed and dangerous and dead, was trying to get the woman pregnant *again*. That means there are other children in that household. How old are they? In high school? Grade school? Still in diapers? If the woman is here and still alive, we have to find her and get her back to her children. If she's dead, those children are now orphans who have been without their parents, have been without any adult care for several days, since *you* delayed informing *anyone* about this. Where are the children, Vera? We have to alert the authorities in that town."

"I don't know what you're talking about."

I stared at her. "You don't give a damn about the children—if there are any children, and that's not part of the bucket of lies you've been spilling on me since you asked for my help."

"I don't lie, Cecily!"

Toxic relationship. One-upmanship. Rivalry.

How many people had been caught in the crossfire of this particular game? Gus, certainly. Barney too? More?

"But you also never tell the truth, do you? All you're really interested in is finding the man. Or are you looking for the person who called his wife and told her he was screwing around and you were the other woman? Called her and got her riled enough to bring a gun to the party?" My smile must have looked scary—or deranged—because I heard Vince suck in a breath. A shallow breath since we were in an interview room, and Vera was definitely heading for the high side of whiffy. "Did she drop the gun after she realized she not only killed you but her husband as well? Did you pick it up and drive to town, choosing the service station as a place to hide while you figured out what sort of story you could spin? Did you shoot Gus because he realized you were an animated dead person and he was going to call the DR office so that someone could come and help you—someone you already knew wouldn't be me because you'd tried to reach me earlier that day and was told I wasn't available?"

"Bull's-eye," Vince whispered, seeing the change in Vera's expression.

Because I'd been conditioned since childhood to believe what Vera said, I'd initially accepted that she and Gus were victims of the same shooter—something my colleagues wouldn't have done, even with the blood and bullet hole as proof.

She'd counted on my acceptance, counted on me not challenging her because of her connection to my mother. That was why she'd waited until I came back to work before informing anyone of the shootings.

Toxic relationship. One-upmanship. Rivalry.

Or had she waited so that I, Elvira Blanque's daughter, would be the DR officer caught up in this twisted game?

Sickened by the thought, I hesitated a moment too long when Vera lunged across the table, reaching for me.

Vince didn't hesitate. He'd been easing the door open in preparation for a fast exit as soon as he realized we had been played. When Vera lunged, he flung open the door, yanked me out of my chair, and shoved me into the corridor. The moment he was out of the room, he spun around to push the door closed just as Vera hit the door with her full weight in an effort to escape.

I joined in the door-pushing effort while Vince shouted for help.

Vera gave the door a hard shove, enough for her hand to get through the opening and grab my wrist.

I screamed in anger—or maybe panic—and jerked my arm out of reach.

She screamed too, pulling her hand back inside the room a moment before Vince secured the door.

I stared at the skin hand that slid off my wrist and plopped on the floor.

"Well," Commissioner Puget said as he joined us, "with that

much skin slippage, it looks like Vera isn't as freshly dead as she claimed to be."

8

VINCE FILLED A PLASTIC CUP WITH WATER AND handed it to me, having decided—correctly—that my hands were shaking too much to hold anything made of glass.

"Not your fault, Blanque," Vince said. "We didn't know about any of this until Vera made contact with you."

"Depending on how long the man had been drinking Neuterville water, there might be an animated dead person running around in a neighboring county."

"How long do Vera's affairs usually last?" Vince countered.

"A few months."

"Possibly long enough for him to be temporarily shooting blanks if he already has two kids, but definitely not long enough for him to become an animated dead person. Assuming he was drinking Neuterville water at all."

"Yeah, there is that." There was also the question of why Vera had been hiding out at the service station instead of asking her bestest best friend for help.

Commissioner Puget walked into the break room. "Officers."

Bad news. Bad, bad news. "You found Barney," I said.

"At the service station, in the trunk of Vera's car." Puget's voice held anger he had under ruthless control. "Most likely, Barney was killed yesterday morning when he reported for work. He is not ADP—and he wasn't shot."

I looked at my boss. "Gus and Barney weren't killed by some rampaging animated dead man from another town."

"I agree." Puget blew out a breath. "Blanque, the police are bringing your mother in for questioning." He held up a hand as if I'd protested. "We need answers, and we're not likely to get those answers from Vera Stanton. Maybe, under the circumstances, your mother will tell us things she was told in confidence."

I drank the water and set the cup aside. "You'll need a hammer. Mom will slither and slide around any questions to do with Vera. That's what she's always done. Slither and slide and take Vera's side—even when doing that ended her marriage to my father. You'll need a hammer to get the truth—or some form of truth—out of Elvira, and I'll need to wield it." I swallowed and wondered if there had been ground glass in that water. Sure felt like it. "And then . . ." I hesitated, remembering other vitriolic episodes when I'd expressed the smallest doubt about Vera.

Puget looked like a thunderstorm about to break. "You think your mother will hurt you?"

"Physically? No. Disown me? Yeah. I expect it will come to that."

"I can question her," Vince said. "No skin off me if she snubs me forever."

"No, you can't. I appreciate the offer, but like Commissioner Puget said, we need answers fast, and I know which buttons to push to get them."

"Whatever you need from us, we'll do," Puget said.

"Thank you, sir."

He nodded. "I'll let you know when your mother is brought to an interview room at the police station."

"What happened to the skin from Vera's hand?" I asked.

"It's in an evidence bag," Vince replied. "Why?"

"I'll need that too."

9

COMMISSIONER PUGET AND A POLICE DETECTIVE WERE standing on either side of the interview room door. I was sitting at the table. So was Elvira Blanque. My mother.

The men had offered—again—to do the questioning. I thanked them—again—and turned down their offer. I was a DR officer, not a cop. What I said didn't have to be taken as official since I could claim, legitimately, that I didn't know all the nuances of the law. This was more like reality TV when people go off script and there's no one around to yell, "Cut!"

Besides, one look at Mom and the telling bruise on her temple, and I knew why Commissioner Puget looked worried about me doing this interview and why the detective's eyes held pity.

Elvira gave me the Glare, then aimed her questions at the men. "What am I doing here? Why am I being treated like a criminal?"

"You are a criminal," I replied. "What we need to determine is if you're an accessory to murder before or after the fact."

"What? *What?*"

"When did Vera start using phrases like 'hairy-chest county' and 'smarmy body parts' to insult the men in the neighboring county?" I asked, sounding like we were chatting in the kitchen at her home. "About the same time she got a new hairstyle and bought some breasts-and-bum fuck-me clothes? She tended to make disparaging remarks when she was interested in something or someone—as if none of us had clued into that behavior. At least we know where to start looking for her victim. Or victims. See, we need to determine how long she'd been having an affair with *this* married man. Because Vera liked to target married men, didn't she? 'How married is he?' was her personal slogan. You preferred men who weren't officially single but weren't going home to sleep with their wives after spending the evening with you."

"You don't know what you're talking about." Elvira glanced at the men. "And you shouldn't be airing our dirty linen in public. It's unseemly, Cecily."

"I've kept some of your secrets for a long time because you're my mother. Now? With what's at stake? I will make banners of our family's dirty linen and string them up on Main Street if that's what it takes to prevent another death."

"I don't know—"

"After Vera was shot and became an animated dead person, she killed two other people, and she did it because of the affair she was having with a married man in another county. Who is he, Mom? Where does he live? Vera would have told you, would have bragged about how she could still bag a man while sympathizing that you couldn't hold on to the one you'd married—and you couldn't net any of the ones you had dated since Dad left."

Mom looked horrified. Then she looked furious that I would reveal her struggle to find a new man. Except at our last weekly dinner, Mom had said she would be out of town the following Thursday, and I would have to make do with Sally's company. Then she took a call from Vera and was all giddy and gushing about going on a happy holiday with "her friend" for a couple of days and how, after that, even Vera's makeup and do-over party wouldn't be enough to make "chubby wifey" sufficiently attractive.

The timing fit too damn well.

"When Vera called this past weekend looking for me, did she tell you she was killed by her enraged lover after someone made a tell-all phone call to his wife?" I waited a beat. "Or maybe it was the wife who killed Vera and that no-good cheating husband who had caught your eye as well. You don't usually target the same man, but this time? Did it turn into a game of 'You saw him first, but I can steal him'?"

"I don't know what you're talking about."

"If the woman did kill her husband, is there another relative who can take the children when the wife goes to prison?"

"What children? Cecily! You're talking crazy! Vera would never endanger children."

"Really? She wasn't concerned about my welfare when she confessed to having the affair with Dad that crashed your marriage. Then again, she claimed Dad wasn't my biological father because he'd sowed his wild oats when he was in college and filled his quota of children before he returned to Neuterville and married you. Did she give you enough hints that you figured out why you weren't getting pregnant? Did she help you find a guy who looked enough like Dad that people wouldn't ask questions?"

"Vera is my friend. You have no right to say such awful things about my best friend." The words were a warning for me to back off.

I didn't back off. Torch the bridges and let the flames light up the sky. "The thing is, after I left home and could make phone calls without you listening in on the extension, I called Dad to give him my new address and phone number. And I asked him if I had any half siblings. Turns out I don't. But you were still happily married to Dad, and Vera had just had another fiancé back out of an engagement, so she lied about Dad's wild oats just to hurt you and balance the scorecard somehow—just like she won points when you'd gone out and gotten pregnant by another man. Just like she won points years later when she'd tearfully confessed to having an affair with Dad—which he strenuously denied, by the way—but Vera was your bestest friend, so you sided with her like you always did, and she was there to comfort you when Dad finally left and filed for divorce."

Torch the bridges. Light up the sky. "You and Vera have been accomplices and enablers to each other's schemes since high school, getting high off the hurt and harm you do to each other as well as the people around you. When you made the phone call last week to your lover's wife in order to cause trouble for Vera since she probably teased you about making a play for him herself, I'm sure you didn't anticipate people being murdered. A bust-up between Vera and your shared lover? Absolutely. A wrecked marriage that can be laid at her door? Bonus points. But now you and Vera are involved in murder. You have to know the name of the woman you called. You have her phone number at the very least. Tell us what you know. It might save someone's life."

I gambled—and I lost. Mom's loyalty to Vera—or to their twisted, toxic games—meant more to her than any other consideration.

"I want to discuss this with Vera," Mom said. "You're making things up, trying to put her in a bad light."

"Vera isn't going to have visitors. She's at the End of Days facility in a containment room." I grabbed the evidence bag that I'd set on the floor beside my chair and slapped it on the table. "Vera is falling apart. Literally."

Mom glanced at the evidence bag, and there was a moment of fierce glee in her eyes.

"You," I continued, "can still be prosecuted to the full extent of the law. However you want to spin it, you started the chain of events that ended with Vera, Gus, and Barney being killed."

"You are an unnatural child." Mom stared at me, cold and accusing. She shifted her stare to Puget and the detective. "I will discuss these vile accusations with my lawyer. He will be in touch."

"Give us his name, and we'll give him a call," Puget said. "Let him know you're here."

"I'm not staying here!"

I didn't have to look at the men to know their stares were equally cold and accusing.

"You're not going anywhere," the detective said.

That wasn't quite true, but no one was going to discuss the transfer while I was still in the room.

"Officer Blanque," Puget said.

I grabbed the evidence bag, pushed back my chair, and walked out of the room.

"You're not my child!" Elvira shouted as the door closed. "No child of mine would say such vile things about me or my friend!"

After I handed over the evidence bag, Commissioner Puget walked me out of the police station.

"I'm sorry it was rough for you, Blanque."

"She didn't give us the woman's name or the town," I said. Right now, I felt emotionally numb, and I was glad for that. The hurting would come later.

"We'll access her phone records and find the woman that way. We'll find out the truth of what happened."

I hoped he was right. All we had right now was a mess of lies and counter-lies.

"Cecily . . . ," Puget said.

I shook my head. "There is something I need to do. Let me pretend a little while longer."

10

"WE DON'T KNOW WHO WE'RE LOOKING FOR," VINCE said as he and I headed out in the van to canvass the town's main streets, "and the animated dead don't usually scamper around where they're easily seen."

"Neuterville residents don't," I agreed. "But I'm not even sure there is an ADP on the loose, since Vera is the one who told us about him. That's not why we took the van. We're going to Elvira's house."

"Why?"

"Because there are some things stored in the attic that I don't want to lose, and this will be my only chance to get them." I hesitated, but Vince was a friend as well as a coworker. "I have keys to the house, so the first thing she'll ask her lawyer to do is call a locksmith and have all the locks changed—if for no other reason than to stop me from finding whatever she hasn't hidden yet that might prove her involvement in this mess."

He gave me a sharp look, then focused on the road. ADPs were notorious for crossing the street without looking both ways. No longer needing to worry about getting killed turned some of them into daredevils who went out and played in traffic.

"How long have you known that your dad wasn't . . . ?" Vince frowned.

"Maybe wasn't. When I talked to him after getting my own place, he said he'd take the DNA test if I needed to be sure, but as far as he was concerned, I was his daughter. Full stop." I looked out the van's passenger window, pretending that I was scanning for an animated dead person I was sure we wouldn't find. "Vera sent me up to the attic one afternoon when she was visiting and my mom wasn't home, claiming that she'd left a box of her stuff up there since her apartment was too small to store anything extra. While I was searching for the box, I 'found' a folder on top of a box of my old books. Letters. Kissy notes on paper napkins. A report from a PI confirming that the man I'd thought was my dad had gotten two girls pregnant while he was away at school and bailed on both of them. There were also letters between Vera and my mom, being very forthcoming about Vera helping Mom find a 'substitute' who looked enough like my dad that there wouldn't be any comments. The thing is, I'm pretty sure Vera created the letters and the kissy notes as supporting evidence of Dad's bad behavior, and I'm sure the PI report was faked because the PI's name on the letterhead belonged to a detective from an old noir movie. I'm not sure Elvira ever slept with the substitute she and Vera had found but just said she had as a kind of brag—and never considered that Vera would tell my dad as a way to sour the marriage."

"She really is a piece of work."

Which one? Mom had a vindictive streak. It was usually short-lived, but it was fierce while it lasted. She might be sorry for her actions later, but later was always too late to fix the damage.

That was why I knew Elvira would blame me for any trouble that landed on her doorstep because of Vera's actions. After all, nothing that happened after Vera arrived in town would have happened if I'd been at work, which was where she thought I would be.

As Vince backed the van up the driveway of my mother's house, curtains twitched in the neighbors' houses. In a couple more minutes, someone would find an excuse to step outside and do a little friendly snooping.

"I'll lay out some fresh plastic in the van and then help you load up the boxes," Vince said. "There wasn't time for a thorough cleaning after you brought in Gus and Vera."

I unlocked the front door, walked into the house . . . and stopped when I saw the hall closet door wasn't properly shut. Mom always said a door that was open invited people to snoop, and she went ballistic whenever a closet door wasn't closed.

Vince walked in. "Blanque?"

"Vera wasn't wearing her own coat," I said as I opened the closet door all the way and studied the coats. "If she'd been wearing her coat when she was shot, it would have been damaged, would have been bloody like her blouse."

"Okay."

"Vera was wearing my mom's coat, the one she said looked like a carpetbag. It didn't match her outfit, and she was always fussy about that, but she'd counted on everyone not noticing that once she'd dramatically revealed the bullet holes and announced that she'd been murdered. And she was right. I didn't notice—until now."

"If she came here first, why go to the service station at all?" Vince eased past me to look at the living room—to look for clues.

"She's here often enough that neighbors would recognize her car. Besides . . ."

I hurried through the house and started up the stairs to the attic. I wasn't a "saver," as we politely called some of the ADP folks who resisted leaving their homes for way too long, but I did have a few boxes of favorite books from childhood, and there was a box of my clothes Mom claimed she had kept for sentimental reasons. Boxes were neatly stacked, with the name of the person written on the side in big black lettering.

I would take the boxes because that was my excuse for being here, but I had another reason for checking the attic—and I found part of the answer when one foot slipped on a stair and I pitched forward, banging my knee before I caught myself with my hands. I eased down a few steps and studied the stair.

"Blanque?" Vince asked.

I held up a hand to stop him before he started up the stairs. "Part of that stair has been greased." I gave him a moment to consider that. "Mom had a thing about stairs. She wouldn't go up the middle. She went up on one side and down on the other side. Not something you would notice on a public staircase, since everyone goes up one side and down the other, but only someone who spent a lot of time with her in the house would realize she did it at home." I looked at Vince. "Only half the stair is greased—the side she would use when she came down, most likely in a hurry." And Vera had been in the house. Taking Mom's coat proved that.

"Crime scene," Vince said.

Did I want to see what was in the attic enough to possibly mess up a crime scene?

"They'll find traces of me here anyway. You stay below the greased stair. I'm going to see what Vera left in the attic."

I hauled all the "Cecily" boxes to the attic stairs, then carefully handed them to Vince so that we both avoided the greased stair. Having completed my excuse, I looked around to see if I could identify whatever Vera had left up here as bait.

I stared at the box that had been pulled to one side instead of being neatly stacked with the others. It had been labeled "Vera" but someone had made a clumsy effort to change the name to "Elvira." I argued with myself over whether I should take the box or call the detective who was working with Commissioner Puget.

I took the box. Unlike the other boxes that were used to store things in the attic, this box had been taped shut, and someone had tried, unsuccessfully, to pull off all the heavy-duty packing tape. While it wasn't likely, all things considered, there was still a possibility that the box and whatever it contained would disappear before the police could obtain a warrant to search the house. Assuming they needed a warrant under the circumstances.

I picked up the box and grunted a little as I walked toward the stairs. I wasn't sure what the box contained, but it wasn't light.

"Be careful with this one," I said when Vince returned from carrying my boxes to the van. I turned my body enough so that he could see the label. "Be careful," I repeated.

"Are we going to turn that one in?" he asked, taking the box from me.

"Yes. But maybe we're going to look through it first."

He didn't point out looking through potential evidence might be considered interference and could get us both in trouble. He just took the box down to the van.

It hadn't taken long to clear out the remnants of my life in my mother's house.

I went into the kitchen and saw enough to guess what had happened, based on watching these two women for so many years. Vera sneaking into the house to set things up before Elvira returned home, and then calling her bestest friend, sounding angry or frantic or scared, telling Elvira she had hidden some evidence in the attic that would prove Elvira had killed her lover in a jealous rage after he dumped her in the middle of their romantic getaway. Elvira running up the attic stairs and finding the box. Unable to tear through the heavy-duty packing tape, she runs down the stairs to get the scissors in the kitchen, slips on the greased stair, and bangs the back of her head hard enough to cause a serious injury—an injury that probably affected her balance and was the reason she fell in the kitchen, hitting her temple on a corner of the island when she went to fetch the scissors.

Whatever else happened in between the time of that fatal fall and when the police showed up to bring her in for questioning, she didn't go back up to the attic.

I took the set of keys for Vera's apartment before I left Elvira's house. Vera didn't live in the town of Neuterville. She was still in the same county, but her apartment complex was in the next village—a gated community with a swimming pool and tennis courts and other amenities for the residents.

As we drove there, I called Commissioner Puget to let him know I had the keys to Vera's apartment and a box I had taken from Elvira's house that might hold evidence of . . . something. I gave him the four-digit code for the keypad at the gate—a code that was attached to the key ring since Mom never remembered it when she was supposed to go over and water plants when Vera was away. And I gave him the address because I didn't remember seeing Vera's purse and didn't know if the police officers had found any ID on her.

I really hoped whoever had to pat her down was fully suited up in the event some bio excitement occurred during the process.

11

VINCE PUNCHED IN THE NUMBERS I GAVE HIM, AND we drove to Vera's apartment complex, parking behind another white van with a police logo that was nowhere near as discreet as our DR logo.

Since there were already police cars from Neuterville and the village where the gated community was located, as well as cars from the security company that watched over the community, our van—and its logo—kind of disappeared.

I hopped out of the van and hurried toward what looked like a heated argument between the Neuterville police and the security company guards over entering Vera's apartment without a warrant, which the police didn't really need since Vera lived alone and was deceased. Except it got tricky with an ADP since their faculties were still intact, more or less, and they weren't all-the-way dead even if their bodies were slip-sliding away, so entering an animated dead person's home without permission was a gray area.

"Detective?" I called, waving the keys. "Since Vera Stanton is a friend of the family, I'm just going in to water her plants and make sure the stove is turned off. Would you like to come in and help me check out the apartment, make sure everything is right and tight while she's away?"

"Thank you, Ms. Blanque. I'm happy to help."

I smiled at the security guard. "My mom usually takes care of the plants when Vera is away, but she's currently unavailable, so I said I would do it."

The detective coughed and came in after me, along with a couple of his officers.

"You know what we're looking for?" he asked.

"Nope." I handed him the keys. "I catch corpses. You catch bad people. I'm going to water the plants. You can lock up when you're done."

He gave me a long look. "Point of information. Barney died of blunt force trauma. A savage attack. We found that weapon, but we're still looking for the gun that killed Vera Stanton and Gus."

I took a deep breath. "I found a suspicious box in my mom's attic and took it to make sure it wouldn't disappear. And I discovered that one of the attic stairs was greased. Fortunately, I was going up instead of down when I discovered that. You should also take a look at the kitchen." I hesitated. "I'd like to see what's in the box in case it's nothing more than embarrassing lingerie."

The detective studied me. Neither of us thought I would find lingerie in that box. "One of my officers will look through it with you. That's for your protection." He signaled to the female officer who came in with him. "Wear gloves."

"Yes, sir."

I quickly watered the plants before the officer and I went out to the van. Vince opened the back doors and said, "Give it a minute to air out."

Yeah. Dead person was a scent that tended to linger.

I was going to have to figure out where to store the boxes I'd taken from the attic. Maybe I could rent a cleaned room at End of Days where I could go through my old stuff while it aired out.

Vince moved the Vera/Elvira box close to the open door, produced a pocketknife, and slit the tape holding the box closed. Then he stepped back and let the officer open the box.

Miscellaneous junk as far as I could see, with two exceptions:

the coat Vera must have been wearing when she was shot—and the gun.

"Fuck," Vince said quietly when he leaned in to take a look. "Cecily . . ."

"Not now. Doesn't matter." And it didn't matter. Couldn't matter yet.

I took the keys to Elvira's house off my key ring and handed them to the officer. "The detective will need those now—or whenever he gets clearance to enter the house. I don't live there anymore, so I'm not sure if I can give that authorization while Elvira is ADP."

The officer eyed the other boxes.

"Those have some of my things," I said, answering the question she didn't ask.

"We'll take them to End of Days and store them there until Blanque has a chance to look through them," Vince said.

"The detective and Commissioner Puget are welcome to open the boxes and take a look," I told the officer.

She nodded. "I'll let them know."

We waited while she fetched the detective and showed him what was in the Vera/Elvira box. They took that box to their own van, and Vince and I drove back to End of Days.

12

ELVIRA BLANQUE WAS FURIOUS WITH EVERYONE, ES-pecially with me for not being at End of Days when the police and Commissioner Puget transferred her to the facility. Because of her "excitability," she'd been put in an interview room that had walls on either side of a table that was bolted to the floor. Above the table was a see-through shield that had a small opening where papers could be passed back and forth and a circle of small holes so that people could talk without shouting.

It was the room where final legal details were settled or friends and family got the last chance to visit.

When I arrived at End of Days, I was told Elvira's lawyer had been fired because he had dared to enter the room wearing a protective mask.

One more thing to do.

I walked into the room and sat in the chair on the other side of the table.

Elvira glared at me. "If you're not going to be around when I need you, don't bother coming around at all."

Same old, same old.

"We found Vera's coat and the gun," I said. "They were hidden in your attic."

"I don't know what you're talking about."

Yes, she did. Vera had made sure of that.

"It doesn't matter if Vera was already having an affair with the man you were meeting for a fun weekend or if she was making a play for him to spoil things for you. Either way, when you realized you might end up sharing him with your bestest best friend, you called your lover's wife and aimed her at Vera. The police will figure out who shot Vera. Someone did, and she was pissed off because she figured out why. Was someone else shot? Is that how she ended up with the gun? Again, the police will figure it out. What matters is that Vera used the gun to kill Gus, then went to your house before you returned home and planted the evidence to make it look like you were responsible for the shootings. Was she watching the house, or did she guess when you would get back from your tryst? Either way, she called and told you about the gun hidden in the attic, and you went running up the stairs to find it."

"I don't know what you're talking about."

"Vera greased the attic stair. That's what caused you to fall and hit your head the first time."

"You're making things up. I want to talk to Vera."

"She burst," I lied. "She's gone."

"Gone?"

"Gone."

It gave me chills to see my mother look so viciously happy.

"Then I won," Elvira said. "I finally got one over on her!" She smacked her hand on the table and left a little skin.

"Yeah, Mom. For what it's worth, you won."

"Now go out and talk to those fools so that I can go home."

Was this denial, or did she really not know? "You died, Mom. You suffered some kind of brain bleed, and you died. You can't go home. The people here will make you as comfortable as possible, but you won't be leaving. You might want to ask them to call your lawyer and have him come back to review your last wishes."

She stared at me. "If you leave me here, you'll get nothing."

"I wasn't expecting anything," I replied as I rose and headed for the door. "I always thought you would leave everything to Vera."

"She always said you were an ungrateful daughter!"

I didn't turn around, and I didn't answer. I had nothing to prove to either of them.

Commissioner Puget waited for me outside the room. "You're on paid leave, starting now."

"For how long?"

"A few days." He glanced at the room. "Until things are resolved."

"It will leave the team down one person."

"Vince and Archie will handle it." Puget's voice softened. "You've had a rough day, Blanque. Go home—and stay home. I'll call you when it's done."

I went home, took a long hot shower, got into my comfiest clothes—and took care of the last task.

"Dad? It's Cecily. There's something you need to know."

13

SALLY SHOWED UP AN HOUR LATER WITH A HUGE ORder of spaghetti and meatballs, garlic bread, and salad, courtesy of Santino's Restaurant.

"Vince talked to his folks, then called me," Sally said, hauling the food into my kitchen and bustling around to set the table. "The Santinos send their condolences—and enough comfort food to last you a few days."

Touched by their concern, I blinked away tears and tried to make a bad joke. "They forgot the chocolate."

"Don't be daft. You don't put chocolate on garlic bread or spaghetti. That goes on the ice cream." Sally opened another bag and set out chocolate syrup, chocolate sprinkles, and chocolate candies. Then she shoved two containers of ice cream into my little freezer.

We ate. We watched a sappy movie Sally had brought because, she said, it was a perfect excuse to cry.

Finally, Sally said, "Why don't you come to the spa for a few days? You can ride horses, swim in the pool, get a massage, take a yoga class, walk in the meditation garden." She waited a beat before adding, "And you can graze at the buffet tables for every meal and never have to wash the dishes."

"Thanks, I might do that—once I run out of spaghetti." I fiddled with the hem of my sweatshirt. "You were right about them. Toxic friends who wrecked each other's lives to prove . . . something."

"They wrecked a lot of lives, not just their own," Sally said gently. "But you'll be okay."

"Yeah, I will be." I sighed. "Did you bring any other movies?"

She reached into her enormous purse and pulled out the other movie.

I blinked. "Zombies? Really?"

"Thrills. Chills. Bodies that blow up. And the good guys win."

Sometimes Sally knew me better than I knew myself. "Put it in the player. I'll get the ice cream—and the chocolate."

POTPOURRI

I call this section Potpourri because it is a mix of stand-alone pieces.

I wrote "The Day Will Come" a few days after 9/11.

"Truth and Story" was part of my Guest of Honor speech at Thylacon in Tasmania.

A piece of music performed at a philharmonic concert inspired the phrase "stands a god within the shadows." That phrase became woven with the idea of a "Lady of Shalott" character in a postapocalyptic world.

"She Moved Through the Fair" had its roots in the folk song by the same name and then took its own turn in the telling of a ghost story.

I was invited to write a YA science fiction story around the same time that three things tapped into my creative well—a quote by Chief Seattle about humankind being one strand in the web of life; the game *SimPark* (which I *always* lost); and a bumper sticker that said, "One Earth, One Chance." I wondered what would happen if you could have a second chance, and my answer was the story "A Strand in the Web."

THE DAY WILL COME

THE DAY WILL COME WHEN THE LAST CHUNK OF concrete and the last piece of steel are hauled away, and there will be empty space where something that was both structure and symbol had been.

The day will come when those who walk near that place will not see the ghost of what was because their eyes cannot see what their hands never touched.

The day will come when there are those among us who do not need to forget because they were too young to remember.

The day will come.

That's why we must hold on to the stories.

We have heard news reports, facts, rumors, details, speculations. We watched a nightmare happen through the camera's eye. We felt numb, and we felt pain, and we felt so much we didn't know how to feel anymore.

We had facts, little blocks of information. Now we are also hearing the stories: the person who stepped out of a subway station into a world of dust and rubble; the people who watched from their office windows, unable to do anything but stand as witnesses; phone calls made to give warning; phone calls made to say good-bye.

In the end, it will be the stories that help us remember and understand and connect with those who came before us and those who will come after. It is the stories that will hold people's thoughts and feelings in words so that a moment in history cannot be looked at from the safe distance of facts.

Share the stories. Write them down before memory is dimmed by healing. Tell the stories to help others understand and remember. Honor the stories. They are our humanity.

The day will come when there will be those among us who do not know the significance of September 11, 2001.

History will give them the facts about that day.

Stories will show them the heart.

—September 14, 2001

TRUTH AND STORY

TRUTH WAS A BEGGAR. HE WORE RAGS THE POOR-
est man in town wouldn't wear. He begged for scraps of
food. He slept wherever he could find shelter.

When Truth approached the people in the town to tell them
the things he knew, they would turn their backs on him, or cross
the street, or go into their houses and close the doors.

After a while, Truth noticed there was a woman in the town
whom everyone wanted to talk to. People greeted her on the
street, and she was welcome in all of their homes, from the
poorest shack to the finest mansion. Sometimes her clothes were
simple, sometimes elegant, sometimes frivolous, and sometimes
fantastic.

Truth didn't know who she was, but he knew she was very
special.

One night, when Truth was wandering through the streets
looking for something to eat, he passed one of the mansions
where there was a party going on. He peeked into the window
and saw all the people laughing and talking, saw the banquet
table loaded with all kinds of wonderful food. He knew if he

knocked on the door, they wouldn't let him in, so he sat on the steps, in the cold, shivering in his rags.

After a while, the door did open. The woman came out, sat down beside him, and asked him why he was sitting out there in the cold.

So Truth told her about how people didn't want to listen to him, how he wasn't welcome in any of their homes.

The woman thought about this and then said, "Why don't we become partners? My name is Story."

And so, from that day to this, Truth and Story have been partners—and they are welcome wherever they go.

STANDS A GOD WITHIN
THE SHADOWS

1

HESITANT TO LEAVE THE SAFETY OF MY BEDROOM, where the windows were shuttered on the outside and let in nothing except a little light and the illusion of fresh air, I hovered in the doorway that opened onto the main chamber of my prison. It was a large, well-furnished room with comfortable chairs, a sofa, and tables of various shapes and sizes. The overlapping carpets were thick enough to challenge the cold that rose from the stone floor. The center of the room was clear of furniture and provided enough space to serve as a little dance floor or exercise area.

Not that I was diligent about exercise—or anything else, for that matter. What difference did it make if I was sloppy-fat and smelled or if I was trim and freshly bathed? *He* wasn't going to care.

As I crossed the room, I kept my eyes averted from the one large window that had shutters on the inside—the one window that looked out on the land beyond my prison. The shutters were safely closed, but I still kept my eyes focused on the chair . . . and the mirror on the wall that matched the window's size exactly.

I was forbidden to look at the world directly. My jailer wouldn't tell me what the penalty would be if I disobeyed. He simply insisted that I would be cursed, and the implied threat was that I would not survive the punishment.

Some days I wondered whether not surviving would be such a bad thing. Would that really be worse than a lifetime of solitary confinement?

No. My confinement was not quite solitary.

I sat in the chair and closed my eyes. A moment later, as some device registered my weight in the chair, I heard the shutters pull back from the window. I opened my eyes, focused on the mirror, and breathed a sigh of relief as I looked upon the world.

I couldn't figure out whether I was on the bottom floor of this gray tower or the top, but I suspected that, if viewed scientifically, the mirror shouldn't be able to reflect what I saw regardless of the room's position. Since I was a writer, a storyteller, and a dreamer, I ignored science and accepted the view.

A piece of the river, flowing clean and clear. Lilies growing near the bank, their buds swelling as they waited for their turn to bloom. A bright fuzz of green that indicated new grass. Then the section of dirt road framed by mirror and window. Beyond that, there was a scattering of trees and a lane that divided two fields, but they looked vague and out of focus.

"Fields of barley and rye?" I asked the mirror, thinking of the old poem.

"Is that what they should be?"

My pulse raced at the sound of his voice. Not because it was *him*, but because I was glad to hear *anyone's* voice.

Steeling myself for whatever would be lurking in the deep alcove that hid the entrance to this prison, I turned my head and looked at the male figure half-hidden in the shadows.

The horned god today, bare chested and barefoot, but wearing jeans that had the softness of long wear.

Oddly enough, the incongruity of his looks and his choice of clothing made it less easy to deny that he was what he seemed— one of the old gods who, for whatever reason, had decided to keep me as a pet.

"Good morning, Eleanor," he said with the same quiet, courteous respect his voice always held when he spoke to me.

When I woke and found myself here and he asked me my name, I had told him I was Eleanor of Aquitaine, a small act of defiance and a shot of courage on my part to claim to be an imprisoned queen who was centuries gone.

He had accepted the name without question, which was when I began wondering a few things about him.

My keeper. My jailer. My only companion. He never came into the room. I had never felt the touch of his hand. Sometimes I wished he would try to touch me, just so I'd know that he was real and not an illusion created by a broken mind.

"I'm not Eleanor," I said, fixing my eyes on the mirror and the world beyond the stone walls.

A silence that asked a question.

"I'm the lily maid."

A different kind of silence before he said, "Ah. The Lady of Shalott."

I struggled not to smile, pleased that he understood the

reference since he understood so few of them. Then I got down to the business of watching the world reflected in the mirror.

Blue sky and some white, puffy clouds. No sign of rain.

Maybe tonight, I thought. *That would make the spring flowers bloom.*

Birds flashed in and out of the mirror. A man on horseback trotted down the road, heading for the village. Then a young woman on a bicycle rode by.

After that moment of distraction, I saw Peggy coming down the lane. She was plump and solid, her quick walk covering the distance and bringing her to the spot where the lane met the road. She crossed the road, looked up, and positioned herself dead center in the mirror. Then she set down the satchel she was carrying in one hand and held up the bouquet filling her other hand.

She was smiling, but even at this distance I could see a weight of sadness in that smile. She knew I was imprisoned in this tower. That was why she came and stood there every morning on her way to the village's school. Maybe, unlike me, she even knew why I was imprisoned. But regardless of why I was there, Peggy would support a friend and do whatever she could to help—even if that meant standing on the edge of the road in all kinds of weather, waving to someone imprisoned in a tower that was set on an island in the middle of a river.

Peggy held up one flower at a time so that I could see them clearly. Daffodils, hyacinths, tulips. Crocus. Wild iris. But . . .

"They're all white," I murmured, trying to hold on to the pleasure of seeing flowers.

"Shouldn't they be?" came the question from the shadows.

I shook my head. "They're a celebration of spring. They should be yellow and orange and red and purple and pink. Even striped. And some," I conceded, "should be white. But not all."

I ignored his thoughtful silence and focused on the scene.

Robert rode up on his bicycle and stopped to chat with Peggy. He pointed to her satchel. She made a dismissive "It's no trouble" wave of her hand that was so typical of Peggy it made me smile.

Robert pointed again, insistent. After going back and forth a couple more times, Peggy put the satchel in the empty carry basket attached to the back of his bicycle. The satchel would be on her desk at the school when she arrived, but she'd have been spared the trouble of lugging . . . whatever she was lugging to the school that day to show her students.

Another minute went by. Then Peggy waved to me and headed down the road to the village.

I spent the morning watching the shadow world reflected in the mirror. Birds. The sparkle of sunlight on the river. Clouds. A few people on the road, but anyone who worked in the village had already reported to their jobs.

Finally tired of staring at fields of grain, I stood up. In the moment before I closed my eyes and the lack of weight on the chair triggered the device that closed the shutters, the mirror reflected something else, something dark.

Something terrible.

A bad angle, I told myself. Nothing more. The mirror was positioned to let me see out the window when I was sitting. Ordinary things wouldn't look the same when I was standing.

Despite what I told myself, I kept my eyes tightly closed until the shutters covered the window completely. Then I turned and walked to my bedroom.

"Will you come back to the mirror after your meal?" he asked.

I paused in the doorway but didn't turn around to look at him. "I don't know."

The bed had been made, and there were clean towels in the bathroom. A meal had been laid out on a small table, a cover over the dish keeping the food hot. The book I was currently reading was next to the dish.

I didn't know who tended these rooms. I never saw anyone but my jailer, but someone kept things tidy and filled the bookshelves with new offerings on a regular basis. And . . .

I lifted the cover on the dish and let out a *whuff* of pleased surprise. In the beginning of my imprisonment, all the food was gray and had a soft mealiness. It was nourishing enough but awful to look at. That was one of the reasons I began reading while I ate. Today's roast beef, red potatoes, and broccoli and carrots were identifiable. Even their tastes were more distinctive.

After the meal, I spent the rest of the day in my bedroom, reading, sleeping, and listening to the music *they* had scrounged from somewhere. I didn't go back to the mirror. Maybe I was mistaken, but when he had asked the question, I thought there had been a hint of yearning in his voice.

THE NEXT MORNING, when I looked in the mirror, Peggy held up a dazzling rainbow of spring flowers.

2

WEEKS PASSED. IN THE EVENINGS, I SOMETIMES SAW the moon reflected and marked the passage of days by its waxing and waning.

Were there others like me, imprisoned in other towers? Even

imprisoned here? Some nights I stamped on the floor, hoping to hear an answering thump that would confirm there was some- one else trapped in this place. Some nights I stood near a win- dow and screamed—and wondered if anyone could hear me.

Except him.

On those nights, I felt his presence in the alcove, but he still didn't enter the room. Didn't even speak to me.

Then one night . . .

I had finished dinner and the current book. My keepers had found some Celtic music, which was more to my taste, so I lis- tened to music for a while. I put another disc in the player, then went over to the bookcase that held the "new" selection of books. I now had a bookcase of favorites that was never dis- turbed by whoever tended the rooms and a bookcase that ro- tated on a regular basis, offering me an eclectic mix of fiction and nonfiction.

A fat leather-bound volume caught my attention. As I pulled it out, I noticed the cover was heavily stained and the pages had a rippled, swollen look. I opened the book and riffled through a few pages.

Dark stains, as if the book had fallen near a puddle of coffee or tea and no one had pulled it away before it had gotten a good soaking.

Not coffee or tea, I decided as I continued riffling the pages, not taking in the content. Then I hit a page . . .

Splashes. A spray of dark blotches on the paper. Not dark like coffee; dark like old . . .

Memories came back in flashing images, like seeing a fast slideshow of stills from a movie that had frightened you badly as a child.

I dropped the book and screamed.

"Not true," I panted as I rushed out of the bedroom, stopping when I reached the chair positioned before the mirror. "It's not true."

I took a step, intending to sit in the chair. Then I turned and looked at the window.

Rage filled me and with it, an insanity that eclipsed madness. I'd been told I would be cursed if I looked upon the world directly. So be it. The answer could not be found in the mirror.

Since the shutters had been opened mechanically each day, I had expected them to resist being opened by hand.

Not so. They flew open with almost no effort.

I looked. I saw. I screamed again, but this sound was full of denial and terror.

I slammed the shutters closed and . . .

"Eleanor? Eleanor!"

He stood at the alcove's threshold, scanning the room until he found me pressed into a corner, curled in a tight ball.

"Eleanor, I'm sorry. They didn't know, didn't understand they shouldn't bring you such things. The book is gone. Eleanor?"

"Go away."

The shock on his face was real, but even that wasn't enough to make him step into the room.

Or maybe he's unable to step into the room.

He studied the shutters over the window as if trying to decide whether they were in the exact same position as when he'd seen them earlier in the day. Then his body sagged. His head sank forward.

"Eleanor," he said as he took a step back.

It wasn't the sorrow in his voice that prodded me. It was the defeat that made me call out, "Wait!"

Still there, but I knew with a heart-deep certainty that if he took another step back into the shadows, he would be gone forever.

"Just for tonight," I told him. "I need to be alone tonight. Come back in the morning."

A hesitation followed by a sigh of relief. "In the morning," he said. Then he was gone.

I uncurled slowly. Holding on to my heart and my courage, I went back to the window and opened the shutters.

No fields, no trees, no grass or flowers. The river flowed sluggishly, choked with bloated, decaying bodies.

Even after all these weeks—maybe months by now—the river was still choked with bodies.

Had some fool finally pushed the button that began the end of the world? Had some storm been Earth's answer to global warming and toxic waste?

Something cataclysmic that caused a chain reaction. Unstoppable once it began. The end of the world I had known. Not even the damn cockroaches had survived.

I couldn't remember the how or why. Maybe that was a blessing. When you're the only survivor, those questions don't matter anymore.

I turned away from the window and walked over to the mirror. It showed me the same image, the same desolation.

Was that the curse? Had I torn away the veil of magic that had given me the illusion that a piece of the world had survived?

What *had* I been seeing in the mirror?

Now that I no longer blindly accepted what I'd been seeing,

I remembered that Peggy had been killed in a car accident several years ago. And Robert? I saw him as I remembered him—a friend of my youth—when he should look middle-aged if I was seeing something besides a memory. As for the land . . .

A country village just down the road. I couldn't see it, but I knew it was there. Something more like the Avonlea in the Anne of Green Gables stories than Arthur's Camelot, but pieces of both those places could be found in the streets and houses and public buildings.

And what about *him*? He came to me most often as the Celtic horned god—the Green Man, the Lord of the Hunt. An earthy, primal male. But he came in other forms as well, and the only reason I knew it was him was because his voice didn't change along with his face or body shape.

What was he? Some old earth spirit that had returned to try to mend a broken world? An alien from another planet whose people were trying to keep the few surviving humans alive and sane for however many years they had left to live?

When I told him to go away, I'd frightened him. Truly frightened him. Why?

Because he needs something from me.

I closed the shutters and returned to the bedroom. The book was gone, as he'd said. But the thought of selecting another book from those shelves made me tremble, so I kicked off my shoes and lay down on the bed fully clothed.

Slowly I became aware of the music that was playing—had been playing in the background.

A hammered dulcimer and other string instruments playing the songs of Turlough O'Carolan, a blind Irish harper and bard who had lived centuries ago. I recognized the song "Mabel Kelly," which had been one of my favorites. I got up long enough to program the player to keep repeating that song. As I listened, the music lanced a wound that had been festering in my heart, and my quiet tears washed the wound clean.

The world I had known was gone, but another world existed—a shadow world I could only see reflected in the mirror. A world that, somehow, had been layered over the real one.

Real world? I was a writer and a dreamer. A storyteller. I had never been chained to the "real world." And since I couldn't touch either one, why should I let desolation be given the solidity of the word "real"?

As the music and the night flowed on, I made some choices, found some answers. Perhaps they were not factually accurate, but they were answers I could live with. That still left me with a question.

When he looked at me, what did he see? Who was I that he thought me so important to *his* people's survival?

3

THE NEXT MORNING, HE WAS WAITING AT THE threshold, wearing a different form.

I walked to the center of the room and studied him, trying to determine if this was a message.

The Celtic horned god was primal, earthy. This male had a youthful maturity and a handsome face with blue eyes and black hair. The feathered white wings brushed the sides of the alcove, and the white jumpsuit he was wearing . . .

"Angels are androgynous," I told him.

"Andro . . ." He frowned as he tried to find the tail end of the word.

"They have no gender."

"No . . . ?"

I circled my hand at a height that vaguely aligned with his groin. "No."

As I walked over to the chair, knowing I was about to change the rules, I heard him mutter, "I don't think I like this form."

Hope. If I'd had to guess at the reason he'd chosen this form from the myriad images or symbols humans had created over millennia, I would have said it was meant to symbolize hope. And hope must walk in the world.

"It's a good form," I said. "As necessary in the world as your other form." I hesitated, then added, "I'm not an expert on angels, so I suppose the ones who deal directly with people would need to look more like people and have . . ." Again I waved vaguely at his groin.

His sigh was gusty and heartfelt. Then he offered a hesitant smile and said, "Good morning, Eleanor."

I met his smile with a grim expression. "There is something I must show you."

I sat down in the chair and watched the shutters being drawn back from the window.

I glanced at him and noticed that his skin had turned sickly pale as he realized what the mirror revealed. He made some inarticulate sound of despair.

I focused on the image in the mirror. "This," I said in a clear, firm voice that would turn words into the stones of truth, "is the Land of Armageddon. It is a dark place. A terrible place born of death and destruction. What oozes out of its festering skin is dangerous, deadly. Know the names of the creatures who call this place home."

"I will learn them," he said, his voice stripped of everything, even hope. Especially hope.

I nodded to acknowledge that I'd heard him. "This is the Land of Armageddon. It is a dark place. A terrible place. It is also far away"—I turned and looked him straight in the eyes—"and it will never again be seen in the mirror."

His eyes widened as he realized what I'd just told him.

I stood up. The shutters closed.

"I must rest today."

He hesitated. "I should return tomorrow?"

"Yes." I smiled. "Return tomorrow." I headed back to my bedroom, truly in need of rest. But I paused at the doorway. "If *they* should come across books about gardening—books that have pictures of flowers and shrubs and trees, I would like to see them. And books on yoga."

"Yoga?" He tried out the word.

I spelled it for him, and he nodded.

He was gone before my bedroom door fully closed.

Gardening and yoga.

I wasn't sure why I had survived or what I was doing in this place, but if I was going to keep the Land of Armageddon far away, it was time to start setting a good example.

4

DURING THE AFTERNOONS, I DID YOGA. AT NIGHT I danced to O'Carolan's music and envisioned a gentler world than had ever existed. I pored over gardening books, fixing the look of flowers and trees in my mind's eye, focusing on how they would look in their own particular seasons.

I remembered the faces of friends and family, conjuring them out of memory until I could recall their voices, their particular way of laughing, the way each of them moved.

And I saw each one of them walk down that little stretch of road that was framed by window and mirror, pausing to wave before they headed for the village and another kind of life.

It wasn't much different from world-building for a story, I thought one afternoon while I was trying to figure out what fruits could be grown in this climate—and then wondered if that was even a consideration anymore. Then I thought, no, it was more like being a stage manager and director for an improv theater. I supplied a description and character sketches for the people and a stage and props that had as much detail as I could bring into focus. After that, it was up to the beings who took on the roles to interact with one another.

So I did yoga; I danced; I studied.

The sloppy fat burned away. The meals, once I concentrated on the gardening books that contained fruits and vegetables, became tastier and offered more variety.

Every day he was there within moments of my leaving the bedroom. He alternated between horned god and angel, on occasion trying on other forms to see what reaction I would have.

The minotaur form, after leaving a steaming pile in the alcove, was banished from the tower, but was allowed to roam the countryside as a "natural disaster."

After all, even the most benign story had to have *some* conflict.

The night I saw a unicorn cantering up the lane between the fields brought tears to my eyes and took my breath away.

The seasons turned. The fields were nothing but stubble

under snow. The river froze. Through the cold winter days, I talked to him about the feel of things, the smell of things, the taste of things.

And then, when the first cracks appeared in the river's ice, I tried to expand my horizon.

5

"WHY CAN'T IT SHOW THE FIELDS ON THE OTHER SIDE of the village?" I asked for the fourth time. My frustration rose in direct proportion to his strained patience.

"The mirror can only reflect what can be seen from this window," he replied.

But it doesn't reflect what is seen from the window, I thought bitterly.

"I cannot change the nature of the mirror," he said after several minutes of stony silence.

His tone came awfully close to a plea, and I felt the jolt of his words. But I still wasn't ready to concede. Except . . .

The nature of the *mirror*.

I had thought that because I was creating the stage set, what I saw reflected in the mirror could be changed simply by wanting it to change. But I had forgotten a basic truth that every storyteller knows: Whether it is science or magic that creates the wonders in a story, there are rules that must be followed—and there are limits to what an object can do.

That was what he had been telling me—the mirror could only do this much and no more.

"It doesn't matter," I said, already feeling the deep ache of disappointment.

Hours passed. I kept my eyes on the mirror but didn't see anything.

Finally, he asked, "Why did you want to see another field?"

"I didn't. Not exactly." How to explain when I still wasn't sure *what* I was talking to every day. "I just thought there might be a field on the other side of the village where the festivals were held and . . ." *And I could see more of the people. I miss the people.*

Of course, I'd be looking at empty ground for much of the year, so maybe seeing a handful of people go up and down the road every day was a better choice after all.

"Festivals?" he asked. "What is festivals?"

As an unspoken apology, because he really did try to make my confinement as comfortable as possible, I told him about fairs and festivals. I told him about competitions that would be typical of a country fair. I told him about the game of horse-shoes. I explained the concept of picnics. I tried to remember the various small celebrations humans had enjoyed, assigning one to every month. And feeling whimsical and impulsive, I told him about the famous rodeo tournaments that had been held in some villages.

His delight was a tangible thread between us, and his thirst for details melded with my flight of imagination.

For the first time, I saw him as something more than a jailer. I saw him as a friend.

When I finally stood up, stiff from so many hours in the chair, he stepped back into the shadows.

"Wait," I said, rushing to the alcove.

He stepped up to the threshold, his alarmed expression warning me even before I felt the invisible barrier that separated the alcove from my rooms.

Whatever supplied me with breathable air, food, and clean water did not extend beyond my rooms. Did not extend into the alcove.

Which meant that whatever he was didn't need those things the way I did. Or maybe it meant that the environment that sustained me would be poison to him.

That was one explanation for why he had never tried to enter the room. But there was another explanation, one I had feared from the very beginning of my imprisonment.

"Are you real?" I asked.

A long pause before he whispered, "I don't know."

Then he was gone. I heard no door close, saw nothing change in the alcove, but I knew he was gone.

THROUGHOUT A LONG, sleepless night, I thought about that moment, and just before I finally fell asleep, I realized something. Even though I was the one who had asked the question, he had been hoping I would also be the one who had the answer.

6

THEY DIDN'T PLANT BARLEY AND RYE THAT YEAR. AT least, not in those fields.

They made a Place of Festivals.

Of course, I couldn't see more than the strip of road and land that could be seen in the mirror. Not with my eyes, anyway. But he came each morning with more information about what was being built and where it was in relation to the road, and as I put the pieces together, I could visualize the place.

They had a racetrack that served as a place for athletic foot-races as well as horse races. They had dug a reflection pond in the center of the racetrack and would use it as a skating rink during the cold months.

They had other areas for games and competitions, but like the racetrack, those were things I couldn't see.

Closer to the road and on one side of the lane, they built an open-sided pavilion that served as both concert hall and dance floor.

They built a small stone building on the other side of the lane. There was a bench along the side of the building that faced my tower, giving me a clear view of whoever sat there.

I understood the purpose of every structure except the stone building, but no matter how I phrased the question, he refused to tell me what it was used for.

I stopped asking once I realized that structure had a deep significance for him or his people. It was enough that the building drew the villagers to my little piece of the world.

They seemed less uniform than when I'd first begun viewing the world through the mirror. Peggy still came every morn-ing. Sometimes she sat alone on the bench outside the build-ing, but, more often, someone else came along to chat for a few minutes. Friends who were no more than shadows and memo-ries I held in my heart were alive again, looking exactly as I'd last seen them. But there were others as well, who had been conjured from some other well of memory. There were the an-gels, who varied in coloring but were all handsome, well-endowed young men. There were no female angels, but there were fairies, equally diverse in coloring and just as lovely as their angel coun-terparts. There were several who walked in the skin of the old

Celtic god and seemed to be the groundskeepers for the Place of Festivals.

Was it their confusion or mine that had declared all these things equally real?

Did it matter?

7

EVERY MONTH THEY HELD A MAJOR FESTIVAL AND A Minor Festival. They used some human celebrations, but most of the celebrations I remembered had no significance for them. So they didn't celebrate Valentine's Day, but there was a Crab Grass Festival in the summer. When I asked why, he said his people remembered crab grass causing a great deal of excitement in certain types of males, so it had to be important. Therefore, its existence was now formally celebrated.

The rodeo tournament was a dubious success. There was no calf roping or bronc riding, and those participating in the jousting tried to strike a target attached to bales of hay rather than strike one another.

When he told me about the barrel races, I agreed that, even though they were bulkier and not as fast on their feet, the centaurs did have an unfair advantage over the Quarter Horses because two heads were not always better than one and that next year there should be a separate event for each kind of participant.

They had a Festival of Trout, a Festival of Deer, and a Festival of Turnips.

I understood the trout and the deer. I didn't want to know about the turnips.

"Apples," I said as I watched Michael and his ever-present toolbox enter the stone building. "Next year you must have an Apple Festival."

"Apple?"

He had become braver, this god who stood in the shadows. More often than not, he stood closer to the barrier, and his expressions were easier to read.

I closed my eyes and remembered *apple*—the glossy red skin, the white meat of the fruit, the sweet juice, and the satisfying crunch. Of course, there were green apples and tarter varieties, but the reds had been my favorites, and for a few moments, I relived the experience of eating an apple.

THAT FALL, PEOPLE gathered at the small orchard that had appeared near the stone building. I spent the day watching them pick apples. Michael, Robert, and William organized the pickers and the distribution of ladders. Nadine and Pat organized the baskets that every family in the village had brought, fairly distributing the fruit, while Julie and Peggy bustled around the orchard with pitchers and glasses, offering water to the pickers. Lorna sat in the shade, playing her harp to entertain people as they came and went, and Merri and Annemarie entertained the children with games and stories.

I barely left the chair that day. And he never left the alcove.

I wasn't sure what he could see from that angle, but he seemed able to watch the reflection just as I did. That day, when I finally forced myself to look away from the mirror . . .

I had never seen him so happy.

That evening, when I reluctantly took a break, I found a bowl of ripe red apples on the table along with my dinner.

8

SEASONS CAME AND WENT, COUNTING OUT THE MEAsured beat of years. The people in the mirror didn't change. Neither did my companion. But I was a canvas upon which time painted.

My health was failing. My body was failing. A walker that had been found somewhere allowed me to shuffle from bedroom to chair. The day was coming when I wouldn't be able to get out of bed. The day was coming. . . .

"What happens when I'm no longer here?" I asked him after I had gotten comfortably settled in my chair.

"No longer here?"

"I'm old," I told him gently. "I'm dying. I won't be here much longer." My gnarled hand pointed at the mirror. "What happens to that when I'm gone?"

A long silence. Then, "Eleanor? Look out the window."

I shook my head.

"Please," he said. "Look out the window."

"Just got myself comfortable," I grumbled. But I hoisted myself out of the chair and shuffled over to the window.

The shutter mechanism was a little stiffer than I remembered. Or maybe I had simply gotten weaker. I got one side of the shutters opened and decided that was enough.

Then I looked out the window and struggled to open the other side.

The Place of Festivals.

Peggy sat on the bench, chatting with Pat and William while Merri crouched nearby, pointing out some wildflowers to her two daughters. Robert and Michael and one of the angels were exchanging news. Nadine was in the pavilion with Julie and Lorna, organizing baskets of something.

"Must be a minor festival," I muttered. But I couldn't remember which one. Couldn't even remember the month.

Didn't matter. The people were all there.

"How?" I asked, not willing to look away. "How can I see them?"

"They're real now. At least, real in this other way."

I shuffled the walker a little so I could look at him but still easily watch the world.

"When Armageddon swallowed the world, some of the Makers survived. Not many, but some."

"Makers?"

"Beings like you."

Like me. "What are you?"

He took a deep breath and let it out in a sigh.

"Are you aliens from another planet?"

That surprised a laugh out of him. "No, Eleanor. We have been here since the world was young, a part of the world but always apart from the world. We did not have form, could not inhabit the space that was already filled. So we only had the shadows, the . . . reflections . . . of the world you knew. We existed, but we could not live. Not like you.

"After Armageddon, the world was empty. There were no reflections. We did not want to exist in a dead place, so when we found some of the Makers, we used what we are to create small places where they could survive."

Four gray walls and four gray towers. A confinement shaped to order by the fevered dreams of a mind trying to save itself from self-destruction.

"You used an image from my mind, didn't you?" I asked. "Something I had projected as a tolerable kind of prison."

"Yes," he said quietly.

"So not every place had the lily maid's mirror."

"No, but each place had something in which to see the world reflected."

"Why?"

"When the Makers looked upon the world directly, they could not see anything but the dead place."

The Land of Armageddon.

But here, now, the river flowed clean and clear. Lilies bloomed along the banks. The people I'd known . . .

"I provided you with shapes to inhabit?"

"That was all most of the Makers were able to do. But a few, like you . . . An . . . echo . . . filled your remembering, so there was more than shape. There was . . . feeling."

An echo of friends long gone but still remembered. A village still inhabited by these good people. That wasn't a bad legacy to give to the world.

"Since you're answering questions, will you tell me what that stone building is?" I asked.

Some strong emotion, there and gone, filled his face. "A . . . temple?" He paused, looking thoughtful. "A place to sit quietly and give thanks."

"To you?"

He jolted. *"Me?"*

"Aren't you the god who stands within the shadows?"

He looked shocked.

"No, Eleanor," he stammered. *"I* am not the god here."

My turn to feel shock.

"They call you the Lady of Shadows," he said quietly. "You are one of the Makers who dreams the world, and the reflection of that dreaming is the place in which we live."

I wasn't sure what to say. If I'd known I'd been assigned the role of deity, would I have done things differently?

Well, I wouldn't have mentioned something as stupid as the rodeo tournament, but that didn't last for more than a few years anyway.

As I mulled over my promotion from prisoner to god, I thought of something. "If I'm the Maker, what are you?"

"Companion?" He pondered for a minute, clearly trying to put his thoughts in order. "These places can only hold one Maker. It was all we could do. But we knew that Makers needed company, so some, like me, were chosen to remain with the Makers."

"Remain? Don't you go down to the village when you leave here?"

"No. I cannot leave this place. I am not like the Tenders who take care of your rooms. They can come and go. But I act as . . . go-between? . . . so I, too, am in between while I am companion. Once I leave here, I cannot come back."

"Then how did the people in the village know any of the things I've told you, described to you?"

"I was the go-between. There were ways to communicate, much like you and I do."

I had thought he'd been free to come and go, but he had been as much a prisoner as me. Had been as isolated as me. All these years, he'd had no one for company but me.

"So I ask the question again: What happens when I'm gone?"

"I will go down to the village and live with the others," he replied. "Our place will stay as it was made."

We kept silent for a while and watched the world, already having said too much—and maybe not quite enough.

When my old legs got too tired to stand, I shuffled back to the chair where I could watch the world in comfort.

"There is something I would like to ask you," he said once I was settled. "We could make a starting place that could be seen as reflection. Besides what we wanted for ourselves, we had wanted to give some comfort, some hope that the world was not so dead. All the Makers were warned not to look out the window. All were warned that they would be cursed if they did. And yet all of them looked. Some resisted for a long time. Some didn't try to resist the temptation for a single turning of the sun. They looked—and nothing was the same. They stopped Making. Some broke and died. Some turned dark, and their Making was a terrible thing."

"What happened to your people?" I asked. "The ones who were caught in the dark Making?"

"They did not inhabit the shapes, and the Making had no substance and faded away. But you. You looked, and you were still able to see the reflection in the mirror. You still continued Making. How did you do this?"

How could I explain? It was more than being a storyteller, more than being accustomed to seeing worlds that didn't exist anywhere except inside my head.

An . . . echo . . . filled your remembering, so there was more than shape. There was . . . feeling.

That's what he had said. And that, I realized, was the answer.

"When I looked in the mirror," I told him, "I didn't see with my eyes. I saw with my heart."

A moment's silence. "Ah," he said, as if I had explained a great mystery.

We watched the world. I couldn't tell if there was supposed to be a specific festival. People came and went, but the people I had loved remained, staying around the pavilion or the stone building, or crossing the road to stand on the river's bank and raise a hand in greeting.

Or farewell?

"This place," I said. "It's an island in a river?"

"Yes."

"What do you call it?"

He smiled. "The Island of Shalott."

"And the village?"

The smile faded, and a touch of anxiety took its place. "It was never named."

I hadn't understood my role. I'd thought of it as the village, assuming it already had a name that I was not aware of.

A legacy. A word that would hold shining hope within its sound.

"Camelot," I said. "The village is called Camelot."

A hesitation. Then, timidly, he asked, "Do I have a name?"

All these years he'd spent patiently waiting. Exiled by choice in order to give as much as he could, not just for my sake but for his own people. I thought of the faces and forms he'd worn over the years.

"You are Lancelot Angel Greenman," I said.

His eyes widened. "So many names."

"You earned them."

Stunned pleasure.

Not much time left. But enough.

"I want you to do one last thing for me, Lancelot."

"Anything that I can."

"I want you to go down to the village. I want you to leave now."

He jerked forward. Reached out. Almost touched the barrier. "No."

"Yes. I want to know you're safely in the village. I want to see you in the mirror, with the rest of my friends. Do this for me."

He lowered his arm but still hesitated. "What form should I wear?"

"You only get to have one form once you go down there?"
He nodded.

"Then you must choose for yourself who you want to be."

He took a step back into the shadows. Took another. "Thank you for our piece of the world," he said softly.

The silence and the solitude had a weight it had never had before. He was gone from the tower.

A few minutes later, a young man stepped onto the part of the road framed by the mirror. He had black hair and blue eyes. He had the face of an angel, but he'd given up the wings of that form in order to look more like the others. When he turned toward the tower and raised a hand in greeting, there was something in his smile and his stance that told me he had kept a bit of the old god too, at least in his heart.

I watched him as the others came over to greet him. I saw his face when the simple act of being touched by the others confirmed that he no longer just existed in the shadows; now he truly lived in that world.

I saw his joy.

Then I breathed out a sigh—and saw no more.

SHE MOVED THROUGH
THE FAIR

F OLLOWING HIS IMPATIENT SONS, JAGAR LANGLEY
strolled toward the banner that read GREENFIELDS
FAIR. His wife's hand was tucked in the crook of his arm,
but with every step he felt another hand wrap around his heart,
ready to squeeze the life from it.

What life was left in it.

He hadn't set foot on this land for fifteen years. If Hadrea's
father hadn't insisted he come to Greenfields to negotiate a
property deal for land on the other side of the lake, and if his
sons, Franklin and David, hadn't turned into whiny brats once
they'd fixed on the idea of seeing the damn fair, he still wouldn't
have set foot in this place.

His father-in-law was a clever man who didn't believe a cold
marriage bed was any excuse for behavior that might queer a
business deal—especially when that marriage bed held secrets
that could queer more than a business deal. So he was being
punished for an affair that hadn't been quite as discreet as he'd
thought, and Hadrea was being reminded that she had wanted
this marriage enough to . . .

"Do you think we'll see the ghost?" David Langley asked eagerly as they passed under the banner.

"Really, David," Hadrea Franklin Langley said, eyeing her nine-year-old son with dislike. "Wherever did you hear such a thing?"

"Franklin told me," David replied. "There's a ghost who walks the fair two days each summer, and this is one of the days."

Hadrea sniffed delicately, a sound that conveyed a frigid contempt. "We send you to one of the finest schools in the country, Franklin. Is that the kind of foolishness they teach you there? If that's so, I'll tell your grandfather he's wasting his money on your tuition."

Color blazed in Franklin's thirteen-year-old face, but he raised his chin and looked at Hadrea with eyes that were as old and as cold as hers. "In point of fact, Mother, it was Grandfather who told me about the ghost."

Jagar glanced at Hadrea, torn between delight and sympathy as he watched her pale. Her father's verbal thrust had been placed perfectly, especially since it had been delivered by the boy. Tell Franklin just enough to intrigue, just enough that he would tell his younger brother, who would bring it out in the open. And bring the memories with it.

Did you take Franklin into the parlor and point out the portrait you had commissioned for Hadrea's eighteenth birthday? Jagar wondered as Hadrea and Franklin looked away from each other, this moment being just another brick in their mutual wall of hate. *Did you bring his attention to that one-of-a-kind dagger with a hilt decorated with inlaid gold and black enamel and a ruby as big as an eye?*

I wish to God I had never seen that dagger. And I wish even more that I didn't know how Hadrea lost it.

Ah, Lucy. Hadrea's father bought a secret with a dowry and a business deal, and I married cold ambition instead of marrying you.

He saw her then. Her dark rose jacket and long skirt were both fifteen years out of fashion. Her blond hair was done up in the simple style that suited her. The hat matched her outfit, accented by one jaunty white feather.

Light and life. Love and joy. That was Lucy McGuire. That had always been Lucy McGuire.

They had been engaged. The wedding day had been set. Then Hadrea had told him something that had changed everything.

Soon it will be our wedding day.

Fifteen years ago, that was the last thing Lucy had said to him before going off to shop at the merchant booths that made up the fair. Buying things with her pin money to set up housekeeping.

The first star was in the sky when she left the fair and headed home, taking the road that followed the lake.

She never reached home. Was never seen again.

He watched her now, as he'd watched her that day, still loving her as he had never loved anyone else before or since.

"Jagar? What on earth are you looking at?" Hadrea asked, her voice oddly shrill.

"Nothing on earth," he replied, his chest aching as Lucy looked right at him. Maybe he'd been mistaken all these years. Maybe she had been here all along, moving through the fair, tending the land her father had owned. If he got close enough, would he see age lines in her face, see proof of the years that had passed?

"Jagar!"

Lucy turned and began walking toward the other end of the fair. Toward the road that followed the lake.

Despite all the other visitors milling around the booths, he never lost sight of her. But when he took a step to follow her, she simply disappeared, as if she were no more than a dream.

Or a ghost.

THIRTY-FIVE YEARS LATER

"NOT MUCH, IS it?" Rayce Langley said as they walked from the parking area to the banner that marked the entrance to the Greenfields Fair.

It's my inheritance, Ellen McGuire thought, wishing she'd come here without Rayce's "helpful" escort. His hold on her arm was more possessive than courteous, and the change in his attitude toward the fair and the village and everything except the expensive "luxury living" community on the other side of the lake was making her more and more uneasy.

Of course, the community on the other side of the lake was owned by Franklin & Langley Inc., the company Rayce's great-grandfather had founded. As the charming man who had chatted her up when she'd checked into the Greenfields Hotel three days ago morphed into a slick wheeler-dealer, she began to suspect that Rayce wasn't interested in helping a divorced thirty-year-old woman find her way around Greenfields and the surrounding area. Rayce was interested in wheeling a deal with the person who now owned *this* side of the lake.

The rents from the current leases won't make you rich, the lawyer had said, *but even after taxes and such, you'll make a fair living from it. Enough that you can do as you please.*

She had a house here in the village—an old place that had a paid-off mortgage and a long list of needed "improvements."

She had a chance to find out what she wanted and who she could be. And as she passed under the banner, she could have sworn the air around her changed, surrounding her with the warmth of welcome.

Or it could have been heatstroke, since the summer weather had been ferocious these past few days. Made her glad she'd chosen to stay at the hotel rather than move into the house—and made her envy the central air-conditioning in one of the luxury condos Rayce had shown her yesterday.

But she wasn't quite as envious, or as gullible, as he seemed to think.

Rayce twisted around. "You doing all right there, Gramps? Madame?"

Ellen looked over her shoulder at the couple trailing behind them. She had never seen two people as unhappy as Jagar and Hadrea Langley and couldn't imagine enduring fifty years in such a bitter marriage. When she'd had lunch with them and Rayce yesterday in the old mansion that had been the Franklin country home and now housed a restaurant and boutiques for the community, she'd had the impression Jagar and Hadrea were each just waiting for the other to die so the survivor would have a few remaining years to live in peace.

And she'd never before seen such undiluted hatred as she'd seen on Jagar's face when Rayce had led them to the room that was now the Activity Center and shown her the portrait of Hadrea Franklin and the dagger.

As Ellen put on the floppy striped hat to protect her face from the afternoon sun, she saw Rayce sneer and heard Hadrea's delicate sniff—a sound that told her clearly enough that she wasn't worthy company for any member of the Langley family.

All right, it wasn't a stylish hat, but Rayce had given her the strong impression that the fair was a grubby place, so she'd worn jeans and a T-shirt—and the floppy hat—instead of something nice. Which meant she felt like the poor relation next to the expensively dressed Langleys.

And that may have been exactly how Rayce had wanted her to feel.

For the first thirty minutes, she let Rayce herd her through the wide lanes bordered with merchants' booths while Hadrea made disparaging remarks about the merchandise in a voice that wasn't loud but was cutting enough to turn heads.

Why should I be the only polite person here? Ellen thought as she came to an abrupt halt.

"Rayce," she said, hoping her face muscles had correctly shifted into "smile" position despite her urge to snarl. "I appreciate all the time you've taken to show me around, but I'd like to wander by myself for a while, and your grandparents look like they could use a break from the heat. There's a refreshment tent right over there. Why don't you get them something to drink, and I'll join you in a little while?"

"Yes, Rayce," Hadrea said. "There's no reason to be trailing after Ellen while she looks over her little kingdom."

Ellen turned on her heel and marched off, not caring where she was headed as long as it was away from *them*.

She finally stopped walking when she realized she had no idea where she was, except that she was still inside the fair. Somewhere. But the booths around her were full of produce instead of trinkets. Apparently, the fair was also a farmers' market.

She scowled at neatly displayed baskets of peppers and carrots and wondered what else might be here that no one had mentioned.

"Oh my," a voice said. "Such a grumpy face. Should I offer to buy you some spun sugar?"

Ellen glanced at the woman standing nearby, then turned to get a better look. A face lit with amusement, but the blue eyes were kind. She wore an old-fashioned skirt and jacket and a matching dark rose hat with a jaunty white feather.

"Sugar is bad for your teeth," Ellen said, then added after a pause, "Is there an ice cream booth here?"

"Doesn't ice cream have sugar?"

"It's different."

"Oooh." The woman tipped her head. "And who might you be?"

"Ellen McGuire." People in Greenfields had looked wary or delighted when they'd heard her name. Now that she thought of it, the reaction seemed to depend on whether Rayce was with her.

The woman smiled. "Then that makes us kin, Ellen McGuire. I'm your cousin Lucy." The smile widened. "Well, a cousin several times removed, but still a relation."

"I'm pleased to meet you. I didn't realize there were any McGuires left in the area."

The smile faltered, then firmed up. "I'm the only one left. But I love it here."

"Are you in costume, Cousin Lucy?"

"No, Cousin Ellen. Are you?" Lucy looked at Ellen's hat and wrinkled her nose. "There is a booth that sells sun bonnets. They're much prettier."

No criticism in the remark. Just light and laughter—and an invitation to have a little fun.

"Fair enough," Ellen said, laughing.

"For the right heart, the fair *can* be enough."

She heard the message, but she wasn't ready to think about

it. Not yet. She followed Lucy to a booth filled with sun bonnets, noted the shocked delight on the merchant's face, and figured the poor woman hadn't sold a thing all day.

She tried on several bonnets. Lucy dismissed every one. The brim wasn't right, or the crown wasn't right, or the ribbons weren't the right color. Ellen couldn't see much difference in the selections—until she put on the one that finally met with Lucy's approval. Subtle differences that made all the difference in how it flattered her face.

Cousin Lucy might be a bit odd, but she knew hats.

Pleased with her purchase, Ellen stuffed her old hat in the bag the merchant provided and moved through the fair with Lucy.

"There's a handsome one," Lucy whispered as they walked toward one of the booths. "A steady heart that hasn't quite found its match."

"Are you the village matchmaker?" Ellen asked.

"Sometimes."

As they passed the booth, Ellen tipped her head to get a better look at the man in question. Handsome enough—and a bit of a flirt, judging by the wink and the grin he gave her.

She'd seen the fair through Rayce's sneering spiel. Now she saw it through Lucy's eyes. It was an orderly hodgepodge of booths and tents that offered a variety of goods. There were tourist lures, like the costume shop where you could rent an outfit for the day or just have your picture taken while wearing clothes from a different era. There were craft booths and antiques booths and the Greenfields souvenir booth. It was all shabby but well-maintained, a deliberate echo of the fair as it had been long ago.

"This is sweet land," Lucy said as they walked toward the

souvenir booth. "My father owned it, as well as the land that is leased to the stables on the lower side of the lake. More practical to have the horses downwind."

The stables now provided pony rides and carriage rides as well as boarding for people's horses—and it was still a practical choice to have them below the fair.

"Look," Ellen said, stopping at the souvenir booth. "These letter openers are replicas of the dagger that belonged to Hadrea Langley. I knew they had lived here, but I hadn't realized the Franklin-Langley family was that much a part of Greenfields's history."

"I remember it," Lucy said, pressing a hand over her heart.

"I'm sorry, Miss Lucy," the merchant said, his jowls quivering. "I'm that sorry. Never expected to see . . . I mean . . ."

The merchant looked ready to keel over as he snatched the letter openers off the counter, then looked around for a place to stash them. Focused on the man, Ellen grabbed the rest of the faux daggers to help get them out of sight.

When she turned back to Lucy, the other woman was gone.

"YOU'RE LOOKING BEFUDDLED, darling. Let me buy you a drink."

Ellen focused first on the voice, then on the man, and then on the booth. "You sell books and postcards." And he'd winked at her when she'd come this way before.

"But I have an ice chest full of water and soda pop, and I'm willing to share a glass."

While he rummaged around for plastic cups and a bottle of something cold, Ellen pouched her cheeks and blew out a breath of frustration. How could someone disappear so fast?

"Have you seen Lucy?" she asked as he set a full plastic cup on the booth's counter.

"Today was my first time, and I thank you for the experience. A lot of people saw her today. We figure it has to do with you."

"She's a relative. A distant cousin." Ellen kept scanning the booths on the other side of the lane.

"So you're the McGuire who has inherited the land on this side of the lake."

She heard something in his voice, that same mix of hope and wariness she'd been hearing since she'd arrived in Greenfields. "Yes, I'm Ellen McGuire. And you are . . . ?"

"Shamus O'Connor. I teach history, and in the summer I work at the fair. I've been coming here since I was a boy, and I've been working here since my teens."

"Why?" Ellen picked up the cup and drank half the soda before the sudden cold began stabbing at her temples.

"For exactly this day," Shamus replied, smiling. "For the chance to see Lucy. She only appears two days each summer—on the day she was last seen leaving the fair and on the day she would have been married to Jagar Langley. Which is today."

"Jagar Langley?"

"I noticed you with Rayce Langley earlier in the afternoon. Did he not tell you the story?"

"He told me there was a mysterious death here fifty years ago, which is why the fair isn't considered prime property."

Shamus looked away for a moment, as if he were having a debate with himself. Then he looked into her eyes. "Rayce Langley has been sniffing around these past three months trying to find out anything he can about the heir to this land. His family owns the other side of the lake; the McGuires have owned this side for generations before either the Franklins or the Langleys set foot in Greenfields."

"What does that have to do with Lucy?"

"Jagar Langley and Lucy McGuire had been engaged, and a wedding day had been set. The whole village had taken an interest in the courtship because the McGuire hadn't been keen on his prospective son-in-law, and Lucy had done a fair share of sweet-talking before her father agreed to the match. Then Hadrea Franklin showed up. The McGuire was more like a well-to-do country squire while Mr. Franklin was Money, if you understand the difference."

Ellen nodded since he seemed to be waiting for some response. "Hadrea set her sights on Jagar."

Now Shamus nodded. "One summer day, Lucy headed home after shopping at the fair and was never seen again. Before a month passed, Jagar Langley, the grieving lover, was married to Hadrea Franklin, who, oddly enough, had lost the one-of-a-kind dagger her father had given her for her eighteenth birthday."

Chilled now, Ellen set the drink on the counter. "There's no proof that Hadrea killed Lucy."

"None at all. It's just a story quietly told—and never within hearing of anyone from the Franklin-Langley clan."

"Thank you for the drink, Mr. O'Connor."

"The pleasure was mine, Ms. McGuire."

Ellen moved through the fair, seeing nothing, her thoughts fixed on the past. Did the villagers really believe that story? Had she really spent time with a ghost? Shamus O'Connor seemed to think so.

Wondering if any of the old books might have a picture of Lucy, she turned back toward Shamus's booth.

Rayce suddenly appeared beside her. He grabbed her arm and hauled her around.

"Where the hell have you been?" He kept the volume down, but that didn't soften the violence in his tone. "I've been looking all over for you."

"I—I'm sorry, Rayce. I got distracted. I should have realized you wouldn't want to spend so much time here. If you want to leave, I can get a ride back to the hotel."

"No." He seemed angry, agitated. "I just wanted to spend some time with you. I thought we could have a little fun."

The man who kept hammering the point that the grungy little fair wasn't worth the cost of the property taxes suddenly wanted to have fun *here*?

"There's the costume shop," Rayce said. "I thought we could dress up, take a stroll, give the tourists a thrill. I've already picked out a costume for you."

"You want to play dress-up in this heat?"

"After all the time I've spent with you, can't you do this one little thing for me?"

She recognized that tone of voice; knew there would be bruises where his fingers dug into her upper arm. So she didn't argue. Her marriage had taught her how to choose her battle-grounds.

The proprietors of the costume shop were nervous and un-happy. She understood why when she saw the outfit Rayce had picked out for her. It was blue instead of dark rose, but the style of the long skirt and short jacket was very similar to the clothes Lucy had worn.

And they would be wicked hot in this weather.

"There are dressing rooms back here," the woman said,

taking the outfit off the rack of reserved costumes. "We also have lockers where people can leave their street clothes."

Ellen followed passively, still feeling Rayce's fingers digging into her arm even though he was no longer touching her. She waited until they were out of sight, then touched the woman's arm.

"It's a lovely outfit, and I would like to wear it someday." Ellen paused. "But not today."

The woman, who was about her age, looked relieved. "Want to use the back entrance?"

"Thank you."

The woman glanced toward the front of the shop, then headed down the hallway to the storage area.

As Ellen followed, her mind circled around some questions. Why would Rayce want her to dress up? And why pick one of the days when, according to village legend, Lucy might be seen? Because he *had* insisted on visiting the fair today.

"Is there another road that leads up to the village?" Ellen asked.

"The road that borders the lake. These days, it's foot and horse traffic only. It's been around since the fair. That's the way Lucy would have gone to reach home." As the woman pushed the back door open, she added, "You remind me of her."

Ellen paused. Considered. "You've seen Lucy?"

The woman smiled. "Yes, I have."

Ellen slipped out the back door and scurried behind the booths, following a trail that connected to a bridle path that, in turn, connected to the road by the lake. Normally, the gentle incline wouldn't tax human or horse, but it did create enough of a cliff that a fall into the lake wouldn't be a welcome experience.

And there, at the crest, she saw Lucy.

She puffed up the incline, sweating from the heat and wishing she'd thought to buy a bottle of water.

"I've been looking for you," she said when she reached the crest.

Lucy just stared at the lake, then looked past Ellen toward the fair that was now below them. "My grandfather started the fair to give the peddlers a place to sell their wares. They set up their wagons where the booths are now and pastured their livestock below. After a while, the fair grew enough that they began building booths for the merchandise and used their wagons as living quarters."

"The wagons were set up where the cottages are now?" Ellen asked. Many of the merchants rented the little cottages as summer homes. Those, too, were part of her inheritance.

Lucy nodded, but she was still looking at memories. "I chased a man through the fair once. He had stolen an old woman's purse, and I was outraged that he would do such a thing at *my* fair. I hauled up my skirts with one hand and had my parasol in the other. My father had guards who kept order, and they were there that day. So were several policemen who were shopping with their families. They all kept pace with us, but not one of them interfered. So there I was, smacking the fool thief with my parasol and him with the stolen purse held over his head, yelling for help. He finally spotted a policeman who was in uniform and ran over to him, begging to be arrested. I broke my favorite parasol on that fool. But the next day, six parasols were delivered to the house, with nary a name or note attached to any of them. My father laughed for days over that."

Lucy sighed. "This was never meant to be a rich man's land, Cousin Ellen. The people on this side of the lake are more interested in living a contented life than having a chest full of gold."

She hesitated, then added quietly, "And the days at the fair were some of the happiest in my life."

"Jagar courted you there, didn't he?"

"Yes. But he loved ambition more than he loved me. The young man who is with him today is like him in face—and in heart. Be careful, Cousin Ellen."

Chilled by the warning, Ellen looked away—and saw something glint at the edge of the cliff.

"Careful!" Lucy said. "We had heavy rains a few days ago. The ground is still soft at the edge."

Testing the ground before shifting her weight, Ellen knelt at the very edge. Something there, poking out of the side of the cliff, not too far from the surface now that the rain had washed away some of the dirt. She found a flat stone and scraped at the softened edge, sending clots of dirt into the lake below.

Stopping to catch her breath and rest her fingers, she noticed the darker shadows in the cliff wall. "Are there caves in the cliff?"

"Hollows below the water. Things get washed into those hollows and end up lost forever."

Hearing restrained panic in Lucy's voice, Ellen went back to work and finally freed the object. She eased away from the cliff's edge before holding it up for a better look.

A hilt decorated with inlaid gold and black enamel. A red stone as big as her thumbnail. The whole thing was crusted with dirt and the blade was rusty, but there was no mistaking what it was.

"I remember what it feels like," Lucy whispered, her hand pressed over her heart. "I remember. . . ."

She vanished.

Ellen realized she'd been holding her breath when she suddenly gasped for air. Nothing she could prove, but . . .

A flutter of white where Lucy had stood. Ellen walked over and picked up the man's handkerchief. She studied the JL monogram, then wrapped the dagger in the handkerchief, making sure the monogram was visible.

She hurried down the incline, then felt a hand on her arm, tugging her toward the bridle path. Yes. Anyone looking for her would come up the road. No one would expect her to know about the bridle path yet.

She jogged down the bridle path until she found the trail behind the booths. She kept moving, stayed hidden. When she finally reached one of the major lanes in the fair, she came out directly across from Shamus O'Connor's booth. And standing in the middle of the lane like an unhappy island were Jagar and Hadrea, looking heat-weary and cross.

Ellen felt the weight of the dagger. Heard the echo of Lucy's whispered "I remember."

She had no proof, but there might be a way to get justice.

RAYCE STRODE UP the road that bordered the lake. Where had the bitch gone to *this* time? The deal was set, or as good as set. He'd done his homework, checked things out. But the McGuire relation who should have been the heir didn't end up *being* the heir all because of a frigging name. Ellen Lucille McGuire had inherited a frigging fortune in land all because of her *middle name.* How unfair was that? The McGuire relation he'd initially contacted was more than willing to sell the land and didn't give a rat's ass for all these pathetic little merchants and their puny ideas about commerce. They were all a blight on a land deal his great-grandfather had begun. And *he* intended to complete that deal and control *all* the lakefront property.

By the end of that first day, when he'd taken a shot at sweet-talking Ellen McGuire, he'd realized the dumpy hitch in his plans had to go.

And there she was, right where he wanted her, standing on the edge of the cliff.

As he moved toward her, he shifted his right hand behind his hip to hide the latex glove—and the souvenir dagger.

"ELLEN." HADREA GAVE her a swift inspection and sniffed. "Have you seen Rayce? This heat is appalling, and I've had quite enough of this place."

"Do you feel well?" Jagar asked Ellen, sounding concerned. "You look . . . flushed."

More like dirty and sweaty. Maybe more than that, judging by the look of alarm on Shamus's face when he saw her. He grabbed something from the ice chest, ducked out of the booth, and headed toward her.

Finish this. Holding out the wrapped bundle, Ellen looked at Hadrea. "I found something that belongs to you."

Hadrea looked at the bundle in disgust and raised one hand to her throat. "Whatever that dirty thing is, it can't be mine. Throw it away."

She glanced at Jagar, noticed him staring at the monogram, his ruddy face turning pale. She also saw Shamus pull up, slow down. Saw other people easing closer.

She flipped the edges of the handkerchief, revealing what she held. "I found it at the cliff. Guess all the rain finally washed away enough soil so that what was buried didn't stay buried."

Hadrea stared at the dagger. "I lost it. I brought it with me to the fair to show some friends, and I lost it."

"You lost it," Jagar growled, his eyes full of hate. "Like you lost the baby that cost me the woman I loved."

Hadrea staggered back a step. "I had a miscarriage!"

"*You had nothing!* Nothing but tricks and lies."

Ellen watched Hadrea. "So you killed Lucy and lied to Jagar about being pregnant so he'd feel obliged to marry you."

"No!" Hadrea slapped the dagger and handkerchief out of Ellen's hand. "I wanted to marry Jagar. I lied about the baby so he'd break things off with Lucy and marry me. But I didn't kill her. I didn't!"

"You did!" Jagar roared. His eyes filled with tears. "If I broke the engagement to Lucy after the McGuire finally gave his consent, no one in this county or the next would have done business with me. And there was *your* father telling me I had to marry his slut of a daughter to protect *his* reputation. If I didn't marry you, he swore he would ruin all my prospects before I'd even begun."

Hadrea stared at Jagar as if she'd never seen him before. "You killed her. You stole the dagger and killed Lucy."

"I had to! The only way to marry you without breaking the engagement to Lucy was if Lucy disappeared."

"You were the one who called attention to the dagger being lost. You implied . . ." Hadrea choked. Her voice dropped to a hoarse whisper. "You implied that you'd seen me kill her. That's why my father set you up to succeed him in his company."

"I had to get *something* out of this marriage. I held the dagger, but it was your lie that killed Lucy. So her blood is on your hands as much as it's on mine."

A terrible silence.

Hadrea looked around, her eyes dulled by pain. She finally focused on Ellen. "I want to go home. Could you find Rayce? I want to go home." When she turned, the crowd that had gathered around them shuffled to get out of her way.

Jagar hesitated, then followed her.

The crowd drifted away.

Shamus bent down and reached for the dagger. Then he paused a long moment before he picked it up. "You're a scary woman, Ellen McGuire. Did you expect your bluff to pay off this much?"

She felt numb. Cold. She'd guessed wrong, but maybe there was a justice to it after all. Jagar and Hadrea had been in a kind of prison for fifty years. Now, whatever happened next, they were free of the lies.

"Bluff?" she said. "I found the dagger on the cliff, buried in the dirt."

"Nothing but glass and gilt, darling," Shamus said, holding it up for her to see. "This isn't the famous dagger. It's one of the souvenir letter openers. Someone must have bought it and dropped it a while back."

She shook her head as she stared at it. "That's not what I dug out of the cliff. That's not what I showed Jagar and Hadrea. That's not what they saw."

"I know," he said softly. "But God as my witness, Ellen, I'm going to swear to any and all authorities that this is what you were holding when you bluffed a confession out of Jagar Langley."

"But what happened to—" A chill went through her, raising the hairs on her arms. "You said Rayce was trying to find out who inherited this land."

Shamus frowned. "That's right."

"He wanted me to dress up like Lucy." She shivered despite

the heat. "I think he intended to kill me. That's what Lucy was trying to tell me when she said Rayce is like his grandfather in face and in heart. Oh God, Shamus."

He caught her as she whirled to run back to the cliff.

"Wait!" Keeping a firm grip on her arm, he handed the letter opener to the merchant in the neighboring booth. "Don't let this out of your sight. And call the police!"

Then they ran toward the cliff.

"YOU LOOK PERFECT," Rayce said as he moved toward her. And being close to the edge, she was perfectly positioned too. There wasn't any way she could get past him. "Dressed like that, it will be easy to convince people of your lifelong obsession with Lucy McGuire. That's why your middle name is Lucille, isn't it? Named for her. But you got too caught up in pretending you were Lucy, and this trip to the fair unhinged your fragile hold on sanity. Don't worry. Your heir will have letters in his possession as proof of your increasing instability. Then I'll finalize the deal for the rest of the lakefront property, and you . . ." He glanced at the lake. "Well, I've heard things can get trapped in the hollows under the cliff for years."

"So like him in face and heart," she said, sorrow as well as anger in her voice.

He took another step toward her. As he whipped the letter opener from behind his back and raised his arm to strike, he felt the hilt change, thicken, grow heavier.

Instead of stepping back, she moved toward him.

"I won't let you kill Ellen," she said. "And I won't be married again to cold steel."

———————

THEY SAW RAYCE tumble off the cliff.

Shamus grabbed Ellen's arm, stopping her rush up the incline. "He's in the water." He cupped his hands around his mouth and shouted to the people hurrying up behind them. "We need boats! Fast!"

Ellen pulled away from Shamus and continued up the incline. Nothing to see. She knew that. But she had to look.

"No, you don't. No, no, no. One person taking a header off the cliff is enough."

Strong arms around her waist swinging her away from the cliff. She didn't protest when Shamus marched her over to the other side of the road.

"Where . . . ?" She wasn't sure what she wanted to ask.

"If they find him, they'll bring the body to the boat launch at the lower end of the lake."

"I need to be there."

A hesitation. A slight withdrawal. "Did he mean something to you, then?"

She shook her head. "Not for his sake. For hers."

"MOTHER OF GOD, I've never seen the like," one of the boatmen said.

Ellen waited as men lifted the tarped bundle out of the boat and set it on the sand. Jagar and Hadrea were there, along with several police officers. Shamus was there too. She didn't know why he was being so kind, and she didn't care. She needed a friend right now.

When they opened the bundle, she was prepared to see Rayce. But she wasn't prepared to see the other.

Buried in Rayce's heart right up to the hilt was a one-of-a-kind dagger with a ruby as big as an eye. And wrapped around Rayce in a lover's embrace, with one hand curled around the dagger's hilt, was a skeleton wearing the tattered remains of a dark rose skirt and jacket.

"CAN WE DRESS up today, Mama?" six-year-old Sally Mc-Guire O'Connor asked. "Can we, please? Pretty please?"

"Yeah!" said four-year-old Lucy Ann. "Pretty please, please, please?"

"Maybe." Ellen kept a firm grip on her daughters' hands. If she didn't, one would be down at the stables talking her way into an afternoon-long pony ride and the other would be hustling souvenirs. Which their father found amusing, so *he* wasn't much help. At least until she got them to the booth. Then she could count on Shamus to ride herd on his darlings.

A handsome man with a steady heart. That's what she had found at the fair.

"*That* lady is dressed up," Sally said, pointing to the woman wearing an old-fashioned skirt and jacket and a dark rose hat with a jaunty white feather.

The woman's smile was full of light and joy and love.

"Of course she's dressed up," Ellen said, returning the smile. "That's Cousin Lucy."

A STRAND IN THE WEB

1

"OH, YUCKIT," ZERX SAID AS SHE LOOKED AT THE CUP in her hand and made squinchy faces. "I asked for it hot, and this is barely even warm!"

"That sounds like the date I had last night," Benj said, snickering as he walked over to his console to begin the morning's work.

No one responded to Benj's remark. That was how we handled these typical morning comments—with polite silence.

"I don't see why the maintenance engineers can't fix this thing," Thanie complained, taking her mug from the food slot. She sniffed it to make sure it held tea, then took a cautious sip.

"I heard Marv finally fixed the warning light problem," Whit said as the data for his part of the project filled the screen in front of his console.

"What warning light problem?" Stev asked.

Whit swiveled his chair to face the rest of us. "A warning light on one of the main panels has been flashing intermittently for the past several weeks, warning of a circuit failure in one of the minor systems."

"It's probably our food slot," Thanie grumbled.

"Of course, the engineers checked the system out every time and didn't find anything wrong," Whit continued. "When the warning light started flashing again yesterday, Marv gave the control panel a thump with his fist. The warning light went out and hasn't come back on since. Problem solved."

The computer chimed quietly, the signal that the morning class had begun.

As the rest of the team members settled into their places, Zerx complained loudly, "Why do *I* have to do the insects?"

Before any of us could remind Zerx—again—that the computer had done a random draw to give us our parts of the assignment and that every part was equally important, Benj said, "Because you *look* like a bug."

Unfortunately, that was true. Zerx had gathered two segments of hair at the front of her head and used some kind of stiffener on them so that they stood straight up and looked quite a bit like insect antennae.

Benj turned away, satisfied with his retort. He didn't see the look on Zerx's face before she went to her own console. Zerx could be very unpleasant when she was in a snit, and that look on her face always meant payback.

Tuning out the usual morning grumbles, I carefully checked my own data, feeling the shiver of excitement go through me as it had for the past month when I sat at this console.

My teammates kept acting like this was another computer simulation that was part of our classwork. Oh, it was part of our classwork all right. In fact, this *was* our classwork now. Only this. But this wasn't a computer simulation where time was accelerated and a planet year was contained within a classroom day. This was *real*.

There were six teams at this stage of our education. We'd had to take an extra year of schoolwork while we waited for our city-ship to reach this world—and *another* extra year after that while we waited for the Restorers to prepare this world for the life we would give back to it.

You couldn't apply for a Restorer's team until you proved you could work in real time and maintain Balance in your part of the project. So we had waited and studied and done the computer simulations and watched our simulated worlds crumble into ecological disaster—much like the worlds the Restorers committed themselves to rebuilding.

Now each team had part of a large island. Each part had a strong force field around it to prevent any accidents or disasters from going beyond the team's designated area. Now we were working in real time. We couldn't just delete plants and animals to make it more convenient when something got out of hand because we were given an allotment from the huge honeycomb chambers holding the genetic material for billions of species from all over the galaxy. That allotment determined how many of each species we could deposit at our site. Now every life counted—not just for our own final scores in the project, but for the well-being of the planet.

I was assigned the trees for this project, which pleased me very much because my name is Willow.

As I scanned my data, I took a deep breath and let out a sigh of satisfaction. The number of trees had increased since I last checked. I had planted some mature trees, but most of my allotment for this area had been used for saplings and seeds, and the seeds were beginning to grow.

I keyed in the coordinates and the command for a planet-side picture on half my screen. A moment later, I was staring at a tiny twig with two leaves—a baby oak tree. Someday its roots would spread deep into the land. Its thick trunk would support the strong branches that would provide nesting areas and shelter for birds. Its acorns would feed chipmunks and squirrels, and it would produce oxygen that the animals needed to breathe.

A tree was a wonderful piece of creation.

"You look pleased," Stev said as he approached my console.

"Tree," I said, grinning like a fool.

"That *is* your assignment, Willow," he replied, trying to maintain a somber expression. Then he glanced at the screen, and his eyes narrowed. He looked at my twig of a tree and then at the numbers for each species. "How'd you get that many trees out of the generation tanks so fast?"

I stiffened a little. But there was nothing in his voice—like there would have been in Benj's or Zerx's—that implied I was getting preferential treatment because both of my parents were Restorers. "I requested twenty percent of the stock as mature trees old enough to begin self-reproduction, thirty percent as saplings, and the rest as seeds."

It could take days for the generation tanks to produce a mature specimen, depending on how fast the growing process was accelerated. But it didn't take the tanks more than a few hours to produce healthy, viable seeds.

Stev whistled softly. He didn't say anything for a minute. Then, with his eyes fixed on the little oak tree still on my screen, he said, "The Blessed All has given you a gift for this kind of work, Willow. You'll be on a Restorer's team the moment you're fully qualified."

With a smile that was a little sad, he went back to his own console. And I went back to staring at the little oak.

Restorers. That's what the eighty-seven people who are the heart of our city-ship are called. They give purpose to what would otherwise be an aimless wandering through the galaxy.

The Scholars say that a very long time ago we lived four score and seven years. Our people now live *forty* score and seventy years—870 years. They say that the Blessed All granted us the knowledge to extend our life spans so that we could make Atonement. That is why the city-ships that are now the home of our people were created—so that we could make Atonement by restoring worlds ravaged either by external disasters or by disasters caused by their inhabitants.

And it is part of our Atonement that we live in a world made of metal, that we never walk on a world we have restored, never feel the breeze that ruffles the leaves, smell the wildflowers . . . or press our hands against the bark of a tree that we planted.

The Scholars never say why we have to make Atonement, but they know. You can see the sorrow that's always in their eyes after they complete their training and are told the Scholars' Secrets.

So this restoration of damaged worlds is our way of making Atonement to the Blessed All for some failure long in our past. The Restorers and their teams are the ones who shoulder that responsibility.

I can't remember a time when I didn't want to be a Restorer—not because of the prestige that goes with the title, but because I love to watch things grow.

My console chirped a query, reminding me that I had work to do.

Blanking my screen, I called up the dot map that would

show me the placement of the trees. I still had acorns, some sapling ash and birch, and one young willow left from my first allotment of trees, and I wanted to use them for the start of a new woodland.

As I brushed my finger over the direction pad on my console, intending to shift the dot map and look at the coastline, my hand jerked. I shook it, wondering why it had done that since the muscles didn't feel cramped.

The Scholars say that sometimes the Blessed All shows us our path in very small ways.

When I looked at the screen, my hand poised above the direction pad to shift position back to my team's designated area, I saw the other island. It was to the west of the students' island and about one-third the size—which didn't make it a small island by any means.

Curious about who the Restorer was, I keyed in the coordinates and asked the question. Every Restorer had a specific code so that other Restorers could quickly find out who was working on a particular section of the planet.

There was no Restorer code for that island.

Thinking I'd made a mistake when I keyed in the coordinates, I tried it again.

No Restorer code.

That wasn't right.

I requested soil analysis data. Maybe the Restorer teams had missed this island when they had carefully laid down the microbes and bacteria that were the first step in restoration. Maybe the land was still too toxic to support life, and that was why no one was working it.

No, the land was fertile and waiting.

I closed my eyes. It was rash. It was foolish. I would never be granted a landmass that size for a special project. And even if I was, I wouldn't be able to achieve Balance without a team to help me.

But I could feel an ache in my bones that I knew was the land's cry to be filled with living things again.

I wanted to answer that cry so much.

A soft warning beep reminded me that I had other land to tend.

I called up the screen that listed the trees and the numbers of each species.

My mouth fell open. For a moment, I couldn't breathe.

During the time when my thoughts had been elsewhere, ten percent of my trees had been destroyed!

Yesterday, Dermi had placed three deer in the meadow that bordered the woodland—which was fine because the meadow was already well established and could feed them.

Now, *fifty* deer had been plunked in the middle of the woodland. There was nothing else for them to eat, so they were devouring my seedling trees.

My fingers raced across the keyboard as I wrote an Urgent request to Dermi for the immediate transfer of the deer to other viable positions within our designated area.

I could have just shouted across the room—and sometimes we did that—but every request had to be backed up with written data. The computer could override any request that *wasn't* formally made because, in part, that trail of requests and memos was what our Instructors used to judge our work. And that was sometimes very frustrating. We weren't graded just on our *individual* work, but on the *team's* ability to maintain Balance.

I sat back, trying not to bite my nails while I waited for Dermi's response. It wouldn't take long. Urgents always got top priority.

Minutes passed.

I swiveled my chair and looked at Dermi. She was sitting there, inputting data as calmly as you please.

I sent another Urgent request . . . and waited.

I attached a verification requirement to the third request to confirm that she *was* receiving the Urgents.

The verification came back. Dermi had gotten the requests and *still* wasn't doing anything.

Throughout the first part of that morning, I continued sending requests while I watched the number of my remaining trees fall . . . and fall . . . and fall.

When midmorning came, I sent an Urgent request to Fallah, who was handling large carnivores, and asked for a sufficient number of predators who ate deer to be brought to the woodland. At that point, I didn't really care what kind of carnivore she used as long as they would start eating the deer before the deer ate the entire woodland down to the ground.

By the time the computer chimed the signal for the midday break, there were 125 deer in a woodland that wasn't ready to support even one and still maintain Balance.

Instead of transferring deer *out*, Dermi had responded to each Urgent request by sending more deer *in*.

And Fallah hadn't sent one carnivore.

I blanked my screen before going to the food court where the older students gathered for the midday meal. When Stev asked me what was wrong, I brushed him off. I didn't mean to be rude; I just couldn't talk to anyone. Still, he brought his plate over and sat at the same table. Not next to me or anything, but he was there, along with Thanie and Whit.

I picked at my food, choking down only enough to give my body fuel for the rest of the day.

As we headed back to our classroom, Thanie tugged on my tunic sleeve to slow me down. Not that I was eager to go back in and find out how much damage had been done in the past hour.

"I overheard Dermi and Fallah talking," Thanie said in a low voice. "You're not going to get any carnivores."

"Why not?" I said loudly enough to have Thanie shushing me.

"Because Dermi's in a snit because Stev went to the concert with you last night, and Fallah is Dermi's best friend."

"Stev didn't go to the concert with *me*," I hissed back at her. "A group of us went together—including you."

"*I* know that. But Dermi wanted Stev to ask *her*. So *she's* not going to give you any help, and neither is Fallah."

I'd spent a month creating that woodland. A month's worth of work, and all that *life* I had drawn from the genetic material so carefully stored. All of it wasted because Dermi was jealous.

As I walked to my console, I looked at Dermi. She and Fallah had their heads together, whispering. There was something smug and mean about the way they stared at me.

I called up the data on my screen, and for the rest of the afternoon, I watched my woodland die.

I didn't give Dermi and Fallah the satisfaction of seeing me cry.

I also didn't plant any trees to replace the ones that had been devoured.

I just sat there . . . and watched.

Toward the end of the day, when we were supposed to write the day's activity report for our Instructors to review, Zerx sprang her nasty little surprise—her payback for Benj's bug remark.

I wasn't paying attention to much of anything until Whit yelled, *"Zerx!"* He sent a planet-side view to each of our consoles.

Swarm after swarm of locusts were descending like black

clouds onto the meadowlands. Zerx must have used almost her entire allotment of insect life to create them.

And there was nothing any of us could do until class began again the next morning.

I think that's why I did it.

Instead of writing my activity report, I used my personal computer pad to write a request for a special project, a piece of land where I would have complete control, where I would be the only one responsible for achieving—and maintaining—Balance.

I asked for the other island.

I requested a Restorer screen around it, which meant that life-forms could be transferred through the force field around the island with my consent, but nothing could slip through on its own. I requested monitor blanking—a Restorer could override that request, but no one else would be able to see what I was doing unless he or she knew my password.

I sent in my request, blanked my console screen, and went to the living quarters I shared with my parents.

Mother always says that a person must have a life beyond the work. She belongs to a musical society. Father belongs to a theater group. They seldom talk shop at dinnertime unless something special has happened. Or they talk about their work as a way to answer the questions that usually spill out of me while I tell them about my classwork.

I didn't talk about what happened in class that day. Since they both seemed concerned about something they were obviously reluctant to talk about while I was there, I also didn't tell them about requesting a special project. After all, I wasn't sure I would get it. Student special projects were usually limited to a few acres of land, not a whole island.

As soon as dinner was finished, I mumbled something about

needing to prep for class tomorrow and went to my room. Normally, I would have spent at least an hour going over details and getting requests ready to submit to the techs who oversaw the generation tanks.

Instead, I took the hologram from its special place on the shelf, set it on my workspace, and turned it on.

WHEN I WAS a little girl, my mother asked me what I wanted for my birthday, which was still a couple of weeks away. I told her I wanted a tree.

The day of my birthday, just before the time when Mother usually programmed the food slot for the evening meal, Father muttered something about having a bit of business to take care of and left.

Before I could express my disappointment that he wasn't going to celebrate my birthday with us, Mother held out her hand and smiled. "We have a bit of business to take care of too."

We went to the room where her team worked. It was the end of the day shift, and there were only a couple of her assistants in the room. When they saw us, they smiled and left. At the time, I was too young to realize that a Restorer's room was *never* left unattended, and there was something unusual about them *all* leaving like that.

Mother led me to the large console where she worked. She sat me on her lap, and with her hand over mine, she opened a screen that showed a planet-side picture of a creek. Her hand guided mine as we set the coordinates and issued the command codes.

A few minutes later, a young willow tree stood near the bank of the creek.

"There's your tree, Willow," Mother said quietly.

I don't know how long we sat there, Mother with her arms around me and her cheek resting against my head, just watching the light breeze flutter the willow's leaves.

When she finally blanked the screen and we returned to our living quarters, Father was waiting for us, his smile a little hesitant.

And I knew then that, just as my mother had arranged for me to plant that tree, my father had personally overseen its growth in the generation tanks. But that wasn't his business that evening.

After dinner and the birthday sweet, I got my other present— a hologram of that young willow by the creek. While Mother and I had been planting the tree, Father had arranged to have the hologram made so that I would be able to keep that moment.

In all the years that have come and gone since then, that hologram has remained my most treasured gift.

I TURNED OFF the hologram and carefully put it back on the shelf.

There was nothing I wanted to do about the class project. There was nothing I *could* do about the special project. So I read for a while and then went to bed.

And spent a restless night full of terrible dreams about destruction.

2

I CHECKED MY PERSONAL COMPUTER PAD THE MOment I woke up. I checked it before I left for class. I checked it the moment I got to the classroom.

Nothing. No confirmation or denial for my special project.

The locusts had been busy since class ended yesterday, and everyone could see this was leading to disaster. Requests zipped back and forth, mostly requests to the Instructor who was our advisor to be allowed to terminate the locusts down to a workable population. The same message came back every single time: termination was unacceptable. Balance had to be restored by natural means—which meant transferring into that area or producing enough birds, reptiles, and mammals to consume the locusts.

Requests for predators poured to Stev's and Whit's consoles since they were the team members who were training to become a Right Hand—a Restorer's primary technical assistant—and had some pull with the generation tank techs. They forwarded the requests, which were acknowledged but put in the queue with the rest of the student requests. That meant all we had to work with was what we already had.

The lack of response caused a lot of muttering and grumbling.

The locusts weren't the only problem. The deer had eaten my young woodland right down to the ground. All I really had left to work with were the mature trees and the acorns and saplings I still hadn't planted. And I had no intention of sacrificing *them*.

Then Benj thought to check the team rating and discovered that it had dropped so low *none* of us would qualify for *any* kind of starting position on a Restorer's team.

That was when the yelling *really* started.

Of course, Zerx, Dermi, and Fallah were the ones who yelled the loudest.

The rest of the morning was filled with scrambled panic. Dermi started transferring the deer any old place within our designated area. Fallah finally released some of her carnivores and plunked them down in the middle of the deer. Benj dumped mice, squirrels, and rabbits into the meadowlands already covered with locusts, not giving any thought to whether any of those animals would help with the locust problem. Thanie transferred her songbirds to that area, and Dayl poured in a load of reptiles.

It was a mess.

I did very little throughout the morning. I politely answered requests for more trees and made no promises. When the requests became more forceful, I said my order for saplings was already in the student queue and I would begin establishing the woodland as soon as trees were available.

It was almost time for the midday break when I keyed in the coordinates for the other island.

I stared at the screen for a long minute, my heart, and my hopes, sinking.

The island now had a Restorer code.

The midday meal was . . . unpleasant. Stev, Thanie, Whit, and I sat at a table by ourselves. None of us wanted to talk. Thanie was the only one who tried—once.

"It's early in the project," she said, looking hopefully at each of us. "We'll be able to restore Balance soon and get our rating back."

"The only good thing about all of this is that the force field won't allow our stupidity to spill into anyone else's area," Stev replied with enough bitterness that none of us dared say anything else.

Judging from the angry looks that were flashing between other tables around the food court, our team wasn't the only one having problems. Which didn't make me feel any better.

It was toward the end of the class day when I finally checked my personal computer pad again. My parents sometimes left messages to let me know if they would be working late or if there was a particular chore I should take care of.

There *was* a message for me. I read it three times before I finally understood what it said.

My request for the island had been granted. The code I had seen was the one that had been assigned to *me* for the duration of the project.

Feeling dizzy, I hugged the computer pad and tried to draw in enough air to breathe properly.

A warm hand settled on my shoulder.

"Willow?" Stev said, sounding concerned. "Are you all right?"

"I'm fine," I said, trying not to gasp out the words.

He studied me carefully. "You don't look fine."

"No, I'm fine. Really." But my hands shook as I tried to remember how to close up my console.

Stev brushed my hand aside and closed the console in the proper sequence.

"Come on," he said. "I'll walk you home."

"I'm fine," I said again. At that moment, I wasn't sure if I was going to dance down the corridors or burst into tears. I *did* know that I really needed to be alone for a while to think this through.

Stev walked me to my family's living quarters. He didn't ask any of the questions I could see in his eyes, and I was grateful.

I spent an hour in my room staring at that message.

The island was mine. *Mine.*

I couldn't possibly build a viable ecosystem for a landmass that size and maintain Balance all by myself. In fact, it would be totally foolish to even *try* to establish an ecosystem over the whole island all at once.

I wasn't sure how much time I would have. Sooner or later, someone would realize that a student had been given an island that should have been handled by a primary Restorer. But if I could establish a full ecosystem in a few thousand acres to *prove* I could do it, maybe I would be allowed to continue—or at least be part of the team that finished restoring the island.

I couldn't do it alone. Life-forms, from the smallest to the largest, had to be established. Each link in the chain of survival had to be formed carefully and in the right order. I needed someone who would act as an RRH—a Restorer's Right Hand. I needed someone who would support my work without trying to change it to suit his own vision, who could work independently, someone who could be counted on to value Balance.

I needed Stev.

Since I had an hour before my parents got home, I keyed in the island's coordinates and requested lists of all the species that were viable for this world and for that particular island.

The computer immediately requested the password.

Huh? I hadn't *set* a password yet.

I went back to the message that had given me the Restorer code. At the bottom of the message was the password: unicorn.

An odd word, I thought as I sounded it out. And it seemed equally odd that the password had been chosen for me. But this was no time to quibble. I made my request for species lists, added the password, and waited.

The lists were daunting. I'd had no idea that so many of the species that were stored in those vast honeycomb chambers were suitable for this world. No wonder the Restorers were looking a little dazed.

The computer chimed the warning that the hour was up. I saved the lists under my password, closed down the computer, and went to make dinner since it was my turn.

When I pressed the pad next to the food slot to indicate I was about to place my order, I was still muttering, "Earthworms, grubs, tadpoles, flies." Fortunately, the computer suggested that I place another order from the available menu. I could just imagine Father's reaction if I set a platter of tadpoles and bugs over earthworm pasta in front of him. No, this wouldn't be a good time for a lecture on keeping my mind focused on the task at hand. Not a good time at all.

I chose meat loaf, which would please Father, and a variety of vegetables to go with it, which would please Mother.

I had the table set when Father came home. Mother arrived a few minutes later, looking distracted.

She filled her plate without any comments, then sat there, pushing her peas around with her fork.

After a few minutes, Father said, "Has Britt made a decision?"

"She's stepping down as a primary Restorer," Mother replied.

"Britt?" I snapped to attention. "Why is Britt stepping down? Is she sick again?" Britt was the oldest Restorer on our ship. Forty score and seventy were the years allotted to us for Atonement. Britt had celebrated her eight hundredth birthday several months ago, shortly before she became very ill. She had recovered and seemed fine whenever I saw her, although I remember Zashi, her RRH and life partner, had been very concerned for a while.

"Zashi is also stepping down," Mother said, still rearranging her peas. "He says he wants to concentrate on his tale telling."

Zashi was a wonderful tale teller. Whenever one of his story hours was listed in the activities, I was there. But if Britt and Zashi were no longer going to lead a team . . .

"What's going to happen to Britt's team?" I asked.

"Oh, they'll help out wherever they're needed for a while," Mother said, sounding vague—which wasn't like Mother at all.

"Then Britt didn't name a successor?" Father asked, frowning at his meat loaf.

"Not yet."

And even if she had, a new Restorer would form a new team, so there would be the inevitable shuffling as people settled into new assignments.

Father sighed. "Looks like some of us will have to shoulder the extra work in order to take care of the area that Britt intended to restore."

"No," Mother said, a funny catch in her voice. "Someone has taken responsibility for restoring Balance to the island."

I choked.

Mother gave me a light thump on the back. "Better?"

I nodded, not trusting myself to speak.

I'd been given Britt's island. *Britt's*. Blessed All, she was the most talented Restorer to come along in several generations. Everyone said so.

"Are you all right, Willow?" Mother brushed her hand over my forehead. "You look pale."

That got Father's full attention.

"I'm fine," I lied. "Really."

Mother smiled, but it wasn't her usual, easy smile. I could tell she was straining not to say a lot of things. Which made me wonder if she knew who had taken responsibility for restoring Balance to Britt's island.

I spent the evening in my room. Father had gone to a rehearsal for a play that his theater group was doing. Mother was listening to music.

My feelings kept going round and round. First feeling overwhelmed by the task I'd been given, then excited, then scared.

Finally, I sat in meditation to become attuned to the Blessed All. In that silence, I found the quiet stillness within me. And then all I felt was joy.

I could do this. I *would* do this. I would bring life back to the island—not only for my sake and the land's sake, but now for Britt as well.

3

THE NEXT MORNING, JUST BEFORE THE COMPUTER chimed the start of class, I sidled over to Stev's console.

"Stev, I've received permission for a special project. Would you help me?"

His eyes lit up with pleasure. "Sure, Willow." Then he added reluctantly, "Will you credit me for my work?"

I hesitated a moment too long. And remembered a moment too late that other people had asked for Stev's help on a project and *hadn't* given him credit for his work. I'm sure the Instructors were aware of his part of it, and there was probably a private note in his file acknowledging the work, but it wasn't *formally* listed on his credits—and that could make a difference in earning the qualifications necessary to work on a Restorer's team.

His eyes dimmed. His face hardened. "Just tell me what you need," he said—and turned his back on me.

He didn't sit with Thanie, Whit, and me during the midday break. He didn't say a thing to me during the whole day.

When the computer chimed the end of the class day, I gathered my courage and approached him.

"Could you stay a few minutes?" I asked quietly, noticing the sullen looks Dermi was giving me and the way she was lingering so that she would leave at the same time Stev did.

She left in a huff when Stev finally noticed her and gave her a cold stare.

Dermi was one of the people who hadn't given him credit for his work on one of her projects. Why she kept expecting him to ask her for a date after pulling that stunt was something the rest of us couldn't figure out.

"What is it?" Stev asked, not sounding the least bit friendly.

I took a deep breath. "If this project succeeds, I'll be very happy to give you credit for your work. But if it doesn't—"

"Succeed or fail, I either get credit or I don't," he snapped.

"I think you should see the project before you say that."

Going to my console, I keyed in the coordinates and asked for a red line to show the boundaries of the project.

When the red line appeared, all I could do was stare. The message granting my request for the special project *had* contained the dimensions of the area that was now my responsibility, but I'd been so stunned and excited about getting the island, I hadn't paid attention to the numbers. It hadn't occurred to me that my designated area would be *larger* than I'd requested.

Not only was I responsible for the island; I was also responsible for a band of salt water that surrounded the island. Which meant I was responsible for a small part of another entirely different ecosystem.

Stev studied my screen for a minute. "You've got that little island off the main one a Restorer is working on?"

"Not exactly," I said weakly. Stev was looking at a tiny island off the east coast. It probably had been connected to my island at one time.

"So what *is* your project, Willow?" Stev said a bit impatiently.

"Well . . ." I gestured vaguely at the screen. "Everything inside the red line."

Stev's mouth fell open. *"Willow!"* He braced himself against the back of my chair. "Do you know how *big* that is?"

I certainly did.

Stev took a couple of deep breaths. "So who do you have for your team?"

"Well . . . Actually . . . You."

It was more luck than intention that he ended up sitting in my chair and not on the floor.

"Are you *crazy*?" he shouted.

I knelt in front of him, grabbed his hands, and held on tight. "We can do it, Stev. I know we can! And we don't have to do *all* of it all at once. Look." I jumped up, keyed in the boundary lines of the area I'd decided to work on first. "We can start here, with just this much. That's enough land to create Balance. We can work out from there."

I wasn't sure if Stev couldn't think of anything to say or didn't dare say what he was thinking.

"We can do it," I said again.

"That's a Restorer code," he said slowly as he studied the image on the screen.

"That's the code I was given for this project."

He took another deep breath. "With a Restorer code, we wouldn't be stuck in the student queue. We could use any generation tank that was available."

"We'll have to start from the ground up," I said as my brain began its stubborn chant of *Earthworms, grubs, tadpoles, flies.*

"This really is crazy." Then he smiled. "Count me in. Have you made any lists for what's suitable for that land?"

"I'll transfer copies to your personal computer pad," I said happily.

Stev looked at the lists. Then he finally looked at me. "You're the Restorer on this project. Where do you want to start?"

I'd already thought of that. Balance. Always Balance. Every living thing needed a food source. "The simpler life-forms, especially the ones that aerate the soil. Seeds for grasses and wildflowers."

Stev nodded. "I'll do some checking. The generation tanks may already be producing some of these for other teams. With life-forms like this, the techs usually use enough genetic material to create in batches, then portion it out. That way no team is dependent on the genetic variables that might be in a single batch. We decide on a total number that we want in the designated area, then ask that a percentage of the total come from each batch until we reach our allotment. The grass seed won't be a problem. I'll go down to the tank rooms now and get that started. There should be some to distribute by tomorrow afternoon."

I smiled. He was talking to himself more than to me, which was what he usually did when he was focused and interested in the task.

He finally stopped, looked at me, let out a shout of laughter, gave me a fast hug, and headed for the door. When I didn't follow, he stopped. "Aren't you coming?"

Still smiling, I shook my head. "I have to close down. Then I'll work at home. You can reach me on my personal pad."

When he was gone, I keyed in the coordinates I had searched for last night. My screen filled with a planet-side picture of a stream dancing over rocks.

Each link in the chain of survival had to be formed carefully and at the right time. But the simpler life-forms and the grasses would not be the first bit of life I gave back to this land.

There, by the stream, I planted the young willow tree that I had saved from my student allotment.

4

I GOT TO CLASS EARLY THE NEXT MORNING. STEV was already there.

"The first batch of grass seed finished early this morning and is now in a holding tank," he said. "There's also a memo asking that the holding tanks be emptied as quickly as possible since there's a lot of material going down to the planet, and full holding tanks will slow up the use of the generation tanks."

"Then let's get to work." I'd spent part of last evening working out where we should start. Accessing the data Stev had sent to my personal pad, we had enough seed to cover several hundred acres. I keyed in coordinates for half the acreage and sent the command to the holding tank for dispersal of half the seed. As the commands were relayed through the city-ship's various systems and dispersal began, a green tint began filling in the dot map that I had called up on my screen. When it was done, I sat back and grinned.

"You've still got the other half of the seeds to plant," Stev pointed out.

"No," I said, "*you've* got the other half to plant."

His eyes widened when I sent the password to his personal pad. His fingers danced through the command codes.

Grinning like fools, we watched the green tint fill in another part of the island.

We both jumped to change the image on our screens when the door slid open and Whit walked in.

"I don't know why the two of you are looking so pleased," he grumbled. "If we can't get this project under control, we'll have to ask for complete termination and start over. And *that* will definitely be on our formal records."

The rest of the team members began to file in. Dermi and Fallah walked past me as if I didn't exist. Thanie slunk into the room, looking like she'd had a very bad night. Even Benj didn't make any of his usual comments. And none of the others had anything to say as they took their places and called up the data for their part of the project.

Whit was right. It was awful. So much of the plant life had been consumed, there wasn't enough for the animals to eat. And there was no chance that the remaining plants would reproduce and repopulate the area fast enough. If we dumped the next class allotment of plant life into the area without doing something to adjust the number of animals and insects, it would be consumed immediately.

What it came down to was this: if we were going to restore Balance, we would have to wait out the depletion of life. That, too, was part of Balance. Creatures consumed one kind of life and were, in turn, consumed.

For a while, the predators—both those that walked on the land and those that soared in the sky—would feast. They would mate and produce young who would also feast. But their prey, who ate the plants and seeds, would starve and produce no young. The predators, in their turn, would starve. And the land would start building the links in the chain of survival again— the grasses and flowers, the shrubs and trees, the insects that would pollinate them, and on and on until, once more, there was Balance.

But sometimes a world goes too far out of Balance. Sometimes too many links in the chain are broken too severely, and a world spirals into destruction.

Those are the worlds we restore to Balance as our Atonement to the Blessed All.

The computer chimed the start of class, and I got to work.

There were several requests from Dermi, of all people, for seedling trees. Checking the coordinates she had indicated, I realized she wanted me to put down seedlings in the middle of the deer herds to give them a food source. My next allotment of trees would feed the deer for only a few days at most, and that wasn't going to help the situation.

But I was still part of the team, and I had to do something to honor the request.

Remembering what Stev had said about the holding tanks, I released all the sapling birch and ash with a Priority attached to the planting command. I planted half the acorns I still had. I ordered the other half for aboveground dispersal. I winced about that, but they *would* provide some food for the nut eaters.

I didn't plant or disperse any of them where the deer concentrations were the highest. I felt bad for the deer, but sustaining them today only to have them starve tomorrow wasn't going to help the team restore Balance to our area.

I also put in a request to Whit's console for oak and beech trees that were mature enough to reproduce. I didn't think it wise to send *all* my requests through Stev, even though I preferred working with his specimens. Whit would use the full acceleration feature of the generation tanks; Stev never did without a very strong reason.

I breathed a sigh of relief when the computer chimed the midday break.

"Well, that was an interesting morn—" Stev started to say as the door slid open and we stepped into the corridor.

It was *cold*.

"Blessed All," Whit said. "Some of the heating system must have gone down." He shivered. "Come on. Let's get to the food court and get some hot food."

"If there *is* any hot food," Thanie grumbled, hurrying after him.

The rest of the team members rushed past us. Stev didn't move.

"Stev?" I put my hand on his arm. His muscles were so tight they didn't feel like flesh anymore. And he was very pale.

"This is how it started the last time," he whispered.

"No, Stev," I said, shaking my head. "*No*. Part of a system went down. The engineers are probably already working on it, and it'll be fixed in no time."

His eyes were haunted when he finally looked at me. "Of course it will," he said.

He didn't believe it. He had reason not to believe it.

But we couldn't afford to believe anything else. As part of

our Atonement, we lived in a world made of metal. If something really *was* wrong with the ship, there was nowhere else for us to go. Nowhere.

DERMI RETURNED FROM the midday break in a major snit. When she checked her data and realized what I'd done, the snit exploded into a prime tantrum.

"You . . . ," she said, stomping across the room toward me. You . . ." She called me a very rude thing. "You did this deliberately."

"I provided what I had available," I replied, trying to remain calm as I stood up to face her. "I've also requisitioned my next tree allotment."

"That's not going to help my deer *now*, is it?" Dermi shouted.

"Hey, Dermi," Zerx said, looking wary and guilty since it was *her* snit that had given us the locust problem. "Willow is just doing what—"

"Stay out of this, bug-brain," Dermi snarled. "She did it on purpose."

The way you poured deer into a woodland that couldn't support them? "I provided what I had available."

"You're doing this just to make me look bad," Dermi said, so angry she was turning pale. "The deer need food, and *you* could have provided it."

I took a deep breath. "You could ask to transfer them. Maybe one of the other student teams needs some deer. One of the Restorer teams might be planning to bring that species of deer into another area. You could—"

"You get *demerits* on your score when you ask to transfer,"

Dermi shouted. Then her voice dropped to a quiet that was far more menacing. "Of course, *you* never get demerits for *anything.*"

Maybe I should have realized this wasn't really about the deer. Maybe I should have remembered that Dermi wanted the special student privileges I had without doing any of the work I'd done to earn them. She always wanted something from people without ever being willing to give anything in return. Maybe I should have realized how much she resented my friendship with Stev. Maybe I would have been prepared for what happened.

But I really didn't expect her to *hit* me, because harming someone violated our strictest rules.

And I can't honestly say which of us was more stunned when her hand connected with my face.

I staggered back into the arm of my chair. As the chair swiveled, my body twisted with it. I reached out to grab the console, but I was too off-balance to catch myself. My right hand slid. My head hit the console with an awful *thud*.

I must have blacked out for a few seconds. When I could see again, Dermi was sitting in the middle of the room, crying her eyes out, and Whit was doing his best to hold on to Stev, who had his teeth bared and his fists clenched.

I tried to push myself into a sitting position, but something was wrong with my right wrist. I yelped in pain and flopped back down on the floor.

At least that made Stev think of something besides punching Dermi, which would have gotten him into trouble.

The next thing I knew, I was cradled against Stev's chest and Thanie was kneeling in front of me, crying quietly, holding out a wadded-up piece of linen that had a lot of colored threads dangling from it. After songbirds, Thanie loved embroidery, and she always carried a little sack of stuff with her.

She tried to press the linen against my face. It hurt, so I tried to push her hand away.

"You're *bleeding*," Thanie said.

Well, that explained why my face felt wet.

At least she had remembered to take the linen out of the embroidery frame. I just hoped she'd also remembered to take the needles out of the cloth.

"Can you walk?" Stev asked.

"Sure," I said, not sure of anything at all.

"Close down our consoles for us," Stev said to someone. It must have been Whit since he was the person who answered.

I wanted to go home. I got walked to sick bay. The medic frowned at the bruise on one side of my face, grumbled about the sprained wrist, and said some very rude things while he took care of the gash on my forehead.

By the time Stev walked me home, my head was pounding so bad it made me sick to my stomach. I barely made it into the bathroom before I threw up.

That didn't make my head feel better. But what made me feel worse was realizing Stev was hovering outside the bathroom door, probably wondering which would be more helpful— coming in or staying out.

If he *really* wanted to be helpful, he would have gone as far away from the bathroom as possible.

Sometimes boys have no understanding at all of how girls think.

Of course, that was what my emotions wanted and not what my body needed. Stev was right to stay close by, and my emotions were wrong for wanting him to go away—which, by the time I left the bathroom, made me very cranky.

Stev told me in a quiet, soothing voice, "The medic said you're going to be fine. You just need to get some rest now." He took my shoes off and tucked me into bed.

Then Father burst into the room.

"The medic contacted your parents," Stev whispered before he stepped away from the bed.

Father had that look on his face—that pale, tight, angry look he got when I was really sick or hurt and there was nothing he could do about it.

He didn't say anything. Not one thing. Not a scold, not a soothe, nothing. He just walked over to the bed and very carefully placed his hand on my head.

"I'm fine," I lied, trying to smile.

Nothing. That was a *very* bad sign. When Father was this angry and wouldn't say *anything*, it meant that he was about to explode.

I wished Mother were there. I didn't think my head could stand Father exploding.

"The medic said someone should stay with her," Stev said quietly. Then he added, "I'll stay, sir."

Father straightened up, turned, and looked at Stev.

Stev straightened up and tensed.

The air between them seemed to crackle.

"I'll check in," Father said. Then he walked out of the room.

Stev let out a deep breath. His fingers lightly brushed my hand. "Get some rest, Willow."

I must have dozed off, because I sort of remember hearing Mother and Stev talking quietly. Then I fell asleep and didn't hear anything at all.

———

I WOKE UP sometime later.

Stev was sitting in front of my computer, quietly working.

All the muscles that had tensed as I fell were now aching along with my head and wrist. My mouth tasted like what I imagined the bottom of a swamp did, judging by pictures I'd seen of swamps. And I couldn't get my body to listen to my request to sit up.

Stev looked at me, saw me struggling, and hurried over to help me up.

"How are you feeling?" he asked.

How was I feeling? Very aware that I was sitting with a boy whom I might like as more than a friend, looking like some swamp dweller and not being well enough to do anything about it. Which Stev wouldn't understand at all, so I said, "Thirsty." I looked at the computer. I just wanted to forget about this afternoon and fuss over my trees for a little while.

"You need to stay warm," Stev said as he went over to the storage cupboard that held my clothes. He came back with my robe—the worn-out robe that was my favorite piece of clothing and that I wouldn't ever let anyone but my parents see me wearing.

Before I could tell him to bring something else, I was bundled into the robe.

"Slippers," he muttered, looking around until he spotted them. Those made him pause.

Mother gave them to me last year as a funny present. I don't know where she got the idea for them or how she got them made, but I loved them.

They were fuzzy, blue bunny slippers. I wore them so much, the "fur" was all matted. The ears, because I tended to play with them while I was thinking through a class assignment, weren't as stiff as they used to be and would wave at people when I walked.

Stev didn't say a thing as he stuffed my feet into the slippers. He helped me to the other chair at my workspace. "I'll get you some tea," he said, then hurried out of the room.

He brought back mugs of chamomile tea for both of us.

"Your mother has been checking in every hour," he said as he sat down. "Your father has been checking in every fifteen minutes." He sounded both annoyed and approving.

"He's worried about my head," I said.

"Your head isn't what he's worried about."

At least, that's what I *thought* Stev muttered. I let it go. I didn't feel well enough to try to figure out why Father and Stev were acting odd about each other.

"Where are we?" I asked as I tried to focus on the screen. That was a mistake. My head immediately started to pound.

Stev hesitated. "Based on where you had indicated woodlands and meadows, I've made a list of the species that will inhabit those areas."

That was good. At least one of us hadn't wasted the afternoon.

"We'll have to wait until we get back to class tomorrow to plant anything," I said. We could do all the planning on our computers or our personal pads, but we needed a console to send requests to the generation tanks or command codes for the distribution of species on the planet.

Stev put his mug down. He took mine and set it down before taking my hands in his.

"Willow . . ." He sighed. "You've been dismissed from the class project. The message came in a little while ago."

"Dismissed?" I stared at him in shock. "I've been *expelled* from the Restorer program?"

"No," he said firmly. "It didn't say you were expelled from the program. It said you were dismissed from the class project."

"But that's the same thing," I wailed. "At this stage of training, it's the same thing." Then I really *looked* at him. "They dismissed you, too, didn't they?"

"Yes." He looked down at our linked hands. "When the message came through your computer, I checked my messages and . . ."

"Was Dermi dismissed?"

"There's no way for me to know that, Willow."

Of course there was—Whit. The team would have to be told that Stev and I were dismissed so that our work could be distributed among the rest of the team. If Dermi had been dismissed as well, Whit would have known by the end of the class day—and he would have told Stev.

So Stev and I were out of the program, and Dermi . . .

"The island," I gasped. "What about the island?"

"Nothing was said about the island. Your code is still there; the password still works. You still have the island."

"*We* still have the island."

Stev smiled slowly. "We still have the island." He looked at my computer. "But we need to find a console to work from."

"We'll find one. And we'll do the work while we can."

He gave me an odd look. "Yes. We'll do the work while we can." Turning away, he started closing down the computer.

"We can still—"

"Do you want anyone else to know about the island yet?"

"No."

He continued closing down. He must have understood something about my father's check-ins that I didn't, because Father arrived home a few minutes later—well before his usual time.

And there I was, sitting next to Stev, wearing my grubby robe and my bunny slippers, my face bruised and bandaged.

When I saw my father, I flung myself at him and burst into tears. "Daddy, I've been *expelled*."

I don't know which startled him more—my calling him Daddy, which I hadn't done since I was a little girl, or crying all over him. But he held me and rocked me and told me everything would be all right. And because for that little while he was once again Daddy, I believed him.

By the time I'd wound down to sniffles, Stev was gone and Mother was home.

They didn't fuss over me too much that evening. That was Mother's doing, I think. I stayed in the living area most of the evening, drifting on the music Mother had selected. I could hear them talking very quietly, but I couldn't focus enough to make out the words.

I drifted on the music and found my way to the deep stillness within me—that place where answers are sometimes found if you're willing to listen.

When I finally fell asleep, I knew exactly where to find a console Stev and I could use.

5

IT TOOK THREE DAYS BEFORE I FELT WELL ENOUGH TO work anywhere other than my room. Stev worked from his room too. It would have been easier if we could have worked in the same place instead of always checking our personal pads for messages, but Stev pointed out that the only way he could have spent the day in my room without Father spending it with us would be to explain the special project.

I could see his point, sort of. Since we didn't have any class-work, it would be difficult to explain why we needed to work together without explaining what we were working on.

So I made lists. I planned. When I had finished working my way through the links in the chain of survival for the land, I switched to the freshwater systems: plants, insects, reptiles, fish. By then I was too restless to do nothing more than make lists that I couldn't turn into reality, so I went hunting for a console.

Every Restorer team had a main room where the respective members worked. Each team also had an auxiliary room with a handful of consoles.

I figured that, since Britt and Zashi had stepped down, the people on Britt's team wouldn't be using the auxiliary room. Any assistance they were providing to other teams could be done from their main room.

So that morning, with my head still a little achy and my nerves stretched tight, I stood in front of Britt's auxiliary room and put my Restorer code into the keypad next to the door. When the door opened, I slipped inside the room.

I wasn't alone.

Britt turned away from one of the consoles. She studied me for a long moment while I tried to think of some way to explain what I was doing there.

"How are you feeling?" Britt asked quietly.

"I'm fine," I replied. Which had been a lot truer before I'd been caught sneaking into an auxiliary room.

Britt's eyes were far too knowing, but all she did was smile as she walked to the door. Then she hesitated.

"I was about the same age you were when I created my unicorn. My horned horse," she added when I stared at her. "Mine didn't have the elegant equine tail yours did, and it had a beard under its chin." She stroked under her own chin to illustrate. "I'd added that bit because my uncle had a beard like that, and I was fond of him." She smiled again.

When the door opened, she started to step through, then stopped. "We need to do more than what is correct for this world, Willow. We need to do what is *right*. This world . . . *this* world is our true Atonement."

When she was gone, I stumbled over to the nearest chair, sat down, and tried to sort out the messages beneath Britt's words.

The horned horse. The unicorn.

One of the projects necessary to qualify for a Restorer team was to create an "oddity"—to take some of the genetic material from the honeycomb chambers and create a new creature that could survive in a natural environment. I suppose the fact that most of the "oddities" couldn't survive outside the lab was supposed to instill in us a realization of the difference between being a Restorer and being the Blessed All who is the Creator. It also showed that there was no room for ego in the work we were choosing to do. When a creature had to be created in order to fill a niche in an ecosystem, it had to be done with care. A world could only tolerate so much ego indulgence before it rebelled.

I had created a horned horse. On the surface, there was nothing else that distinguished it from other equine species, but it *was* different.

I remember when Britt was a guest Instructor for one of my classes. She had said that sometimes all the barriers between a person and the Blessed All were flung open. When that happened, it wasn't something that could be described, but it was something that you recognized. And when that happened, what flowed from you was more than what you could point to on the surface, was more than you could knowingly create.

I remember that feeling, that dreamlike quality. It had flowed through me the day I created the horned horse. And when the specimen had been grown and all its data inputted into computer simulations to observe how it reacted to its environment, I had no explanation for why things were the way they were.

In every simulation, wherever a unicorn lived, there was Balance. Somehow, its presence kept omnivores from overfeeding in an area so there was always food for every creature that lived within its territory. Predators wouldn't touch it while it lived. When it became old and was ready to return to the Blessed All, predators would follow it at a distance and wait. It would finally choose a spot and lie down. As it took its last breath, the horn would fall off. Then the predators would approach the offered flesh. But before any of them consumed so much as a bite, one of them would dig a hole nearby and bury the horn. It didn't matter what kind of predator it was, whether it traveled in packs or alone. It would bury the horn.

The Scholars and the head Instructors were more than a little startled when they reviewed my project—and some of them were openly upset. But nothing was said to me, and I was accelerated through a couple of levels of study because of that project.

Stev, on the other hand, had almost been thrown out of the program because of his bumbler bee.

It was a bee, a pollinator like other species of bees. Except that it was bigger and looked a little furry. Its wings weren't in proportion to its body size, but it was still able to fly. It "bum-bled" from flower to flower, which is why he'd named it a bumbler bee.

The Scholars had grilled him mercilessly because of that bee. What research had he used, where had he gotten it, what sealed files had he accessed. When he insisted that he'd followed the project instructions and had come up with the bumbler bee on his own, they didn't believe him. They acted as though he had found a way to look at the files that contained the Scholars' Secrets—or had done something equally bad. Because of that project, Stev wasn't advanced with the rest of his group. And shortly after that, he switched from the Restorer program to the Restorer's Right Hand program.

No one at that time or since then has ever explained what it was about the bumbler bee that had gotten him into so much trouble.

But it left a scar on Stev's heart that still wasn't healed.

Now, thinking about what Britt had said, I wondered how much she'd had to do with my acceleration through the Restorer program—and how much she'd had to do with making sure Stev hadn't been dismissed from the program altogether.

I sent a message to Stev's personal pad, telling him I had a console and where to meet me.

When he arrived a few minutes later, he looked nervous. "Willow . . . if we get caught in an auxiliary room . . ."

"We won't get caught," I said, then added silently, *Britt will see to that*. I couldn't have explained why I was so certain of that, but while I'd been waiting for him, I'd reached two conclusions: Britt knew who had taken responsibility for restoring Balance to the island that had been hers before she had decided to step down as a primary Restorer. And Britt approved.

———

AS SOON AS I accessed the console, there were three polite, but somewhat impatient, requests that I remove my material from the holding tanks.

"I don't *have* any material," I muttered as I double-checked to make sure the requests were meant for me.

"Willow." There was a funny catch in Stev's voice.

As we reviewed what was in the holding tanks against the lists we had made, we realized that what we had available was exactly what we needed. Oh, the quantities didn't *quite* match Stev's figures, but close enough. The grass, clover, wildflowers, and ground cover that were at the top of our lists were waiting for us. There was also an unsigned suggestion that we increase the percentage of mature trees.

"Let's think of this as a gift," I said. And, really, that's what it was. By using what was already there, the three days when we couldn't do anything for the land hadn't been lost.

Stev spent the morning working through our lists and sending requests down to the generation tanks for the rest of the "foundation" life-forms—that is, the insects—as well as a variety of shrubs and berry bushes. I spent that time dispersing the seed that was in the holding tanks.

By the time the midday meal came around, a light rain had begun over the island—just enough to give the seeds the water they needed and also settle them into the earth.

The food slot, which had been a bit whimsical all morning about what it chose to give us, decided to quit altogether when we tried to get a more substantial meal.

"Come on," Stev said, steering me toward the door. "We'll go to one of the food courts."

"But—" I didn't want to go to a food court, especially the one for the older students. It was going to take a while before I could bear to sit in the same room as Dermi.

"Your eyes—and the rest of your head—need a break from staring at that console screen all morning," Stev said firmly.

What was it about Stev that made me the most annoyed with him when he was right?

I began to wonder how much of a break my eyes *really* needed when we met up with Thanie and Whit outside the older students' food court.

"Why don't we go to another food court," Whit said as he glanced nervously at the other students who were going through the door. "There's another one a little way down the corridor."

"We can't go there," Thanie said in a hushed voice. "*That* one is used by the Restorer teams."

"Well, we can't go into *this* one," Whit snapped.

So we went to the other food court, feeling very self-conscious when we walked through the door. There were a few glances, a few polite smiles. It wasn't that we weren't *allowed* in this food court. It was just that this was a gathering place for the adults.

We got our food and chose a table as far away from everyone else as we could get.

The first bite was enough to remind me that I really was hungry, so I applied myself to my meal. I was halfway through it when Thanie blurted out something that made me lose my appetite.

"As soon as she heard you were dismissed from the class project, Dermi asked to handle the trees," Thanie said.

"*Thanie*," Whit said in a warning voice.

Thanie was too upset to heed the warning. "She used the whole allotment of genetic material to create seedlings."

My fork slipped out of my hand. My stomach began to hurt. "So the deer got their food after all," I said dully.

"She hasn't done a *thing* about bringing the deer population into Balance. By this morning, they'd eaten all the seedlings. Dermi requested another allotment of trees and was told her next allotment wouldn't be available for another thirty days, so now she's in a *major,* major snit." Thanie paused. "And she blames you."

Whit glared at Thanie while Stev said *very* rude things.

"Why does she blame *me?*"

Finally realizing how angry Stev and Whit were at that moment, Thanie hunched into herself.

"She blames you because she's more of a bug-brain than Zerx," Whit finally growled. "If Dermi had bothered to read the project parameters, she would have *known* that tree allotments are given out in thirty-day cycles. And what's worse is Fallah, who's supposed to be her best friend, keeps encouraging her rash decisions. The results will put our team score right into the waste recycler, but it will sure make Fallah's individual score look good compared to everyone else's."

"Excuse me," I said, pushing away from the table. "I— excuse me."

When Stev started to rise, I put my hand on his shoulder to keep him in his chair.

As I headed for the door, I glanced to my left.

Zashi was watching me, a concerned look on his face.

I tried to smile in greeting. I couldn't quite manage it, so I hurried out of the room.

I sat in the auxiliary room, glad to be alone for a while. I told myself over and over that the student project was no longer my concern, that *those* trees were no longer *my* trees, that I had other work to do—other land to restore to Balance.

I understood that Balance was give-and-take, that life-forms lived . . . and life-forms died. I understood that some life-forms became extinct, not because of carelessness or indulgence, but because their time in the world had come to an end. When extinction was a natural part of the ebb and flow of the world, something else would come along to fill that space. It was when a life-form ceased to exist before its time was done that a hole was left in the world. That was when Balance itself could become extinct.

By the time Stev returned from the food court, I had pretty much convinced myself that one allotment of trees used foolishly wouldn't *really* make any difference to this world.

That night, one of the generation tanks failed completely, and there was nothing any of the techs could do to save the life-forms that had been growing inside it.

6

OVER THE NEXT FEW DAYS, WE WORKED. THE GRASS seed we had initially dispersed had sprouted and was growing well. Some of the flowers had begun to sprout. Following my directives, Stev began accelerating some new plants to the point where they were in flower.

During that time, two more generation tanks developed problems. The techs, who were now extremely vigilant, immediately sounded the alarm. The engineers were able to stop the system failure on those tanks, but a memo came through from the techs strongly recommending that those two tanks not be used at more than fifty percent capacity.

A lot of ants could be created in a tank that could function only at half capacity, but that recommendation would have a serious effect when it came to larger life-forms.

During that same time, the problem with the heating system had spread from the corridors into the living quarters. My room would change within the space of an hour from freezing cold to being hot enough to make me sweat.

Stev didn't say a thing about the heating system or the problems with the generation tanks, but I knew what he was thinking.

Our city-ships are very, very old. Our people had been wandering through space for many, many of our generations. There were spaceports that belonged to other races where we could stop and make repairs once in a while. But we couldn't build new ships to take the place of the old ones because the generation tanks wouldn't work in any ship but the ones they had been built for, and we no longer had the skill to make new tanks.

It was as if, for one brief point in our people's history, we had been given the gift of knowledge to create the piece of technology that would give our people a chance to make Atonement. Once the ships, and the generation tanks, were built, that knowledge faded away, never to return.

Our engineers could maintain and repair the tanks, and they understood *in theory* how to build them. But they simply couldn't build one the size and complexity of the original tanks. The engineers have been trying for generations. Sometimes a very small tank was built and actually worked, but it could only produce one small specimen at a time. The results of trying to grow anything larger than a rabbit were ghastly. And trying to grow more than one specimen of *anything* in one of those tanks . . .

Sometimes one healthy specimen survived. Sometimes.

Everything has a life span. Even a ship.

Slowly, one by one, our city-ships have been dying.

We seldom meet another ship that belongs to our people. When we do, we travel together for a while. These rare meetings are the only way for us to bring new blood into our population. Sometimes people want to leave their own city-ship because of some unhappiness in their lives. Some people leave because they fall in love, and one partner is willing to give up family and friends to be with the other.

It takes courage and deep feelings to make such a choice because the chances are very slim that they'll ever meet up again with the city-ship that had once been home.

And then there are the survivors.

I was barely old enough at the time to remember when our ship picked up a weak distress call from a sister ship. It took weeks to reach it even though we had headed for it with all possible speed.

When we got there, we noticed that the small shuttle ships were missing, and there was some speculation that a few people had tried to use them to escape. But shuttle ships, which were capable of transporting us between one ship and another, were not meant for long journeys. There had been no world within range that they could have reached.

The people of that ship had done what they could. What little power was left had been channeled to the honeycomb chambers that held the genetic material—and it had been channeled to the cryotubes. These tubes usually stored specimens that had been carefully grown so that fresh genetic material could be added to the honeycomb chambers to replace material that had become too old to be viable.

When the team members from our ship had gone over to look for any sign of life, they had found the two hundred cryo-tubes filled with children. Only eight of those tubes were still functioning. Those eight children were brought to our ship.

One of them was Stev.

So I didn't offer him assurances neither of us could believe. We just did the work while we could.

I DISCOVERED THE problem in the honeycomb chambers when I put in my request for bees. A few minutes after I sent the request, the console chimed that I had an urgent message.

> If not used immediately, there may not be enough viable material available to produce requested number of specimens.

Muttering to myself, I spent close to an hour working my way through the command series that would allow me to view the honeycomb chambers that stored the genetic material.

Obviously, there had been a mistake. Somehow the computer had misread my request. Bees weren't some exotic species. They were *bees*. They went *buzz*; they helped pollinate plants as they gathered pollen for food; they made honey. And I had *checked* the amount of available genetic material just two days ago to make sure there would be enough, since I figured every Restorer team would want to disperse bees.

When I finally got to view the honeycomb chambers that held the genetic material for bees, I just stared at the screen. A shiver went through me—a shiver that grew and grew until I began to shake.

The honeycomb chambers had a color code. Green chambers held genetic material. White meant the chamber had been emptied; the material had been completely used. Pink meant the computer was picking up a problem within that cell that could damage the material. Red was a major alert that the genetic material was in danger. Black meant the material within that cell had died.

The area designated for bees was spotted with black and red cells. As I watched, two red cells turned black, and several pink cells changed to red.

With my heart pounding, I keyed in a Priority Urgent message warning every Restorer team that there was a problem with the honeycomb chambers. I also sent the message to the techs' consoles at the generation tanks. At that point, I didn't care who knew I had a Restorer code or that I was handling the island. The teams had to be warned.

As soon as I sent that message, I sent a Priority Urgent to Stev, who had gone down to the generation tanks to oversee the transfer of genetic material to start the field mice we would add to the meadows. I told him to put a hold on the mice and draw *all* the genetic material available for bees and get it into a generation tank.

A minute later, as I watched more green cells change to pink, I got back the query: ??

DON'T ARGUE. JUST DO IT!!! I sent that message twice.

Stev didn't respond.

"Hurry, Stev," I whispered, clenching my hands so hard they began to cramp. "Please hurry."

More pink cells turned red. Some red cells turned black.

Then, finally, one by one, the red cells turned white. The pink cells turned white. Last, the green cells turned white.

I finally managed to take a deep breath—and realized I was crying.

There was a strong possibility that the material in the red cells wouldn't be able to create healthy bees anymore. Stev, being Stev, would have put that material in another tank so that it wouldn't contaminate the rest if it was no longer viable.

Whatever bees we managed to grow would have to be shared among the Restorer teams that needed them. There wouldn't be enough. We would need another pollinator.

I got a cup of tea from the food slot. Thought it over carefully—and followed my intuition.

When I did a little checking, I discovered that someone had taken Stev's little "oddity" and had been carefully growing more specimens from it. There were several dozen cells filled with its genetic material.

I waited until Stev sent a message that he was returning to the auxiliary room.

Then I sent another Priority message to the techs overseeing the generation tanks.

I was the Restorer for the island. I was the only one who chose what was given to that land, and I was the only one who would be held responsible for that choice.

Before Stev arrived, I got back confirmation from one of the techs.

When the next generation tank became available, it would be growing Stev's bumbler bees.

WHEN I GOT home, Mother was crying her heart out and holding on to Father as if he were her entire world.

"There was nothing we could have done, Rista," Father said

quietly as he rubbed her back, trying to soothe her. "Even if we had known about the problem before today, there was nothing we could have done. Those species aren't right for this world. They would have always been out of Balance."

"I know. I know. But . . . Jeromi . . . *Extinct*."

"We don't know that. There might be another ship—"

Father saw me at that moment and didn't continue. It had been a long time since we had heard from another city-ship. There was no certainty that there *were* any others out there anymore.

I don't know what he saw in my eyes, but I saw the conflict in his. He wanted to take care of the two people he loved, but he wasn't sure which one of us needed him more at that moment.

I smiled at him and went to my room—not because I didn't need the comfort or the hug, but because Mother needed him more and deserved to have him all to herself for a little while.

Because Mother was from one of those other city-ships. She'd given up everything she had known out of love for another person.

I took my hologram down from its shelf and turned it on, watched it for a while.

An overloaded circuit was the reason that the warning about the cells never reached the techs' consoles. There had been a few erratic warnings a week ago, but the diagnostics showed no problem with the system, and the techs concluded that the warnings were a computer error.

Nobody understood why my accessing the information at that moment triggered the warning circuit, but my sounding the alarm produced an awful scramble in the tank rooms. In fact, my request for bumbler bees was the last confirmed request for the rest of the day.

While the techs were checking out the system, they discovered how much genetic material had already been destroyed. Fortunately, none of the now-extinct species were vital to this world, and some couldn't even have lived on the planet under any condition, but that didn't make the loss any better.

"Extinct" was the most terrible word we knew.

And if we *were* the last surviving city-ship, it was a word that would apply to us very soon.

7

A COUPLE OF DAYS LATER, WHILE STEV AND I WERE eating the midday meal in the Restorers' food court, Whit showed up. He got a plate of food and then just sat and stared at it for several minutes.

"Thanie resigned from the program," he said abruptly. "So did I."

"*What?*" I put my glass down so I wouldn't drop it.

"What happened?" Stev asked sharply.

"The . . . the songbirds were being destroyed from every direction. They were starving, and there were so many predators after them, the ones who weren't actually killed as prey were dying from fright and exhaustion. She just couldn't stand watching it anymore. So this morning, she sent in a request to have all the remaining songbirds transferred out of the area. The approval came in about an hour before the midday break. When the rest of the team realized what she'd done, you should have heard the way they shrieked about it. Dermi and Fallah were still yelling at her when she keyed in her resignation from the program, shut down her console, and left."

"What about you, Whit?" I asked.

His eyes were bright with tears. "What's the point of putting up with bug-brains like Zerx and Dermi and Fallah—or even Benj, for that matter? The ship is dying. Everyone knows it even if no one will admit it. There's no reason to do this since it's not going to make any difference."

His voice had risen to the point where several people around us had turned to look at us with not-too-pleased expressions on their faces.

"Not the Restorer teams," he said, his voice dropping back to normal. "I don't mean them. They're doing *real* work, and they *are* making a difference to this world. But there's no reason for me to keep gritting my teeth and trying to work with the rest of those *people* in order to earn my qualification. There's no future in it." He tried to smile at a joke that was, in its honesty, obscene.

None of us finished our meal. Stev took Whit off to talk for a while. I went over to Thanie's and ended up saying useless things while she cried.

IT WAS A couple of hours before I got back to the auxiliary room. Out of habit, I called up the screen that listed the species that were now in the area we were restoring. Several names popped up on the screen with the "new species" symbol next to them.

I stared at the screen. Birds? *Birds?* I hadn't *requested* birds yet. There weren't supposed to *be* any birds yet.

I keyed in the command for the computer to locate and provide a planet-side view of one of these birds.

There it was, a little sparrow that was barely able to hold on to the branch of a sapling oak tree.

"What's going on here? The Restorer screen is supposed to *prevent* things like this from happening," I muttered as I started to key in a demand to remove those birds. Granted, in a few more days, I intended to request birds from the generation tanks, but . . .

That was when it occurred to me to check my messages *before* I sent that demand to the tank techs.

There was a directive accepting a transfer of songbirds. The directive had a Restorer code that wasn't mine. It also had very specific instructions about the placement of the birds. They had been scattered over the several thousand acres of land that Stev and I were restoring. Despite being added prematurely, the birds really wouldn't be consuming more food than the land could provide.

Which wasn't the point, I assured myself as I muttered my way through the directive. Those birds shouldn't *be* there until *I* decided they should be there.

And then I got to the end of the directive. The Restorer code was repeated. Under it was simply—*Britt.*

I sat back, no longer sure what to think.

I checked my other messages—which I hadn't bothered to do since I hadn't expected any to come through on this console—and found the transfer request. It had been an open request. That meant it had been sent to every Restorer code the computer recognized, and anyone who wanted any of those birds could request them to be sent to the area that person was restoring.

Britt, for whatever reason, had initiated the transfer of the birds to the island.

No. Not "for whatever reason." They were living creatures. The person who had requested the transfer had done so in order to save them. In a few more days, I would have requested the same species. And I still would in order to bring the numbers up to a viable population.

But I think Britt, who sometimes understood too well, knew exactly what my decision would have been if I'd read the transfer request when it first came in.

Just as she understood exactly how Thanie would feel if she knew her beloved songbirds were safe with me.

8

"WILLOW? WHERE ARE YOU GOING?"

Glancing over my shoulder, I saw Thanie hurrying to catch up with me.

"I have some . . . stuff . . . to do," I said lamely as I continued walking toward the auxiliary room.

"Can I help?" Thanie said. "It's just . . . well, I thought since you didn't have class either . . ."

The entire walk was filled with her unfinished sentences, but I understood the gist of it. Thanie didn't want to sit home doing nothing while there was an entire world aching to be restored. She had no idea how I had been filling my days since I'd been dismissed from the class project and probably figured that two people doing nothing might create more of the illusion of doing *something*.

I was still trying to figure out what kind of excuse to give her when we reached the auxiliary room. As it turned out, I didn't need an excuse. As I approached the auxiliary room from one direction with Thanie, Stev approached it from the other direction with Whit, who had the same lost look that Thanie did.

I looked at Stev. Stev looked at me.

"Well," I said. "Four can do more than two." I put my code into the keypad. The door opened. "Let's get to work."

"Willow . . . ," Thanie said as she followed me into the room. "Students aren't supposed to be in auxiliary rooms."

"We're not students anymore, remember?" I replied as Stev and I started opening our consoles. "Thanie, why don't you take that console." I indicated the one immediately on my left. "Whit, you take the one next to Stev."

Whit looked around the small room. "You got permission to do a special project?" he asked, looking hopeful. "Could I—" He glanced at Thanie. "Could we help? Not for credit or anything."

That made me pause. I looked at Thanie.

This wasn't about getting credit. This wasn't about getting points on a score—or even getting formally qualified. They just wanted to do the work.

Stev was the one who broke the silence. "If you're going to be here," he said dryly, "we don't expect you to just sit there and play with your fingers."

"So . . . what's the project?" Whit asked.

Stev and I braced ourselves to catch them as I called up the screen that showed the entire project. We didn't want to start the day with a trip to sick bay because someone hit the floor.

Whit and Thanie just stared at the screen, their mouths hanging open.

"Blessed All," Whit finally said. "You've done that much by yourselves?"

Pain and fury flashed in his eyes for a moment before he regained control. He was seeing the difference between what a *real* team, even if it consisted of only two people, could accomplish compared to what was done by one that was a team in name only.

"We've done that much," I said, feeling the pleasure of our accomplishment warm me. "And we've got a lot more to do. Thanie, you've got the birds."

"Willow . . ."

Since I was already at my console, transferring the data to *her* console, she took her seat. When she looked at the number of birds, tears filled her eyes. She knew where they had come from.

She sniffed a couple of times and then firmed up. "You don't have any hawks or falcons."

"They'll have to be added . . . along with the other bird species that are designated as being appropriate for this ecosystem."

I watched her take that in. She would be handling *all* the birds—and that included the birds that would eat the songbirds.

She closed her eyes for a moment, took a deep breath, and nodded.

In a land that had Balance, Thanie would be able to accept the give-and-take of life.

While Thanie and Whit spent the next couple of hours acquainting themselves with the project, Stev continued to work through the lists of species we would need, and I went through the messages that had been sent to this console.

Most of them were from the Restorers, basically offering understated praise for saving the bees. They also carefully indicated that they would like some of the bees if any were available.

Since I had initiated the order to grow the bees, I was entitled to keep as many as I wanted or needed. If I kept all of them, I would have a full population of bees for the island, but everyone else would have to scramble to find something else to take the bees' place in the ecosystems they were restoring. So we would share them.

Besides, I had the bumblers, which no one but the tank techs knew about yet.

The next message was from a tank tech informing me that all the genetic material for the bumblers had been placed in a generation tank and was being grown at the same slow acceleration rate that Stev had ordered for the other bees.

The message after that was from another tank tech informing me that the bees would be ready for dispersal in twenty hours. That message was copied to Stev.

The last message was from Zashi, who warmly praised my quick action concerning the bees and then gently offered his assistance. If I was willing to release the equivalent of two small hives—queens, drones, and workers—he would personally oversee using them as the genetic base to create more bees.

That was a tough decision to make. The generation tanks didn't require large amounts of material to start growing another specimen, but it seemed unfair to create something and then turn around and use it to create more of its kind without ever giving it a chance to live. But I was also aware that two queen bees would provide enough material to create close to fifty more queen bees. And fifty hives, which could then produce more bees on their own, would go a lot further toward giving every Restorer team starter hives.

I keyed in a message to Zashi taking him up on his offer. I copied the message to Stev, with an additional note that listed the Restorer teams who had requested bees. He would see that each team got an equal number of bees—or as close to it as possible.

By the time we were ready for a midday break, Thanie was bubbling over with enthusiasm. "Just wait until—"

"*No.*" I blocked the door. "This project is need-to-know *only*, Thanie. It doesn't get discussed with anyone who isn't working on it."

I knew she wanted to rub Dermi's and Fallah's noses in the fact that we were working on a major project, but there was still a chance that we could be shut down if this came to *too* many people's attention.

I saw her struggle with the disappointment. That was my real reservation about having Thanie work on this project. When pushed, she tended to blurt out confidential information in order to regain some emotional ground.

"What about my parents?" Thanie finally asked. "Can I tell—"

"They aren't need-to-know when it comes to this project," Stev said firmly.

Whit shifted uneasily. "You *do* have approval for this, don't you? I mean, you didn't . . . lift . . . the Restorer code or anything?"

"I have approval," I replied. "And there is a primary Restorer who is . . . aware . . . of the work."

That was enough for Whit and, apparently, Thanie.

Stev just gave me a searching look. After getting a message from Zashi, it wasn't hard for him to figure out who the Restorer was who was aware of our work. But I wasn't prepared to tell even Stev just *how* aware Britt was of our work.

And I wasn't going to start wondering *why* she was so interested in what I would do with the land.

9

A COUPLE OF DAYS LATER, WHILE THE FOUR OF US were eating what the food slots in the Restorers' food court had decided to offer for a midday meal, Zashi stopped by our table.

"The new bees are growing very nicely," he said, smiling at me. "They'll be distributed tomorrow." Then he gave me a speculative look. "I just came from the tank rooms. Since I was assisting you with the bees, one of the techs didn't see any harm in mentioning that your other specimens were nicely grown and ready for dispersal. I believe you'll find a message to that effect when you get back to work. I gather you want to give them a chance to prove themselves before offering them to anyone else?"

"Yes," I said, feeling my smile become brittle. "That's it exactly."

"I don't think you'll find that to be an issue—at least, not with any Restorer." He lifted his hand in farewell and went to join friends at another table.

"What other specimens?" Stev asked.

"I'll explain later," I muttered, not daring to look at him.

There had been a blend of amusement and sympathy in Zashi's eyes before he left us that clearly told me he knew as well as I did who was going to make an issue out of this.

WHEN WE GOT back to the auxiliary room, Stev read the message waiting for us and threw a fit.

"How could you?" he shouted. "How *could* you? I have spent *years* trying to put that behind me."

"They're pollinators. They're viable. They work in this eco-system. We *need* them," I shouted back.

"They *aren't* viable. They *don't* fit! The Scholars and Instructors made that very clear when they reviewed the project."

"*I'm* the Restorer for this team, and *I* say they fit!" If there wasn't so much hurt under the anger, I could have punched him for being so stubborn. "They're *bees*, Stev, and *we need bees*."

He turned away from me.

Whit quietly cleared his throat. "Uh . . . Thanie and I have some . . . stuff . . . to do. We'll be back in a little while." Taking a firm grip on Thanie's arm, he dragged her out of the room.

I barely noticed them leave.

"They'll chew on you for this, Willow," Stev said bitterly.

"Let them try." I waited until he turned to face me. "I'll put our work up against *any* Restorer team. I don't know why the Scholars and Instructors made such a fuss over the bumblers. I don't care why they did. They were *wrong*, Stev." I was so angry at that point, I started to cry. "They were *wrong*."

"Willow . . ." Stev put his arms around me. "Don't cry, Willow. Please don't cry."

I did my best to stop, not because I was ready to, but mostly because seeing me cry made Stev feel helpless.

Stev sighed. "I guess no one will really notice a handful of bumblers."

Obviously, he had gotten only far enough into the message to read "bumbler bees" and hadn't actually taken in the *number* of specimens that were ready for dispersal. Once he did that, hopefully he, too, would start wondering why someone had taken the time and trouble to produce that much genetic material for an oddity that had no value.

Now there was just the little problem of dispersing the

bumblers. As much as I cared about Stev and would trust him without question at any other time, I couldn't be sure he wouldn't dump the bumblers under six inches of water somewhere if he was the one handling the dispersal. Since I'd ordered *all* the genetic material for the bumblers to be drawn from the honeycomb chambers, if Stev did something rash out of some misguided idea of saving the rest of the project, there wouldn't be any way of starting over and producing bumblers again.

Wiping my eyes with my sleeve, I checked my own console for messages while Stev slumped in his chair.

There was one message—from Zashi. All it said was, Bumblers??

Thank the Blessed All for Zashi. That message was an offer to handle the dispersal. Stev would have had another fit if I had asked Whit to take care of the bumblers, but there wasn't much he could say when a primary Restorer's Right Hand offered to handle it.

Yes, please, I answered.

A few minutes after Thanie and Whit returned, a message came in from Zashi, copied to Stev, thanking me for allowing him to participate a little and make use of his skills.

I busily avoided Stev's stare until he settled back to work.

And I smiled when, much later that evening after Stev had already gone home, I watched a bumbler land on a flower.

10

WE WORKED AS LONG AS WE COULD AND AS HARD AS we could. It still wasn't enough.

Every day there was a circuit failure in yet another system.

The engineers would just get one repaired and two more would go down. The tank techs were sending messages every morning, warning the Restorer teams about continued failures in the honeycomb chambers and which species were threatened. And every Restorer team was using the generation tanks at full acceleration now, even though there was more risk that a fully accelerated specimen might have less reproductive capability.

We just wanted to get as much life down on the planet as possible before a vital system in the ship failed—like life support or the ability to maintain orbit.

I was alone in the auxiliary room. I'd sent Whit and Thanie home because there was nothing else that could be done at the moment, and Stev had gone to check out something in the tank rooms before getting some sleep.

I was tired enough that I had slipped into that state of waking dreams. I stared at the screen in front of me, not really seeing it anymore.

Every link in the chain of survival had to be built in the right order and at the right time. That was what we'd been taught in every Restorer class. That idea was fine when there was more than enough time, but it wasn't going to work now. If I waited until I reached a particular link in the chain at this point, the genetic material might not still exist when I needed it. But if I *didn't* follow procedure, I risked the Balance the island now had.

As I stared at the screen, I felt a surge of energy flow through my body. I sat up. I really *looked* at the planet-side picture that was on the screen.

For several minutes, I watched a spider build a web and saw all my lists and plans in a new way.

Not a *chain* of survival—a *web* of *life*. A link was only connected to the links on either side of it. But a web . . . Each strand affected *every* strand in the overall scheme of the web, but in the end, there was Balance.

With the image of a web kept firmly in my mind, I looked over my lists again.

With the city-ship breaking down a little more every day, I might not be able to send enough of each animal and plant down to the planet in time to ensure that each species would be able to sustain itself in the future. But now I knew how to fully restore a part of that island so that, for a shining moment, there would be Balance.

11

THE NEXT MORNING, WHIT AND THANIE LOOKED very confused as they reviewed the list of species I had requested from the generation tanks. Stev looked very concerned.

I knew what he was thinking: that I'd been working too hard and something inside me had snapped.

There was no way I could explain to him, but something inside me hadn't snapped; it was now wide open. Balance flowed through me in a way it never had before. I was no longer following the rules that had been laid down for us in class. I was the Restorer—and I finally understood what that really meant.

"Willow . . . ," Stev said. Before he could go on, the door opened. Britt and Zashi stepped inside.

Britt's eyes met mine and held.

She had been waiting for this moment, had been wondering if it would come.

"Would you like some help?" she asked.

I just smiled.

Britt, Zashi, and I slipped into working together as if we'd always done so. After a couple of hours, Stev was almost in stride with us. Whit and Thanie were bewildered by the change in the project's direction and a little dazed at suddenly working in such close quarters with the most respected Restorer and Restorer's Right Hand on the ship.

At midday, Britt and Zashi excused themselves, saying they had other commitments during the afternoon. I thanked them both—and was greatly relieved when they assured me they would be back the next morning.

As they were about to leave, I overheard Zashi say to Stev, "Give yourself some time. You'll get used to working with someone like her."

12

LATER THAT EVENING, WHEN I HAD FINALLY GONE home to get some sleep, I opened a file that had been sent to my personal computer pad. It was a picture of an old document followed by a plain copy of the text. I didn't need to be told that the document had come from the Scholars' secret files. I also didn't need to be told that the sender had taken great care to make sure access to this particular file couldn't be traced to me.

The document was a long list. A terrible list. At the top was the heading *Lab Specimens Are the Only Specimens Now Available.*

Wolf, crow, hawk, falcon. Salmon, dolphin, fox, panda. Bison, zebra, elk, tiger. Nightingale, otter, cobra, seal. The list went on and on, naming plants and insects as well as animals. If I compared it to the list of species that were suitable for this world and were stored as genetic material in the honeycomb chambers, they would match. I was certain of it.

The next part of the list was much, much longer. Its heading simply read *Extinct*.

Near the bottom of that list, I found the reason why the Scholars had been so upset with Stev—and why they had suspected him of accessing their secret files. The entry said *Bumblebee*.

Stev had re-created a creature that had become extinct before its time in the world was done. If the Scholars hadn't slapped him down to the point that he would never be willing to try again, who knows what other creatures he might have given back to the world?

The last part of the list said *Myths*. The very last entry was the unicorn.

I looked at that entry for a long time. Then I deleted the file. I understood why Britt had sent it to me, and I understood that the list, as well as the underlying message, wasn't meant to be seen by anyone but me.

13

WE WORKED FOR ANOTHER MONTH WHILE THE SHIP failed around us. Whit continued to disperse grass seed and wildflowers over the rest of the island whenever we could get them. Thanie dispersed seeds to build young woodlands while I planted the saplings that would give those woodlands an anchor. Britt added the deer. She had insisted on using the genetic material that was still available instead of transferring animals from another location. I was grateful to her for understanding that I could never have felt impartial about the deer if they had originally been Dermi's.

We had six breeds of horses. There were cows and sheep, hawks and falcons, foxes and hares, mice and owls. We had salmon and trout in the streams, and frogs lived among the cattails and water lilies in the ponds. We had woodlands and shrubs and meadows. We planted fields of oats and barley as well as plots of every other vegetable the land would support. Parsley and thyme were among the herbs that had taken root. There was a small population of every kind of creature that belonged to this land. And we had the plant life to support it all.

In that one portion of the island, we had Balance.

We hugged each other. We cheered. We laughed until we cried.

We had Balance.

Over time, the plants and animals would spread out over the rest of the island and grow in number.

We wouldn't see it. But that didn't matter.

And then, the next evening, Stev told me something that changed everything.

STEV WAITED UNTIL the others had left for the day. Then he put his hands on my shoulders.

"Willow . . ." It took him a moment to try again. "Willow, I was talking to one of the tank techs today. In order to try to save the specimens that are needed to restore this world, they're going to start cutting the power to the rest of the honeycomb chambers. All the genetic material in those cells will die."

I felt a deep sorrow, but I understood the necessity. We wouldn't be traveling to any other worlds. We had to do what we could for this one.

"That includes the student projects," Stev said softly.

It took me a moment to understand.

"The unicorns," I whispered.

"I'm so sorry, Willow."

I closed my eyes and tried to wait out the pain.

"They can't die," I said. *Not again.*

I don't know why that thought filled my head, but once it was there, there was nothing else.

Turning away from Stev, I worked my way through the commands that would show me the honeycomb chamber that held the genetic material for my unicorns. When I found it, I couldn't say anything.

There was just enough material to create a small but viable population of unicorns. But if even one cell was lost . . .

Then I remembered something else. It took a few minutes more before I found the cells I needed.

Half of the cells containing the genetic material had turned black.

"If we made them all weaned foals, there would be just enough material for a small population. And *my* adult unicorns would look after them along with the other foals."

"We can't do it, Willow," he said, his voice thick with regret. "We can't put a species on this world that doesn't belong here."

I knew what he was thinking. I had saved his bumbler bees, and he had to be the one to tell me that I couldn't save something I had loved ever since I'd seen that one specimen that had been grown in the generation tanks.

He cared—and I loved him for it.

He was also wrong.

"They don't belong here, Willow."

I thought about the list of Myths I had seen. I thought about how, in the simulations, there was Balance where a unicorn lived. I smiled sadly. "Yes, they do. This is where they came from, Stev. This is their home."

His eyes widened. He stared at me as if he'd never seen me before. Then he looked at the screen and frowned. "Why did they put your genetic material into two different honeycomb chambers?"

"They didn't. Those are Britt's unicorns."

He seemed to have trouble breathing for a minute. "Blessed All," he whispered.

I waited.

He took a deep breath. Blew it out. "I'd better get down to the tanks and do this myself. You stay here and send me the cell numbers. That way I won't have to go through any of the tech consoles where this might get traced."

When he reached the door, he paused and looked back at me. "Zashi was right. It will take a bit of time to get used to working with you."

14

SINCE THEY WERE THE ONLY ONES AVAILABLE AT THE time, Stev used the two generation tanks that were working at half capacity. He set them at full growth acceleration so that they would be available again as fast as possible.

When a fully operational tank became available, he insisted on placing some of my unicorns in it.

I couldn't argue with him. The speed at which the cells were changing from green to pink to red to black was terrifying.

The techs weren't interested in what he was doing. They

were scrambling to take care of what they could for the Restorer teams and were happy that he was willing to do his own work.

Whenever he could, he jumped in and filled another generation tank before the techs could put other material into it. As soon as a tank finished the growth process, I issued the command code to send the unicorns down to the island.

I don't think either of us really slept for days.

Finally, the moment came when Stev placed the last surviving material into the generation tanks.

A couple of days after that, we sent the last of the unicorns down to the island.

The day after that, an angry group of Scholars and Instructors showed up at the auxiliary room door.

15

THANIE WAS WRACKED WITH GUILT AND KEPT APOLogizing in between bouts of tears.

We'd warned her, again and again. But a couple of verbal jabs from Dermi and Fallah were all it had taken for her to lash out and tell them about the special project.

Of course, Dermi and Fallah immediately went to the Head Instructor and told *him* everything—including the fact that there were bumbler bees on the island. Which was what brought in the Scholars.

Stev and I were still groggy from lack of sleep. We were just sitting at our consoles, drinking tea and trying to wake up enough to function, when Whit and Thanie were herded into the room, followed by the primary Scholars and the Head Instructor. Behind *them* came Britt and Zashi.

Stev jumped to his feet. A younger person was supposed to rise whenever a Scholar or Instructor came into the room.

I remained seated. I sipped my tea and stared them down.

That made them furious. And, for some reason, nervous.

Accusations filled the room. I had deceived my Instructor by falsifying the information when I made the request for the special project. A *student* would never have been given a restoration project the size of the island. I had deceived the tank techs into believing I was a qualified Restorer and entitled to the special considerations I was given. I had *lied* to them in order to remove unsuitable genetic material.

During this harangue, Britt watched me.

I just sat there drinking my tea.

When the yelling finally wound down, the Head Instructor said, "Well? What do you have to say to us?"

"Nothing," I replied calmly. "I have nothing to say to you. I do not answer to you."

"Oh?" said the Head Scholar. "If not to us, then whom *do* you answer to?"

"The Blessed All."

They stared at me. Britt pressed a hand over her mouth.

I smiled at her. "I have something to show you."

I keyed in the coordinates and requested a planet-side picture.

A meadow, on the edge of a woodland. Butterflies flitted by. Birds flew from tree to tree. A bumbler went from one flower to another, doing its duty.

A minute passed. Two minutes.

Then from among the trees came a white unicorn mare. Beside her were two fillies. One of the fillies had a beard under her chin.

Tears filled Britt's eyes. Then she started to laugh—a joyous, heart-deep laugh. "I knew you were the one. I knew."

"You took a risk," I said. "You could have gotten more of them out in time. We saved what we could."

Britt smiled at me. Zashi's eyes began to twinkle.

Somewhere—perhaps on the part of the student island that *hadn't* been designated for the students—there were more of Britt's unicorns. If I had failed this last test, there might not have been enough of them to survive. Britt had been willing to take that risk . . . because she needed the certainty of this last test.

"Willow is my successor," Britt said. She walked out of the room.

Zashi winked at me, smiled at Stev, and followed her.

The Scholars and the Head Instructor turned pale. Without another word, they left, taking Whit and Thanie with them.

It had come to me last night, just before I fell asleep for a few hours. All the other Restorers were referred to as *a* Restorer. Britt was referred to as *the* Restorer. She answered to no one but the Blessed All—because Britt was always in Balance.

And because Britt would not just do what was correct; she would do what was right.

16

TOMORROW WE ARE GOING TO ATTEMPT TO LAND our ship on the planet's surface.

The engineers have reluctantly admitted that it's *possible*, but they aren't sure we can do it. But if we *don't* try it, we won't survive another month out in space. If we succeed, we'll gain a few more years to continue our work before the ship dies completely.

The Scholars, of course, argued against it.

It was Britt who decided.

I've wondered if her decision would have been different if I hadn't saved the unicorns. If, without someone to take her place as *the* Restorer, she would have let her own people die rather than risk the world that is still slowly being restored to Balance.

I think I know the answer. That is why I will never ask her.

We have lived in a world made of metal, wandering the galaxy and restoring worlds to Balance because we have to make Atonement for something we did long ago.

Now we have a chance to feel the earth beneath our feet, to feel the wind on our skin, to smell the wildflowers, to press our hands against the bark of a tree. We have a chance to live as one strand in the web. And we can never afford to forget that we *are* only one strand.

I don't think my people will ever again have the knowledge or the skill to go into space. This world is all we will have. If we fail it, we will be among the species that are listed as extinct.

Tomorrow we will land on the planet.

Britt was right.

This world *is* our true Atonement.

ACKNOWLEDGMENTS

My thanks to all the editors and publishers who took a chance on my work and have published my stories over the years.

My thanks to Blair Boone, Neil Schmitz, Nadine Fallacaro, Charles de Lint, and other friends who gave me encouragement during the early years and all the years since.

A big hug to all the friends who celebrate with me each time a book is released.

And finally, my thanks to all the readers who have felt a special connection to or affection for the stories I tell. You're a big reason why I continue to hone my skills as a writer, and I hope to entertain you all for many years to come.